*. . . so she obeyed. Rather like a zombie, or a robot.
Thinking repeatedly, this can't be happening . . .
such things do not happen to people like us . . .*

But in a world that has created so many serial killers
like Colin Asch, such things do happen . . . even to
nice, well-off, normal people . . . people like us.

SOUL/MATE

"DARK AND BROODING . . . A FRIGHTENING
PSYCHO-THRILLER."—*Chicago Tribune*

"DEMONIC . . . NEARLY UNBEARABLE
SUSPENSE . . . CAREFULLY PLOTTED,
PASSIONATELY WRITTEN . . . CHARACTERS
WHO COME QUICKLY TO LIFE . . .
UNPUTDOWNABLE!"
　　　　　—*The Atlanta Journal and Constitution*

"SOMETHING YOU RARELY FIND . . . A HAIR-
RAISER AS LITERATURE . . . I LOVED IT!"
　　　　　—Elmore Leonard

SOUL/MATE

ROSAMOND SMITH

AN ONYX BOOK

NEW AMERICAN LIBRARY

A DIVISION OF PENGUIN BOOKS USA INC.

ONYX
Published by the Penguin Group
Penguin Books USA Inc., 375 Hudson Street, New York, New York,
10014 U.S.A.
Penguin Books Ltd, 27 Wrights Lane, London W8 5TZ, England
Penguin Books Australia Ltd, Ringwood, Victoria, Australia
Penguin Books Canada Ltd, 2801 John Street, Markham, Ontario,
Canada L3R 1B4
Penguin Books (N.Z.) Ltd, 182-190 Wairau Road, Auckland 10,
New Zealand

Penguin Books Ltd, Registered Offices:
Harmondsworth, Middlesex, England

SOUL/MATE was previously published in a Dutton edition.

First Onyx Printing, June, 1990
10 9 8 7 6 5 4 3 2

Printed in Canada

PUBLISHER'S NOTE
This is a work of fiction. Names, characters, places, and incidents
either are the product of the author's imagination or are used
fictitiously, and any resemblance to actual persons, living or dead,
events, or locales is entirely coincidental.

BOOKS ARE AVAILABLE AT QUANTITY DISCOUNTS WHEN USED TO
PROMOTE PRODUCTS OR SERVICES. FOR INFORMATION PLEASE WRITE
TO PREMIUM MARKETING DIVISION, PENGUIN BOOKS USA INC., 375
HUDSON STREET, NEW YORK, NEW YORK 10014.

For Han and Bill Heyen,
"soul mates"

PART ONE

1

Dorothea Deverell knew herself at a disadvantage.

On this drizzly misty evening of November 14, driving in her secondhand Mercedes to the dinner party that would forever alter the course of her life, Dorothea—thirty-nine years old, widowed for fourteen years, and for all of those years childless—felt the sharpness of disadvantage like an early, ominous, shivering presage of the flu: and did not like the feeling. She did not like it because it was too familiar.

She was already twenty minutes late for the Weidmanns' dinner party (which she did not much want to attend, in any case, since her lover and her lover's wife were also to be guests), and she had been so delayed in leaving the Institute (where she was assistant to the Director, a charmingly incompetent gentleman who not only publicly claimed he could do nothing without Miss Deverell's help but saw to it that the extravagant claim was daily, even hourly, substantiated) she had not had time to hurry home, bathe, calm her thoughts, and change into something more formal, and more feminine, than the navy cashmere suit she had worn that day to work—a Chanel ten years out of date, elegantly shabby, with raised slightly knobby shoulders and long sweeping skirt to mid-calf that gave her the look, as her lover, Charles, once remarked, of a sweetly befuddled prioress in a nineteenth-century French novel. Dorothea dreaded being late for any occasion, however innocently, out of a fear that those awaiting her might guess she really did not want to come at all; sociable gatherings, though the very life's blood of the unmarried and the staple, so to speak, of her administrative work at the Institute—she was in charge of scheduling lectures, chamber music concerts, art exhibits, trustees' meetings, charity functions, luncheons, receptions, and many another gregarious event at the community-minded Morris T. Brannon Institute—often filled her with a mysterious malaise.

That morning Charles had telephoned her in her office to ask if she was going to the Weidmanns' tonight, and Dorothea had said in a weakly ebullient voice, "Of course—I wouldn't miss one of Ginny's lovely parties for the world, would you?" "God, yes," Charles said. He spoke with more than usual vehemence; he was no more naturally sociable than Dorothea, though, like Dorothea, he usually managed to acquit himself well at such events; even, upon occasion, to shine. He was a tall lean greyhound sort of man, in his late forties, with sandy-silvery hair, a fair face splashed with pale freckles, a frowning smile, somber pebble-colored eyes beneath rather prominent brows—trained in the law but reserved, even shy. Ah, yes, enormously shy! He and Dorothea Deverell had been romantically involved with each other, to the ambiguous degree that they *were* romantically involved with each other, for more years than Dorothea cared to recall. "And is Agnes coming too?" Dorothea heard herself ask, rubbing harshly at an eye; and Charles said, "She plans to be, yes," with a just perceptible sigh, an exhalation of breath Dorothea would not have noted had she not had so many years' prac-

tice. "Well," she said. "Well," Charles said. The
line went silent, though not yet dead; like two shy,
bumbling adolescents they did not want to say goodbye. Finally Dorothea said, in a resolutely neutral
voice, "I'd heard from Ginny that Agnes was sick,"
and Charles said quickly, "She *was,* last week, with
a migraine headache, and nerves, and—the usual. But
she's better now. And she intends to come to dinner
tonight; she wouldn't miss one of Ginny Weidmann's
parties, she says, for the world." "How nice," Dorothea said dryly. Her lips twitched in a fierce little
smile, but of course Charles Carpenter, miles away on
the far side of town, could not see.

Ginny and Martin Weidmann, whom Dorothea had
known from the days of her marriage—her young,
doomed husband had been in fact a classmate of Martin's at Williams College—lived in the most fashionable section of town, in a splendid old "Italianate
Victorian" house with a square central tower, tall narrow framework-framed windows, steep shingled roof.
The very street was antique and otherworldly: cob-
bled, in chronic need of repair, banked in so severely
at the curb that Dorothea invariably scraped the lower
edges of the Mercedes' fenders whenever she parked
in front of the house—as she was now doing. "Why
am I here?" she cried aloud. She foresaw that it would
be one of those evenings when nothing would happen
that had not happened countless times before.

Judging by the cars parked on the street and in the
Weidmanns' circular driveway, all the other guests
were here. She recognized the Carpenters' white Cadillac, on the opposite side of the street, poised as if
for a quick getaway. Impractical eye-catching white had
been Agnes' choice though she rarely drove the car;
Charles did all the driving.

Dorothea rang the doorbell breathlessly and smiled
her bright beautiful smile as Ginny embraced her and

scoldingly greeted her—"You're almost half an hour late, Dorothea! It isn't like you! We were all worried!" Inside, the hum and buzz of conversation filled the downstairs, like a familiar piece of music; there was a delicious odor of roasting lamb; smells of wine, flowers, fruit. The Weidmanns' black maid, Tula, came to take her coat away, and for a blurred instant Dorothea had a consoling glimpse of herself in Ginny's antique Venetian mirror—she did not look nearly so haggard as she felt. Her burnished-mahogany hair fell smoothly about her face as if it had been conscientiously brushed, her large intelligent brown eyes shone with expectation. "How lovely you look, Dorothea, all the same!" Ginny said ambiguously. "That suit is so becoming!"—with a fleeting frown that cut Dorothea's heart. (For it meant, didn't it, that the suit had become by now too familiar? that it wasn't at all the sort of thing Dorothea should have worn this evening?) Ginny was perfumy, chatty, Junoesque, her hostess gown as splotched with color as chintz wallpaper. She was a dear friend of Dorothea's who did not in truth know Dorothea very well; one of those older, dauntingly generous married women who see it as their task to find the perfect mates for their unmarried female friends. Over the years Ginny had introduced Dorothea to so many eligible bachelors, Dorothea swung between a sense of guilt for having failed her and a sense of outrage for being so frequently hauled up on the auction block, against her will and, indeed, often without her knowing what was going on—until it was too late. She had begun to feel like one of those suddenly stubborn mares who at a certain weary age refuse to "stand" for a stallion and have to be impregnated, if at all, by artificial means.

Thus Ginny Weidmann—who meant, of course, only well—was now hurriedly briefing Dorothea on the subject of tonight's candidate, another in her seemingly inexhaustible store of very nice men, gentlemanly men, business associates of Martin's. "Why do you look so surprised, Dorothea? Surely you haven't forgotten? I *told* you I was inviting Jerome Gallagher tonight, didn't I?" Ginny asked.

"Yes, I'm sure you did," Dorothea said quickly.

Wineglass in hand, husky voice lowered, Ginny provided Dorothea with a hurried compendium of facts regarding Mr. Gallagher to which Dorothea made a spirited pretense of listening. Surely this too was familiar? She understood that, remaining unmarried for so long, she was a sort of enigma to her friends and that after a certain period of time there is something disquieting, even disagreeable, about an enigma. She was trained as an art historian at Yale; traveled and studied abroad in her early twenties; came home and met, fell in love with, and married a young French architect, newly an American citizen, named Michel Deverell, who died in an automobile accident on a Boston expressway, aged twenty-eight, when Dorothea was herself only twenty-five years old and recovering from a miscarriage suffered in the seventh month of a difficult pregnancy. And how quickly the subsequent years had passed, how swiftly and seemingly without event her life was passing from her! There was Charles Carpenter, whom she had known since her marriage, and whom, for the past eight or nine years, she had loved, but their affair, their friendship, was a strictly private matter, suspected perhaps by some—by Agnes Carpenter? by sharp-eyed Ginny Weidmann herself?— but not known: decidedly not known. It was Dorothea's custom, when asked discomfortingly personal questions, to say simply, "I was married once, a long time ago; my husband died when I was twenty-five. I've worked for the Brannon Institute since 1982." She did not willingly elaborate; though shy, she was also stubborn, the sort of person, usually female, who so subtly shifts the subject away from herself, and onto others, the finesse of the maneuver goes unremarked. Vaguely it was thought that Dorothea Deverell had been pregnant when her young husband had died and had lost her baby as a consequence, was thus a doubly tragic figure, and this misconception Dorothea could scarcely correct, for it belonged to the genteel mythologizing of her life to which she had no access: like the belief that she was, for all her well-bred delicacy of manner, actually a woman of enormous unexercised passion (like the proverbial virginal prioress) and that she was an heiress of considerable means who did not therefore require serious advancements in position or salary at the Institute—this, the most invidious notion of all, based on the evidence of haphazard items inherited years ago from an elderly great-aunt, including the 1979 Mercedes-Benz 500 SEL, which was always stalling on the expressway, a well-worn natural stone marten coat several sizes too large for her, and various pieces of costume jewelry, furniture, and household goods. If the mythologizing did not represent her, neither did it betray her, and Dorothea took care not to contradict its general outline. She knew that she was locally admired, even, to a warming degree, well liked: she was lovely, she was reliable, she was beautifully mannered, she was *good*. Yet even to her face people evinced airs of pity, for, having such advantages, why then did Dorothea Deverell appear so disadvantaged? At the last dinner party at the Weidmanns' she'd attended, not so many months ago, at which, thank God, Charles Carpenter and his wife had not been guests, a well-intentioned older gentleman had inquired of her at the dinner table, in full hearing of the others, why a pretty girl like herself wasn't married, his very words being, unblushing, in fact quite forceful and accusing: "Why isn't a pretty girl like you *married?*" And Dorothea had smiled and had replied, sweetly enough, though inwardly trembling and feeling a rude hot blush rise up into her face, "I was, once—when I *was* a girl."

And the entire table went silent, eyes averted. For a space of several awkward seconds.

Now Ginny was saying, "Oh, and another thing. What *is* this campaign of Roger Krauss's against you? I hear such—"

They were midway in the Weidmanns' polished and sparkling foyer, about to join the festive group in the living room, when, to Dorothea's dismay, Ginny did a characteristic thing—even to laying an exclamatory hand on Dorothea's arm and squeezing. Having just thought of this new subject, Ginny, who was all spontaneity, emotion, and thoughtlessness, not unlike an overgrown bullying child, could not keep it to herself for a more felicitous moment but had to thrust it immediately at Dorothea, as if, indeed, thrusting it into her appalled face: "I hear such disturbing things, Dorothea, *really!* We must talk!"

"But now? Must we talk of that terrible man now?" Dorothea cried with a despairing little laugh.

The older woman, regarding her with some concern, relented and merely shook her head, making her diamond earrings flash and her splendidly glowing red-rinsed hair catch the light. Dorothea's heart panicked in her breast. She had now to compose her face, her very self, as best as she could, entering the living room in which her unacknowledged lover awaited her—her lover, and the others. Ah, how she did not want to appear in their eyes as she so sadly, emphatically, felt: one of those persons of whom the world says with surprise and pity, But how unfair! how unfair, her life!

Dorothea Deverell had fallen in love with Charles Carpenter by degrees; even, it might be said, against her will. She was a woman of principle and she did not

believe in provoking others to violate principle—and
Charles was of course a married man. However unhappily and pointlessly, a married man. At every step
she had warned herself, *You'll regret this!* like a brash
child venturing out onto thin ice, ever outward onto
thin thin ice, wind wailing in her ears and heart pump-
ing: *You'll regret this! You'll regret this!* How very
unlike the precipitous headlong plunge into passion,
emotion, and eventually grief she had experienced with
the young French architect. (Dorothea had known her
husband so briefly, if tenderly, it seemed natural for
her to think of him in formal terms. And, dead at
twenty-eight, he would remain forever young.) Charles
Carpenter was a partner in a prestigious Boston law
firm for which Michel Deverell's architectural firm had
done some work; thus the two couples came to know
one another socially, if not intimately; but it was during Dorothea's first flush of local renown, when she
was establishing herself as a new bright cultural presence in Lathrup Farms (a suburban village, resplendent on Boston's North Shore) that she became
reacquainted with the Carpenters: with Charles in particular.

One Sunday afternoon he had appeared seemingly
out of nowhere close beside her to touch her shoulder
and murmur, ''Dorothea? Might we talk? alone?—for
a minute—back along here?'' as with a surprisingly
forcible grip of her elbow he led her along a rather
slippery marble walkway out of sight and earshot of a
crowd of others; and Dorothea, frightened, excited,
guilty, had known at once what the man intended and
how she would respond. The occasion was a large
cocktail reception for some charity purpose held in
one of the area's stately old homes, a neo-Georgian
mansion overlooking the Bay, one of those from which
Mrs. Carpenter had mysteriously absented herself, requiring of her husband that he convey her apologies

and offer, never quite convincingly, an explanation of
some kind—usually having to do with health. It would
be false to say that Dorothea had not been aware of
Charles Carpenter for some time, and aware of his
interest in her; that she did not bloom in his company,
enlivened by his wit and the vigor of his conversation;
that she had not in fact often sought him out at such
gatherings, as a way of establishing that the gathering,
for her, had some human validity. And now Charles
was saying in a hurried undertone, staring at Dorothea's face, "I don't want to embarrass you, Dorothea,
and I certainly don't want to alarm you, but I seem to
have fallen in love with you, and I thought that you
should know."

Dorothea said softly, wonderingly, "Yes."

So it began, their romance, their mildly adulterous
friendship, with Charles talking and Dorothea listening: an attractive couple in young middle age whose
rapt interest in each other would have been (perhaps
was?) self-evident to any incidental observer. So long
a widow in her own and the world's imagination, Dorothea had felt herself comfortably a virgin again; her
womb, emptied of any substance, was again a virgin's
womb, chaste, tight, and inviolate. Hearing Charles
Carpenter's faltering, agitated, but finally quite moving declaration of love and his desire to see her pri-
vately, as soon as possible, if only she would allow it,
Dorothea remained strangely calm: as (so memory
cruelly tossed up to her) she'd been, at first, when
news came of Michel's death, and she had stood in
their little rented Beacon Street apartment listening,
nodding, head bowed, nothing to say, only a few practical questions to ask. If her eyes had flooded with
tears they were not so much tears of emotion as simply
a nervous response, as if she had been slapped hard
across the face. *You'll regret this!* she told herself
coolly, but there she was agreeing just the same to see

Charles Carpenter, a married man, the very next evening. And to tell him, as he loomed dangerously near to her, squeezing her hand in his, that she was very fond of him too: she'd long thought of him, she said, as a special friend, to whom she might have turned in time of trouble.

Yet, after the early delirium of intimacy, the fierce whispered declarations, vows, promises, proposals, their feelings for each other quickly acquired a kind of equilibrium, or stasis. Charles telephoned—or did not telephone; they met surreptitiously once, or twice, or three times a week—or did not meet at all. So weeks yielded to months, and months to years. Eight years? Nine? There were periods when Dorothea seemed in retreat, as if gripped by conscience; there were periods when Charles seemed in retreat, as if nettled or hurt by Dorothea's display of conscience or stricken by his own. As passion waxed in one it was likely to wane in the other, following a melancholy law of human paradox, so that if Charles suggested telling Agnes everything and asking for a divorce, Dorothea was likely to resist, uneasily reminding him that his wife was not a well woman and would be humiliated by such an event; if Dorothea in an outburst of temper suggested that she'd had enough of subterfuge, she would be seen with Charles publicly or not at all, Charles might point out, reasonably enough, that it was she, with her sensitive position at the Institute, who would suffer the more—"Of course I want us to marry, I want it with all my heart, but is this the right time? Have you thought it through seriously? Have you considered the consequences?" Not for nothing was Charles Carpenter trained in the law.

And so—the years. Dorothea had her work (she was generally believed to be next in line for the directorship at the Institute, when the current director, Mr. Howard Morland, retired: Mr. Morland was sixty-six, no longer much engaged in his position, and very fond of Dorothea Deverell); and Dorothea had her friends, her numerous friends, one of whom was Charles Carpenter. She had the vague hazy warmly comforting conviction that, yes, she and Charles would one day be married, and there would be, in town, a new Mr. and Mrs. Charles Carpenter; perhaps they would live in a new house, in her fantasy one of the fine old restored eighteenth-century houses in the Weidmanns' neighborhood. When the time was "right." (Or had Charles said "ripe"?—his voice often dropped to a murmur in Dorothea's presence.)

Charles's wife, Agnes, remained oblivious of her husband's love for Dorothea Deverell. Or, if suspecting, had made up her mind not to care. She had become with the years one of those women, not uncommon in tightly knit social circles, who exudes an air of disappointment and irony like a pungent perfume assailing the nostrils of others. She dressed expensively but carelessly; her skin was sallow and unhealthy, and her eyes puffy-lidded; her round stolid face was a defiant pug's face, with the liverish cast of a being of action who has for mysterious reasons refused to act, so that her energy, her very life, had backed up in her, choking her. It was not known in Lathrup Farms whether she drank because of chronic ill health or whether her chronic ill health was the result of her drinking; whether she was "difficult" because she drank or drank because she was "difficult," trusting to alcohol to free instincts that social decorum would otherwise have suppressed.

In the many years of their acquaintance, Dorothea's only intimate encounter with Agnes Carpenter had been an embarrassing one. She had come upon the woman in a powder room one evening at one or another party, the wife of her lover, whom she envied, and feared, and hated, and often pitied, and there was

Agnes Carpenter in a gold lamé pants suit leaning and swaying over a sink, so drunk her eyes were squeezed shut and her skin had gone a dead doughy ghastly white, and when Dorothea offered to help Agnes pushed her hands away blindly, crying, "Don't touch! Don't touch!" but then, a moment later, she begged, "Oh, God, help me please—" turning and staggering as Dorothea caught her in her arms and, in one of the toilet stalls, held the poor woman's shoulders while she retched into a toilet bowl, vomiting in long shuddering heaves. The bout of sickness had lasted perhaps ten minutes, during which time other women, venturing into the powder room, discreetly backed out again, leaving Dorothea Deverell to the task: which of course she acquitted ably, like a nurse's aide, hardly seeming to mind (though of course she minded terribly) that her black silk dress with the countless shimmering pleats was splashed with Agnes Carpenter's foul-smelling vomit while Agnes Carpenter's gold lamé came through unscathed. And after that unfortunate incident Agnes Carpenter's public manner with Dorothea Deverell was distinctly formal, if not chill.

Telling Ginny Weidmann about it (for she'd been, for all her scruples, unable to keep it to herself), Dorothea had said with a nervous laugh, "Now the woman is my enemy for life!" and Ginny had agreed, though not laughingly. Ginny said, "Agnes Carpenter is the kind of person you wouldn't choose for an enemy, any more than you'd choose her for a friend."

At the Weidmanns' elegantly set dining room table, amid the flutter of candle flames and the sparkle of silverware and the rich fragrance of rack of lamb and vegetables, Agnes Carpenter sat in a pose of polite attention, not swiftly but methodically draining her wineglass and allowing it, as if absentmindedly, to be refilled by Martin Weidmann. Talk ranged up and down the table—politics, a local art exhibit, mutual friends, a best-selling novel, the latest real estate development scandal—while Agnes Carpenter fussed unconvincingly with the food on her plate, cutting it up, Dorothea noted, into small pieces, and mucking the pieces about and leaving most of them. If Charles saw he naturally gave no sign; but perhaps, caught up in the conversation, glancing frequently at Dorothea, he did not see, exactly—for what after all could he do? She is a strong-willed woman, Charles had remarked to Dorothea once, rather vaguely, and Dorothea had not disagreed. Though thinking, What of me? Have I no will at all?

But she was determined to enjoy herself. As always, at the Weidmanns' table, the atmosphere was lively, exclamatory, irreverent, a bit loose at the edges, punctuated by Ginny's interruptions—"You did *what?* You said *what?*"—and by Martin's braying laughter. The food was superb, the wines delicious (and expensive); in twin etched-glass bowls at the center were pale yellow rosebuds that gave off a muted fragrance. In addition to the Weidmanns, the Carpenters, and Dorothea, there were three other guests: a striking Cleopatra-looking young woman in her late twenties named Hartley Evans, a new friend of Ginny's who worked for a Boston television station; a youngish jowly man named David Schmidt, who worked, as he rather too frequently mentioned, for a prominent brokerage firm in the city; and Jerome Gallagher, Dorothea's dinner companion for the evening, a tax lawyer whose habitual expression was sharply quizzical, as if he were hard of hearing, and whose bald head shone fiercely in the candlelight, like polished stone. We have all been brought together for a purpose, Dorothea thought, but what is the purpose? Is life, even in a world of couples, too lonely otherwise? Tonight she felt more than ordinarily on display since she and

Charles were seated almost directly across from each
other and obliged either to talk or, pointedly, not to
talk to each other; and there was the distraction of
Jerome Gallagher, Ginny's eligible bachelor of the
evening, introduced to Dorothea with the aside, "You
two have so much in common, I *envy* you!" So blunt
a prognosis had the temporary effect of making them
both tongue-tied, frowning Mr. Gallagher in particular, but, after some awkward false starts, Dorothea at
last asked the inevitable question, "What sort of work
do you do?" And Jerome Gallagher proceeded to tell
her. She knew she could relax for the duration since
as a female listener she was hardly required to respond
except in monosyllables of agreement, enthusiasm, or
wonder. Except for Charles Carpenter, men never
asked Dorothea about her work.

Mr. Gallagher talked and Dorothea half listened,
observing Charles and thinking how odd, how ironic;
in the man's actual presence she often felt estranged
from him, as in her reveries (indulged in daily, or
rather nightly) she did not, even as she acknowledged
his attractiveness: that angular fine-boned face, the
light splash of freckles like raindrops, the alert intelligent eyes. And he dressed inconspicuously well, not
stylishly but decently, wearing, Dorothea saw to her
pleasure, a beautiful silk necktie she'd given him (and
which Charles had had to mention to Agnes as an impulsive purchase of his own) and a fine bluish-gray
pinstripe suit that fitted his tall lean frame elegantly.
A man one might kill for, Dorothea thought, if one
were that sort. That morning Charles had said he
would rather have stayed home, except for seeing her,
but he seemed to be enjoying the dinner party as much
as anyone at the table, having struck up a spirited debate with Schmidt, a very vocal and opinionated young
man (conservative, Republican, scornful of "federal
restraints"), and the exotically made-up Hartley Evans

(inky black hair smooth and synthetic as a wig, enormous blue-lidded eyes wide in perpetual surprise), in which Ginny Weidmann participated and to which Agnes Carpenter made a perfunctory pretense of listening, using the excuse of a change of plates to light a cigarette: parchment-colored cigarettes, Egyptian, which gave off a sharp acrid stench and within seconds drifted to Dorothea's sensitive nostrils and eyes. If Agnes had eaten little she had drunk much; her fleshy face seemed about to shift its contours; she laughed for no specific reason and raised a chunky hand to her brow—her enormous dinner ring, a square-cut jade bordered with diamonds, catching the light aggressively. Her damp derisive gaze shifted to Dorothea's face without taking hold, as if Dorothea's place were empty.

Why will you not give him up? Dorothea silently pleaded. When you don't love him? When you are standing in the way of others' happiness?

Then, to Dorothea's horror, conversation at the table shifted suddenly, like a landslide, and within seconds the subject was the "power struggle" at the Brannon Institute, in particular the unconscionable tactics employed by a new member of the board of trustees named Roger Krauss, in promoting a protégé of his while systematically denigrating Dorothea Deverell—from the position of being, as Krauss insisted, not at all anti*woman* but anti*feminist*. Krauss, who had been named to the board the previous spring, had taken public exception to several of the programs Dorothea had scheduled, most notoriously (for he had published an attack in the Lathrup Farms weekly paper) a traveling exhibit of women's sculpture; he was condescending or outright rude to Dorothea when they were thrown together, talked behind her back to other members of the board and to the director, Mr. Morland. That Krauss had his own candidate for the directorship, a nephew-in-law currently working at the Whitney Museum, was part of his campaign against Dorothea, but he was clever enough to present it only as a part; his real objection to her taking over the directorship, he said, was ideological. He would not trust her, he'd several times declared, not to "subvert" the Institute for her own political ends. . . . Dorothea laid down her fork in dismay, felt her face go painfully hot and her heart beat sullenly against her ribs. This was the very topic she dreaded their taking up, and the worst of it was they were obviously not so much taking it up as reverting back to it, as if, before Dorothea's belated arrival, they had been discussing it, and her, at length.

Her eyes snatched at Charles's, seeking solace. He was staring down at his plate as if sharing her discomfort. It pained Dorothea the more, wounded her in her pride, that her lover had learned of her predicament before she had explained it to him, before she had transformed it into a dryly amusing little anecdote, to mitigate her shame. Ginny was saying angrily, "It just seems to me so outrageously unfair that Dorothea, who has done a damned good job at the Institute, should be obliged to defend herself after all these years—and to defend herself against such spiteful attacks!"

Martin agreed, and so of course did Charles, who was still staring down at his plate, his lips pursed; the new people—David Schmidt, Hartley Evans, Jerome Gallagher—looked thoughtful if rather neutral; but Agnes Carpenter, exhaling smoke through both nostrils in a lavish gesture, said, "But Roger *is* excessive. It isn't his nature to do things by halves."

Ginny said, "A scorpion has its nature too!"

Unperturbed, Agnes Carpenter said, "Scorpions aren't required to be lovable. Only to be scorpions."

At this rather unthinking remark there was a startled silence; then Martin Weidmann came gallantly to Dorothea's rescue, and Charles said something impatient, and Ginny, excited, held forth at some length, the words *unfair, unjust, outrageous, misogynist* flying about Dorothea's head like crazed wasps. She tried not to listen; tried to smile, as if not minding in the slightest; wondered how it would be received if she simply rose from the table and left the room and stayed away until the subject was changed. The problem of Roger Krauss and his heartbreaking campaign against her was one Dorothea dealt with by not thinking about it at all: simply blanking the horror out, as a dirtied wall is whitewashed, crudely and expediently.

Social life! Dorothea glanced at her watch and saw that it was only five minutes to ten. It seemed much later. There was a salad course yet to come, probably cheese and fruit, and of course dessert, coffee and liqueurs, and the rest, another hour at least to be endured before she could slip away home to fall exhausted into bed to dream of one day marrying Charles Carpenter and living a normal blessed life in a lovely old Lathrup Farms house, with a walled garden perhaps, and in cold windy weather Charles would build a fire in the fireplace, applewood for fragrance, and they would sit close together on the sofa clasping hands staring mesmerized at the dancing flames thinking *How lucky we are! How happy we are! How did such good fortune befall us?* Dorothea's eyes flooded with moisture as if flames were indeed singeing her eyeballs. Beside her Jerome was saying stiffly, "This fellow Krauss sounds like bad news. You might think about bringing a lawsuit against your employer, you know, if they do ease you out, if there really were promises made about advancement. Women are doing it all the time, these days."

Dorothea excused herself and hid away in the Weidmanns' gold-wallpapered little guest bathroom as long as she dared, and when she returned to the table, thank

God, the subject of Krauss had been dropped and a fresh subject taken up. The salad course was just being served, and Martin Weidmann was opening another bottle of wine, and Agnes Carpenter was lighting up another parchment-colored cigarette and exhaling smoke through her nostrils. Dorothea thought of Toulouse-Lautrec, who dined frequently at the Eiffel Tower, and who said, "One place I do not have to see the Eiffel Tower is inside the thing."

And then the doorbell rang. And everyone went silent. And Ginny cried, "Who can that be?" as if, her table being full, no one else could possibly turn up at her door.

They listened as Tula went to answer.

"What a surprise! What an enormous, *lovely* surprise!"

The unexpected visitor was a great-nephew of Ginny Weidmann's named Colin Asch: a tall too-thin boy with shadowed eyes, a delicate-boned asymmetrical face, lank pale hair that fell nearly to his shoulders. Dorothea, quite taken by his appearance, would have put his age at twenty-three or -four. He wore a soiled sheepskin windbreaker with a broken zipper, khaki trousers, a black cashmere sweater badly stretched at the neck, and no shirt beneath; his skin was sallow as if with fatigue, and his chin and cheeks were lightly stubbled; pulled reluctantly into the dining room to meet his aunt's friends, he blinked, and frowned, and squirmed, like a nocturnal animal rudely confronted with light. With a maternal solicitude in which delight and accusation contended, Ginny several times exclaimed, "But we were expecting you *last* week, Colin! Weren't we, Martin? Where on earth *were* you last week? Of course it's all so vague, the way you young people live your lives!''

Except that Ginny's arm was linked through his, the boy looked as if, in a paroxysm of embarrassment, he would have liked to run out of the room. Dorothea felt sorry for him, hauled like a prize of some sort into his aunt's dining room, exhibited to her friends. (Ginny's own grown children, about whom Dorothea heard a good deal, were well adjusted, happy, moderately successful, and not in much need of their mother's fervent attention.) The boy stammered an apology and said he hadn't meant to interrupt a party, but by now Martin too was on his feet and insisting Colin should join them at the table; it was unthinkable that Colin not join them, plenty of room and plenty of food and surely Colin had not eaten: ''You look,'' Martin said jovially, ''as if you haven't eaten in weeks!''

''But maybe Colin would like to freshen up a bit first,'' Ginny said, belatedly noticing her nephew's disheveled appearance and the look of pained pinched fright about his eyes. ''Would you, dear? And then have a little something to eat? Why don't you take him upstairs, Martin? He can change, if he'd like to, into something of yours.''

With a desperate shoulder-squirming maneuver the boy wriggled free of Ginny's grasp, repeating that he hadn't meant to interrupt a party; he never went where he wasn't invited; he'd see them again some other time.

''But you *are* invited,'' Ginny persisted.

And Martin, laying a heavy paternal arm across the boy's narrow shoulders, said warmly, ''You can't run away when you've only now arrived!''

Colin Asch stammered and resisted a bit longer, but the Weidmanns, united, were clearly too much for him, too practiced at this sort of benevolent bullying. Though Dorothea exchanged a swift amused look with Charles—how like Ginny and Martin this scene was!—

she felt relieved at the outcome: that this lonely appearing melancholy young man should be cared for, at least temporarily, and made to join their company. There was something striking about him, his eyes, his face, his very stance, to which she could not have given a name, yet which seemed to her both exciting and familiar. In any case his presence in the Weidmanns' overheated dining room would give the evening a distinct note of validity.

In a flurry of excitement Ginny and Tula laid another place at the table, close beside Ginny at the head, and in a dramatic undertone Ginny said, "The poor boy! Poor Colin! He had had such a tragic life!" All her guests leaned forward expectantly; Ginny glanced toward the foyer and the stairs, as if to reassure herself that Colin and Martin were safely out of earshot.

"The first thing, which some of you may have read about, or I've told you about, years ago—it must have been fifteen years ago—Colin's parents' death and the way they died; it was too ghastly! Too terrible! My niece and her husband and Colin, who was twelve at the time, were in their car, my niece's husband was driving, and it was raining, and they were going over a bridge in the Adirondacks, just south of Lake Placid, one of those metallic-mesh bridges, or whatever you might call them—you know the kind, so particularly slippery—and this bridge was narrow and not in good repair and there was another car coming from the opposite direction and somehow my niece's husband lost control of his car—I really do think the other driver must have been speeding, or driving dangerously, but that was never established—and struck the railing, and the railing broke, and they plunged into the river. The boy managed to get out and swim to the surface, but his father and mother were trapped inside the car, in only about eight feet of water, so the boy tried to save them, diving back down trying to get the doors of the car open, trying to pull his mother free, and then his father; he'd dived back into the water a dozen times by the time police arrived, isn't it just hellish to imagine? My poor niece, who was so sweet! Her poor husband! But the poor boy most of all, to endure such a nightmare! Because he'd tried to save his parents and he'd failed, and''—here Ginny's voice dropped tremulously, and she glanced again back toward the stairs, one beringed hand pressed against her breasts—''and they said he'd been raving and delirious when the police came; he'd fought the police, insisting his parents were still alive and he could save them; the poor child, imagine, only twelve at the time and always so sensitive—he had musical talent, a lovely soprano voice, he had a talent for drawing and painting; my niece herself was an artist, she'd taught for a while at Holyoke—and it was said that Colin had gone mad in those minutes, that his mind simply shattered.''

The very candles on the table seemed to shiver; Dorothea felt a pang of creaturely sympathy and horror, recalling in that instant the black engulfing wave not of madness but of the acquiescence to madness, to whim, accident, chance, fate, that had swept over her and threatened to drown her when Michel Deverell died. . . . I know now that God, as principle or presence, is sheerly madness, Dorothea had thought calmly.

In the silence that followed Ginny's account, Agnes Carpenter said, in the vague surprised tone of one who, expecting to be bored, is not after all bored, ''Yes, I remember that. That freak accident. The boy trying to rescue his parents from the submerged car. It was in all the papers. There were photographs. I remember.''

As if delivering a coup de grace Ginny said quietly, ''But that isn't all. There is more.''

A few minutes later Martin returned to the table, having left Colin Asch upstairs to shower and change, and hearing Ginny's recitation of yet more tragedy, or wretched bad luck—following his parents' death Colin had been sent to a boarding school for boys in New Hampshire, at which the headmaster was discovered to have "preyed" upon certain of his young charges, evidently including Colin—he said in a reproving voice, "Ginny, I really don't think Colin would feel comfortable if he knew you were talking about him. He was quite anxious to leave, and I assured him it would be a quiet evening."

"But he can't hear us, he won't know," Ginny said.

"The important thing is he's so much better now," Martin said, "compared to the last time we saw him. We wouldn't want to upset him."

As if Martin had merely confirmed her point, Ginny said passionately, "That's the courageous part of it. The noble part. How the boy has been in and out of hospitals half his life, not exactly mental hospitals, please don't misunderstand me, but clinics of one kind or another, being treated for depression and anorexia and God knows what all else. After the scandal at the boarding school—the headmaster committed suicide, in fact—Colin had a breakdown and couldn't eat, couldn't sleep, refused to talk or respond to anyone, even had to be fed intravenously for a while, against his will. Then he recovered, to a degree, and was sent off to live with relatives in Baltimore, but that didn't work out for some reason, so he went back to another boarding school. Over the years most of the family has chipped in to help, and there was some insurance, of course, from his parents' deaths, and even a lawsuit some of the boys' parents brought against the school in New Hampshire—what is the name of that place, Martin?"

"Monmouth Academy," Martin said reluctantly, "but I really don't think you—"

"—which the school settled out of court, and all of

this helped the financial problem somewhat, but only somewhat. Fortunately Colin is so bright and quick and serious about his studies, at least initially, he has managed to win several scholarships since graduating from high school—if in fact he ever did graduate from high school; I'm not sure on that point.'' Ginny paused breathlessly, glancing again toward the upstairs. There was no sound, no evidence of movement; Dorothea had a sudden surrealist vision of the fated boy, having overheard his aunt's somehow too animated voice, deciding on the spur of the moment to take revenge against her by slashing his throat in her bathroom. ''But he has done well in recent years. I mean, fairly well. His life is a bit mysterious actually. He had a scholarship to the Rhode Island School of Design, and then he disappeared and turned up in New Mexico living with a colony of artists, and then he was backpacking through Europe and no one knew his whereabouts for months, and then—do you remember, Martin?—we ran into him, almost literally ran into him, in San Francisco, when we were out there for a convention of yours. He seemed to be alone, and he said he had a job as a salesman of some kind, door to door. He didn't seem eager to spend much time with us.''

There was a pause. Hartley Evans asked, ''Where does he live now?''

Ginny said, ''That's it—no one exactly knows! He was in Europe this past summer, Amsterdam and Heidelberg mainly; then he backpacked through Germany and Italy and wound up somehow in northern Africa; and then a few weeks ago he telephoned us saying he was going to be driving through Boston, but the evening we expected him he didn't show up. Knowing Colin, we didn't worry too much, but Martin did check with the police, and there was nothing, and he never called of course to explain, and now tonight: here he is. He's such a sweet boy—you can see it in his eyes. And the tragedy of his young life—you can see *that* in his eyes. I wish there were more he would allow Martin and me to do, to help. But he has his pride too. He's twenty-seven years old, a grown man. He has his pride.''

Martin said jovially, ''Now, dear, I think that's enough.''

Dorothea had listened intently to Ginny's account, wondering why she was so strangely moved. She recalled the philosopher's cryptic observation: Terrible experiences give one cause to speculate whether the one who experiences them may not be something terrible. She could not remember the name of the philosopher but knew he must be German.

When Colin returned to the dining room and was again rapidly introduced to the Weidmanns' guests, he had so radically altered his appearance—having showered, shaved, combed his damp pale hair back from his forehead, put on a fresh white shirt and a navy-knit tie of Martin's—Dorothea did not think she would have recognized him. Though exceedingly self-conscious, a bit embarrassed, even sullen, about the mouth, he managed to take his place at the head of the table, beside his beaming aunt, and he managed to smile—even, shyly, to laugh—as he began to eat. (He was clearly hungry, yet picked about in his food like a fastidious child.) Dorothea saw that his eyes moved quickly and ceaselessly from one guest to another, one face to another; she imagined that for a beat or two he lingered at her own, frankly stared, and then moved on. He knows we have been talking about him, Dorothea thought uneasily. *He had gone mad, in those minutes. His mind had simply shattered.*

But he was hardly mad now: edgy and self-conscious but subdued; in his uncle's clothes, several sizes too big for him, he looked mysteriously chastised. He was a handsome young man, very nearly a beautiful young man, Dorothea thought, with his long Roman nose, waxy pale at the tip, and his well-shaped mouth, like something sculpted in stone. Indeed, there was something lapidary about him, particularly in profile; of whom or of what was Dorothea reminded, by his profile? Had he lived to be born, my own son might be sitting in that place, Dorothea thought. It was a wholly senseless thought which she discounted and forgot at once.

With unsteady fingers she reached for her wineglass and saw to her surprise that it was empty.

The subject of Germany was raised (presumably because Colin Asch had recently been there?), and the men at the table, and Hartley Evans, were discussing it: the political phenomenon of the "two Germanys," the division of East and West ("like warring twins," Charles thoughtfully said), the primitive or mystical belief in a special destiny for that nation—or for any other nation, in fact. Martin asked Colin's opinion, and there was an awkward pause during which it appeared that Colin might not have been listening; then he glanced up, shifted his shoulders like a recalcitrant schoolboy, and gave, in a rapid murmured voice, a most remarkable little précis—succinct, pointed, intelligent. So far as he knew, he said, from talking with people his age, particularly in Heidelberg where he'd studied for a while, the younger generation did not think in such outdated mythic terms at all: for them, East Germany and West Germany were two quite separate nations, and the fact that they would never be united did not trouble them, or deeply engage them, in the least. "They are more concerned with ecological matters," he said. "They are concerned with American and Soviet missiles." He paused. His mouth worked oddly. "The future. Not the past."

"Oh, but I find that so hard to believe, knowing

what we do of the Teutonic character,'' Hartley Evans
said, pursing her glossy scarlet lips and frowning pe-
dantically. Wine and rich food and the excitement of
an attractive young man at the table—more obviously
attractive, in any case, than David Schmidt, the bro-
ker's assistant, to whom Ginny had pointedly introduced her—had enlivened the young woman, loosened
her, brought even more color into her cheeks. She was
one of those women who perceive of social intercourse
in such circumstances as a near variant of the sexual,
requiring some of the same feints, jousts, and rejoin-
ders. But Colin Asch did no more than glance at her,
and mumbled something inaudible, and stared down
at his plate, fumbling his fork; and the subject was
snatched up, like a football, by David Schmidt, who
had spent six weeks in Munich recently and who knew
a good deal about ''the Federal Republic—and the
other'' and was not shy about informing his listeners
of what he knew.

For everyone excepting Colin Asch the salad course
was now over, and a delicious salad it had been, with
several kinds of greens, including arugula—a favorite
of Charles Carpenter's which Dorothea never failed to
serve him when he ate dinner at her home, as he sometimes, though infrequently and always surreptitiously,
did—and indeed the subsequent course was cheese and
fruit, pungent imported cheeses and luscious Concord
grapes; though by now Dorothea's appetite was quite
quenched. She noticed that Colin Asch was eating
oddly, even furtively, rather like a sick cat Dorothea
had once owned—the poor creature, afflicted with what
turned out to be pneumonitis, had been starving but
had been unable to eat, repeatedly lowering her head
to her food and then looking up helplessly at Dorothea. The sight had filled Dorothea with a terrible anxiety, for what could be done? So too did Colin Asch
bring his fork to his mouth, then lower it; raise it again

and take a small quick bite, chewing with an expression of scarcely concealed distaste.

Sharp-eyed Ginny Weidmann, just returning to the table from the kitchen, cried, "Colin, is something wrong? You aren't eating."

Colin shook his head and mumbled no, nothing was wrong.

"The meat? The *lamb?*" Ginny asked, as if something crucial were at stake. "Can't you *eat* it?"

Again Colin replied in a mumble, lowering his head. A panicky expression crossed his face.

"But you seem to have eaten some of the vegetables, haven't you?" Ginny persisted. "Oh, dear, are you a *vegetarian?* Colin? Is *that* it?"

Colin shifted his narrow shoulders in a paroxysm of embarrassment or annoyance, meaning possibly yes, possibly no; meaning, Leave me alone. But Ginny Weidmann would not let him off so easily. He was hungry, she said; he must eat. He was alarmingly *thin.* So Tula was charged with taking away his meat- and gravy-contaminated plate (though with a stiff sort of dignity Colin had not acquiesced to this) and bringing another, heaped with steaming vegetables in almost comical profusion. A harsh ruddy blush by now mottled the young man's face, prominent as a birthmark. To draw attention away from him, so that he could, if he wished, eat, Dorothea threw out a remark on some cheerful neutral subject, which was taken up hopefully by Charles Carpenter, but unfortunately Agnes Carpenter was not to be deterred and asked of Colin Asch, in a voice both belligerent and coquettish, whether he belonged to a religious cult that forbade the eating of meat or whether not eating meat was—well, a quirk of his own?

This, Colin simply did not answer, not rudely, but as if he had not heard; and Agnes Carpenter asked her question again, louder, and added. "But do you eat

eggs? Or cheese? Do you wear *leather?* I bet you're
wearing leather *shoes!* A leather *belt!* What I find so
annoying about vegetarians is their self-righteousness;
I mean, we don't harangue them, why should they harangue *us?*" She appealed to the table, as if inviting
complicity. "It's like those people who do volunteer
work with the homeless, feeding the homeless, that
sort of thing, and make the rest of us feel guilty simply
for existing."

"Well," Martin Weidmann said with an embarrassed laugh, as if summing up the subject, "these
things are controversial, of course. Like abortion, or
air pollution. But who would like more wine? Jerry?
Dorothea? Your glass is empty."

Agnes Carpenter persisted, looking at Colin Asch.
"But do you belong to a cult? One of those exotic
Indian religions, with the gurus who own Rolls-
Royces? I hope not!"

Colin Asch, impassive, his face stony, said, with a
patience that struck Dorothea as heroic, that, no, he
did not belong to any cult, but he did belong to the
Animal Rights League; and he was a vegetarian, but
he didn't make a habit of haranguing others to believe,
or to behave, as he did. He added, mumbling, "As
you would, if you knew."

" 'Knew'?" Agnes Carpenter asked sharply. "What
does that mean, 'knew'?"

"That we are all sentient creatures. That, in our
consciousness, we are one."

"Including animals?"

"Yes. Including animals."

"And what does the—whatever it is, that you belong
to—"

"The Animal Rights League."

"—and what is *that?* Do you campaign against lab-
oratory experiments; do you break into zoos, that sort
of thing?"

"Agnes, why don't you let Colin eat his dinner?" Charles Carpenter said, suddenly exasperated.

"But I am simply *asking*. I'm sure he would like to *tell* us."

"Our organization is based upon the premise that human beings are not superior to animals," Colin said, beginning to speak agitatedly, "but that human beings *are* animals. It is not a pejorative term, 'animal,' but a simple description of biological reality. Animals have personalities, animals have emotions and beliefs, and some animals have languages—"

"Does a sponge have 'personality'?" Agnes interrupted.

And David Schmidt, meaning to be amusing, said, in an undertone, "A spider? A slug? What about bacteria?" Hartley Evans giggled. Jerome Gallagher laughed.

No one meant to be cruel, but the effect upon Colin Asch was to silence him, in mid-sentence. He laid down his fork—dropped it, really—and made a gesture of pushing his plate away from him. His mouth was working as if words churned inside, unable to break free. Though Martin Weidmann was saying loudly, affably, in the voice of a well-practiced host, that no one need defend himself and no one need take offense, Colin pushed his chair back from the table, and stood, and said in a quavering voice, *"Homo sapiens* is not the only species on earth. *Homo sapiens* has the power to destroy many of the other species and to destroy itself, but it is not the only species on earth, nor is it above and beyond and superior to creation, as you would know if you looked within yourself, if you made an attempt to transcend your vile human selfishness—"

"Colin, dear," Ginny cried, "do sit down! Please!"

With a strange tight smile Colin said, "The suffering of animals is no less because it lacks a language. Like the suffering of infants.''

There was a pause. Agnes Carpenter, startled, relenting, murmured something conciliatory; Martin repeated that no one should take offense; Ginny, roused to maternal solicitude, pleaded with Colin Asch to sit down and to finish his meal. There was salad to come, she said pleadingly, and dessert; surely he wanted dessert? Pecan pie with whipped cream? ''We understand about the animals, Colin, really we do,'' she said. ''Animals do have personalities, dogs and cats certainly do, and horses; they're quite strong-willed really, we all know that. Won't you sit down, dear? We promise you can eat your meal in peace.''

''Do you!'' Colin Asch said angrily.

The atmosphere was highly charged; everyone was looking at everyone else in alarm. What had happened? And why? In the silence Dorothea spoke, in a peculiar slow voice, as if the words were being coaxed from her against her will, ''But animals too eat one another. We, I mean—since we are animals. It is something of which we should be ashamed, but even shame is not enough to defeat hunger.''

Colin Asch looked at her steadily, stared at her. His lips had gone white, like a wound from which blood has drained. After a long moment he said, simply, ''Yes. You are right.'' Yet he continued to stare at Dorothea for another beat or two, while the others shifted uneasily in their seats.

In the end Colin Asch allowed his aunt to coerce him into resuming his meal; true to her word, she saw to it that he completed it in peace. He said nothing further. He did not so much as glance at Dorothea. Then he excused himself, and went away upstairs, and was gone. And by midnight Dorothea Deverell was safely home, by a quarter past midnight she was soaking in her bath (for going immediately to bed, tonight, would have been unthinkable), giddy with exhaustion yet queerly exhilarated, stirred. Why had she said the strange words she'd said to Ginny's great-nephew? And why had he looked at her so intently, his eyes narrowed and damp, the skin about them appearing bruised? Saying good night in the Weidmanns' foyer, Charles Carpenter had pressed Dorothea's hand hard; and he too had looked at her intently, with a flattering sort of interest, his warm gaze one of tenderness and affection, yet mute. Why could he not speak except in pleasantries? Banalities? She supposed he would telephone in the morning as he frequently did, and she supposed she knew of what their conversation would consist. *I love you, you know. Yes—and I love you.* He would want to know more about hateful Roger Krauss and the "campaign" against Dorothea, and Dorothea, wincing, would assure him it was nothing, really; nothing at all, really; had not Mr. Morland virtually assured Dorothea his position when he stepped down . . . ?

(But perhaps I will bring a lawsuit against the Institute after all, Dorothea thought, amused. As my lawyer friend Mr. Gallagher has suggested. For why not? What's to be lost? My precious "femininity"?)

Soaking in her bath, belatedly a little drunk, Dorothea breathed in the warm fragrant steam that smelled like narcissi; she imagined she could hear the telephone ringing in the next room but of course that could not be. Charles would never call her this late; that wasn't in his character.

When was the last time they'd made love, like real lovers? Weeks ago. Back in September. In Dorothea's chaste white wicker bed, enclosed by Dorothea's chaste Laura Ashley floral wallpaper. *I love you, you know. Ah, yes!—and I love you.* They had not spoken of marrying for some time, not even to advise each other solemnly against it. They had not spoken of Agnes Carpenter for some time except in the most general of terms.

Dorothea lay luxuriously in her bath in the warm fragrant water, noting idly that her breasts, her creamy-pale unused breasts, floated gently, like balloons, and that the dark wiry hair between her legs, scratchy to the touch, was obscured by the water's rippling soap-bubbled surface. She stretched her rather long legs, pressed her toes against the hard rim of the bathtub. *I love you. His mind had simply shattered.* The gentleman to whom Ginny Weidmann had introduced her tonight had asked if he might telephone her sometime the following week; might she be free for dinner sometime soon, perhaps a concert in the city? She'd been vague and polite, not quite looking him in the eye. Thank you, yes. Perhaps. Sometime.

She was nodding off to sleep, in the bath. The day had been so incalculably long.

A boy's face appeared suddenly: blunt, bold . . . the eyes searing, knowing. Not a human boy but an angel: a fierce bellicose archangel, out of Michelangelo perhaps, blowing his doomsday trumpet, cheeks puffed and forehead cruelly creased. Colin, his name. He'd stared at her, in front of the others. But what was his last name? She was too drowsy to remember.

2

Colin Asch had been forced to kill before but never so dispassionately. So without premeditation.

A clean sort of XXX, he was to note in his Blue Ledger in carefully printed block letters, *uncontaminated by desire.*

It had happened in innocence. It had been the consequence of actions not within his control. He'd left Sea Breeze Village (several acres of condominiums) early in the morning of November 10, driving out of Fort Lauderdale in the red '87 Mustang with the sliding sun roof the woman had given him, which she surely wouldn't call the police to get returned, and just south of Daytona Beach on I-95, maintaining his usual steady unobtrusive speed of sixty-five miles an hour, he happened to see, one lane over to the right, one car length ahead, a car he thought at first to be identical with his, lipstick-red, two-door coupe, good condition except for streaks of corrosion on the fenders, but it turned out to be a Toyota of about that year, and what drew his attention to it like a magnet was it had a sliding sun roof too *and the roof was partway open and there was a hand stuck through it wriggling the fingers to taunt him.*

Or was it a signal?

(In the open air! Drivers on all sides! The Florida State Highway police patrolling in unmarked cars!)

Colin's immediate and instinctive response was to brake, slow his speed, let the Toyota move ahead. Because the disembodied hand (it was the driver's hand: he had only one hand on the steering wheel) was so distracting, vertical in the air like that. Because the eye is drawn irresistibly to such a thing, against the mind's will. Because looking at it while he was driving, staring at it, was dangerous; what if he had an accident? Colin Asch was by temperament and choice the sort of person who neither shrinks from trouble nor seeks it *but if this was a taunt or a signal what then?*

Slowing his speed didn't help: the Toyota slowed too. Kept the distance fixed between them. Aloud he murmured, half sobbing, "Why don't they leave me alone!" He had cash on his person, nearly $1,000 in various denominations, thus a form of anonymity, thus clean and pure, but there were credit cards too. Certain goods in the trunk of the car.

You need to concentrate at such times. Need to be alert at every pore.

The Toyota in the right-hand lane was a mirror twin of his car, and in it a driver (male, alone) was arrogantly sticking his hand up through the sun roof, making a fist, flexing the fingers. What did it mean? Was it directed at Colin Asch, or simply at the driver of the red '87 Mustang? It might have been a fag sign too, Colin thought. He speeded up to pass, but the sight of the disembodied hand through the roof was *so distracting so insulting so dangerous* he lost his nerve and fell back. He was in a sudden panic, fearing the loss of control of his car.

But he played it cool. Inside, he wasn't emotional really; he could enter the Blue Room, breathe in its chill numbing air; he was going to be untouched. Had not he impressed Dr. X (the most recent of Colin Asch's many psychiatrists, psychotherapists, spiritual counselors, et al.) with his "integral" personality? his maturity? his healthy optimism tempered by a healthy sense of realism? That look in the eyes (so important to make eye contact with the fuckers) that meant intelligence, patience, humor? Pointless to risk so much. And the credit cards, one of them for Neiman-Marcus of Palm Beach, in a name clearly not his. And the goods in the trunk which *were* his by rights, but still it was risky.

North of Daytona Beach, about thirty miles from Jacksonville, the driver of the Toyota exited at a rest stop. Colin Asch followed. For some miles he had not been taunted by the disembodied hand, but the point had been established. To prepare himself he'd whistled flawlessly from start to finish, not missing a note or a beat, the languorous first movement of that Beethoven piano sonata known as the "Moonlight." An insipid sentimental title, not Beethoven's. But it had stuck.

There he was, suddenly, the driver of the Toyota: medium height, medium build, black bushy hair, glasses, teacherly, short-trimmed beard, denim jacket, jeans . . . not so much as glancing over at Colin as Colin nosed the Mustang into the space beside his. Cool. He'd locked his car and gone off in the direction of the men's lavatory.

On the rear bumper of the Toyota was a sticker: ANIMALS ARE ONLY HUMAN TOO. What was that supposed to mean? Was it some kind of joke? Colin Asch detested bumper-sticker jokes; they interfered with your thoughts. The Toyota had District of Columbia license plates and a Georgetown University parking decal. In the back seat were scattered books, pamphlets, articles of clothing. Though Colin Asch stretched and yawned, a lazy relaxed look should anyone be watching, in fact he was scrutinizing the rest area: just about deserted except for a station wagon with Iowa license plates, a camper with Ontario license plates, and a diesel with its motor running on the far side of the rest rooms. The place smelled of damp and loneliness.

Stealthily, Colin's fingers tried the door on the passenger's side of the Toyota. But it was locked. And the sun roof too was shut.

In the men's lavatory with its powerful stench of disinfectant, Colin Asch struck up a conversation with the driver of the Toyota, remarking on the bumper sticker—What's that mean, *animals are only human too?*—and the young man said he was an activist with an organization called the Animal Rights League; the bumper sticker was just a sort of joke. Easygoing enough but he didn't seem inclined to linger so Colin asked another question or two, learning that the organization was comprised of a coalition of animal lovers, conservationists, philosophers (academic), and lawyers; their project was to "define" and "protect" animal rights, to expose inhumane practices regarding animals in our society, and to publicize abuses *all the while behaving as if on the road there'd been no signal between them,* so Colin too played it ingenuously, nodding and smiling his boyish sweet attentive smile, beautifully lashed russet eyes fixed to the other's ordinary mud-brown eyes behind the lenses of his glasses, two youngish males measuring each other maybe, but it was a public place; anyone could walk in at any time.

The guy was a fag but not acknowledging it? Seeing that Colin Asch was not the man he'd thought he was?

Or was it something else entirely?

The animal rights man, a professor at Georgetown, philosophy, might have thought it strange that Colin Asch was so absorbed in their talk that he followed him out of the lavatory without using it, but he gave no sign, captivated perhaps by Colin's bright flattering sincerity and the evidence he gave as if off the cuff that he too was a sharpie, remarking how he'd always thought it disgusting the way animals were exploited by man, raised to be slaughtered and eaten, tortured in laboratories in the name of science, but the tricky thing was as Jeremy Bentham argued (wasn't it Bentham? one of those hard-nosed Utilitarians?) that there are no rights outside the law, you can't have "rights" without "law" since there is no natural law, no moral law, only transcribed manmade laws in certain carefully delimited political contexts—which took Colin's listener so by surprise he really opened up, talking warmly and excitedly as if he'd found some long-lost friend or brother. That was the effect Colin Asch generally had on people when he tried.

The man's name was Lionel Block; they even shook hands. Colin showed great interest in reading Animal Rights League literature, thanked Block kindly for giving him a pamphlet ("The Metaphysics of Animal Awareness" by Lionel Block), stood beside the Toyota turning pages, seeing photographs of hideously burned, scarred, mutilated animals . . . including wild creatures that had gnawed off their own paws to free themselves from traps. Block was talking but Colin Asch wasn't listening. Tears of hurt and rage slowly filled his eyes. He said quietly, "You will go to any extreme, won't you?—people like you."

There was a startled silence. Colin grinned at Lionel Block, who was frowning at him as if he hadn't heard.

Overhead, high, an airliner was passing. On the interstate, traffic passed in a steady droning stream. The diesel was starting up on the other side of the rest rooms, heaving into noisy motion like a prehistoric beast. The station wagon was gone, the camper too.

Colin said, "That signal you were making back on the road—what did it mean?"

"Signal? What signal?"

"With your hand. You know. Through the sun roof of your car."

Block adjusted his glasses on his nose, peering at Colin as if he didn't understand. His hair, bushy and kinky, was receding from his forehead; he wasn't Colin Asch's age after all but some years older. When he asked again, "What signal?" Colin made the gesture himself, with his right hand, flexing the fingers lewdly. Block stared. He said, "I wasn't making any signal. I was trying to keep myself awake."

"Awake?"

"The cold air, the wind—it's just a way of keeping from dozing off," Block said uneasily. "When I drive alone I get hypnotized from watching the pavement, so sometimes I open the sun roof a little. Just some crazy thing I do."

Colin regarded him levelly, smiling as if they shared a secret understanding. "So that was it!" he said. "All those miles I thought you were making a signal."

They stared at each other. The rest stop was a desolate place, back far enough from the highway so that no one driving past could see, or would care to make the effort of seeing. At any instant, however, someone could exit, drive right up to within a few yards of Colin and Lionel Block, and this Colin liked, sort of. It kept him on his toes. He had the wire loop prepared in the right-hand pocket of his sheepskin jacket, and his finger crept in, to caress it. He winked, and grinned, and said, "You certainly fooled me! Made a fool of *me!* Misreading you the way I did."

Block licked his lips, trying to smile as if mirroring Colin Asch's smile but with little success. His eyes gave him away; they were the eyes of a badly frightened man. He said, "Well, I guess you did. Misread me. I'm sorry.'' He rubbed at his nose with blunt stubby fingers, and a gold signet ring gleamed on his left hand. ''Now if you'll excuse me—I have to leave.''

''That sort of thing is distracting, you know,'' Colin said. ''At high speeds. Making signals to other drivers and confusing them.''

''But I wasn't making signals! Jesus Christ, I never dreamt anyone was watching. Or, if watching''—Block swallowed clumsily in mid-sentence—''paying any attention.''

''It was a false signal, then,'' Colin said brightly. ''A false alarm.''

''I—I guess so.''

''You just said it was, didn't you?''

Colin stood quietly, unmoving, his head slightly lowered as if he were preparing himself for a struggle. He had tied his longish hair back in a careless ponytail at the nape of his neck, but several strands had worked free and were blowing across his face. He brushed them irritably away from his lips; he couldn't bear hair on his mouth, his own or anyone else's. Then he returned his right hand to his pocket, fingering the wire loop. He carried an eight-inch switchblade in an inside pocket, and there was, in the trunk of the car, the woman's snub-nosed little .38-caliber Smith & Wesson revolver, but it would be the wire loop, the wire noose, this morning. He said softly, ''No one likes to be manipulated.''

Block stammered, ''No one was manipulating anyone! I'm sorry if you misunderstood!'' He would have pushed his way to his car, pushed Colin Asch aside, but courage failed him. Thus far they had not so much as touched. ''Look,'' he said, pleading, ''this is crazy, isn't it? Are you joking? Are *you* crazy? You must know I didn't mean . . . if it was some sort of hand signal, some sort of secret signal, Christ, I swear I didn't know, I've never heard of such a thing. Don't

you believe me? Anything I did I did in absolute innocence! And I certainly wasn't aware of keeping pace
with you, you and your car.''

Colin said, winking, ''OK, but tell me. Why did
you select me? I mean, why me? How did you know?''

''Look, I'm going to have to get some help, help
from the police, if you don't let me by.'' A rim of
white showed above the dark dilated pupils of his eyes.
His breathing was harsh. *At this point,* Colin would
afterward note in the Ledger, *he seemed to comprehend his error and the fact that there would be no
turning back.*

Still they discussed the matter further. Like reasonable men. Colin was saying that Block wasn't going
anywhere until he explained, and Block persisted in
saying there was nothing to explain, and Colin said,
what the signal meant, and how he knew Colin was in
the car behind him, *how he'd known when Colin himself could not have known.* He was gripping the wire
noose, calculating the motions he'd make, observing
himself from a distance or, as if it had already happened, on film. Block might have been a match for
him if he'd tried, but like most men of his type (Colin
Asch knew the type) he wasn't going to try, scared
shitless just by some stranger looking at him the wrong
way and saying things he wasn't prepared to hear. Thus
Block was backing off, looking confusedly around for
help while at the same time hardly daring to take his
eyes off Colin's face. But there was no help. No one
would come. Out of a mottled bluish sky fat raindrops
fell as if idly, erratically, striking the asphalt pavement, the men's red-matched cars. Block was saying
in a broken voice, ''Let me alone—I'll get the police,'' and Colin said, following him, though not yet
hurried, ''Hey, man, I only want to know why of everybody out there on the road you selected *me,* why
me?'' and Block said, ''But I didn't,'' and Colin said,

"Why, for this? For now? For what you're forcing me to do?" and Block lost control at last and shouted, "But what am I forcing you to do?"

Four days later, late in the evening of November 14, Colin Asch arrived at the Weidmanns' home in Lathrup Farms, Massachusetts. He was driving the red '87 Mustang. He was spaced out and tired—hadn't eaten in a long time. Hadn't washed (except for his hands), hadn't shaved (hadn't had the opportunity). He'd planned on stopping in Baltimore (where, guilty and reluctant, and maybe a little scared, they'd have to take him in) but for some reason kept on driving. North to New York, north to Massachusetts. Boston. Reasoning it was wisest under the circumstances. No one would ever catch up with him, but distance helps.

He'd promised his Aunt Ginny he would visit them anyway; she loved him and would take care of him, and even if she asked too many bossy questions he could handle that, no problem about that. The husband he could handle too. No problem. He didn't lack for cash—he had now about $1,075 in his wallet—but that wouldn't last forever and he was tired, suddenly so tired. The good feeling had propelled him for days, but now it had left him as it always did like water draining out of a sink and there he was in Lathrup Farms, at his aunt's house, knowing she'd take him in. "She is one of the few people who believes in me," he said aloud, as if to another party. And it was true. The other sons of bitches were always waiting for him to make a misstep, waiting to find fault, commit him to medical treatment. But his Aunt Ginny loved and trusted him; she'd taken him in for a while after the scandal broke at school, Mr. Kreuzer found dead and all that. Just to think of her was to forget, sort of, his actual age, and to half think (as in a dream) that he was some other age, years younger. But it was all subjective, after all.

In the Blue Ledger where he kept account of his life he'd noted only *B.L. 781011Alf.* regarding what had happened in Florida, reversing initials and numerals in case anyone ever read what he'd written. He knew there were professional code breakers who worked for police and the FBI, but that didn't worry Colin Asch in the slightest. To break your code they first have to find your code. They have to find you.

There were guests at the Weidmanns', seated at the dining room table, but everything was stopped for Colin as soon as he stepped inside the door. His aunt greeted him as if she'd been waiting for him all these days, hugged him hard, fussed over him. Powerful waves of shyness and pleasure alternated in him, raising heat into his face.

Ginny Weidmann was a large soft perfumy woman, not bad-looking for her age—about fifty, Colin guessed—with a bright made-up face and intense eyes. The kind of female who, if you closed your fingers around her upper arm, you'd leave prints in the flesh. But sharp-eyed and no fool: she was biting her lip, trying to gauge the extent of his hunger, his tiredness, all he'd been through these past few days. Even noticed the marks on his hands, the shallow reddened scratches, saying half accusingly, as if Colin were much younger than his age, "Oh, Colin—what on earth have you done to yourself? And where have you been?"

She sent him away upstairs to shower and change; his Uncle Martin was a good generous-hearted guy taking him in hand—here's the bathroom, he told Colin, and here's a closet of shirts and things; anything you need give me a holler, you promise?—and

Colin, a little breathless, promised. His eyes were filling with tears at this welcome. When he was alone in
the shower, lifting his face to the hot stinging spray,
he said, "They know they can trust me—they're not
like the others." If he'd barged in on his uncle down
in Baltimore, the old fart might have sent him away
again; Colin wouldn't have put it past him. I'll go
away, I didn't mean to interrupt, he'd have said, polite
as he was with the Weidmanns, and the old bastard
might have taken him at his word. Which was why he
hadn't gone to Baltimore after all. Or one of the reasons.

It was six or seven years since Colin had been in the
Weidmanns' house, but he remembered it clearly. In
certain respects he was gifted with a photographic
memory: he gathered, from things people told him and
from things he read, that his mind wasn't like other
people's minds but capable of summoning back memories vivid as dreams, frequently so real they left him
shaken and aroused. So the Weidmanns' big Victorian
house entered, came flooding back as if he'd left it
only last week. The carved archways and molding, the
tall narrow many-paned windows with their elaborate
curtains and draw drapes; everywhere you looked, antique furniture and Oriental carpets and polished hardwood floors. Cut-crystal chandeliers, stained-glass
window in the foyer. The smell of freshly polished
silverware. Of freshly cut flowers. Of money.

There'd been talk of the Weidmanns taking Colin
Asch in after the accident in which his parents drowned
(which he thought of as simply the Accident—when he
thought of it at all), and again after the trouble at the
Monmouth Academy and Colin's breakdown and hos-
pitalization. But their children, a boy and a girl Colin's
age, he'd blanked out their names, had opposed it.
They'd been jealous of him, pretended to be afraid of
him. The little fuckers.

"But I'm here now."

He was grateful for the hot splashing water, the fragrant soap. It was the least they could do for him—his own blood kin, after all. He shampooed his hair roughly and rinsed it, surprised at its length. He didn't want to be mistaken for some hippie queer. Out of the shower, dripping, he dried himself in an enormous towel the size of a beach towel and combed through his snarled hair with a stainless steel comb that must have belonged to his Uncle Martin—this was Martin's bathroom—then shaved with a razor he found in the medicine cabinet—his uncle's too, he assumed—hands shaking slightly so he had to go slow, didn't want to nick himself. In the mirror his expression was guarded, self-critical. He'd always been aware of his remarkable good looks—a Nordic angel, Mr. Kreuzer used to call him, mocking and loving—but he knew that good looks can be lost rapidly, in a few months, a few days, a single hour if it's the right hour. His eyes looked shadowed even in the bright overhead light, and the whites were lightly threaded with blood as if he hadn't slept in days. (About that—sleeping—he wasn't too clear. He guessed he'd slept in the car in hidden places off the highway, curled up in the back seat with the .38 revolver under him.) They would feed him here in this house, and they would see to it that he slept, rested, regained his equilibrium. They were good people, the Weidmanns: Ginny especially. If only she wouldn't try to overdo it.

Colin's hands ached where the wire had cut in deepest. He had not noticed at the time or afterward, driving gripping the steering wheel tight. He had not wanted to use gloves with the wire noose because it was tricky enough handling it with his bare hands. He thought of surgeons, their manual skill, precision: required to wear the thinnest of gloves when they operate, because they need to feel what they're doing and the instruments are so delicate. And if the membrane of the glove is pricked, and if blood from the patient seeps through, there is the danger of AIDS. Except for AIDS he'd go to medical school and train to be a surgeon. You're born with the touch, it's said, or you are not. You are or you're not. Like musical talent, which Colin Asch had had too, as a child.

"It's so fucking *unfair.*"

He couldn't have said what was unfair but he felt it keenly, and he knew too that they were talking about him downstairs, hearing of his "tragic" life, et cetera, shaking their heads and murmuring the usual banalities. If the Weidmanns went too far with that shit they'd regret it.

It burned his ass too that his Uncle Martin (so-called uncle: the two of them weren't related by blood, and even if they had been he'd be Colin's mother's uncle, not Colin's) just naturally assumed he hadn't any decent or even clean clothes of his own. Wear anything you like, anything that comes close to fitting, the smug old fart had said, showing him shirts, a rack of neckties, letting his beefy hand fall on Colin's shoulder as if he had the right. Maybe he was queer too, like the bastard back at the rest stop. His uncle's age, you might as well try anything.

So Colin, his heart beating sullenly, selected a plain white cotton shirt, a plain navy-knit tie; the neck and shoulders of the shirt were too big for him but he liked it, sort of, when clothes didn't exactly fit, gave him a boyish even a waiflike look, a real advantage. He'd always been young, and he'd always looked younger than his age. There was a real advantage in that; he thought of it as a kind of lever.

He sat on the edge of the Weidmanns' bed, pulling on black silk socks. Wild! A few days ago he was on the beach in Lauderdale, greasy hair blowing in his mouth, and now he was here! The master bedroom was a spacious high-ceilinged room with green silk wallpaper, thick white wall-to-wall carpeting, most of the furniture oversized—big four-poster antique bed, big bureau, big full-length mirror. If he had time he'd investigate but he hadn't time, they were awaiting him downstairs; he *was* hungry. In his uncle's cuff link box he found a pair of gold and onyx cuff links which he slipped into his pocket; in his aunt's jewelry box he found a pair of gold and diamond earrings which he also slipped into his pocket, reasoning that, with all the Weidmanns had—and of course Ginny's really expensive jewelry was locked safely away—they wouldn't miss these small items. In a dressing room alcove he found his aunt's handbag, or one of her handbags, a red leather Gucci, quickly extracted the wallet and from that a few bills, two tens, a twenty, a five, reasoning they wouldn't be missed, so many bills remained. And the bitch had credit cards, of course. They all did.

"It's the least you owe me. Fuckers."

When, downstairs, he entered the dining room it was like stepping out onto a stage: he could feel the electrically charged air, his mere approach giving off sparks. Ginny with her big mouth and probably Martin too had set him up perfectly so now there were these assholes, solemn-faced, gaping at *him*: Colin Asch. He just took over; he had them all. But he played it cool, knowing everybody likes sweet shy boys, tongue-tied boys, *orphan* etched into their faces. And no reason he could have named except he'd actually looked through some of the material in the back seat of the Toyota, felt a sudden kinship of sorts with the victimized animals, legs in traps, wired up for experiments in laboratories, chickens with their beaks chopped off, monkeys with skulls sawed open—*Christ, what a world of suffering! Why does God allow it to happen!*—so when he picked up his fork it seemed to him that he'd be the kind of person who couldn't eat meat, who was too pure to eat meat, and the rest of them would have to acknowledge it. Thus within seconds the taste and even the smell of the lamb roast was nauseating.

This caused a flurry of excitement too, his aunt fussing over him and sending the little black girl away for a clean plate; Colin liked it but squirmed with embarrassment. Sons of bitches looking at him imagining themselves so superior, taking pity on Colin Asch.

One by one he took them in. Tried to memorize names—his short-term memory was fantastic when there was some purpose for it.

The youngest woman at the table was "Hartley," about thirty years old, little-girl good-looking, black glossy hair, bangs to her eyebrows, fleshy red mouth he imaged sucking him off, and that expertly; and within days. "Charles Carpenter," a mild-mannered but probably shrewd-minded coldhearted son of a bitch, mid- or late forties, lawyer, and well-to-do. His wife, "Agnes," a drunk with a soft ruined face, heavy-lidded eyes, too much jewelry hanging on her with a mineral glitter as if out of spite (the woman's jade dinner ring was the size of a robin's egg), but Colin connected with something in her, something sour and peevish waiting its turn. And there was a guy his age or a year or two older, "Schmidt," by the look of him a young lawyer or a young stockbroker, nattily dressed, smug, hopeful, trying to impress the table (trying to impress "Hartley") with some crap about West Germany. And there was another man whose name Colin hadn't caught—he'd have to ask before the evening broke up—pinch-faced, bald except for patches of grizzled gray around his ears, nervous, sad, heavy-hearted, Colin could see, or sense; in his early fifties maybe, or older. And quietest of them all a woman named "Dorothea Deverell" who was a friend of Colin's aunt, creamy-pale skin, large intelligent eyes,

watchful too, very still, hard to estimate her age but
Colin supposed she must be in her mid-thirties . . .
who did she remind him of? She wore her dark hair
brushed back from her face and fastened neatly at the
nape of her neck by a tortoiseshell clip. She looked
down the table at him intently, he had the idea respectfully. It occurred to him that she was a good person,
she had a good kind decent generous soul; like a spark
the idea ignited in his heart, pulsing warmly through
his blood. Later that night he would note in the Blue
Ledger, *I think so. Of course I can't be sure.*

Though probably little or nothing would have come
of this insight—Colin Asch was visited with so many
insights, sometimes within a single hour—had not, a
little later, this woman spoken so strangely, and so
. . . purposefully. To him. In front of the entire table.

Exactly how it happened he wouldn't be able to recall, afterward, trying to record the episode in the Blue
Ledger. Carpenter's wife, Agnes, had been questioning him about vegetarianism, asking did he belong to
a cult, coming fairly close to insulting him—it was
really surprising how hostile the bitch was *for no reason at all simply for the hell of it,* which Colin Asch
could understand but which didn't mean he liked it or
liked being mocked in front of a little audience including the hot-looking girl with the eyes and the pouty
luscious mouth and Miss Deverell, who looked pained
at the attack—but he maintained his composure, observing himself carefully as if indeed he were on stage
as years ago he'd studied a videotape of Colin Asch
on an actual stage—he'd played the role of Mark An-
tony in Shakespeare's tragedy at the Monmouth Academy and everyone marveled over his acting skills, most
of all Mr. Kreuzer who had directed the play—so there
was no temptation to lose control, start stammering,
saying things he'd afterward regret. In fact the nastier
Mrs. Carpenter became the nicer Colin Asch could

be; there was a palpable rhythm to it, like two people on a teeter-totter, or fucking; which was maybe why Mrs. Carpenter persisted, when everyone else was on Colin Asch's side and casting her disapproving looks. Colin got to his feet so agitated he didn't know what he would say; the words just came out of him: "The suffering of animals is no less because it lacks a language. Like the suffering of infants."

That got them. That got them! Agnes Carpenter had to back down, knowing she'd pressed him too far. And the others said things, tried to gloss over the awkward moment, fat blowsy Ginny Weidmann trying to slide her arm through his as if she had the right. "We understand about the animals, Colin, really we do," she said anxiously. "Won't you sit down, dear? We promise you can eat your meal in peace."

Colin wrenched away from her. "Do you!" he said.

Thinking: You can all go fuck yourselves.

It was at that moment, in the startled silence, that the woman Dorothea Deverell spoke. A stranger to Colin Asch yet clearly sensing his inner distress. Saying *in a weird quiet premeditated voice* words of a higher consolation: "But animals eat one another too. We, I mean—since we are animals. It is something of which we should be ashamed, but even shame is not enough to defeat hunger."

Colin stared at her through a watery red haze. How strangely she'd spoken, how unexpectedly! To him! Piercing his heart!

There had never been anything like it before in his life.

Thus the ugly moment passed, and Colin Asch was able, with dignity, to resume his place at the table, and his meal: for which he was indeed ravenously hungry. And afterward, upstairs in the room these kindest of people had provided for him, he had recorded the incident in the Blue Ledger as best, considering his exhaustion and agitation, as he could. *Animals eat one another too. We, I mean . . . Even shame is not enough.*

A beautiful woman. "Dorothea Deverell." A stranger to Colin Asch *yet mysteriously knowing him;* knowing how he craved understanding, sympathy, consolation. *The gist of it is, hunger sanctifies!* he recorded.

An utterly simple truth which it was required a stranger tell him, lest false guilt contaminate his soul.

So Colin Asch, though by nature the roving kind—or is it roaming?—restless to the very marrow of his bones and drawn, it sometimes seemed, by the sun's westward movement across the sky, to movement of his own, allowed himself to be cajoled by the Weidmanns into staying on in Lathrup Farms for a while. Through Thanksgiving, at least. Until he knew more clearly what his plans for the future were. (He wanted, he said, to look for a job. Maybe later return to school. There were so many good schools in the Boston area. Many job prospects too, he guessed. At RISDE—the Rhode Island School of Design—Colin Asch had been an outstanding student; certain of his instructors had praised and encouraged his talent, as an artist and as a graphics designer. There was a future awaiting him, they'd said.)

So he said yes. So he said Thank you from the bottom of my heart.

And meant it! God, yes.

"Everybody else treats me like"—he paused, reflecting—"dirt."

"Oh, now, Colin dear, that can't be true," Aunt Ginny said reprovingly. "Can it?"

* * *

He was twenty-seven years old, in December to be twenty-eight years old. Alone. Unmarried. No true family. In Europe it was several times said of him he was "so uniquely American," but in America what could be said of him? He carried innocence about him like a radiant heat, shining in his beautiful eyes, coursing through his veins. His handshake, his touch, communicated warmth, strength, modesty, a special destiny. Knowing nothing of his tragic background, women adored him for the hurt in his face, and his manliness. Some men too adored him, and some men feared him. *And with good cause!* as he noted, amused.

Of the several XXX incidents recorded in the Blue Ledger, only one was female. And that, in one of the western states, in so blurred a passage of Colin Asch's life (someone had turned on Colin Asch to the powerful visions of mescaline) it scarcely counted. Might in fact have been a dream. Contemplating the cryptic abbreviations in the Ledger regarding that incident Colin Asch was as puzzled, or nearly, as a stranger to the Ledger might have been. He'd forgotten the girl's name, the girl's face, even the means of death! Which was not consistent with his character.

Before Fort Lauderdale and the sixth-floor condo in Sea Breeze Village, Colin Asch had been living in Miami, and before Miami he'd been living in Houston, and before Houston he'd been traveling in Morocco (where one evening in Tangier he knocked on the door of the American expatriate writer Paul Bowles—and was admitted), and before Morocco he'd been traveling in Greece, Germany, Holland. . . . Before that was the United States: a brownstone in Brooklyn Heights where he'd lived with some of the members of an experimental troupe of actors. And before that a string of shitty manual jobs, servile jobs, in the New York area. And before that . . . things were vague. Patches of his adult life were shifting out of focus like his childhood, which was so distant from him as to have happened to another person. Barely remembered on the far side of a river.

These things he yearned to tell the Weidmanns' friend Dorothea Deverell. How he was cursed with too many talents. Music, art, writing, acting, science, "the art of human relations" . . . all beckoned. Yet in none thus far had he managed to succeed while others, less talented, had forged careers. "So damned fucking *unfair.*"

The truth was that much that had happened to Colin Asch in the course of his life, beginning with the Accident surely, but perhaps beginning at birth, had happened merely in his vicinity. Apart from his will *and without his guidance.*

Thus "praise" and "blame" are equally unmerited.

Thus "he" (agent) and "it" (action) are falsely separated.

Thus even the most general time demarcations— "past," "present," "future"—are invalid.

For in the Blue Room (which at certain times Colin Asch was privileged to enter) all things become one. The fierce blue light erases all shadow. There is no gravity, no weight. Not even "up" and "down"!

Purification is the goal. The means scarcely matter.
Absolution.
Sanction.

As Colin Asch would explain to Dorothea Deverell. When he saw her again.

Each day Colin Asch scanned the newspapers hoping to find an account of the episode recorded in the Blue Ledger as *B.L. 781011Alf.* But there was nothing. Days passed, and a week—and there was nothing!

"Fuckers."

It angered him that his victim Block, who had in the end put up a desperate struggle to live, like a maddened animal, and had given Colin Asch quite a workout, should not merit even an inch of newsprint here in the North. Nor was there anything in *Newsweek,* to which the Weidmanns subscribed. You would think the Florida state police and the highway patrol would talk to reporters about having come upon a "perfect crime"—for, if it was not perfect, where was the perpetrator?

"Yeah," Colin said, snorting in derision. *"Where is he?"*

He considered writing messages to the police down there. Maybe the Jacksonville police too—maybe they were involved. Just to burn their asses a little. Give them a hint who they were dealing with. And maybe to Georgetown University where Block had taught— ANIMALS ARE ONLY HUMAN TOO might make a good cryptic message.

But why do the bastards any favors?

Also, Colin was getting absorbed in matters up here. Looking for a job. Making contacts. Making the right connections.

It did not worry him in the slightest that police might in some way trace him . . . as if they could trace his footprints in the sand leading them right to *him!* Not once since the age of fifteen, when he had first killed, or been forced to kill, had Colin Asch been linked to any of his murders; so far as he knew (admittedly, he could not absolutely know), his name had never been on any list of police suspects. The police, like everyone else, or nearly everyone (for there was the one tenth of one percent who stood apart from the herd), were just too stupid.

Colin Asch had in fact always relied upon the world's stupidity as a factor in his own talent. Amid a herd of slow-witted bovine beasts he was a leopard capable of running at speeds up to seventy-five miles an hour—a flash of burnished flaming light. In Florida he had not been rushed; he had been methodical as always, knowing that, as soon as he returned to his car and drove away, he could enter the Blue Room and float weightless there for miles, hours, in an utter bliss of childlike innocence; thus he followed his self-prescribed stratagem of the Baffle . . . meaning that he deliberately, and with boyish pleasure, fucked up the scene. He dragged the body into a scrubby littered area behind the rest rooms (scolding it for its heaviness and its inclination to snag on tree roots, bushes, and the like, as if even in death Block was being uncooperative) and there pinned a page torn out of a magazine from Block's car onto Block's sweater, reasoning that, when police discovered the body, they would think that the photograph on the page (of AIDS patients in a Washington clinic) had some relevance to the victim's death. Next he found several lipstick-stained cigarettes where someone had dumped them in the gravel, and these he tossed into the Toyota, on the floor by the passenger's seat and in the rear. A condom from his own wallet he tore out of its foil wrapper and tossed both condom and wrapper into the back seat. Then, with Block's car keys, he scratched nonsensical letters and zodiac signs on the hood of the Toyota; then locked the car doors; and, still not hurrying (though a car with Georgia license plates, heavily weighted with children, had just driven into the rest area to park some distance away), he wiped the surface of the Toyota everywhere his fingerprints might conceivably be found. Then he got into the red '87 Mustang and drove away—and did indeed enter the Blue Room almost immediately, sucked breathless into it, like a soul into heaven.

3

Poor man, Dorothea Deverell thought, staring. But surely he can't be totally blind? Out by himself like this?

The gentleman in question, a timid rather stooped figure in dark glasses, wearing a tweed cap, a loosely belted trench coat, and unbuckled galoshes, was making his way across the foyer of the Brannon Institute, tapping the marble floor with a white-tipped cane and following at a slant in the wake of others entering the recital hall; it was nearly 4 P.M. of a dark wintry Sunday at the end of November, and people had come to hear, in larger numbers than Dorothea Deverell had dared hope, the British soprano Natalya Lowe sing Schumann, Brahms, and Poulenc. Always anxious before such events (as indeed before any event that might be said to be her responsibility or, in retrospect, her fault), Dorothea found herself more anxious than usual this afternoon: a pitiable figure, no doubt, to those who knew her, in her elegantly cut black silk dress with the high neckline and the countless shimmering pleats. There were pearls screwed into her ears, and pearls around her slender neck, and she was very pale and smiled steadily. She had worried that no one would show up for the recital, though the event was advertised as free. She had worried that Miss Lowe, known to be temperamental, would not herself show up. Or that her accompanist would raise further objections to the conditions of the recital hall and the piano he was obliged to play. (This high-handed individual had decided, late Friday afternoon, to reject the Institute's Steinway concert grand, insisting that another be rented for the performance.) And Roger Krauss, who hated Dorothea Deverell, had come, with another trustee and his wife; and Charles Carpenter, who loved Dorothea Deverell, had not yet come—and perhaps would not. Standing by the entrance, smiling and waving and calling out greetings to friends, she felt her heart congealing to ice; she could not have been more uneasy if she herself were going to sing. And it was all so absurd. And so excessive. And futile.

Which of the philosophers was it who observed that the natural bent of things is toward chaos, and that order itself is unnatural? For there is only one way for things to go ideally, and any number of ways for things to go wrong.

Seeing that the man in the dark glasses was headed waveringly in her direction, Dorothea quickly came forward to assist him. "Sir? May I?"

Though startled, he acquiesced immediately to her hand on his arm, smiling inside his gingery-gray beard and murmuring, "Ah! Thank you! You're very kind." Had he been standing at his true height he would have been a head taller than Dorothea Deverell, but he walked in a hunched, crablike manner; it would have been difficult to determine his age. Not young, certainly. But how old? As Dorothea led him slowly down the wide center aisle of the hall and to a choice seat in the third row he apologized for being a nuisance; he wasn't, he said, totally blind, but had a fair amount of vision in his left eye, at least if the light was good; most of the time he had no difficulty getting around.

"You aren't a nuisance," Dorothea protested.

"We're very happy to have you here." In her excitable mood she spoke almost gaily; she had no idea what she said. (For perhaps Charles Carpenter had arrived by now? was watching her help a blind man settle into his seat?)

Though Dorothea would have liked to flee, the man in the dark glasses unexpectedly thrust out his hand at her and said, "My name is Lionel Ashton—may I ask yours?"

"Dorothea Deverell," Dorothea said.

Mr. Ashton did not release her hand quite so quickly as she might have wished; his grip was strong. He had heard of her, he said; didn't she have something to do with the Brannon Institute, wasn't she well known in Lathrup Farms? He squinted frowningly up at her through the smoky black lenses of his glasses; you could see nothing of his eyes inside. In the foyer he had seemed timid and hesitant, but he exuded a curious sort of authority now, bent upon deterring Dorothea though he sensed her eagerness to hurry off. His voice was husky as if unnaturally lowered and much of his face was concealed, by the glasses, and the tweed cap (in style though not in quality resembling a British workingman's cap) pulled low over his forehead, and the bristling little beard that reminded Dorothea of a Scotch terrier's fur. How odd that I have never seen him here before, Dorothea thought. When she finally excused herself to back away, he called after her, "Thank you again, Miss Deverell! I'm not a man who forgets kindness!"

It was just past 4 P.M. and the recital hall was agreeably filled. Dorothea dismissed the girls who were handing out programs in the foyer and remained to hand them out herself to last-minute stragglers. But there were few. She stood smiling vaguely toward the front doors, waiting. As she so often waited. Perhaps I am of that breed of women uniquely qualified for waiting, she thought. Behind her the doors of the recital hall were shut; after a pause the first vigorous notes of Schumann's "Widmung" were sounded; a powerful soprano voice, so much larger than life, seized control of all imaginations. That is the way to do it, Dorothea thought, staring toward the entrance. Though she had signed on Natalya Lowe for this engagement back in March and had been quite pleased at the prospect of bringing the soprano to Lathrup Farms, in Dorothea Deverell's own Sunday afternoon recital series, now, she scarcely heard—

The outer doors opened another, final time, and two Lathrup Farms matrons, sumptuously clad in fur coats and hats, hurried inside, bearing with them a bone-chilling gust of air.

Dorothea Deverell took her place inside, at the rear of the little hall, sitting alone, hands clasped on her knees. She was thinking that since Roger Krauss had begun his systematic campaign against her she had become conscious of doing many things wrong.

It was like proofreading for the dozenth time a passage of her own careful prose to discover, to her chagrin, that she'd made a typographical error of the most blatant kind. . . . The other day, doing galleys for next season's calendar, she had come upon "arists" where "artists" was meant. And she had read this so many times. . . . The error was trivial yet it filled her with dread: for if the eye trickily fills in where there is a significant absence, what does that portend for our reading of the world? and our sense of ourselves in the world?

Where previously, at the Institute, Dorothea had carried on in a bliss of well-being, assuming that, underpaid as she was and uncomplainingly overworked, she had the general support of the community behind her, now she supposed that was not the case at all and never had been. She was well liked, of course—how many times had people said, conspicuously in her hearing, *Isn't Dorothea Deverell marvelous!*— but she was liked as other civic-minded women in the community were liked, and her talents, such as they were, set beside those of a man—any man?—were likely to be discounted. In this affluent suburban village many women, the wives of prominent citizens, exerted themselves in volunteer work; yet their exertions were likely to be erratic, unreliable, and even, in certain comical instances, seasonal. With these, Dorothea Deverell was surely lumped: which was, she supposed, no one's fault but her own. For in what ways *am* I different?

She was keenly aware too of the many missteps and blunders of her daily life. Returning from the grocery store with fruit already bruised, overpriced items she must have selected without seeing. Mislaying things, losing things. Forgetting things. Spilling things. Allowing herself to be cheated in stores because she was absentminded, inattentive . . . for her life pushed forward in its subterranean way with little vigilance and self-protection. She believed, at times, that she was under the spell of an interior voice she did not quite recognize: chiding, nagging, questioning, narrating. The voice passed judgment on Dorothea Deverell, and this judgment had the power to silence her. Ah, what would it be, Dorothea thought, to have the confidence to so powerfully (yet tenderly) declare oneself to the world as the soprano Natalya Lowe declared herself? (Miss Lowe was now singing Poulenc's beautiful little cycle "Tel Jour, Telle Nuit.") Does the power of one's voice come first, or is confidence required for power? Dorothea wondered.

Over the telephone Charles Carpenter, to whose elusive figure Dorothea Deverell's hopes for "emotional happiness" were affixed, had murmured apologetically that he would not know until the last minute if he could come to the recital. "If I'm not there—I suppose I won't be coming," he had said. Dorothea laughed. "Your logic is amazing." "But I do want to come. You know I do." Adding, after a wistful pause, "Just to see you, Dorothea." Carelessly, Dorothea Deverell said, "Ah, Charles, you can see me any time!"

When the recital ended and Miss Lowe and her accompanist were warmly applauded, Dorothea woke from her trance and applauded happily with the rest. Despite her distracting thoughts she had noticed that the middle-aged singer, still flamboyantly beautiful, or at any rate "striking," had developed a slight hoarseness at lower levels; and her upper register of passion and substance seemed rather willed—if not frankly simulated. In the middle range Natalya Lowe was most effective; thus in the middle range she poured out her soul, or gave a convincing impression of doing so. In any case we are an audience of amateurs and not difficult to please, Dorothea thought. She clapped and clapped until her hands stung.

Overall, she was so pleased with the event she had herself arranged that she did not even dread the wine and cheese reception to follow, at which Dorothea Deverell would function as hostess for two hundred-odd people. The color had returned to her cheeks, the light to her eyes. The dry cleaner's had done a superb job with her black silk dress. She had forgotten her enemy Roger Krauss entirely. She had forgotten the importunate blind man whose grip had been so insistent. She had forgotten—almost—that Charles Carpenter had again disappointed her.

Next day at noon, crossing the small park attached to the Institute (the Morris T. Brannon Institute was housed in the English Tudor mansion that had been the home of the wealthy industrialist-philanthropist Josiah Brannon, and the property included several acres of land), Dorothea happened by chance to notice a solitary figure on one of the park benches . . . bareheaded, very blond . . . in a patch of wintry sunshine, *The Selected Poems of Shelley* in his hands. It was the very paperback edition Dorothea had owned since college, thus the cover was familiar; and familiar, too, the young man who sat so intently reading. He was long-limbed, lean, boyish, with a bright blue scarf around his neck and a soiled sheepskin jacket: ah, Ginny Weidmann's nephew Colin. Dorothea hesitated, wondering if she should say hello; but he *was* so absorbed in his book and had not seen her. Dorothea Deverell was the kind of person, inexplicably shy at selected times, who, seeing even old friends and acquaintances on the street, was inclined to turn quickly away if she herself had not been detected.

Afterward, however, she thought of the young man with pleasure: so romantically alone, in a chilly deserted park, in the middle of the day, reading the poems of Shelley! I envy him, I suppose, she thought.

That night she felt urged to telephone Ginny Weidmann, to thank her, belatedly, for the dinner party; and to apologize for not having telephoned sooner. As a single woman in a world dominated by couples Dorothea Deverell could not dispel the notion that any social invitation made to her was proffered out of kindness, if not charity; she had to keep in check a propensity for excessive, guilty gratitude. But Ginny Weidmann was primarily interested in critiquing Agnes Carpenter's behavior that evening—like other Lathrup Farms women, she did rather resent the fact that Agnes Carpenter was Charles Carpenter's wife, now that the woman had grown so charmless, and so unapologetic as well. ''I simply can't forgive her for attacking my nephew after I'd confided in her, in her and in all of you, about his—his sensitivity," Ginny said. "The poor boy has had breakdowns, he's been hospitalized, and he has made such a—I really don't think it's excessive to say he has made a valiant effort, a heroic effort, to live in the world. The vegetarianism is only a phase, I'm sure, and it isn't after all *criminal.*"

There was a pause. Dorothea too felt a thrill of maternal, or perhaps sisterly, solicitude for the beleaguered young man. "How is he?" she asked. "I assume he's staying with you and Martin for a while?"

Unhearing, with passion, Ginny said, *"How* do you think Charles endures that woman? He is such a superior human being himself—but I do think he carries loyalty rather too far, don't you? There is something so annoyingly old-fashioned about Charles Carpenter, don't you think?" Dorothea murmured mere sound: neither assent nor dissent. The subject of Charles Carpenter, as conversation, filled her with a profound unease. Ginny plunged on. "Martin believes that Charles is a 'desperately stoical' man and that it is his religion that keeps him from divorcing her. These old Episcopalian families, these stubborn old *Bostonians!*"

Dorothea thought, Charles Carpenter is no more religious than I am. She said, "Well, you can see that Agnes was a very attractive woman at one time. She still would be, in fact, if—"

"Oh, Dorothea! Just *stop!*" Ginny said. "You carry that sort of thing too far!"

What sort of thing? Dorothea Deverell wondered.

Ginny Weidmann went on to speak in a hostess's effusive terms of Jerome Gallagher, who had been "quite taken" with Dorothea—"As I'd predicted, Dorothea; why were you so worried?"—and of her glamorous young friend Hartley Evans: "Isn't Hartley beautiful? Just so—sharp and quick and *contemporary.* She telephoned last week to ask if Colin might be willing to be interviewed on one of the television station's talk shows, about his animal rights work and vegetarianism. Martin and I were delighted—Colin needs to be involved more with the world, the work-a-day 'real' world—and to our surprise he agreed. 'If you give me moral support, Aunt Ginny,' he said. He's such a shy boy at heart, but as you might have noticed he can be amazingly articulate, even eloquent, at times. And he's *smart*. He hopes to get a job in the public sector of some kind, so meeting people at Hartley's station will be a step in the right direction, we think—actually, he happened to mention just sort of casually that he had been an assistant to a German public television producer in Heidelberg, a sort of American consultant, I gather. Isn't he remarkable, really? And so sweet.''

Dorothea said, as if she had been bullied into it, ''Yes.''

''He's going to be staying with Martin and me for a while—there are so many excellent universities and art schools and God knows what all else in this area, and he intends to go back to school in a year or so. The awkward thing is, he hasn't much money but he doesn't want to be a burden on us. Becoming an orphan at the age of twelve was probably more traumatic in certain ways than having been an orphan at birth would have been, since the boy has his pride after all.''

''Yes,'' Dorothea said, not certain that this was true but for some reason keen upon pursuing the subject. ''But does he have many friends? Girlfriends?''

Ginny said, ''No—and yes. Because he's so itinerant he doesn't have friends in the usual sense, I mean they're all scattered, but as soon as he settles down he starts attracting them. Hartley, for instance—she's such a sophisticated young woman, but she seems quite taken by Colin.'' She paused. ''I do wish he'd find the right girl and marry her. I'm conventional enough to think that might be the only solution to his problem.''

"His problem?"

"The trouble is, Colin is so damned trusting. He's an idealist. He has always wanted people to be perfect, and when that doesn't work out he becomes disillusioned, sometimes bitterly. I'm not clear on the details, but evidently when he was living with one of his father's brothers in Baltimore and going to college—the state university, not Hopkins; he'd applied at but been rejected by Hopkins, which hurt him a great deal; after all, he *is* so bright!—he was involved with a man or men later arrested for drug dealing, and check forging, and somehow poor Colin got roped in with the others and actually arrested. It was a mistake of course and the charges were later dropped but it *was* upsetting. And there were other things," Ginny said vaguely, thoughtfully, "other unfortunate incidents that grew out of his naïveté. In some respects, you see, Colin Asch is still a child. An unspoiled, *natural* child. What is that European term, it applies to children abandoned in the wilds, and brought up by animals—"

" 'L'enfant sauvage'—"

"For instance, day before yesterday Colin insisted upon taking Martin and me out to dinner, to celebrate, he said, just the fact we were all alive—it was so touching. He has surprised me with flowers several times—the other day I walked into the bedroom and there was a bouquet, lovely red roses, waiting for me; I simply broke down and cried; my own children, you know, would never, *never* have—well, you know. They completely take Martin and me for granted. But Colin, it seems, takes nothing for granted. He is so eager, so hungry somehow—so curious. He has been asking, for instance, Dorothea, about *you.*"

"About me?"

"Asking how long we've known you. What sort of

work you do, what sort of life you lead. I told him just a bit—I hope you don't mind."

"Oh, no," Dorothea said. "Not at all." Though thinking, My marriage. My "tragic" marriage. She could envision the gusto with which Ginny Weidmann told of Michel Deverell's death; recounted the old, now so very maudlin tale of Dorothea Deverell's miscarriage, which she was sure to place after the death. Yet it did not fail to please her, even as it discomfited her, that Colin Asch, that intriguing young man, should inquire after Dorothea Deverell at all. The situation was a mirror of sorts in which Dorothea might view herself from a new and unexpected—and possibly advantageous—angle, but she did not want to pursue it. Her vanity was to deny all impulses of vanity in herself.

Before they hung up Dorothea said she hoped to have the Weidmanns over for dinner soon, before Christmas certainly: "And your nephew too. If it wouldn't bore him to join us."

"Oh, I'm sure Colin would be delighted," Ginny said, though her voice had gone slightly vague. "Actually he's gone a good deal—says he is acquainting himself with this 'new untouched part of the world'— he usually comes home after Martin and I are asleep. During the day he is job-hunting, and at night I suppose he's making friends, meeting other young people. We've given him a key of course and he's perfectly considerate—never makes the slightest noise—moves through the house like a ghost."

"Excuse me? Miss Deverell?"

Dorothea Deverell looked up from her desk to see, poised in her doorway, having somehow slipped past her secretary, Colin Asch himself—the young man's expression tense, his jaws set, as if he had been steeling himself for some time for this moment. Afterward

Dorothea would recall how unmistakably, how seemingly naturally, their eyes had locked; how immediate her own reaction had been, of surprise, recognition, embarrassment. She felt a rude hot blush rise into her face.

It crossed her mind, perhaps unreasonably, that Ginny Weidmann was responsible; she'd sent her nephew over to say hello to Dorothea Deverell.

But Colin had plans, it seemed, of his own. Tall, lanky, very nervous, with the bright blue scarf wound about his throat, looking both shy and in a way belligerent, he had come to ask Dorothea if she remembered him? and would she like to join him for lunch?

"I just happened to be in the neighborhood, Miss Deverell," he said quickly, as if an explanation were required. "In fact I was just looking at the watercolor exhibit here, it's very good, I think; whoever chose the show has excellent taste—watercolor is the most difficult medium of all, you know. In art. The painting has to be done almost in a single gesture; there isn't any room for error or hesitation. But—but I guess you know all this." In Dorothea's little office the young man's voice had taken on a raw adolescent soaring tone; he stopped speaking abruptly.

Dorothea told Colin Asch that she was terribly sorry—"I'm afraid I haven't planned on eating out today." She was so taken by surprise that she too stammered a bit. Her reply, curter than she'd intended, threw Colin Asch into a blushing confusion; he apologized several times; he should have known, he said, that a person in Dorothea's position would be busy. Dorothea said perhaps they could have lunch another time—for she saw the hurt in his face and did not want to send him away so rudely. She asked after the Weidmanns; she asked how Colin was getting along in his job search and drew him out further on the subject of the watercolor exhibit at the Institute (the paintings were early, minor work by John Marin which Dorothea thought interesting, if not profound—others had their doubts), which allowed him to speak with more purpose, in fact quite impressively. His favorite watercolors, he declared, were those of Winslow Homer.

"And of his it's the Maine ones I prefer, and the ones painted in the Caribbean. The Adirondack paintings look like superior magazine illustrations, don't you think?"

Dorothea, startled, said that she thought so, yes. Yes, she'd always thought so.

So they began to talk more easily. Almost casually. And Dorothea invited Colin Asch to have a seat (there was a cushioned ladderback chair, not often used, perpendicular to her desk), feeling a belated regret that she had so precipitously declined his invitation. Clearly Ginny Weidmann's nephew was one of those persons, rather like Dorothea Deverell herself, who not only dreads being rejected but dreads the yet more subtle social circumstance of forcing another to do the rejecting.

(But why was her heart beating so erratically, and why the unpleasant heat in her face? Was it that Colin Asch's awkward manner—so at odds with his striking face and the slapdash youthfulness of his clothes— reminded Dorothea of the boys of her remote youth who had acutely embarrassed both herself and themselves by asking for "dates" in high school?)

When, ten or fifteen minutes later, it might have seemed time for Colin Asch to leave—when he had in fact risen slowly, with a look of abstraction, to his feet, looming tall above Dorothea's desk—he again surprised her by saying, with a wistful boyish smile, "Are you sure, Miss Deverell, you won't join me for lunch? Somewhere close? It wouldn't really take long."

Dorothea laughed hesitantly and heard herself say,

"Well—I guess we could." For there was no reason after all why not. Adding, as Colin Asch helped her with her coat, "But please do call me Dorothea."

"Dorothea!" the young man said happily, as if testing the very syllables.

Outside, in the chill thin winter sunshine, there was some hesitation about whether they should simply walk to "a tearoom sort of place" two blocks away, where Dorothea often had lunch with friends, or whether they should, as Colin Asch suggested, go to a restaurant he'd passed a short distance away, L'Auberge, since, after all, he had his car, and it was no trouble to drive. Dorothea protested that L'Auberge was too expensive but somehow it came about that she acquiesced, and a minute later they were driving along the boulevard in a handsomely gleaming silvery-green automobile for which, nonetheless, Colin Asch felt obliged to apologize: it was a second- or third-hand Olds Cutlass Calais which he had recently bought on a trade-in and, now that he was its owner, did not altogether like. To make conversation Dorothea volunteered information about her inherited Mercedes, which so frequently stalled at crucial moments, like expressway ramps, and Colin Asch nodded vigorously and said, "Yes. Aunt Ginny was telling me. All sorts of good things come your way—you're the kind of human being they happen to."

Dorothea said laughingly, "Ah, hardly!" But Colin Asch was unhearing.

At L'Auberge there was valet parking, but Colin Asch did not care to entrust his car to the black-liveried "valet," insisting upon dropping Dorothea off at the canopied entrance and parking his car himself; and, inside, in the rather romantically murky twilight, it developed that, though Colin Asch had made a reservation, and the table indeed was in readiness, he was not dressed "in appropriate attire"—that is, he was not wearing a coat. That he wore jeans, that he was tie-less, seemed not to matter—but he was not wearing a coat. In the exigency of the moment Dorothea did not have time to think it odd about the table reservation, for now there was a spirited exchange—good-humored for the most part, yet quite serious too, like a game of tennis between well-matched players—between Colin Asch and the maitre d', the former insisting that his clothes would be wholly appropriate in the most chic, exclusive clubs in Manhattan, hence why not here in suburban Lathrup Farms, the latter insisting that the dress code was not of his invention but it *was* his responsibility to enforce. Catching sight of Dorothea's look of sympathetic worry, Colin Asch decided abruptly to give in and wear the dullish gray shoulder-padded "sports coat" provided by the management, though it was far too large for him and, as he laughingly said, not his style. Thus the early part of their conversation at lunch was taken up with the absurdity of conformist behavior, which in lightning-quick leaps Colin Asch related to the Inquisition, and the Holocaust, and the subjugation of women through the centuries, and the stoning of Socrates—or did Socrates die some other way? Colin asked, seeing perhaps the merest flicker of an expression on Dorothea Deverell's face. She said, "He was given hemlock to drink." And added, for the situation seemed to require such grand, summary, thoughtful statements, "He died nobly."

"He *did,*" Colin Asch said emphatically. "He absolutely *did.*"

And then they were talking—or at any rate, and very animatedly, Colin Asch was talking—of Percy Shelley: of *his* death; of the ignorance of the world that had so vilified him, the English establishment in particular, how they'd virtually driven him to his death by drowning, a death Colin Asch thought as clearly a suicide as

Chatterton's. "In my opinion," he said emphatically, "both suicides were mistakes: poets of such genius had not the right to cut off their lives so prematurely and give counsel to their enemies."

Dorothea, who had been talked into sharing a carafe of rather delicious red wine with Colin Asch, agreed, and said, "Who was the poet—I think he's a contemporary—who said that suicide is pointless; 'it happens anyway'?"

At this Colin Asch laughed with enormous appreciation, as if Dorothea had said something very witty. Which perhaps she had?

Though Dorothea Deverell had been taken to dine at L'Auberge any number of times since moving to Lathrup Farms she did feel, in its pointedly "gracious" atmosphere, distinctly out of place; not in her manner, or in her appearance (for in fact Dorothea was perfectly if accidentally dressed for the occasion in a dove-gray silken wool dress with a belt that emphasized her slender waist, and good patent leather pumps, and a necklace of amber stones Charles Carpenter had given her for her thirty-seventh birthday), but in her temperament: for places that seem to require of one an obeisance to their pretensions ran against the grain of her spirit; and, more practicably, she worried that Colin Asch—so touchingly anxious that wine, food, the table, Dorothea's seat at the table, be perfect— would spend far too much money on this supposedly casual and impromptu occasion, even if, as she would insist, she paid half the bill. (She began to worry too that he would not allow it.) Yet it did stir her vanity that, so unexpectedly, on an ordinary weekday, she *was* here, and not at the clattering female-thronged tearoom where the management and the waitresses smiled at her familiarly and knew beforehand the dishes she would order; or, worse, at her cluttered desk at the Institute, distractedly spooning yogurt into her mouth or gnawing at an apple, or a croissant, while frowning over material that Mr. Morland, in what Dorothea thought of as the man's wholly factitious premature senility, had dumped into her lap. Here at least, in this elegant setting, amid the flash of cutlery and gilt-edged china and the murmurous intonations of the wine steward—and had not Dorothea, entering, glimpsed several acquaintances dining here today too? including, even, a ripple-haired gentleman who at first glance resembled Mr. Roger Krauss, the trustee who bore her such spirited ill will?—Dorothea Deverell might be mistaken as a person of consequence. For why otherwise would so striking a young man, in a modish black silk shirt and very casual jeans, a young man not related to her or in any way obliged to her, be addressing her with such interest and exuberance? Why would he listen so attentively to her every word, as if he meant to memorize it?

Colin Asch was saying, "I was afraid you wouldn't remember me, Dorothea."

Dorothea said, as if in gentle reproof, "Of course I remembered you."

"But you must meet so many people, in your position—so many important people."

"Not so very many. And not so consistently important."

"Ah, but I find that hard to believe!"

Colin leaned eagerly forward, his elbows on the table, regarding Dorothea with intense, rather quizzical, warmly brown eyes. His face with its fine-cut features seemed illuminated from within; he smiled repeatedly. He had brushed his long pale hair deftly back from his forehead so that it fell, in languid waves, behind his ears and curled over his collar. He had shaved carefully and anointed himself with a faintly scented lotion. His fingernails were short, as if bitten, but scrupulously clean; on the third finger of his right hand he wore a gold signet ring; a high-tech digital watch with an iridescent black face gleamed on his left wrist. In the oversized sports coat with its bulky shoulders and wide lapels he looked like a boy whimsically disguised in his father's clothing.

As the meal progressed without incident—the smiling young Italian-looking waiter had shrewdly deferred to Colin Asch's authority from the start—Colin visibly relaxed, as did Dorothea. There was, even, no fuss about the menu, or the food; since the vegetarian dishes did not seem particularly appealing, Colin Asch ordered soft-shelled crabs, saying that, since coming to stay with the Weidmanns, he had had to modify his vegetarian diet to a degree. "I didn't want Aunt Ginny to be preparing special meals for me," he said.

They talked for a brief while about vegetarianism, and animal rights, and the philosophical problem of what constitutes consciousness, personality, and selfhood: if the ability to use language is necessary to a definition of "selfhood," what then of brain-damaged human beings who have no language? Are they any more "animals" than normal human beings? Are animals who respond to or (in the case of certain celebrated chimpanzees) actually learn to use language more "human" than these afflicted people? But then— for Colin Asch's transitions were abrupt—they were talking about the Marin watercolor exhibit again, and about "great art" and its effect upon the soul, and what art schools in the area would Dorothea recommend? Colin intended to apply sometime soon. He asked about her background, her training, and wondered if he too might apply to Yale, then discarded the notion; Yale was probably one of these snobbish intellectual places, like Johns Hopkins, Harvard, Princeton, that looked down their noses at you if you didn't have the right degree. "It must be wonderful, Dorothea," he said, smiling quizzically, "the kind of job you have. At the Brannon Institute. Aunt Ginny was telling me a little about it.'' He paused. ''And about you.''

Dorothea's face, which showed her emotions far too nakedly, must have stiffened in apprehension, or in pain, for Colin Asch quickly amended, with a delicate sort of tact, ''I mean—how active you are in the community. How much everyone likes you, how many friends you have.''

The words hovered oddly in the air as if challenging Dorothea to refute them. But they were true enough, she supposed. Hardly the whole truth but true enough.

With a queer ducking smile she said, ''And not a word about my 'tragic' life?''

Colin Asch laughed, baring his teeth in a sweet spontaneous gesture, like a muscular reflex. ''Ah, my aunt is very good at 'tragic' lives!''

To Dorothea's relief he did not pursue the subject but went on to talk, with his characteristic effervescence, of other things, and Dorothea was spared the obligatory recital of personal facts that had so sadly but inevitably calcified, with time, into mere facts— the romance of the ''whirlwind'' courtship, the brief marriage, the subsequent widowhood. In telling new acquaintances about her background—for, invariably, they asked, as Dorothea Deverell asked after theirs— Dorothea found herself in the ironic position of stimulating sympathy, even, in her more sensitive listeners, emotion, in which she could no longer truly share. Thus in their early rather giddy rather disorganized meetings Charles Carpenter would allude as if guiltily to the shock she'd had to bear so many years before, and how brave she'd been, and so on and so forth, embracing her, kissing her, in a passion that seemed as much reverential as sexual, so that Dorothea had to resist the impulse to say, in healthy exasperation, ''But

Michel has been dead for a long time! *You* are the man I adore!''

Near the end of the meal it seemed to Dorothea that Colin Asch began to speak more rapidly; his talk was bright, brilliant, funny, electric. It was late—nearly two o'clock—but he insisted that Dorothea share a small light fruit soufflé with him and have coffee, or tea—herbal tea?—which the smiling young waiter went to fetch. When Dorothea dared broach the subject of halving the bill—''You can't really afford this, aren't you looking for a job?''—Colin Asch stared at her for a startled, hurt instant, as if she had said something incomprehensible. ''But of course not, Dorothea,'' he said softly. ''Of course *not.*''

As they were leaving the restaurant Dorothea encountered, to her extreme embarrassment, Roger Krauss, in the boisterous company of several men, doubtless businessmen like himself, and Mr. Krauss, a thickset bulldog-looking man in his late fifties, with dark thick hair rippled across the crest of his head and sharp shrewd maliciously merry eyes, not only advanced upon Dorothea with an exuberant mock-friendly greeting—''Miss Deverell! I *thought* that was you inside!''—but stood in such a position in front of the coat check counter, unbudging, that Dorothea had no choice but to introduce him to Colin Asch, with the low murmured words, ''Colin is Ginny Weidmann's nephew, he's visiting them for a while,'' though there was no reason surely—surely!—for any explanation. Colin Asch, flush-faced from the excitement of the meal, just zipping up his soiled sheepskin jacket, flashed Krauss an eerily beautiful smile, like a muscular reflex, and shook his hand too, vigorously. In the company of his grinning friends (to whom, Dorothea knew, he'd been speaking of her) Krauss backed off, pulling a sporty black lamb's-wool astrakhan hat down low on his brow and saying, "How nice of *you*, Dorothea, to entertain the boy!"

The riposte was pointless but cruel; cruel because pointless; and Dorothea was so silent on the drive back to the Institute that at last Colin Asch said, in an almost frightened voice, "That man—is he an evil man?"

Dorothea laughed and said, "Oh, hardly evil! Just not so very nice."

"He seemed to know you," Colin said hesitantly.

And Dorothea said, "He's someone connected with the Institute—one of the trustees," but because the day was so brightly sunny, the mere fact of driving in Colin Asch's handsome Cutlass Calais so innocently pleasurable, she decided to say nothing more of Roger Krauss; or even, so long as it could be postponed, to think of him. There would be ample time for Krauss later, at home. In her bath. In her bed. In the blurry hallucinatory hours of the night when Dorothea Deverell was so frequently wakened from sleep as by an urgent voice in the very room with her: and lay awake, most nights, for a long time, stiff and resistant and helpless.

Colin Asch persisted, glancing at Dorothea, "He seems to have upset you, though. What was the name? Roger Krauss?"

Dorothea said, almost gaily, "He didn't upset me at all. I'm not that easily upset."

At the Institute she thanked Colin Asch for the elegant lunch—overpriced as she'd feared, but delicious. "Now I hope you and the Weidmanns will come to my house for dinner sometime soon, before Christmas at least," she said, shaking the young man's hand; and he, frowning, purse-lipped, retaining her hand just a fraction of a second too long, said, "Christmas is a long way off, Dorothea."

* * *

Dorothea Deverell lived, alone, seemingly by perverse choice, at the curve of a cul-de-sac called Marten Lane; there were no more than six or seven houses on the lane, each old, made of brick or stone, possessed of a crumbly storybook sort of quaintness though not—yet—certifiably "historic." Dorothea's house, bought with a small legacy when she was thirty-one, was made of an alveolate gray stone; the date 1878 had been chipped into one of the front steps. There were, facing the street, two square-cut windows on each of the floors, framed by black shutters in need of fresh paint; the roof was black-shingled, with a look of pushing downward, like a low brow. Inside, the first-floor rooms were large enough, without being spacious; the upstairs rooms, three bedrooms and an old-fashioned bath, were rather cramped. The single staircase at the center of the house was narrow and steep as farmhouse stairs—"Of course this was a country place when it was built," Dorothea felt obliged to inform visitors new to the house. "It was probably a farm; this area was outside the village limits." There came then the inevitable exclamations—how lovely, how perfect for you, how lucky you were to find it—and these facts Dorothea knew to be true. An irony of her circumstance was that, at the time she had been distractedly house hunting, she had resolved she would find a place, for herself, for life; she would never remarry, would never again expose herself to the risk (now needless: for wasn't she self-supporting?) of unspeakable loss. And it was Agnes Carpenter, at that time more generally sociable and even, it had seemed, tolerably fond of Dorothea, who had told her about the house, urged her to telephone the elderly owner (a widow) before the house was officially listed with a realtor.

Though renovated at some expense by previous owners—new kitchen, new electrical fixtures, new plate glass windows to the rear—Dorothea's house exuded, still, a broody damp air, as if sullen secrets were retained in its walls that no amount of light or cheery interior decorating could dispel. And the ceilings, while not literally low, had the look of so being; Dorothea's guests, entering her dining room, nearly always glanced up at the ceiling, and the taller men had an instinct to duck. Entering Dorothea's bedroom, Charles Carpenter too glanced upward, a faint nervous smile on his lips. He was a tall man, about six foot two, and low doorways made him uneasy.

In the house, Dorothea's favorite room was not her bedroom, despite its romantic memories and hopes, but her living room downstairs, which centered upon a large fieldstone fireplace, and which she had furnished with a mélange of things, some from the days of her marriage, some inherited, some newly purchased: a marble-topped coffee table with Italian Provincial legs, a pair of Queen Anne chairs cushioned in dusty rose, an impractically cream-colored sofa in spirit like a chaise lounge, outfitted with numerous pillows, upon which, in the evening, she liked to lie. There was a faded Chinese rug laid upon the hardwood floor that was too small for the room, but no matter. There were hanging plants, plants on windowsills, potted plants listing in corners. There were four antique clocks of which three were in working order but struck the hour at unexpected times; Dorothea liked their waywardness, suggesting as it did that time did not matter but might be a function of individual eccentricity. The coffee table was heaped with magazines and books, for Dorothea Deverell had become one of those persons who begins one book, lays it down and begins another, lays that down and begins yet another, and so until several are in orbit simultaneously; none powerful enough to dispel the others, yet none so negligible as to be shelved or tossed away.

Since girlhood Dorothea felt obscurely that to open a book—a serious book, at least—was to enter voluntarily into a contractual relationship of sorts with its author: one was obliged to stay with it until the end, or, at the least, out of civility, one was obliged to make that effort. She read too with an almost fervid concentration, a groping sort of intensity, as if in pursuit of elusive life-altering truths or ghostly images of herself tossed up in distant mirrors in unknown rooms. And the old romance of reading returned to her, that evening, curled up on the sofa in her rather shabby cashmere bathrobe, her paperback of Shelley's *Selected Poems* in her lap.

She read, pausing now and then to recall that day's so very unexpected excursion and to wonder at Ginny's young nephew, who had orchestrated it—in fact (recalling the reservation, made without Dorothea's knowledge) engineered it. In his presence Dorothea had felt alternately charmed and overwhelmed; now she was left, as with the aftertaste of too much wine drunk at too early an hour, slightly disoriented. The flamelike intensity of his being was admirable but exhausting: she would not want to see Colin Asch again soon, or too frequently—the remainder of her afternoon at the Institute was headachy and fatigued, as if the hour and a half spent at L'Auberge's darkened interior had sucked her vitality from her even as it nourished her. (For the food had indeed been delicious, quashing the need for Dorothea to prepare any evening meal for herself at all.) At one point, driving her back to the Institute, Colin Asch had said apologetically that he hoped he hadn't talked too much and hadn't interrupted her too frequently—it was an old habit of his, he said, but only when he was in the presence of certain people. Most of the time, he said, he spent by himself, in silence, and that silence spilled over—he had used those actual words, "spilled over"—into time spent in company with other people; but when he was in the presence of certain people something seemed to happen. "I guess I'm just lonely. For the right kind of friend." This, Dorothea had not wanted to pursue. She'd murmured something about his aunt's having told her that he had a good many friends—hadn't that young woman Hartley Evans telephoned him?—but this Colin Asch himself did not care to pursue, as if unworthy of their attention or as if in fact he hadn't given it much thought.

Like many quiet, intelligent, congenitally introverted people, Dorothea Deverell prided herself on her powers of analysis, of self and others. They were not assertive powers in any public sense, but they gave her solace at such times, for it seemed to her that the puzzle Colin Asch represented—Ginny Weidmann had referred to him as a "mystery" but surely that was exaggeration?—could be logically worked out if Dorothea applied herself to it. For one thing, the young man's attraction for her, very likely temporary, was that of a son for a mother. (It would not surprise Dorothea in the slightest if she resembled the long-dead Mrs. Asch. She would ask Ginny to show her snapshots.) But the primary fact about Colin Asch was not really that he was an orphan—there are many orphans, after all—but that he was a remarkable person: possessed of a lightning-quick mind, a true if mercurial intelligence, a lively tireless curiosity, and, rare in a young person, a respect for the feelings of others that had seemed, at times, almost morbidly heightened. He had watched Dorothea's face closely; he had stared almost greedily—like an infant staring up at the adult faces above it, equipped by nature with the neurological mechanisms that would provide in time a decoding of their bizarre utterances, but only in time.

How exhausting, though, such sympathy! Dorothea thought. Her impetuous young escort had several times, and always successfully, made a stab at guessing her thoughts.

Like Dorothea Deverell herself, though in a more extreme fashion, Colin Asch had yet to "connect" with life. You could see it in his frank innocent open gaze before he opened his mouth to say a word. He had no career, and his prospects were as unformed as those of a bright eighth-grader. Too much attracted him—indeed, enthralled him. A young man of his gifts who spent his time driving aimlessly about the country, dropping in on relatives on the spur of the moment, or backpacking through Europe or northern Africa—clearly, no one had taken him in hand; no one had forced him to apply himself to the effort of growing up. It was admirable perhaps that he was looking for a job—Ginny Weidmann seemed to think so—but for what sort of job was he suited? His chatter about himself that day, both evasive and artless, had indicated he had never completed any course of study, had never earned any degree. Art school seemed the most pathetic sort of chimera.

Dorothea perceived in Colin Asch, as in herself, a fatal lack of strength, drive, ambition. Not an excess but a deficiency of ego was the problem. He was a young man who could assert himself with parking-lot attendants and waiters but had clearly failed at asserting himself in the matter of life. A tempestuous uncharted energy, like that of Shelley's West Wind, seemed to blow him about from place to place, and Dorothea had winced slightly at his ready employment of the word "evil"—even while doubting that he meant it in any literal sense. It was a child's word, and it had sprung childishly from his lips. But he had not meant it, Dorothea concluded—he was too like herself.

When Charles Carpenter telephoned that evening (by the ease of his voice Dorothea knew he was not at home but at his office in Boston, perhaps, or in some neutral place) and asked Dorothea about her day, she did not tell him about Colin Asch, reasoning that the little excursion would never be repeated, but she did tell him how cozily content she was, how almost blissfully happy, curled up on her sofa, reading a yellowed paperback book dating from her Bryn Mawr days; and what was his opinion of such verse—

Drive my dead thoughts over the universe
Like withered leaves to quicken a new birth!
And, by the incantation of this verse,

Scatter, as from an unextinguished hearth
Ashes and sparks, my words among mankind!
Be through my lips to unawakened earth
The trumpet of a prophecy! O Wind,
If Winter comes, can Spring be far behind?

"Beautiful, isn't it?" Dorothea asked, a little breathless. "We take Shelley for granted."

"Yes. Beautiful," Charles Carpenter said.

4

"**B**eautiful."

Colin Asch's breath streamed whitely from him,
warm blood-heated vapor that immediately turned
cold. Almost directly overhead a full moon shone:
bone-white, powerful as a beacon of light, making his
eyes ache pleasurably. Moonstruck: what did it mean?
Was it real, was it a scientific fact or some old archaic
superstition? *I was moonstruck*, Colin Asch would afterward record in the Blue Ledger, but he would not
record his nervous excitement, his hopeful smile as he
lifted the heavy binoculars another time. *Not to blame:
MOONSTRUCK.*

Inside the warm-lit house some fifty or sixty feet
from where Colin Asch stood in the shelter of a snowy
Douglas fir, she lay curled on a sofa in the innocence
of believing herself unobserved. Colin understood by
her position, bare feet tucked beneath the hem of the
beautiful green robe, pillow behind her at about the
height of her shoulder blades, that this was a familiar
pose, a favored place: *no one had ever seen Dorothea
Deverell quite like that, nor had she ever seen herself
thus*.

The telephone had just rung, and Dorothea Deverell
had set aside her book, and now she lay back with the
telephone receiver crooked against her left shoulder,

the fingers of her right hand twining . . . nervously? happily? . . . in the phone's tight-curled cord. Colin wondered to whom she was speaking, but it was true wonder, not jealousy, for it made him happy that she was happy, if those were the valid signs of happiness he observed in her face.

This was not the first time that Colin Asch had positioned himself shrewdly in such a way as to observe unobserved Dorothea Deverell, but it was the first time he had trespassed on her property, the first time he had watched her in the sanctuary of her home *where, that night, she was doubly safe,* protected by the walls of the house and by her friend outside. Thus he felt no guilt, or nearly none. He guessed that, if Dorothea Deverell suspected his presence, she would throw open the door of the house to call to him. *Colin, is that you? Colin? Why are you outside in the cold, why don't you come in here . . . ?*

He could imagine her voice, that lovely lifting bell-like voice.

But of course she was still on the telephone, still curled up so comfortably on the sofa, her mahogany-dark hair glossy in the lamplight, her pale skin with a look of alabaster radiance, for even if one day Dorothea Deverell should suspect that Colin Asch was observing her at such private times or more public times, he understood that she was the kind of woman, a natural-born lady, who would never want Colin to know that she knew . . . for the specialness between them was just this: that each "knew" while appearing not to "know." For this knowledge if too crudely revealed would ruin everything, the very sacredness of the understanding . . . like acting in a play while simultaneously "acting" and aware of both the audience and yourself, thus the danger of forgetting entire passages of dialogue, bringing the play itself to a premature end.

But she knew. Didn't she know? She knew—in a way. As Colin Asch had known immediately. Weeks ago. The first exchange of glances, the startled recognition. *Soul-mate* was Shelley's word, *soul-mate* the word of the poets. *Mate of one's soul,* and it is through the eyes the souls initially declare themselves, while words, groping, barely adequate, can only follow.

And that day—their time together. When she'd listened so kindly, with such sympathy. Her smile, her warm intelligent eyes, her small hand warm and dry in his, yes thank you, thank you it has been a lovely surprise, though he understood she'd shrunk a little from him too; he would have to be careful in the future not to overwhelm her.

Talking too much, asshole. Cool it.

Guess I'm just lonely. For a friend.

Afterward for a long time he was scared and excited, eyes kept filling up with moisture, spilling over, running down his face, and his pulse was fast, faster than he liked, as if he'd swallowed something unknowingly or been injected in a vein without his knowledge or signed consent. Driving the Olds along streets he didn't know, on the expressway going west for a while, laughing, talking to himself, for a while singing fragments of church songs ("Come, O Holy Redeemer" was the one he seemed to know best) from his days in the boy choir before his voice changed, those days (years) remote to Colin Asch now and indifferent as a scene in a photograph or glimpsed on the far side of a river, and you can look at it, even hear it, without the contamination of emotion or desire; it is all other people, and they have nothing to do with you. Toward night when the streetlights switched on—*how he loved that instant! like the first instant of creation!*—the mania began to stabilize; he was able to meet H.E. as they'd planned in Luigi's near the television studio and she had good news for him about the job he'd interviewed for, though she was pouty and sullen at first because out of innocent forgetfulness and not calculation he was almost half an hour late, but he was so sweet he was so apologetic so loving she forgave him of course and they went back to her place and Colin Asch was laid and that stabilized him a little more, *You're so beautiful Christ I'm crazy about you can't get enough of you love love love you baby,* so sincere and almost pleading as if he were frightened of her of the power she'd have over him when all the while his brain was working fast and smooth as a machine and he explained that he couldn't stay the night since his aunt and uncle were expecting him and he was already late. Thus he got away just past 10 P.M., kissing her at the elevator his arm so tight crooked around her head she winced in startled pain and their mouths bruised together, tongues sucking like the real thing *oh sweetheart I'll call you tomorrow try to see you tomorrow if I can wait that long* in the elevator descending wiping lipstick and spittle from his mouth but he liked her really, *did* like her—she'd kept her word about helping him and the job would be his *Colin Asch's first step in the television business* though he'd have to hold out for a slightly higher salary, he'd earned more than that as a taxi dispatcher and a lot more than that working on an offshore oil rig in the Gulf of Mexico a couple of years ago. "Are you serious about that salary?" he'd ask, smiling his sweet quizzical smile; then he'd say with a soft little laugh, "Well—I guess you are." He got in the Olds and drove up to Lathrup Farms, parked at the mouth of Marten Lane in the shadows where no one was likely to notice the car, then crossed silently slantwise through lots neighboring 33 Marten Lane where Dorothea Deverell lived— tall beautiful fragrant trees lightly encrusted with snow, and the rears of the houses exposed like sawing through a skull: wild!—but he took no unnecessary risks, this wasn't the time, eyes dilated in the dark and senses alert as a wild animal's in the presence of its enemies, until he was at the rear of Dorothea Deverell's stone house where he'd never been before (though he had twice during the day when he knew Dorothea Deverell wouldn't have been home strolled past the front with no intention other than simply recording with his eyes), standing crouched in the shelter of an evergreen, raising the binoculars shakily to his eyes. And there suddenly she *was*. There—she *was*.

Lying on the creamy-colored sofa, scattered pillows around her, vivid green robe, the peep of bare toes, expression somber, intense, wholly surrendered to the book she was reading—which he saw with a thrill of pleasure was Shelley's *Selected Poems*: his very book! She knew nothing of him of course. Sensed no alien presence. He would stay only a few minutes, then leave as quietly as he'd come, for the last thing on earth Colin Asch wanted was to frighten or upset or in any way embarrass Dorothea Deverell: "I'd rather blow out my brains."

In the stark unflattering sunshine of midday Dorothea Deverell had looked to Colin Asch's sharp eye slightly less beautiful than he recalled from the evening when he'd first seen her, and on the afternoon of the music recital through his magical smoked lenses, but now by lamplight the woman's youthful beauty was restored. Alabaster-smooth skin, eyes so dark as to appear black . . . the curve of the brow, and the narrow curve of the nose . . . the perfect slightly pursed (wetted?) lips. As she read Shelley's poetry she was sounding the words to herself like music. She read the poetry as if by that means she were reading Colin Asch.

No human face but the sculpted face of Saint Teresa. The Italian sculptor Bernini. Was it Bernini? The perfect face—*was* it Saint Teresa?—lifted in dreamy ecstasy, sleepy eyelids hooded, and there stood before her a smiling angel with a golden spear just drawn back from plunging the weapon into her heart—or was it Leonardo? In that instant Colin Asch was excited *but made no move to touch himself not wanting to desecrate the moment.*

Moonstruck.

He lowered the binoculars to give his numbed forearms a rest, then raised them again. Old-fashioned heavy binoculars but high-powered: he'd found them poking around in the Weidmanns' basement gathering dust on a shelf with broken-stringed old tennis racquets, the kind with wooden frames. If he had asked his aunt or uncle for the use of the binoculars they would have said yes of course but he was too shrewd to ask: never ask any more favors than you require. Just take. *And keep your mouth shut.* (Colin intended to replace the binoculars as discreetly as he had replaced the diamond earrings and the onyx cuff links when he decided to stay with the Weidmanns as their guest . . . though he hadn't troubled to replace the money in Aunt Ginny's purse, knowing, rich bitch, she'd never miss such small change, and she hadn't, and even if she had would she dare accuse him to his face . . . *him?*)

Inside the house, the telephone conversation had acquired a new urgency. Dorothea Deverell no longer twined her fingers in the cord but was gesturing with that hand, sitting up, speaking intently . . . frowning, and smiling, and smiling frowningly, even nodding, baring her teeth in a grimace of emotion. What was she saying? Was it a quarrel? Suddenly, the perversity of the situation struck Colin Asch: for Dorothea Deverell, showing emotion, waving her hand in the air, behaved, as people do in such instances, as if the party at the other end of the line could see her while knowing of course that he (or she) could *not*—yet, simultaneously, unknowingly, *she was in fact being observed through binoculars*. And for the first time Colin Asch felt a wave of guilt, shame. For he was taking advantage of the woman he admired most in the world, and he could not rationalize that this would have given her pleasure—ah, hardly!

Yet he did not lower the binoculars. It was late—nearing midnight. The white-glaring moon had shifted its position overhead. As if sensing his presence, Dorothea Deverell glanced upward, staring at the window, frowning severely—but Colin knew she could not see him; he was too far away, and hidden; and, in any case, the windowpane of a lighted room, at night, reflects only the interior of the room. Dorothea Deverell ran her fingers through her hair in a sudden impatient gesture that seemed to Colin out of character. Was she about to cry? Was she laughing? A spasm of unreadable emotion passed over her face. *What was she saying? To whom was she saying it? And at so late an hour? A lover? Did Dorothea Deverell have a lover?*

Colin Asch took a step backward as if someone had shoved him.

"I wouldn't like that."

This was not the first time in Colin Asch's life that he had been drawn powerless to resist into the orbit (as he thought of it, and wrote of it in the Blue Ledger) of Woman; for there had been, many years before Dorothea Deverell, the summer when Colin Asch was thirteen years old living with relatives and he'd gone with them to their Wyoming ranch where there was a woman named Mindy—or was it Mandy?—the young blond wife of a neighboring rancher with whom Colin's relatives were friends, and this woman taught Colin to ride a horse, and this woman saw in Colin's face what no others wished to see. *Too bad you aren't my kid!* she'd joke, roughing his hair, giving him a

poke in the arm as boys do with one another, but she
had her own children, horse-riding loud-mouthed children who hated Colin Asch, and that summer he'd followed her with his wide staring sleepless eyes and was
discovered several times outside her house in the early
morning before sunrise where he hadn't any reason to
be or any right so there were cruel jokey things said
and she stopped coming around and Colin knew they
all talked behind his back; thus before they left at the
end of August he took his revenge and though no one
could prove it had been Colin Asch who had set the
fire they seemed all of them to know; thus he came to
hate Mindy (or was it Mandy?—he hated even the
name) and the family he'd lived with, whose name
he had never recorded in the Blue Ledger. And at the
Monmouth Academy there was Mrs. Kendrich, the chap-
lain's wife who had befriended Colin Asch from the
start, giving him books to read and offering critiques
of his poetry and praying with him, and when the rumors began of the headmaster's secret circle it was
Mrs. Kendrich who went to Mr. Kreuzer; thus there
was bitterness between them and division at the school
. . . and the night that Colin Asch discovered the body
in the bloody bedclothes and ran outside barefoot in
the snow it was Mrs. Kendrich who found him . . .
who saved his life. And at the inquest she had protected him.

And there were one or two others recorded in the
Blue Ledger—no more. In the course of fifteen years,
no more. And none of the women had been so wonderful as Dorothea Deverell: none so beautiful, and
none so well-bred and ladylike, so refined, so intelligent too—*for Dorothea Deverell was a match in intel-
lect for any man.* (Only by chance, by way of a remark
of Colin's aunt, had he learned that Dorothea was the
author of three small art books: monographs, with
color plates, on the American artists Isabel Bishop,

Charles Demuth, and Arthur Dove! Of course she was too modest to have mentioned them herself when Colin had asked about her work.)

And she is an heiress. One day (perhaps) to inherit yet more.

And she is independent of any man.

And she is pure. And good. And yet unjudging.

Of the one tenth of one percent of the world's population that stands apart from the rest she is clearly one of us—yet speaks softly and sympathetically.

Her influence is palpable as the moon's on the tide but it is an influence for peace, for calm, for love, for surrender. Not the fierce pounding surf but the gentle lapping on the beach like the approach of sleep. Like the joy of the Blue Room itself—no sound, no shadows! No gravity!

So Colin Asch recorded in the Ledger, sitting on his bed, 4 A.M. and as awake as at midday and writing, writing . . . his pen moving rapidly across the page as if entranced with no regard for lines, margins, red-inked columns. (The Ledger, appropriated from a closet of office supplies at the Monmouth Academy, was an accountant's book, of an awkward size, its covers of stiff cardboard and much battered and stained over the years. Especially toward the front pages were missing, crudely torn out. Other pages were covered in handwritings of various types, in various shades of ink, predominantly blue but also green, red, purple, and crimson; there were erasures that had resulted in serious tears, mended with transparent tape; there were sections crossed out so elaborately that *no one not even Colin Asch himself could have deciphered them.* For the past six years or so the code Colin used had been consistent but before that he'd used other far more tricky codes; thus if he looked back to earlier entries he was often stymied by their meaning though he never doubted that, had he the time and patience to puzzle over them, he could crack his own ingenuity!) Like a man running with a pyramid of eggs in his hands, heartstoppingly beautiful exotic eggs he saw them, the aqua of robins' eggs but larger, painted eggs perhaps as at Easter, like a man entrusted with beauty of exquisite fragility he was desperate to record certain wonders, *to set down permanently certain visions and revelations entrusted to him*, which had their focus entirely upon Dorothea Deverell and granted no significance at all to the fact or facts that so pleased others— that of the numerous job interviews Colin Asch had had in the past two weeks several offers had been made to him *and excellent offers too for prospective employers were bowled over by the young man's appearance manner intelligence sensitivity wide-ranging background and experience in many walks of life above all by his ability to speak and to "relate,"* and he had decided after all to accept the position at WWBC-TV though the beginning salary was modest and might forestall for a while Colin Asch's moving to an apartment of his own. How exciting, dear, how lovely, Aunt Ginny'd said, clasping his hands warmly; you could see the affection shining in the old girl's eyes, Aunt Ginny was one of the few people on this shitty planet who gave a shit for Colin Asch and he knew he could rely on her, if there was some stiffness beginning with Martin Weidmann—and Colin Asch's powers of detection were raised to the nth power in such matters, *just try to put something over on this boy you cocksuckers*—he knew she would protect him, take his side, for it would come to that eventually, in such circumstances living in such close quarters like a family though the Weidmanns had had sense enough to give Colin his own key and to allow him complete privacy,

still it always came to that in the end—a woman bravely
defending Colin Asch against some detractor or enemy.

"Fuckers."

And then, a moment later, since the hoarse word
hung strangely in the air: "But things are changed
now."

It was true: Colin Asch had a job in television, he'd
performed so charismatically on the talk show—Dave
Slattery's *On Your Toes*—calls to the studio Hartley
said were five to one in his favor which was "fantastic" and "unprecedented" because Slattery's viewing
audience was usually conservative if not reactionary
and Slattery did his best to trip people up on camera
but Colin Asch maintained his good-natured calm
smiling dignity remembering always to look directly
into the camera with the red light burning *to make eye
contact with the invisible television audience;* thus he
won even Slattery's grudging respect it seemed—and
viewers you would not predict to be tolerant of weird
ideas like vegetarianism and the "rights" of animals,
not least Colin Asch's long shining Christly pale hair,
were wild for him as Hartley Evans said. And she
said, each time she introduced Colin Asch to one of
her co-workers, "He's a natural for the medium."

And indeed Hartley Evans's co-workers liked Colin
Asch very much too. Shook his hand warmly and sincerely. Congratulated him. A few days later in the studio the manager interviewed him just casually over
coffee in Styrofoam cups; yes there was an opening, a
sort of assistant's assistant, you could say it was a sort
of internship, not much salary to begin with but
"there's definitely a future," and Colin told him of his
experience in Germany and also a job he'd had with a
small television station in Galveston, Texas, sure he
could get references if that was necessary, if that

wouldn't hold things up—"I'm eager, you know, to get *started.*" The manager shrugged off the need for references in this instance, the job was practically on-the-job training after all, a handshake and it was settled, and Hartley Evans slid her arms around his neck afterward, nuzzling and biting his lower lip, fiddling her fingers in his hair as if she had the right, but Colin Asch was suffused with pleasure and allowed it, allowed her anything she wished, childishly passive even malleable in her hands until of course it was time for him to assert his dominance, enter her between her legs, "make love" as it was called—his mind floating and skittering free of his laboring body there between the slightly fattish white thighs opening and closing in an increasingly frenzied rhythm until with a scream (Colin Asch could not have said it was from her throat, or from his) it was over, and an hour later it seemed, though in fact it must have been the next morning just before noon, he dropped by the old renovated Tudor mansion that was the Brannon Institute just to inform Dorothea Deverell quietly but proudly that he had a job—"I'll probably be on camera in about six months"—with WWBC-TV in downtown Boston, his face lighting up happily *at her face lighting up happily* at his good news. He was mildly disappointed when she confessed she hadn't seen the talk show, rarely watched television she said, but clearly she was impressed by the position, by what it meant for Colin Asch's future in the media; he heard himself saying excitedly that "the electronic media is the soul of America, the communal soul," and with this Dorothea Deverell puzzlingly concurred, and though he'd meant to mention her books to her—that he intended to buy them, to read them, to discuss them with her—he'd had time only to skim through his aunt's copies thus far—it was wild! so many interviews for jobs, so many telephone calls, in the past five or six days!—all that slipped from his mind in the exigency of the moment but he came to his senses quickly when Dorothea Deverell invited him to sit for a few minutes, realizing that he'd better be discreet and get the hell out: he knew she was busy (the telephone had rung on her desk, she'd put the call on hold) *and he was busy too*, expected down at the studio early that afternoon. Just thought I'd drop by to say hello, he said, and Dorothea Deverell smiled and said, Any time, Colin, and all accomplished smoothly *absolutely naturally with not a single misstep*. At the door hesitating, glancing back—"I suppose I share your disdain for television, Dorothea, but it *is* a job: a beginning."

And she said at once, "Oh, yes, of course."

The world is a lonely place, lonely as the grave. We live in silence primarily—and in solitude—and this fact the "media" would deny. From this flows the power of the "media" for both evil and good.

These observations Colin Asch recorded thoughtfully in the Blue Ledger, after his first week of assistant manager's assistant at the station. One day soon he would reveal his findings to the television audience—if the fuckers who ran WWBC gave him a chance.

"—I mean it just seems so damned unjust that a woman of Dorothea's qualifications and, let's face it, her *quality* should be treated like that," Ginny Weidmann was saying into the telephone, as Colin casually passed the door. "Especially since Howard Morland has always been so fond of her and these past few years—*is* it his health? is it his heart?—he has certainly taken advantage of her goodwill, and, you know, her capacity for—*I* don't know—her capacity for not wanting to see the truth of the situation. I'm not saying of course—who am I to say?—that Roger Krauss's nephew or whoever he is isn't qualified, for all any of us knows even more qualified—no, but I *didn't* say that, Sandra! For God's sake don't misquote me!—but I *am* saying that Dorothea has a right to the directorship, a moral right, quite apart from her qualifications, and the board of trustees should be forcibly reminded of that if necessary." She paused; she listened; Colin Asch, hovering just beyond the doorway, paused too, his heart going hard but slow in his chest. Ginny said with a harsh exhalation of breath that might have been a sigh, "No, nothing is definite, it's all just rumor. Martin says we should let things develop as they will— for one thing, Howard hasn't officially announced his retirement—and Dorothea's programs this season have been so successful, I'm sure even Roger Krauss can't fault them—I really can't see, you know, how the board could vote against offering her the directorship, how, you know, they could actually *do* it. I mean, Evelyn Mercer is a trustee and she is such a sweet, basically a sweet decent fair-minded woman—of course she *is* the only woman; that's one of the problems. Roger Krauss has made it into such an issue of sex—of gender—talking so irresponsibly as if Dorothea has her present position only because she *is* a woman and that the board did her a favor by hiring her!"

Colin, in his car, driving in early evening traffic along the boulevard, on his way to inspect an apartment in Lathrup Farms Mews—a brand-new apartment-condominium complex actually located in the suburb of Danvers, immediately adjacent to Lathrup Farms: Colin was "looking at" apartments now— whistled from start to finish, flawlessly, that classic song of Schumann's, "Widmung."

* * *

December 19: Colin Asch is twenty-eight years old.

Lying awake sweating and calculating . . . if there were some tactful way of allowing Dorothea Deverell to know of the birthday he was sure she'd want to have him, and the Weidmanns of course, to her house for dinner, for hadn't she promised weeks ago and she surely did not seem to be the kind of person, the kind of woman, who fails to honor her promises, he has happened—ah, really just by chance! *really* by chance!—to see her now and then in the village, in Lyman's (the quality grocer where Ginny Weidmann shops too, and Colin cheerfully goes on errands when he's in the mood) and in the dry cleaner's and in the library where it's clear everyone knows her name, everyone likes her—*faces lighting up as she approaches, as if she were bringing a warmth of pure radiant light*—and in the drugstore making purchases, her back to him poised and straight in the attractive black cloth coat with the filmy fur collar, then crossing Main Street to the parking lot to her car, the classy Burgundy-red Mercedes Colin Asch has come to know so well, he observes quietly from a post near a building just to see: if the car's motor starts, or if, you can't always tell, the car's wheels might spin in the ice; there is a treacherous layer of hard rippled ice beneath the powdery snow, and Dorothea Deverell might need help. . . .

Colin Asch broached the subject casually to his Aunt Ginny, not that Dorothea Deverell might want to have a birthday party for him of course but that he, Colin, wanted to celebrate by taking the Weidmanns out to dinner—the restaurant of their choice, and perhaps Dorothea Deverell would like to join them?—but as Colin should have known, Ginny insisted she would have the dinner herself, at home; she hadn't known the nineteenth was Colin's birthday—and it was coming up so quickly! why hadn't he given her warning?—and he really was spending too much money on restaurants, wasn't he—her fond worried eyes searching his—but Colin wasn't listening to every syllable; he nodded, winced, said a little impatiently, "OK, but do you think your friend Dorothea would like to join us?" and Ginny hesitated a moment before saying of course, she'd call Dorothea, that *was* a good idea, but she'd thought—again searching his eyes quizzically—"Probably you would like me to invite Hartley? Aren't you and Hartley . . . ?" and her voice trailed off discreetly and in a moment of hauteur Colin said, "Hartley and I are—" as if really he couldn't imagine what Ginny was thinking of, what the precise literal even clinical term was; thus it fell to the fatfaced busybody cunt to supply it, not "fucking" (as perhaps she was thinking; the old girl knew which end was up) but "—seeing each other? Quite often? That's the impression I have—am I mistaken?"

Colin was back on his heels now. Cool it. Easy. Saying, smiling, "I guess that's right, Aunt Ginny. I'm so grateful to you for introducing us." He paused, and they smiled happily at each other, like conspirators. "Hartley is such a special person."

"She is, she is!" Ginny said, as if the issue had been in some doubt. "So you'd like me to call her, then? For Saturday evening?"

"And your friend Miss Deverell too?"

"And Dorothea too—of course."

Afterward Ginny said almost accusingly, "Colin, I'm really so glad you told me your birthday was imminent. It would have been a pity for none of us to know. Are there other things about you, dear, you should tell us?"—smiling, as if teasing—"other secrets?"

Colin laughed. "Not a one, Aunt!"

* * *

But to Colin's regret Dorothea Deverell could not come to his birthday party: terribly sorry, she told Ginny, she had another engagement that night.

Mailed him a birthday card, however: tasteful, attractive, but just a commercial card. From a gift shop. No present, no other acknowledgment. If he was disappointed—and, yes, he was—he hid his disappointment so thoroughly that everyone (the Weidmanns, H.E. looking prettier than usual in something soft, lacy, pastel; Colin Asch often had that effect upon even the strongest-minded ''career woman'') had a great time, a memorable time, Colin Asch telling amusing fantastical stories about travel in Europe, travel in North Africa, the vicissitudes of life ''on the bum'' on the open road, and truly he liked making people laugh, especially people who were fond of him, people who were on his side; you could see the excited emotion shining in H.E.'s big sensational mascaraed eyes: now this was a girl (not a girl, precisely: thirty-one years old) who adored him, adored his cock, anything he wanted to do to her he'd be welcome to do, in time, if (as of course he would: Colin Asch was no jerk-off asshole male chauvinist) he took it slow enough, gradual enough, didn't lose his cool with her little-girl simpering and not wanting him to see her in the shower, the droopy big-veined breasts, the lardish thighs, potbelly, and her skin a little coarse without the thick pancake makeup, Jesus how he resented her going crazy the way she did as if for the show of it coming to orgasm like he was killing her or something breaking his rhythm and concentration which really pissed him off it tempted him to the cruel cruel thought of jerking his cock right out of her at the crucial moment as he'd done with one or two cunts in the past taking Colin Asch for granted, or why not—just a casual quicksilver thought: *not serious!*—actually kill the

cunt closing his two big thumbs around her throat—
the carotid artery, is it?—see how she likes it then,
moaning and gasping and screaming bloody murder in
his ear then sobbing afterward saying his name like an
incantation *like she had the right* simply because he'd
told her he thought he was in love with her he'd never
met a girl like her and so on and so forth, it pissed
him off too that she was that eager to believe, wrung
his heart with pity and *he hated pity: all it did was
weaken*.

"Thank you all very much . . . this is maybe"—
eyes filling with tears like genuine pain—"the happiest
birthday of my life."

So that's it, asshole.
Colin Asch's twenty-eighth fucking birthday.

And Christmas too came and went and Colin Asch saw
nothing of Dorothea Deverell but was relieved to hear
she'd gone somewhere to visit relatives—"distant relatives I think," a woman friend of the Weidmanns told
them, "poor thing, distant relatives is all she *has*"—
so he felt better immediately and in the Blue Ledger
charted his plans for the New Year. Impatiently he
thumbed through the earlier pages seeking, what was
it, that Roman saying Mr. Kreuzer had printed on the
blackboard, how the class had shivered when he translated it, and the strange knowing set of his eyes drifting as invariably they did onto C.A., the tall stiff pretty
boy in the first row, what the fuck *was* it, and where?—
then suddenly he'd found it, was staring at it. Hand-
printed block letters in smudged India ink: *Mors tua,
vita mea*.

He smiled; he saw what he must do. And she would
never know—never know a thing!

"Your death, my life."

PART TWO

5

"Yes? Who is it?—What?"

Dorothea Deverell, heart beating rapidly, fists instinctively raised as if to protect her face, was wakened from a deep, near-narcoleptic sleep by a sound as of something, or someone, in the room with her. A murmured word, a sharp inhalation of breath, a shifting (not precisely a creaking) of her bedroom floorboards . . . and suddenly she was awake and badly frightened.

She lay shrewd and unmoving. She heard nothing. She told herself calmly, There is no one in this room with you and there is no one in this house with you . . . as you know. As always at such moments of crisis Dorothea Deverell's interior voice was brisk, pragmatic, and scolding, though her vision, struck so rudely from sleep, was blurred as if she were peering through an element dense as water. What had she heard, if she'd heard anything? It was early, still dark, too early for mourning doves in the eaves to disturb her with their melancholy cooing, or for the notorious sanitation truck, or the newspaper delivery. . . . A jetliner passing overhead, perhaps. Yes. Making windowpanes vibrate, casting a malevolent fibrillation to the very air. That seemed the most likely explanation.

Dorothea's fear retreated but did not vanish, like

shadows dimmed by light. She drew the covers up to her head, tried a childish maneuver of hiding her eyes, pressing her face against the pillow. . . . She tried to take comfort, as ordinarily she would have done, that she was in her own bed: returned home after ten days' absence, amid her own cherished things, beneath her own ceiling, set soon to embark upon one of Dorothea Deverell's flawlessly executed professional days. But these thoughts aroused an unexpected pang of dismay, like muck unwisely stirred. Today was January 4, the first Monday of the new year, and though she had fled the holidays in Lathrup Farms to force herself to a decision about her future, she had failed to come to any decision: the new year, stretching off interminably, would be a more strained variation of the old.

She'd gone away, in dread of the "holidays"—that debilitating season in America when stable men and women begin to quaver, and the unmarried, like Dorothea Deverell, are made most keenly to feel the pathos of their situation—to a small inn in Framington, Vermont, telling no one except Charles Carpenter about where she was going; she'd gone away alone to contemplate her life: as she thought of it, wryly, when in the mood for wryness, the ruins of her life. For she knew very well—how could she not know?—that her days at the Brannon Institute, where she had been so happy, were numbered and rapidly diminishing, and she could not much longer deceive herself about Charles Carpenter—that happiness of any sane sort lay in that direction. They had quarreled bitterly over the telephone; they had said bitter things. Dorothea Deverell, gentlest of women, had heard herself say to the person whom of all the world she loved the most, "To put it crudely, Charles, you seem to be waiting for Agnes to get seriously sick and die—*you* won't take the first step either to divorce her or to break with me."

Before Dorothea left for Vermont, Charles Carpenter had insisted on seeing her, to plead with her another time—not to lose patience with him, or faith in him, not to cease to love him: for what would his life be, without her? "What exactly is your life *with* me?" Dorothea had inquired, not archly but quietly, with the air of one asking a quite serious question; and Charles Carpenter, burying his face in her neck, had murmured, "Just—my life." He had tried to talk her out of going to Vermont by herself, especially at such a time. It would make her all the more lonely. It would make her morbid. (Charles knew that, during the first summer of their marriage, Dorothea and her husband had driven together through New England, had stayed in romantic country inns.) But most of all, he would miss her enormously: "It's so much more painful at this time of year to feel yourself alone," Charles said, rubbing his eyes with both hands, "when you can't actually find any time to *be* alone, to breathe. When you're jammed up against other people and obliged, like them, to be having a good time."

Dorothea ignored Charles's gentle attempt at wit; such attempts, on both their parts, were also usually gestures at reconciliation. She said, unfairly, "You could come with me." He said, staring, "Ah, but Dorothea—that's what I can't do." And so it went, for they had had this conversation or its variants many times before; if one spoke impetuously, like Dorothea, the other had hardly any serious need to reply in defense—for in this case Dorothea knew that Charles Carpenter was not a man who took his responsibilities lightly: he had an emotionally unstable wife who did not so much threaten as to indicate, by her reckless behavior, the continuous possibility of suicide, and he had (the burden, Dorothea thought, of "had"!) aging parents in Boston, supremely nice people, for whom he represented the sole means of emotional support.

As a partner at Bell, Carpenter, Smith & Lowe he had also, at this time of year, the duty to put in an appearance at any number of festive holiday affairs, ranging from black-tie dinners to the company's annual Christmas party for its employees. Running away to a romantic inn in the Green Mountains had the appeal only of the impossible.

Dorothea said, "What I really intend is to spend some uninterrupted time being depressed. I realized, the other day, with the telephone ringing a half dozen times in an hour, it's been a while since I've had the solitude for it. When you're working you really can't settle into being depressed in any systematic way."

Charles laughed as if startled. Though he knew Dorothea Deverell more intimately than any other living person knew her, he professed frequently to be startled by her most candid remarks, as if they were out of character. He said, "You're joking of course?"

"Oh, of course." Dorothea laughed.

They kissed, shyly at first, then with increasing urgency. Dorothea felt her lover's suddenly aroused desire with a pang of unease and excitement. For Charles Carpenter *was* another woman's husband: Dorothea Deverell *was* trespassing; surely this constituted transgression? surely both were behaving criminally? Charles murmured, "Should we go upstairs? Dorothea—darling? Could we?—at least for a while?" but Dorothea said unexpectedly, "No, please—it would only make leaving harder." "But which of us is leaving?" Charles said, hurt. And then, seeing Dorothea's face, "I seem to have ruined your life after all. And I meant, you know, only good." Dorothea said impatiently, "Don't talk like that—you speak as if I were a victim, that my life were over! We both knew you were married, from the start. We both knew." "But I'm preventing you from—from meeting other men," Charles said humbly. And Dorothea, stepping away

from him, laughing, a catch of despair in her throat,
said, "I meet other men all the time! I wouldn't lack
for escorts, really! It's just that, compared to you, they
exert no special fascination." The image of Ginny
Weidmann's young nephew flashed to Dorothea's
mind—the fine cheekbones, the intense intelligent
eyes—but was as swiftly banished. She paused. She
said, "Jerome Gallagher called the other evening."
"Who?" "Jerome Gallagher, you remember—the man
Ginny introduced me to, back in November. At that
dinner at their house." Charles frowned as if suddenly
vexed. "Yes. That dinner," he said flatly. "The evening Ginny Weidmann's strange nephew appeared,"
Dorothea said, as if it were necessary to elaborate.
She knew Charles did not want to be reminded of the
evening since, by the end of it, his wife had drunk so
much that she swayed visibly on her feet and had to
be helped by Charles simply to rise from her place;
yet she heard herself saying, in a bright, neutral tone,
"What did you think of him, Charles? We never really
talked about him: Colin Asch." Charles passed a hand
over his eyes; his skin was unevenly flushed, almost
ruddy. He was standing in Dorothea Deverell's charmingly furnished living room, on her exquisite old Chinese rug, as if, for the fraction of an instant, he himself
were about to sway on his feet—to pass so rapidly
from the exigency of sexual desire to the ellipsis of
discourse might not be, Dorothea was afterward, repentant, to think, altogether healthy. But his voice was
clear enough, if not indeed brusque: "I didn't think
anything of him at all."

Charles Carpenter had extracted from Dorothea Deverell a vague sort of promise that she would telephone
him from Vermont sometime during the holidays; but
this, after all, she did not do: to her vast defiant relief
she did not do. (How many times in recent years Dor-

othea Deverell had been reduced to the shameful act of telephoning her lover and hanging up quietly when his wife answered, she would not have wanted to calculate, nor would she in her pride want to acknowledge, even to herself, how frequently, with no excuse whatsoever, she had driven past the Carpenters' handsome old colonnaded house on West Fairway Drive.) So for the duration of her retreat they had been chastely out of contact, which seemed to Dorothea both bracing and very sad, for she missed him terribly, missed even the special pang of not seeing him that we feel only when living in close proximity with the one whom we are forbidden to see—for distance, in matters of romance, is a powerful analgesic.

She was therefore relieved to discover, amid the pile of cards, letters, and packages of various sizes that had accumulated in her absence, a handwritten letter from Charles Carpenter, which she ripped open at once and quickly scanned: but it told her, in its carefully chosen, rather Augustan diction, nothing she did not already know. Her heartbeat, painful at first, had subsided by the end of the letter to its normal rhythm. *Did I expect him to break it off?* Dorothea wondered. *Charles is not after all the one to break things off.* One of the packages was auspiciously large, gift-wrapped, from Saks, with no other return address and no signature on the MERRY CHRISTMAS card from the store; Dorothea opened it slowly and lifted enthralled out of the tissue paper a white lace formal blouse—or was it a little jacket?—exquisitely beautiful, and in her size— size 6—and there was a matching skirt, floor-length, silken wool, dazzlingly white. It was so lovely a gift, so unexpected—Dorothea had bought nothing for Charles, had insisted they not exchange presents this year—she began to cry in hoarse gasping sobs.

"It's too good for me; I don't deserve it!"

Upstairs in bed she had been so besieged by unwanted thoughts she'd given up trying to get back to sleep; and rose, and showered, and dressed, and began the long day, setting herself in motion like a clockwork doll though it was not yet 7 A.M. In the inn at Framington, in her single rather chilly room with its impeccable antique-imitation furniture and windows overlooking the village green, Dorothea had managed to sleep heavily; yet she had not on the whole felt refreshed, but groggy, headachy, edgy, apprehensive—as if her flight from home had been perilous, exposing her to hairline fractures of the psyche she might not otherwise have noticed. Sleeping was always a problem for Dorothea: if she slept well she tended to feel guilty for having done so, as if it were a symptom of encroaching sloth and deterioration; if she slept poorly, she spent the better part of the day yearning to return to sleep. In Vermont she had not wanted to think that there might simply be something wrong . . . some growing unease in her soul, as of premonitory alarm. Waking several times in the night as she'd wakened this morning, as if something, or someone, were in the room with her. Or watching her. Or merely thinking of her.

And when, twice a day, except on the very coldest days, she left the hotel to trudge along the snowy country roads, she had to fight the panicky sensation that she was being followed. Followed! Dorothea Deverell in an old-fashioned fur coat, fur hat pulled down low on her forehead, knee-high boots . . . so bundled up as to appear ageless, sexless. She knew it was absurd; she knew it was groundless, such fear, such bone-deep *apprehension*. In a stained old volume of Montaigne's *Essays* found on a shelf in her room she discovered a poisonous gem set in the midst of Montaigne's affable prose, a quotation from Pythagoras, translated as *Good is finite and certain, evil is infinite and uncertain*. The insight made a sudden, sickening impression on her—"Of course!"

Yet she managed to enjoy herself nonetheless. She was tough, hardy, resilient: yes, and stubborn to the core. She'd brought along an entire suitcase of work—Institute matters, and correspondence, and notecards, slides, and drafts of a book-length essay on Charles Burchfield for which she had signed a contract with a New York publisher of fine art books—and she managed, on those long uninterrupted winter days in her room, to accomplish a good deal. Her meals were provided, her room briskly cleaned and aired and restored to her. There was no television set in the room. There was no telephone. The Brannon Institute was closed for the holidays so there was no pressing need for her to think of it. Or of Mr. Morland, who for all his sweetness seemed to be avoiding her lately. Or of Mr. Krauss, who, that day in the French restaurant, had so pointedly not avoided her. ("How nice of *you*, Dorothea, to entertain the boy!") After a late dinner in the inn's low-beamed dining room Dorothea propped herself up cozily on her bed and read one or another of the numerous books she'd brought along with her, the majority of them newly purchased novels in smart bright eye-catching jackets. She favored long, weighty novels, novels densely textured (if not snarled and knotted) as life, in which she might lose herself for hours at a stretch. And she had, too, her old companionable edition of Shelley's poems.

And now it was January 4, a blowsy overcast Monday morning, and Dorothea Deverell was back in Lathrup Farms, set in motion, in perpetual motion she sometimes thought it, but determined to acquit herself fully. She might resign her position at the Institute before it was required of her—before Mr. Morland called her in for that embarrassed regretful conversation. She might send out letters looking for new employment, she might put her house on the market, might move away; anything was possible since there was no one to prevent it. She switched on the lights she customarily switched on when preparing to leave the house for the entire day, these truncated winter days, and turned up the volume on the radio (as Michel had insisted: loud voices in a house discourage would-be intruders). She went into the freezing garage and climbed into her car, breath steaming, gloved hands cold on the steering wheel, wondering why, in this familiar setting, she felt so apprehensive, so anxious . . . as if the very silence surrounding her were taut with expectation. And opaque, and dense. Impermeable even to her screams.

Something is going to happen, she thought. Or has already happened.

Dorothea Deverell, much praised for the quality and efficiency of her work and her unfaltering good grace in its execution, had never wished to confront her admirers with the rejoinder: But what is the alternative? My efforts are in the service of a single grand effort, the combating of loneliness.

It had been so since early childhood, interrupted for the space of some swift-passing months during her brief marriage (and briefer pregnancy); then resumed again, with pitiless exactitude, after her husband's death. Work was the blessed anodyne, the *there* to which, in times of stress or despair regarding the worth of her own being, she might retreat. It was the inevitable completion of the task, and the resumption of the life to which it was presumably marginal, that constituted the problem.

Yet at times of supreme concentration, Dorothea Deverell was energized, even quite happy—and it was this mood, intensified by the solitude of the early hour at the Brannon Institute and the agreeable surroundings of her office (a surprisingly capacious room with lustrous cherrywood paneling and old-fashioned mullioned windows reaching nearly to the fifteen-foot ceiling), that Dorothea's assistant, Jacqueline, interrupted at 8:55 A.M. when, still in her coat, breathless from the stairs, her fox-slanted eyes moist from the January cold, she burst in upon Dorothea Deverell to say, "Dorothea! You've been away! Have you heard? Did you read? About Roger Krauss—?" Jacqueline was a solidly built flamboyant attractive woman in her midforties, mysteriously married yet hinting of an acute disappointment in marriage, given to irreverent asides meant to placate, or support, or entertain Dorothea Deverell, to whom she was wonderfully loyal and with whom she must have felt her fortunes at the Institute bound. They had worked together for six years, and though Dorothea did not wholly trust Jacqueline in matters requiring tact and diplomacy, especially over the telephone, she could hardly imagine the Institute without the woman's ebullient presence.

Now Dorothea Deverell and Jacqueline stared at each other, and Dorothea felt her heart clutch, for she saw in Jacqueline's excited glistening eyes—ah, what did she see? Jacqueline, still breathless, was saying, "It was in the papers day before last, how he died— Mr. Krauss; one of our trustees, you know," she said unnecessarily, as if, at this date, Dorothea Deverell might not know who Roger Krauss was, "—the victim of some sort of sex thing, not just robbery, and there's all sorts of rumors, but anyway, the thing is," Jacqueline said, now briskly unbuttoning her coat, "the man is *dead.*"

Dorothea had hardly taken all this in. "What? What has happened?" she asked faintly.

"The night of New Year's Day. In a parking garage, in the city. Mr. Krauss was killed."

"Mr. Krauss?"

"Yes. Him. They don't know who did it yet." Jacqueline was trying very hard not to exude an air of cruel satisfaction. "But they didn't mention us, they didn't mention the Brannon Institute—in the papers, I mean—mainly his business reputation, who his father was in Boston, and things like that, and it was on the television news too, of course, like it's all some sort of big scandal that might open up." Jacqueline paused, regarding Dorothea Deverell intently. "So that's the man who tried to pass judgment on *us*, Dorothea, on *you*, writing such nasty things in the paper about our exhibit last spring, and *now*—look what has happened to *him!*"

"Roger Krauss is dead? He has *died?*"

"Not just died," Jacqueline said impatiently, drawing a newspaper out of her handbag with a flourish, "but been *killed*. 'Garroted,' the police called it."

"Garroted!"

The word hung in the air of Dorothea Deverell's office like an exotic obscenity.

Alone in her office, door shut, telephone off its hook, Dorothea with trembling fingers spread open the creased pages of the *Boston Globe* that Jacqueline had provided her, to read, with shock, dismay, and an incredulity that deepened, rather than diminished, with the passing minutes, of the violent death of Roger Krauss, fifty-six years old, "area businessman and philanthropist": he had been strangled with a wire bound tightly around his neck and also wantonly stabbed in the eyes and groin; robbed of his wallet, wristwatch, cuff links, tie clip, ring, even his belt, hat, and necktie; found in his car, a two-month-old Lincoln Continental, at 4:40 A.M. of January 2, behind the wheel, in a pose very like that of a living man, by the attendant on duty at the high-rise parking garage on Providence Street near Tremont. Krauss's car was

on the third level of the garage and no one had heard
any struggle. His parking ticket had been stamped for
8:15 P.M.; the attendant then on duty had no memory
of him, since business had been brisk at that time, but
the late-night attendant remembered his returning on
foot sometime around 3 A.M. and taking the elevator,
though there had been no exchange of words between
them. He also remembered having seen a young, or
youngish, black man wearing dark glasses, a goatee,
stylish fawn-colored suede clothes, and carrying what
appeared to be a clarinet case, around that time too,
but he had not caught a very clear glimpse of the man.
Police detectives said that Krauss's murder did not
seem to have been simply a mugging death, on the
evidence of the extreme violence done to the victim
(Krauss's eyes had been "severely gouged" with his
own car keys, and the murderer had razor-slashed his
groin through his trousers) and other details, which at
the present time, in the interests of their investigation,
they did not care to divulge.

In the earlier part of the evening Krauss had had
drinks with friends at the Ritz-Carlton and had spoken
of going on to have dinner with other friends, un-
named. Divorced for the past eleven years, he had
maintained a small apartment on Beacon Street but
spent most of his time in his Lathrup Farms residence.
Dorothea read that he had been active in civic, church,
and charity organizations. He had graduated from
Harvard Business School. He had served in the U.S.
Air Force as a first lieutenant. He was survived by two
sons, Roger Jr. and Harold.

"How horrible!" Dorothea whispered.

The accompanying photograph was of a younger
Roger Krauss, hair darker, features sharper, expression more affable than Dorothea recalled. She studied
it and could not see in that face the face of the man
who had mocked her so openly a few weeks ago; she

decided she would expel that unfortunate memory from consciousness since it did not do the poor dead man any credit, nor did it do Dorothea Deverell credit, to insist upon remembering. It is enough that he is dead, Dorothea thought, not knowing, perhaps, what she meant. She felt only pain for Roger Krauss now, a rush of sympathy, and pity for the ignominy of his death— its slightly shady aura, against which he could not protect himself.

So Dorothea Deverell read the article, and reread it, and sat at her desk for a long while, as if entranced or struck dumb. Then she folded the paper carefully up, put her telephone back on its hook, and resumed her day.

But it was not so easy!—there were telephone calls from friends; there were messages for Dorothea to return calls (one of them from "C.C." at his business number—a rare request); there was above all the sparked-up presence of Jacqueline, who, though Dorothea pleaded with her to let the subject drop, could not forbear hurrying out at noon to buy the late-morning edition of the *Globe*. "They caught him! The killer! It looks like!" Jacqueline reported, again breathless, and laying, uninvited, the newspaper across Dorothea's desk. Two other secretaries joined them to read of the newest development in the Krauss case: police had arrested a suspect who answered to the general description of the killer, a black man, unshaven, thirty-two years old, with a record of several convictions for muggings and armed robbery, picked up on a street two miles from the parking garage on Providence at 1 A.M. of January 4. The man had been in an "intoxicated state" and had "offered resistance" to police officers. He was wearing a new suede jacket similar to the one worn by the killer and could give no satisfactory explanation of how he'd come into the possession of Roger Krauss's wallet and credit cards. No photographs accompanied this article. "Well, that was quick!" Jacqueline said, mildly disappointed.

Dorothea Deverell leaned forward suddenly and pressed the palms of her hands against her eyes, as if she felt faint, an uncharacteristic gesture in the presence of others. Asked if anything was wrong she said, almost inaudibly, "Of course something is wrong—a man is *dead.*" Her reply was prim, not quite what she'd intended; Jacqueline and the secretaries retreated, as if chastised. She heard them whispering in the corridor outside her office and went to close her door. She telephoned Charles Carpenter but was told of course that he wasn't in—it was twelve-thirty and he wasn't expected back in the office until after two and who is calling please? Dorothea said quickly, "Thank you, it isn't important, I'll try another time."

Next, she would have liked to see Howard Morland, not to discuss the death of Roger Krauss of course (that would have been unthinkable) but to exchange New Year's greetings perhaps, and to take from the elder man some measure of patrician calm or consolation; but as Mr. Morland's secretary explained, he would not be returning for two weeks—he was vacationing in the Caribbean. "Of course," Dorothea said. "I'd forgotten."

For the remainder of the afternoon she worked with sporadic flashes of efficiency and zeal, trying not to be distracted by thoughts of the dead man, or of the ugly circumstances of his death, but haunted by such words as *garroted, eyes gouged, razor-slashed, mutilation.* She tried too not to hear, as if echoing lewdly in a closed corridor, *How nice of* you, *Dorothea, to entertain him!* I do not want to think ill of the dead, Dorothea Deverell instructed herself, but what is to be done if the dead thought so ill of me? But at 4:00 P.M., when most of the Institute staff was still working,

Dorothea gave up the effort, which had brought on a headache and an inexplicable sense of malaise, and shut up her office and drove out of the parking lot as if released from a prison.

Yet she did not want to go home. She was fearful, for some reason, of going home.

The lovely white outfit Charles Carpenter had given her—did it not resemble a bridal gown?

Was it a bridal gown?

"And we promised we wouldn't exchange presents this year," Dorothea said aloud, in a tone of faint protest. But of course she was quite excited too. She would not have wanted to say *quite* how excited.

Charles must have repented, then, for allowing her to go off by herself to Vermont.

Yet his letter—so staid and circumspect, so typically *lawyerly*—had made no reference to the gift at all.

"He bought it at the last minute," Dorothea said aloud. "He bought it on impulse."

Driving in her car she began almost immediately to feel better, much better: as if the phenomenon of even moderate speeds, the achievement of even a modest number of miles between herself and the Brannon Institute, were mysteriously tonic. And she'd driven so many miles the previous afternoon, from Vermont! Soon she found herself beyond Prides Crossing, beyond Beverly Farms, headed, it almost seemed, for Maine. . . . She parked her car at the end of one of the cliff roads, on a high bluff overlooking the Atlantic, and sat there dazed and exhilarated, as if she had come an enormous distance simply for this: this brilliant waterscape of purples, blues, and greens, choppy and white-crested with foam, like a Winslow Homer painting. Despite the cold she got out of the car, standing for a while looking—staring—at the ice-bound shore, and the riotous waves, and the glowering winter sky, her hair whipping crazily in the wind and her eyes filling with tears. This was not like her, was it! This was not like Dorothea Deverell, was it! She felt an uncanny sort of life, *livingness,* thrumming through her . . . she felt flooded with strength, purpose, hope, resolve. Her enemy was dead and she was alive. It was so simple a thing it might have been overlooked.

She stood there for a while, hugging herself, shivering, her face damp with tears that began, in a light film, to freeze on her cheeks. She stood there until the air turned dark, gradually at first and then abruptly, as with the rushing of thousands upon thousands of dark-feathered wings. But there were no birds, were there? She glanced up, startled. Only the massive snow-laden clouds. Only the oncoming night.

"Wasn't it shocking! Yet, at the same time, you know, not really surprising," Ginny Weidmann was saying. Her manner was somber, even grave, but resolute; she glanced up to take in Dorothea Deverell with the others. "It seems the man led a double life."

"Why? What do you mean?" one of the women asked.

"Sit down, Dorothea, and let Martin get you a drink; you look lovely," Ginny said. She lowered her voice. "The police found pornographic material in his car, you know. It wasn't in the newspapers. Videocassettes, magazines." She lowered her voice even further. *"Male* pornography. *Homosexual."*

"Really?"

"Roger *Krauss?"*

"They found a ticket stub in his pocket, too, from some X-rated theater," Ginny said. "Martin doesn't like me to speculate," she went on hurriedly, while Martin was out of the room, "but the police themselves have speculated that he might have picked up the man, the young black man, you know, in the the-

ater, and was bringing him back home with him.
Which would explain—certain things."

"Oh, but it's so hard to believe of—"

"—so hard to believe of *him*—"

"Roger Krauss, of all people—"

"Oh but, these days, you can't *tell*—"

"—can't predict—"

"Yet with Roger you could, actually," Ginny Weidmann said reprovingly. "Remember his campaign
against Dorothea? Against 'feminists'? Clearly, there
was an emotional bias against women."

The gathering of some six or seven people looked
to Dorothea for confirmation; but she murmured only
a few ambiguous words and must have shown her discomfort, for they let her off lightly and returned to
their spirited analysis of the "mystery" of Roger
Krauss without her—clearly the subject was in full
throttle and must be allowed to run its course. Several
times Ginny Weidmann interrupted to say passionately, as if in Dorothea Deverell's stead, "None of it
surprised *me*. There was a logic to it all along, to
me."

"But has the black man confessed yet? I heard on
the news this morning—"

"He claims he is innocent, of course—what can you
expect?"

"The evidence does certainly seem—"

"—*very* damaging!"

There was a collective pause. The doorbell rang;
another friend or neighbor had arrived. Again it was
murmured, in an air of amazement, "But who would
ever have thought it—of *Roger Krauss?*"

It was Sunday evening. Ginny Weidmann had telephoned Dorothea Deverell the day before, inviting her
to drop by for a drink, just a handful of friends were
coming over, not a party but an impromptu gathering;
we haven't seen you since before Christmas, Doro-

thea, where on earth have you been keeping yourself? So, with mild reluctance, Dorothea came to the Weidmanns', both dreading and anticipating further talk of Roger Krauss, about whom she had heard so much this past week from various sources and with whose name her own seemed, at least temporarily, so unhappily bound. The "homosexual" details Ginny Weidmann had just now supplied were new, however, to Dorothea, and affected her more powerfully than she would have wished to acknowledge. As talk swirled about her head she sat unmoving on the sofa, her drink untouched in her hand, thinking, So that was it. It was nothing personal, then.

Dorothea had come to her friends' home for consolation of this sort, perhaps; or out of simple loneliness; or fear; or guilt. (Though why should she feel guilty?) Since the Carpenters' white Cadillac was not parked outside, Dorothea knew that Charles would not be here; yet she had unconsciously prepared herself, stiffening slightly, for the man's possible presence—his eyes, narrowed, moving quickly and warmly onto her, as, invariably, they did, in these sociable circumstances. But there was no one. That is—there were several men, including (Dorothea saw belatedly) Jerome Gallagher; but there was no Charles Carpenter.

Dorothea had seen her lover, however, the night before last, briefly, and had several times this week spoken with him on the phone. He had been very kind and understanding about what he called, with an air of mild repugnance, the "Krauss affair"; had not pursued the subject with Dorothea, as if sensing (ah, Charles knew her so well!) how she would have begun to feel guilty about it. (Though why should *she* feel guilty?) And there was the tantalizing, one might say unnerving, puzzle of the Christmas presents: the one Charles Carpenter had indeed sent her (a kidskin jewelry box trimmed in sterling and tortoise) and the one

Charles Carpenter had *not* sent her (the white lace jacket and matching skirt). The little jewelry box had been gift-wrapped and mailed from a prominent Boston jeweler's with a card enclosed, *Love always, C.*, and this Dorothea had discovered on Monday evening when she opened the remainder of her mail. Two presents, then? She had been, in her absence, the recipient of not one but two Christmas presents? "If you gave me the jewelry box, then who gave me the—other?" Dorothea had asked, for a moment almost frightened; and Charles Carpenter said with a careless, hurt laugh, "If *you* don't know, Dorothea, how the hell should *I?*"

But Dorothea had not wanted to guess.

Just as she was preparing to leave the Weidmanns', for the others were going on to dinner at a local restaurant and she did not care to join them, there appeared, belatedly, with boyish smiling apologies, Ginny's nephew Colin Asch, in the company of the glamorous Cleopatra-looking girl, whose name, for the moment, Dorothea could not remember; and she understood, suddenly, by way of her absurdly pounding heart, that it had been an error for her to have come here. For here, so abruptly, was the boy—the young man—Colin Asch: with his uncannily lapidary features, like a brash Renaissance archangel come to life, the shock of his white-gold hair, his beautiful crafty eyes . . . looking at Dorothea Deverell with a curious intimate intensity, as if they were old, very old friends, or blood relatives, or a kind that scarcely need greet one another in public. But there were handshakes all around, there were introductions, for not all of Ginny's guests had met her nephew—"really my grand-nephew"—nor had they met Hartley Evans, who was, it quickly developed, the new anchorwoman for the weekday evening news on WWBC-TV, thus locally known, and the object of immediate and spirited attention. Dorothea Deverell, on her feet, meaning to leave, had nonetheless to linger, to smile and listen and disguise the queer emotion she felt at the sight of seeing—ah, so companionably! so *easily!*—Colin Asch with Hartley Evans, or Hartley Evans with Colin Asch (the young woman was standing close beside him, had entered the room with her arm conspicuously linked through his, as if to proclaim they were lovers)—these tall, attractive, radiantly happy young people who, by contrast merely, made everyone else in the Weidmanns' living room appear dimmed and middle-aged. Dorothea Deverell felt a stab of—was it envy? jealousy? simple dismay? or a vicarious sort of pleasure, harsh and unexamined, in the young lovers' very physical presence?

Both were buoyant, nerved up, like performers who find it difficult to leave the stage; or perhaps they'd been recently quarreling—or making love. Dorothea, smiling, looked from one to the other. Hartley wore more jewelry than, even, she'd worn on the evening of the Weidmanns' dinner party, and her glossy black hair framed her face perfectly, sleek as a helmet; her eyes and eyebrows were elaborately traced, her eyelids shadowed in pale silvery blue; her fleshy lips a perfect luscious crimson. And her skin, her young skin—in the lamplight, at least, it was virtually poreless: perfect. Yet the surprise of the evening was Colin Asch, who had had his long hair cut and styled, perhaps with an eye toward television performance, and who wore not his slapdash late-adolescent's outfit but a camel-hair blazer with gold-glinting buttons, a creamy-beige turtleneck sweater, impeccably creased navy-blue trousers. On his right hand was the gold signet ring, on his left wrist a handsome platinum-faced watch Dorothea had not seen before. Studying him as, for the moment, he stared smiling at Hartley Evans (who was entertaining them all with an anecdote about having met recently, and interviewed, former Secretary of State Henry A. Kissinger), Dorothea began to feel uneasily that something was wrong: or was not, in any case, altogether right; for how could *this* young man—healthy, energetic, eyes shining with scarcely suppressed excitement, fingers twitching as if in rhythm with an interior music—have stepped from that *other* young man, Ginny Weidmann's "tragic" nephew, who had seemingly washed ashore at the Weidmanns' home back in November, barely two months ago? That evening, Colin Asch had been a lost soul: dazed, bedraggled, sallow-skinned, quixotically idealistic. (Is he still involved so passionately in animal rights? Dorothea wondered. She'd heard no word of it from Ginny in some time.) Now he looked supremely like a young professional man, confident in his own abilities but respectful—even, seemingly, reverent—of his elders. The two cannot be the same person, Dorothea Deverell thought, amazed.

At this moment Colin Asch glanced at her as if, indeed, he'd heard her speak; and their eyes held; and, feeling a wave of faintness suddenly, Dorothea Deverell explained that she was leaving—was already late for her next engagement. Colin Asch said, simply, "I'll walk you to your car, then, Miss Deverell—I mean Dorothea," taking her elbow gently and escorting her from the room, turning away with such unstudied abruptness from his girlfriend and her charming banter that one had the sense, a rather chilling sense, that he hadn't been listening to her at all, or to anyone. He was vivacious, keyed up, as if pleasantly intoxicated, and indeed Dorothea smelled alcohol on his breath; he was chatting of cheery inconsequential matters, complaining funnily about WWBC-TV and the "media mentality" with which he had to contend, but they were anxious to keep him, promising him he'd be broadcasting soon, but maybe he'd quit anyway, go to work for a competitor—*"That'd shake them up, the buffoons"*—glancing at Dorothea with a sudden liquid look. "But you don't watch television, do you, Miss Deverell? Dorothea? And why should you, with your superior sensitivity, your mind on *other things?"* Dorothea laughed, as if with fond familiarity the young man were teasing her, parodying her high-flown cultural pretensions, but of course he was not; he spoke with absolute sincerity.

In the Weidmanns' foyer Colin Asch helped Dorothea on with her coat, the heavy gleaming beautiful old stone marten fur, and she prepared nervously to explain it to him, the fact of it, an inheritance from an aunt—for she herself did not believe in the cruel custom of raising and slaughtering animals for their skins—but he was humming happily, as if taking no notice; then he broke off to remark that he hadn't seen her in a very long time he missed her sort of he'd liked that lunch that day he'd been disappointed Dorothea hadn't been able to come to his birthday party of course it was planned at the last minute and why Aunt Ginny hadn't called Dorothea sooner he didn't know, that's about the only thing in Aunt Ginny's character that could stand some improvement—"Her habit, you know, of tossing things together at the last minute, telephoning people, as I guess she did yesterday, to invite you all over." He was standing behind Dorothea, tall and suddenly very still, his hands on her shoulders. "But it was very thoughtful of you, Dorothea. That card. That birthday card," he said quietly. "I've kept it, I'm treasuring it. I won't forget it."

Dorothea laughed again, uneasily, and their eyes met in the mirror beside the door, and she thought, He is the person who sent me the present—of course; but at the same instant two facts were unmistakably clear: she had not the courage at this moment to mention the present to him and to ask for an explanation, and Colin

Asch, sensing that she knew, was too tactful, or too crafty, to bring it up himself. Our secret remains our secret, he might have been thinking, smiling dreamily into the mirror.

Colin Asch walked Dorothea Deverell out to her car, which was parked in the Weidmanns' circular driveway, fresh-shoveled snow on all sides; his step was ebullient, and he was whistling the opening bars of a familiar melody—hauntingly familiar—was it a song of Schumann's? He hadn't troubled to put on his topcoat but he'd placed jauntily atop his head a black lamb's wool astrakhan hat—"Do you like my new hat, Dorothea?" he asked with a boyish hopeful smile. "I just bought it, at a post-Christmas sale, in the village—one of those fancy men's shops where Aunt Ginny buys things for Martin."

An excess of information seemed, here, to be proffered; yet Colin Asch's manner was wholly ingenuous, and Dorothea said, as if praising a child, "Yes, I do like it, it's very—handsome."

"You know, Dorothea," Colin said, opening the door of her Mercedes, mimicking a bow from the waist, "I sort of thought you might like it."

Dorothea Deverell gathered her skirt around her—it was a multipleated hunter-green jersey-wool skirt, a rich beautiful fabric hardly at all eroded by time—and slipped into the car. She was breathing rather quickly, like a girl; and Colin Asch, not unlike an impetuous suitor, leaned on her car door and peered down smilingly at her. His breath steamed and faded, steamed and faded. His lips seemed to twitch involuntarily, lifting upward in a white wolfish grin. As if they'd been quietly talking about this subject, he said, "Yes, it's strange how, sometimes, a despicably evil person who doesn't deserve life has it taken from him. As if there were after all justice in the world, as certain of

our great visionaries and poets have believed.'' He
paused, and added, *''As if.''*

Dorothea shivered and fumbled in her purse for her
car keys. Were they talking now of Roger Krauss? She
nodded vaguely; she murmured a vague assent. Thinking to change the subject, to make a kind of closure,
she said, almost gaily, ''You and your young woman
are a very striking couple—you seem so happy together.''

''Do you like that type? Really? Ah, I see you're
being polite, Dorothea.'' Colin Asch was leaning over
Dorothea's car door, pensive, quizzical, arms dan-
gling. The astrakhan hat gave him an exotic, foreign
look and had slid forward on his head, as if it were a
size or two too large for him. In a lowered voice he
said, ''She imagines that she is in love with me—wants
to have my child, and all that! She'd suck my life from
me if she could. The marrow out of my bones.''

This sudden unsolicited confidence left Dorothea
Deverell nonplused. What to say? Why was Colin Asch
looking at her so oddly, as if inviting complicity? She
had begun to feel rather nervous, wishing that this
strange young man would step back from her car and
allow her to drive away. He was gazing down at her at
such an angle, he had all the advantage; Dorothea
could only crane her neck and squint uncomfortably
up at him.

''I don't take the flesh that seriously, to tell the
truth,'' Colin Asch said with a negligent shrug of his
shoulders. ''Only the spirit. The soul.''

Pointedly, Dorothea lifted her car keys out of her
purse; her smile had grown strained.

''But you, Miss Deverell—Dorothea—is there someone you're in love with?'' Colin Asch asked suddenly,
impulsively, as in a headlong plunge of unconsidered
words. ''That no one knows about—except him?''

Dorothea flinched, as if the impetuous young man had reached out to strike her.

He added quickly, "Look: you can tell me. You can trust me. *I can keep a secret.*"

Though she was inwardly trembling, with fear, with indignation, with simple shock, Dorothea managed to say quietly, "I don't divulge secrets promiscuously, my own or anyone else's. Now may I close my car door? I must leave."

Like a hurt, obstinate child Colin Asch persisted. "I *can* keep a secret, Dorothea. No force on earth can pry a secret out of *me.*"

Dorothea Deverell made no reply, switching on the car engine. She was terrified suddenly that Colin Asch would touch her—would reach down gropingly, like a blind man, and stroke her hair.

Instead he sighed, and settled the hat more firmly on his head, and said apologetically, moving to shut Dorothea's door, "The primary thing is, you *are* happy—these days—with the coming of the New Year and all that? You *are* happy, Dorothea?"

"Yes," Dorothea Deverell said, almost angrily. "Very."

For so, after all, she was.

6

It made him happy if she was happy if those were the valid signs of happiness observed in her face.

But she seemed not to trust him yet, fully—he had not proven himself to her all the way.

After he was promoted at the station maybe, or quit and got a better job somewhere else. Maybe. After he moved into the new apartment. Champagne celebration! Black tie! A limousine to bring her! And she'd wear the beautiful clothes he bought her, dazzling white, pure, perfect on her. "La Belle Dame sans Merci." (Which Mr. Kreuzer read to the class slowly mesmerizingly so you could feel the beat, the diminished stress in the final line of each stanza, and his eyes had drifted out to young C.A. slouched in his seat by the window staring down at his hands impassive, transfixed, *I saw their starved lips in the gloam, / With horrid warning gaped wide, / And I awoke, and found me here, / On the cold hill's side,* and after the last words faded there was a silence so tense so haunted he wanted to scream to scream to scream to destroy it utterly but he'd only stared, impassive, at his hands.)

But should Colin Asch do the preparation of the food himself, or should he buy it? The greatest chefs in the world were men; it required a special touch. Not just

any asshole could prepare gourmet food or even make
the wine selection. Or should he order it from a caterer? His aunt would know. There were places like
that all over in the well-to-do suburbs: food caterers.
Thriving businesses. ''The fuckers have so much
money out here they have to eat it, shit it.'' One thing
was certain, they wouldn't cheat *him*.

And what about furniture for the apartment? Didn't
you have to order it weeks ahead of time? Months? It
was going to be tricky getting more $$$ from his sev-
eral sources when he hadn't made a move to repay any
of it. The $$$ from K.R.'s wallet (for so in the Blue
Ledger he was officially recorded) was a nice surprise
but hadn't gone far, and the credit cards were worth-
less in such a circumstance; you'd have to be high on
crack or coke or some other kind of shit to try it, like
the black guy they picked up, poor sad dumb moth-
erfucker asshole what'd he *think*—it was manna from
heaven? and the fancy suede gusset-sleeved jacket too?
There was H., and there was S. (whom he'd just met,
out here in Lathrup Farms in the village bookstore),
and there was X, Y, Z; he'd never lack for ways of
picking up small change, but G. was getting worried,
drawing out cash for him (last time $1,500: for the
camel-hair jacket, shirts, merino wool sweater, decent
haircut—it hadn't gone far) on her credit card, fearful
of writing another check though she had her own personal account: ''Now don't breathe a word of this to
Martin, please!'' she'd warned, as if C.A. of all people required warning. In childlike gratitude he'd
smiled, lifting the old girl's hand with its glittering
diamond ring; he'd pressed his forehead against the
back of her hand in childlike fucking gratitude, Don't
know what I would do without you, dear aunt, you
saved my life when I came here and you took me in,
not like the others: there is no one like you in all the
world. Oh, dear Aunt G.

Now if M. died, one of these days? Mugged in the street, shot in his car, *not* in the vicinity of Lathrup Farms however—you wouldn't want anyone to think it had anything to do with his home. Even breaking and entering, and he's shot defending himself, because G. too might be involved and you wouldn't want that; no, that was out, or at least that was somewhere ahead in the future. Too many things to think at once.

Also, it's always riskier where there is a blood relation, where they can figure out motives. XXX uncontaminated by desire is the highest achievement. But emotions intrude. Like with K.R., he'd hated the fucker so, by the time he got to him. And other things too. Other things intrude.

"I saw that."

"Saw what?"

"You and her. The one you've got a crush on."

"What—?"

"You know!"

"No, I don't know. You tell me."

"That woman with the pale moony face—the stuck-up one. Your aunt's friend."

"What about her?"

"What's her name?"

"Never mind her name, what about her?"

"I said I saw you. You and her."

"Saw what, cunt?"

"You and her! *You and her!* You never look at me like that!"

Colin Asch stood tall as if on stilts, cracking his knuckles that were suddenly very bony, and sort of magnified: first the left, then the right. Eyelids slid over dry achy eyes. They were high—but rapidly descending. All that $$$ and the bitch was bringing them down. As she'd done, stupid cunt, too many times. Wild wet hurt eyes that looked almost crossed, and the mascara blurring. And the nostrils wet with liquidy snot. And the wet red mouth dribbling.

"Sweetheart, I look at you like that all the time."

"Fuck that! Fuck you! I want you out of here!"

Colin Asch began suddenly to whistle. It seemed the necessary response. Head thrown back and lips pursed as for a sucky sucky kiss of the highest order. Whistling "The Bolero"; otherwise there was the danger of something happening. *They tempt you with loss of control. It is that above all to be RESISTED.*

He'd lied to her about where he was the night before and why he'd missed work—the third or was it the fourth time he'd failed to show up, and who got blamed but her? Was there another woman, was it *that woman?* "She looks old enough almost to be your mother." And what about the apartment he was looking for, why wasn't she being kept abreast of what was going on? Or was he planning to move and not inform her?

Her voice went on and on, beyond "The Bolero." He stripped to his underwear, he was so fucking warm. Beads of sweat on his forehead, trickling down his sides. She was saying, laughing angrily, "Sometimes there's a part missing in you, Colin; sometimes you scare me, you're so—" though he'd explained it all smoothly and satisfactorily, he thought, and now in her wildness the cunt was mucking it up again, which he could not allow to upset him. His thumbs deftly pressing against the big bluish throbbing arteries in her neck . . . or maybe he'd take hold of her shoulders and slam her against the wall, the floor, the door-frame, anything hard enough to crack her skull. At a certain point of spiritual intensity *all becomes unbearable—or bearable. It is that point that must be reached.*

He'd stripped to his undershorts, sweating and panting. The whistling was fading out the way a radio station fades, then suddenly it's gone. In the doorway of her cheap glitzy bathroom he switched on the fluorescent tubing and said, "What are you doing in there, sweetheart? What're you doing in the tub like that?"

He came closer, peering. His nostrils were widened with the smell of it.

Behind him she was saying, "Colin? What? What are you—?"

He played at the half horror he actually did feel. Peering at the spectacle through his fingers.

"Sweetheart? Hartley? *What did you do to yourself?*"

She came up behind him, scared, padding barefoot, heavy on her heels but not daring to touch him. Saying, "Colin? What's wrong?"—trying to look over his shoulder at what was in there, in the tub. *Sometimes there's a part missing in you Colin you're so—.* Then she did touch him, her fingers brushing his wrist, but he didn't feel it.

"One side of your head is broken," he said. "There's blood in the water. Hartley? Sweetheart? What happened? *What did you do to yourself?*"

High and wobbly on stilts he freaked her out, seeing it there in the tub, seeing her, the vision so powerful she saw it herself, or almost. Begging him to stop. Begging him for Christ's sake please stop. He advanced to the bathtub talking to what was almost there, the dead female lying naked in the scummy water, big breasts floating, nipples like bruised eyes. There was coagulated blood from the gash from the rim where the skull had cracked; the fingernails and toenails had turned blue. In amazement and pity Colin Asch crouched over the corpse, speaking to it while Hartley Evans tugged at his arm, laughing shrilly, begging him please for Christ's sake to stop—"You're driving me crazy. *You're crazy.*"

They were in an elevator together and the cable'd snapped. Was that it? Next time she spoke of D.D. he would kill her—it was that simple. He guessed she knew. Or maybe, cow cunt, she didn't know. In bed afterward burying his face in her neck saying Love, love, love, having trouble staying hard enough to enter her then when he did she winced as if in pain and he lost it, started to slip out, he thought of hurting her finally and unmistakably so she'd let him go but then he thought of D.D. and of how *she* would be saddened by this, if she knew . . . shocked, saddened, disgusted. After all she expected so much more of Colin Asch. *Please Dorothea I want to be good. I am trying to be good.* Deciding then not to fuck H. or to frighten her but begging her instead for forgiveness, like a child sobbing; she knew he was an orphan didn't she, she'd wrap him in her arms in forgiveness wouldn't she, of course she would. *Please help me Dorothea to be good.* And as if by a miracle the meanness drained from him.

And in the morning neither C. nor H. would remember a thing. Or almost.

K.R.8821Am was the notation. So terse, elliptical. A code not even the FBI could crack.

But inadequate to convey all he'd felt. After so many hours, days, of stalking. *And then the world became so suddenly perfect. PERFECT.*

Someday he would share his secrets with her; he would lay the Blue Ledger itself in her lap and invite her to read. In a calm lucid voice like a broadcaster's skilled voice he would say, "You see, it's like Euclid discovering the truths of geometry. The pure inviolate absolute truths of geometry. Not *inventing— discovering.*"

And the euphoria that followed, though it was finite, was so very real. The blueness of the Blue Room: he'd take her there too. Someday.

She looks old enough almost to be your mother: the

words flung out haphazardly, cruelly—inaccurately.
For D.D. hardly looked old enough to be Colin Asch's
mother, nor did she in the slightest resemble Colin
Asch's mother so far as he could recall her. Mrs. Asch,
dead, drowned, so many years ago. A soft-bodied
vague woman with artistic pretensions, a coarse
braided rope of blond hair like a peasant girl's,
nervous squinty eyes and nothing of Colin Asch's
fine-boned features in her face: nothing. He had the
snapshots to prove it! She'd smoked cigarettes com-
pulsively; she stank of cigarette smoke. She'd smoked
cigarettes *while bearing Colin Asch in her womb*. If
she loved him he did not remember. If she loved him,
"it wasn't anything personal; she'd had loved anyone
in the same circumstances." Mr. Kreuzer had made
the boys snigger, shocked, quoting them some ancient
king or soldier who'd disparaged his brother—*Why
should I honor him just because the two of us came
out of the same hole?*

And then there was Mr. Asch, whom Colin Asch
remembered even less clearly. Dead, drowned. A
Manhattan textbook publisher of whom no one had
ever heard until the news went out over the syndicate
wires about the submerged car, the twelve-year-old boy
who'd dived and dived and dived from the riverbank
to save his doomed parents. . . . Colin Asch remembered none of it afterward, or very little, knowing
mainly what police and others chose to tell him, and
he hadn't asked questions because he'd never been that
kind of child. *Think of your mother and father in a
better, finer world, with God,* Mrs. Kendrich said,
touching his cheek. *Drive your cart over the bones of
the dead,* Mr. Kreuzer said, touching his cheek. There
was a burial site, a joint grave marker, in Katonah,
New York, but it wasn't Colin Asch's responsibility
and he had neither seen it nor thought of it in years.

"And the body's cells change completely every seven years."

The $638 cash out of K.R.'s wallet was his reward, also the platinum wristwatch fancy tie clip crocodile belt cuff links silk rep tie shoes fancy fur astrakhan hat the fucker'd been wearing—*to the victor go the spoils*. The hat especially: you couldn't say that Colin Asch was timid, wearing the hat for all to see should they *see*. But no one save D.D.—of course—had the power to *see* Colin Asch in his truest self.

He'd stood close behind her easing the fur coat onto her, helping her with the sleeves. Lovely silky blackly iridescent fur—was it maybe mink? Nearly a head taller than the woman, he'd observed her greedily in the mirror, her dark beautiful worried eyes, the faintest of white lines bracketing her mouth, gaze veiled by thought; he was saying how thoughtful of her it had been, sending him a birthday card—"I've kept it, I'm treasuring it. I won't forget it." His voice close to quavering.

For of all the world, who had treated him decently, like a human being—like a human *soul*—and not some piece of mere shit you could slight, and insult, and forget, and cast disapproving looks at (like his asshole "Uncle" Martin'd begun to do), or tell to get out, go away and crawl into a hole maybe and die? *Of all the world no one save D.D. cared for him, or knew him.*

She knew of course that Colin Asch was the person who'd sent her the Christmas gift: the lace jacket, the floor-length skirt. The instant their eyes had met *despite the presence of the jabbering others* that fact was established. Thus there was no need for the woman to press Colin Asch's hand and whisper "Thank you" to him, though when they did shake hands—this being the style of affluent America, vigorous sincere-seeming handshakes all around, men and women both—the communication came to him by way of the warmth and surprising strength of her hand. *Our secret remains our secret—ours alone.*

And when he'd popped the hat on his head, feeling buoyant, nerved up, just the slightest bit crazy with the risk of it, and the joke of it too, D.D. had taken it in knowingly, those dark worried eyes lifting to his (for of course she would fear for his safety, having no knowledge of his past accomplishments or of the ingeniousness of the Baffle, no practical knowledge of the stupidity of the police) and had said she'd liked it: "It's very handsome!"

At her car they'd spoken quite directly. Now she knew, if she had not previously known; now he knew that she knew—*there was forever that bond between them* as if when he'd lowered the wire noose so swiftly and cleanly over the fucker's head, when instantaneously he'd jerked it tight, tight, tight, her fingers had guided his own, had fitted themselves to his, warm, soft, surprisingly strong. Thus with Colin Asch's sworn enemies: he'd known what he wanted to do and he had done it! and it was *done!* She would not have wished to witness the actual event, for pity was a fault in her perhaps, as in Colin Asch, or was it rather a magnanimity of spirit—like the great poets and visionaries who seek to embrace the All—so the actuality, the fact of it, would have frightened her, dismayed her, that Death after all is but a feeble word, a mere syllable, to set beside Dying—its physicality, its awful ignoble convulsive struggle—and the sudden stench of shit in the fucker's pants, the transformation of R.K. into K.R., into mere meat. The man had been strong, but Colin Asch with his rockhard shoulder and arm muscles, the powerful tight muscles of his thighs too which, by way of leverage, he brought to bear upon the victim; ah, Colin Asch that radiant angel boy was stronger!—always stronger!

"Did you doubt me, Dorothea? Because I seemed to be taking so long? You should never doubt me, Dorothea."

She had allowed him to know, in parting, that she would never divulge his secret—of course. For it was her own secret as well. And that, yes, he'd made her happy—"*very.*"

Which, after all, had been the point of it.

ANYTHING DONE HENCEFORTH IS BLESSED
BECAUSE IT EMANATES FROM THE SOUL

Thus Colin Asch wrote in the Blue Ledger that night.

The Blue Ledger, precious as Colin Asch's very life, for in a sense it *was* his life, was sometimes carried in his duffel bag, sometimes locked in the trunk of the Olds, less frequently hidden between the bedsprings and the mattress of his bed in the spacious silken-wallpapered guest room the Weidmanns had given him, rent-free, since his arrival in November. But it was there, in that room, that the Blue Ledger showed signs of having been disturbed—taken from its secret place, probably looked into, if not minutely scrutinized, then replaced, *but clumsily replaced!* so that Colin Asch with his sharp eye and instinct for danger knew what had happened at once. His nostrils contracted as with a sudden virulent odor.

"I will have to kill her after all—if she was the one."

The thought upset him, and saddened him—his aunt was one of the few human beings on the planet he'd thought he could *trust.*

But when he went to her, speaking quietly, smiling, his shut fists hidden behind his thighs, the woman professed such innocence, and ignorance, Colin understood she hadn't seen the Ledger after all; she knew nothing about it. Shrewdly Colin had not mentioned the notebook, only the fact that someone had been in his room going through his things rearranging his things without his knowledge or permission *and he didn't like it.* "I thought, you know, Aunt Ginny," he said, beginning to get a little breathless, "that no one would dare violate my privacy in this house. That I could trust people in this house of all the fucking places in the world." Ginny Weidmann's eyes widened and grew moist. She said, "I suppose—it might have been Tula."

Colin said, still quietly, "I asked you not to let her in my room didn't I."

"Yes, dear, and I explained to her, but—"

"I said I'd do my own fucking cleaning, didn't I."

"Colin, dear, please—please don't be angry," Ginny Weidmann said. "I'm sure it was an innocent mistake. I'm sure that Tula just forgot. Or she may have misunderstood my—"

"You told her to clean in there, didn't you? 'Cause you were worried I wasn't cleaning up my own crap, weren't you?"

"No, dear, I'm sure that I—I don't remember *precisely*—"

" 'Cause you didn't trust me. To keep things clean. And I told you the first day, I told you, I can't bear it that a black woman has to clean up after me, I can't bear it; I *told* you, I *explained,* and you said you understood." The injustice of it ran like a flame over his brain, his soul. Still, he managed to control his voice. "Just because we have white skins and they have black skins, and we've exploited them through the centuries, and the conditions are still slave conditions, *only the proportions have been altered.*"

"But Colin," Ginny Weidmann said, removing her half-moon reading glasses and setting them nervously aside, "Tula has worked for us for years! I'm sure she is very fond of us!"

" 'Tula,' as you call her—though she doesn't call you 'Ginny,' does she—hasn't worked for *me* for years."

"But she—"

"She hasn't worked for me for years!"

He backed out of the room and she followed him, apologizing, weakly protesting, her nephew who was rapidly losing control of himself *for as sudden sometimes as sexual desire it sprang up in him: the need to do hurt! to restore balance! justice!* Literally wringing her hands, and her pop eyes swimming with tears. "Colin? Do you really think it's—wrong?"

In another part of the house the black maid was vacuuming. The sound ran through Colin Asch, pulsing with the rage of his own blood.

"For us to hire them? Whites? *Blacks?*"

Colin Asch backed away from the woman, his hands in front of him now in a gesture of angry submission. He wasn't going to hurt her; *she was one of those he wasn't going to hurt* no matter how she tempted him. Blowsy cow with her face all gummed up, fifty-five years old and the "red rinse" glimmering in her hair, not to mention the diamonds—*ah yes the diamonds*—on her left hand winking and jeering at him. He'd helped himself to small change out of her purse now and then, and he'd walked off with tiny crap items no one'd ever miss around the house, a three-inch carved jade elephant on the mantel, a little silver bowl or cup some businessman had given Martin Weidmann in 1977, plus some tacky gold cuff links in the bottom of Martin's jewelry drawer in the bedroom with a look of never being used, but the big things he'd drawn magic circles around *not to cross into and violate* since Colin Asch knew from past experience that once he got started it was very difficult to stop. "The final thing is, you've got to mash in their brains." But the bitch had a nerve—you had to hand it to her—waving her jewels in his face when she knew Colin Asch had nothing, and no prospects: hadn't been able to enroll in a fancy Ivy League college like her shithead children; thus he was fated to occupy an inferior position for life—or was he?

He'd run upstairs to the room to get his duffel bag (in which the Blue Ledger was carefully secreted; hand over hand he tossed things in, panting, as Ginny Weidmann, frightened, tried to placate him. But Colin Asch was not a man to be placated. *His integrity would not allow it. His very soul was sickened.* So upset he'd begun to stammer, telling the ignorant white woman who was his aunt that she and her kind should be ashamed of their exploitation of the black underclass—
"Paying an entire class of human beings to shovel up your shit for you. And boasting it's 'employment'! And boasting it's 'wages'!"

Here was Ginny Weidmann crying at last, Ginny Weidmann who'd never in her blind complacent life been so attacked, so *exposed,* it was like he'd slapped the bitch in the face the way she cringed, staring at him, like Moses and the burning bush you'd think, like Jacob and the angel, so Colin Asch felt sorry for her—almost—as she pleaded, "Colin? Colin? I'm sure that Tula likes us, forgives *us.* And she needs the money I pay her, and I tip her too, Colin, I try to be generous."

Colin felt a stab of pity for his aunt, sympathy almost; he was yanking the new merino sweater down over his head, heather-colored it was, beautiful hand-knit wool, $198 marked down to a bargain $125 for the post-Christmas sale in the Village Haberdashery where he'd bought it; he was brushing his hair irritably out of his eyes, trying to explain to his aunt patiently as you'd explain to a child or a retarded adult that it was the capitalist class structure that was the tragedy, that she and Martin were as much victims of it as

Tula—"If her people were trained for decent-paying jobs, if they were college-educated like most middle-class whites, they wouldn't have to work as slaves for you, or starve."

Ginny Weidmann stood watching Colin Asch, a crumpled tissue pressed against her mouth. Her eyes, swimming in hurt, followed him as if without comprehension. She cried, "Colin, dear—what are you doing? Are you packing your things? *Are you leaving?*"

Politely but emphatically he shifted her out of his path and went to the closet. Fuck it: he'd have to make several trips, what with the new clothes and the books, and that pissed him, definitely—it'd have been the shrewdest maneuver to pack up the car on the sly, then simply walk out, shutting the door behind him. Or could he talk Aunt Ginny into giving him a hand?

"You're—leaving? Like this? Just walking out? Like this? Without even saying goodbye to Martin?"

Colin Asch cast the woman a look meaning yes. Meaning *how can you ask?* Meaning *you are the one who has forced this, not I.*

Of course he had a place to go, he had places—Christ! more than he could count!—but he hadn't yet signed the lease for the apartment, he'd been about to sign then got worried then made an appointment to see the other apartment, Sylvan Towers was one, Fairleigh Place the other, couldn't decide between the two since the rent was about the same and both buildings advertised "no fee"; then Susannah—Mrs. Hunt; he'd met her in the Bookworm—the sable coat attracted him first then the strong snubbed profile then the quick-darting eyes with a look of something knowing, ribald, in them—and she'd been attracted (that was obvious) to him: mop-headed and a bit sullen like a college kid home on vacation and had been quarreling with his parents wandering now in the only bookstore in town with an expression of faint incredulity *You call* this *a bookstore!—this?*—and he'd been on one crutch, his right foot bandaged, a skiing accident at Vail, or was it Switzerland—"People like you better if you're crippled or maimed somehow"—then Susannah Hunt insisted he look at an apartment in her building, Normandy Court, which he liked a lot; it sort of bowled him over with the view of the edge of a park and a balcony where, mornings, he could have breakfast, and the walls were such a pure spotless white and the hardwood floors so gleaming—two bedrooms, two baths, unfurnished—a long living room with glass along one wall where he'd have the celebration party for Dorothea Deverell when she got her promotion— you could fit fifty people in there without much trouble—and the kitchen, though small, was all modern fixtures and really cool: "This place could turn me domestic," he'd said, rocking back on his heels, and Mrs. Hunt, laughing through her cigarette smoke, squeezed his wrist and said, "I have the identical kitchen, Colin, and it hasn't done a thing for *me.*"

So he went there. Not to the apartment but to Normandy Court, where Susannah took him in. The Weidmanns he told her had this weird marriage where the wife drank all day and the husband had his own life practically; it sort of reminded Colin of this man who'd been killed in the city—what was his name, Robert Krauss? Roger?—a successful businessman and all that but unraveling at the edges, hanging out with weird people, rough trade maybe; yeah he'd made a pass at Colin, sort of, but tentative enough to pretend that wasn't it at all; he felt sorry for them they were well-intentioned people basically very nice very kind very generous but pathetic like so many people out here— "I guess you don't fit the pattern at all, Susannah, *you* must be lonely here aren't you?"—and that was the right thing to say since Mr. Hunt was gone (gone where? married a younger woman?) and the kids were grown up and gone and there was bad blood all around, Colin Asch could smell it.

He would tell her *there is no door but the way in is everywhere. Like God whose center is nowhere and everywhere at once.*

Long ago, on the far side of the river . . . coming in breathless out of the freezing wind into the hotel lobby grand as the interior of a cathedral, and his mittened hand had slipped free of his mother's gloved hand, and he was drawn forward staring at the enormous Christmas tree which was like no other Christmas tree he had ever seen because it was not *green* but *white,* and covered in eye-sized blue lights that winked on and off to a quick nervous beat, and glittering blue glass ornaments the size of a man's fist . . . and the air pulsed a chilly blue, finely vibrating with the voices of strangers and their heavy footsteps. He had stared in astonishment at what wasn't a real Christmas tree or even the idea of a real tree but the representation of a wholly artificial tree that nullified the idea of a real tree because it was perfect . . . it was white, it was manmade, it would never die. The entire domed alcove of the lobby in which it stood was blue, a thin cold artificial blue, and there were mirrored walls lightly frosted with artificial snow in which a child with pale blond hair and a small pale face stood transfixed, as if paralyzed by the sinister wonder in which he was enclosed: there was a child in the mirror and a child in a mirror in that mirror reflected from the opposite and adjoining walls, and in these other walls there was a child in a mirror contemplating a multiplication of children in mirrors seen from the side, from the rear, seen full-face, seen in their entirety and in fractured segments, a child repeated endlessly yet always the same child, identical and unmistakable, the eyes snatching here and there, and back again and there, finally staring aghast into Colin Asch's stricken face. How could it be? And yet it *was!* The front of his head as it was ordinarily seen in a mirror yet every other angle of vision simultaneously as God would see so that the child was both inside himself and outside, and there was no child! And the air thrummed blue and was beautiful!

Like dying, he would tell her, *but not needing to go away to see what it would be like, after you were gone.*

In the Blue Room he could float for hours. For hours stretched like days, like an unbroken stream of fat clouds stretched across the sky. *And no one could touch him: he was bodiless, weightless, shadowless. Floating.*

He'd known what he had wanted to do, and he had done it. Thus it was *done.*

And it could never be undone.

Not by any power on earth.

Not by any power in the universe.

Not by the power of God—if there was a God.

XXX performed deftly and with precision, after days of admitted frustration, anger that interfered with his sleep and even his digestion since he'd been unable to get close to the target or, if he'd been able to get close, the circumstances (other people close by, witnesses) weren't congenial for what he wanted to do. He knew that Miss Deverell might be waiting . . . wondering. Why was it taking Colin Asch so long to intercede in her behalf? After that lascivious look the fucker had dared give them, slitting his eyes and oily mouth in insult, as if, for that alone, he wouldn't be punished!— as if for that instant's assault, which pierced Miss Deverell sharp as a blade *as Colin Asch with his senses keenly alert understood,* he wouldn't be punished by all means available! ''Though he was dead, the fucker, when I did the other, I guess''—meaning the gouging of the eyes, which was an impulsive thing, sort of wild, whimsical, and cutting him up as he'd done with the razor, which he'd more or less planned depending upon the circumstances. For split-second timing of course was crucial. You had to know what you wanted to do, and you had to know how to do it. Fast.

And then you had to know how to make yourself vanish. *Fast.*

But for days prior to the execution of the plan he'd been balked and made a fool of, sort of. Like he had a hard on that couldn't be discharged and he was getting meaner and nastier almost in a frenzy in that state. Like it was R.K.'s fault that C.A. couldn't get close to him, to use either the wire or the razor, not one not two but three actual times he'd thought *This is it* calmly and methodically, but the situation had shifted at the very last moment like a picture suddenly blurring out of focus . . . which had surprised him so much he hadn't had time to be scared until afterward, thinking of it. For if Colin Asch's luck had not held, if he hadn't a special destiny but was just an ordinary man, he'd be under arrest now, maybe, or he'd have been forced to kill another person, or more than one other person . . . not skillfully but desperately, in a panic.

"But of course Colin Asch's luck held."

It had been a sign of genius to darken his face as he'd done with theatrical makeup, and wear the woolly little goatee, which he'd worn once before with success, and of course the dark glasses that were practically wraparounds so his eyes were totally hidden . . . and a black wool cap fitted like a swim cap on his head, to hide his hair . . . and the fawn-colored suede outfit meaning he was a certain class of black, had money, taste, personal style. And the clarinet case. *Genius shows itself in detail; in detail is the mark of the artist.*

So Colin Asch allowed himself to be glimpsed by the parking attendant who would be the only witness. The only surviving witness.

R.K. had taken the elevator up into the parking structure so C.A. took the stairs, not altogether certain which level R.K. was on but there was no problem locating him—in his dark topcoat and asshole astrakhan hat, weaving a little as he approached his car, drew his keys out of his pocket to unlock the door. The lateness of the hour and the semideserted garage made everything still. *A certain holy quality to it. Shadowless.* C.A. swallowed hard, feeling that little kick or trip to his heart that meant he was approaching the edge of what he'd been born for, *what was necessary to exact, to restore balance.* The secret was control. The secret was easing into the Death axis where you become the agent of Death in full control of Death, not its accidental victim or witness. So there appeared on level 3B of the parking structure this light-skinned youngish but old-fashioned kind of affable Negro, middle class you'd guess, professional class, strolling openly and in no hurry toward a Datsun hatchback parked a few spaces from R.K.'s Lincoln, a coincidence the two men were going to their cars at the same time but nothing more than a coincidence surely, and when R.K.'s eyes lifted narrowing a bit in his direction the black man nodded respectfully and glanced away as you'd naturally do in such circumstances; then he glanced back as if in recognition, smiled tentatively, said in a lilting friendly absolutely unintimidating voice, "Mr. Krauss, is it?" and Krauss it was, thick-bodied, thick-necked, eyelids mildly inflamed with a long night of holiday drinking, lips pursed, baffled but not wanting to make a social blunder, so the black man said quickly, in his rich low melodic voice, "Wouldn't expect you to remember me, Mr. Krauss, but we met a few weeks ago, I think, out in Lathrup

Farms, at a concert, a recital, at the arts center—wasn't it Howard Morland who introduced us?''

So, the setup: and R.K. naturally fell for it, it *was* innocent-seeming certainly, even in such deserted surroundings smelling of concrete and cold and dirt, and there's a well-dressed artsy-type black man extending his hand for a brotherly handshake and R.K. has no choice but to shift to a magnanimous liberal-hearted white in fact nodding in a semblance of recognition, friendly too and extending his gloved hand in that automatic response you can trigger in strangers if the right cues have been signaled as, here, with clockwork precision, they have been signaled. And easing in snaky-quick and close the affable black begins a smile not to be completed as a smile, exactly.

''Fucker! Did you think you could escape *me!*''

The assault by the agent of Death is so swift, so unexpected, the fur hat knocked from the head, the wire noose forced down and tightened in the same fluid motion, there is no time for anything more than a faint gurgling protest, a muffled dreamlike shriek of astonishment as the eyes bulge outward, the skin darkens with blood swelling within seconds like the skin of an overripe tomato about to burst, then the victim is on his knees flailing, convulsing, tearing with his nails at the unbelievable pressure around his neck choking the life out of him in beats in perfectly calibrated beats—*clockwork that can run in one direction only and can never be controverted not even by the power of God*.

Thus the victorious hunter stands over his fallen prey whose death he has earned, whose death is *his*. Legs apart, knees bent, muscles strained to their fullest, expression thoughtful, patient—for the death convulsions are the *streaming-out of life* in the one that yields to the *streaming-in of life* in the other.

Did you think you could escape *me?*

* * *

Mr. Kreuzer had revealed to C.A. and a very small
number of other privileged boys the secret of the
X-factor, which democracy and Christianity and "archaic ethical remnants" sought to deny, but which
manifested itself in the very genes and chromosomes
of the biological organism—that approximately one
tenth of one percent of the species *Homo sapiens* was
destined to rule the rest, by way of superiority of in-
tellect, personality, spiritual and physical strength, and
that intangible element in the human psyche known as
will. "Will is the conduit of fate," Mr. Kreuzer said.
C.A. had not at first—for he was very young, a mere
boy, a mere *angel boy* in whom his *devil twin* still
slumbered!—comprehended. *Will is the conduit of
fate.*

Thus when one is beset by emotion, by raw unme-
diated impulses flying like maddened wasps about
one's head, it is *will* that must prevail, as *will* prevailed
in Colin Asch, after the XXX on January 2, successfully completed, and the life that had luridly coursed
up into him by way of his tingling hands and arms was
almost too potent to be contained, he wanted to shriek,
he wanted to laugh, to shout!—wanted to proclaim to
the world what he had done and the justice of it! At
the same time he wanted to get out of there as quickly
as he could and had to resist the panicky instinct to
run (for what if someone should step out of the elevator, push open the door to the stairs? What if the
parking attendant below should have heard the sounds
of struggle and was coming up to investigate?), but he
had *plans*, he had a *method*, he had a *discipline* that
could not be violated. So he willed himself to perform
those acts that in his imagination he had already performed, calmly, even coolly, despite his pounding
heart and the sweat running in tiny tickly streams down
his sides, despite his shaking hands: the appropriation

of certain items of clothing and jewelry, and of course the wallet (thick with bills and credit cards), *to the victor go the spoils,* and he had time too for punishing in certain requisite ways, the eyes that had given her insult, the groin, the fat cock, no matter the heaviness of the body in death, mere insensate *deadness*. For the revenge was hers, and must be exacted in full.

"I am the mere agent."

Then he placed the ticket stub he'd shrewdly acquired earlier that evening (at a porno movie house showing the double New Year's Day feature *Boys of the Night* and *Secrets of the Nazi Storm Troopers*) deep in the dead man's trouser pocket; then he heaved the body up and into the Lincoln, positioning it behind the wheel, head back against the headrest as if, indeed, merely resting, and stiffening arms crossed in the bloody lap. Then he removed from its Saran Wrap wrapper a wadded rag soaked in paint thinner, which he tossed into the back seat of the car; then he placed, in the car's trunk, beneath a rubber mat, three fag porn magazines purchased several weeks before, when he had first fashioned his plan—one of them dated January 1988, the others older, stained and rumpled, secondhand.

The genius of the Baffle is simplicity: *give the fuckers one main thing to think and they will think it*.

These actions Colin Asch performed deftly and pleasurably in less time in fact than it would afterward require him, in his aunt's home, sitting Indian-fashion on his bed, to record them, codified, in the Blue Ledger.

And then he took the stairs swiftly down to the ground level of the parking structure, encountering no one, being seen by no one, and on the ground level he waited patiently, perhaps ten minutes, until the attendant was occupied with a customer, and then he walked unhesitatingly out onto Providence Street—a free man. At this late hour (the dead man's watch, slipped on Colin Asch's wrist, read 3:20) the street was deserted except for a scattering of parked cars and a solitary police car easing through the intersection. By now Colin Asch felt so cleansed of all emotion, so pure, so childlike, so righteous, so spiritually replenished—*XXX performed to balance injustice, "eye for an eye, tooth for a tooth"*—that the sight of the patrol car made no special impression. And, in any case, it was headed in the opposite direction.

7

On a snowy Monday in early February, Mr. Howard Morland, tanned and rested from a protracted vacation in Barbados, dropped by Dorothea Deverell's office at the Institute to invite her, as if impulsively, to have lunch with him at his club that day. "The two of us have," he said, with the faintest of embarrassed smiles, "a little catching up to do."

Dorothea Deverell said without thinking, "Oh, but I'm afraid I can't, Howard—not today. I really have too much work to do. I wasn't intending to go out for lunch at all." Seeing Mr. Morland's look of gentlemanly disappointment—or was it, yet more subtly, a look of commingled pity and impatience—Dorothea felt her face begin to burn, as if she had been caught out in a social error. Yet she persisted. "I mean," she said, in a faltering voice, "there really is so much that should be done."

Mr. Morland merely laughed and backed off, with a dapper little salute. "Of course, Dorothea," he said, "I understand. But perhaps you could see me in my office? Sometime this morning? I promise not to encroach upon your time."

"I can," Dorothea said, swallowing hard. For of course this was the summons she had been awaiting. "I mean, I will."

When, an hour later, Dorothea entered the director's office, ushered inside by his smiling secretary, she found Mr. Morland seated not at his desk but in a black leather recliner with a raised footrest; he unwound himself from it and made a sort of belated gesture of getting to his feet, even as Dorothea told him not to bother. They were old associates after all: never intimate, but perhaps familial. "How lovely you look today, Dorothea!" Mr. Morland said, as he almost always did, shaking Dorothea's hand, as he almost always did, with a boyish vigor that never seemed less than genuine. Standing hardly taller than Dorothea Deverell at five feet five inches, Howard Morland was the sort of smallish compactly wiry man who, adept at such ferocious games as squash, racquetball, and handball, enjoys making larger men, and some women, wince at the strength of his handshake. But Dorothea had long ago learned to brace herself against it.

The first several minutes of any conversation with Mr. Morland in his capacity as director of the Brannon Institute were invariably given over to obfuscatory chatter, involving an exchange of social information: health, recent activities, news of mutual friends. Dorothea complimented Mr. Morland on his tan and asked an apposite question or two about the Morlands' house in Barbados. Where usually this preliminary ritual of talk chafed at Dorothea's nerves, for Mr. Morland with his feckless aristocrat's poise seemed to consider everything with equal seriousness, this morning she was grateful for it. Though she smiled readily and laughed at Mr. Morland's jokes—for Dorothea Deverell too had poise—the blood had drained out of her fingers and toes with startling abruptness, and she suspected that she looked rather pale. She was uneasy about the conversation to follow and could not imagine what course it would take.

She knew, however, that Roger Krauss's name would

never be mentioned. It had never crossed Mr. Morland's lips in the past, when Krauss was so pointedly alive, and it would never cross his lips now that Krauss was dead.

Howard Morland's office, originally a drawing room in the Brannon mansion, was half again as large as Dorothea's, with the same elegantly high ceilings, tall narrow windows, and fine woodwork. In addition, Mr. Morland's office had antique furnishings from the estate, including, on the walls, costly works of art—an exquisite sun-drenched Bonnard, a small murky Corot oil. There were long Spanish lace curtains framed by heavy velvet drapes, there was an Irish crystal chandelier, there was a stately travertine marble fireplace of the hue and seeming texture of curdled cream. A model of the old ideal of connoisseurship, Mr. Morland's office was less an "office"—with vulgar connotations of practicability, routine, *work*—than a self-regarding display of wealth and taste. Entering it, seated in it, Dorothea Deverell had never once thought, in her six years as Howard Morland's assistant, that she might some day inherit it; her hopes for advancement had always been abstract. For certainly she did not deserve such splendor.

Just as Howard Morland was known for his habits of obfuscation, so too was he known, by his professional colleagues at least, for sudden, sometimes dizzying transitions of subject. One moment he was chatting amiably, and at length, about the "marvelous wild monkeys—so shy" of the Windward Islands; the next he was telling Dorothea Deverell, in the same tone, his smile undiminished, that he had, at the previous Friday's meeting of the board of trustees of the Institute, made the date of his retirement official: June 1. "And I requested of them, and they concurred—I should say, Dorothea, unanimously and enthusiastically concurred—that you be named the next director." His smile deepened; his beautifully capped teeth shone whitely. Because of his tanned face his hair too shone white, a benign snowy innocent sort of white, still quite thick. "Dorothea? Did you hear? We want you to be the next director of the Institute."

Dorothea Deverell, listening intently, had not, somehow, heard.

But she managed to smile and to nod, murmured a few confused words of assent, felt her eyes fill quickly with tears, as if swelling. She had to resist the impulse to say to Howard Morland, whom, suddenly, she saw as a beneficent father, her friend and protector all along, "But the directorship is too good for me—I don't deserve it."

She said instead, "I'm very honored."

Mr. Morland went on expansively to tell Dorothea of the circumstances of the board meeting, in which, of course, he had played the major role: what was said, and by whom; how very highly Dorothea's unique talents were regarded; their fear that (for there had been recent rumors) Dorothea might seek employment elsewhere. He told Dorothea the board hoped, if she accepted the terms of the directorship, that she might want to take over the responsibilities of "acting director" in a few weeks, to make the transition less difficult.

"With an immediate adjustment in salary, of course," Mr. Morland quickly added, misinterpreting Dorothea's lowered gaze.

So they spoke of practical matters, and problems that had accumulated in Mr. Morland's absence; and the remainder of the historic conversation, for Dorothea, passed in a drunken sort of blur—for she feared she might burst into tears, and Mr. Morland would be obliged to comfort her. Yet she was not untouched by a sense of irony, knowing that, had not Roger Krauss been removed from the board of trustees by death, and had not the circumstances of his death been so ines-capably lurid, it was quite doubtful—ah, quite!—that the director of the Brannon Institute would be having this particular happy conversation with his assistant; he might indeed be having a very different sort of con-versation altogether. (Yet he is not aware of this at all, Dorothea thought. The fact of Roger Krauss has been removed from his memory entirely.)

She thought it amusing too, more innocently so, that Mr. Morland should solemnly propose an interim as-signment as acting director as if, for the past several years, that had not been, *de facto*, Dorothea Deverell's very position at the Brannon Institute.

Yet when she rose to leave and Mr. Morland again shook her hand, or, rather, clasped it almost tenderly, Dorothea felt tears of gratitude rush into her eyes, tears of relief, of sheer girlish joy. Now my future is clear, she thought. A part of my future at least.

"I had always intended this, you know, Dorothea," Mr. Morland said warmly. "You to succeed me, I mean. I hope, dear, you never had any cause to doubt—?"

In a tone of equal warmth, her eyes shining with emotion, Dorothea Deverell exclaimed, "Never!"

When she returned to her office on the second floor, there stood Jacqueline happily awaiting her, and sev-eral other staff members—for of course the secretarial staff had known, since the board's meeting on Friday, of Dorothea Deverell's promotion. *"This,"* Jacqueline said half accusingly, handing Dorothea a single long-stemmed rose, ruby-red, in a slender glass vase. "Why did you think *this* was on my desk? Did you think I just bought it, for myself, for no reason? To liven up Monday mornings?"

Dorothea accepted it from her, blushing with plea-sure. She hadn't noticed the rose on Jacqueline's desk at all.

Later, she telephoned Charles Carpenter at his office, to tell him her remarkable news, which, to Charles Carpenter, did not seem so very remarkable. "It's about time," he said. Grimly, with a husbandly sort of loyalty, adding, "Those bastards." But Dorothea refused to allow him to take that tone and spoke of how exceedingly gracious Howard Morland had been, and sincere; and not a word of course of her old enemy Roger Krauss. "I should hope not," Charles Carpenter said. "I should think, rather, they all owe you an apology—starting with Howard. He has been slipping by on charm for the past sixty-odd years."

In recent weeks, since Dorothea's retreat to Vermont, she and Charles Carpenter seemed to have drifted closer together; they were in one of their cycles of intense, almost sibling intimacy, speaking with each other daily, sometimes twice daily, on the telephone, though they usually did not see each other more than once a week. Charles confided in her that he spoke to her more frequently than he spoke to his wife, and always about more significant things. For which, I suppose, Dorothea thought, I should be grateful: *there is that at least*.

Charles did congratulate her on the promotion, however; he was happy, he said, that she was happy. "Now my future is clear, in Lathrup Farms," Dorothea said jubilantly. Then added, lest her lover be hurt or alarmed, "A part of my future at least."

(Though Roger Krauss had been dead hardly more than a month, the subject of his death, and its shocking circumstances, was no longer much discussed in Lathrup Farms; other matters, less scandalous but gratifyingly local, had come to the fore. Out of a dread of seeming to delight in another's ill fortune, Dorothea Deverell did not follow news of the police investigation in the papers, if, indeed, there was news; nor did she participate in conversations that drifted onto that topic. In time she might even convince herself that Mr. Krauss had merely been baiting her, taking a devil's advocate sort of stand vis-à-vis "feminism," as often, in social situations, meaning no real harm, otherwise good-hearted men will do. To think of him as her enemy was surely to exaggerate? "I must guard against that sort of thing."

It was Dorothea's vague understanding that the mystery of the murder was more or less solved; that the police had their man; that there would eventually be a trial. And this too, this public posthumous death ritual, she would make every effort to ignore in the interest of maintaining that purity of conscience, or soul, that seemed to her as much a part of Dorothea Deverell's identity as her dark brown eyes, her dark brown hair, her creamy-pale skin, her delicate frame.)

On the day that Dorothea Deverell's promotion to Director of the Brannon Institute was made public—by "public" meaning simply its release to the Lathrup Farms weekly, where it was featured in a prominent article—she arrived home from the Institute at about 6:30 P.M. and had scarcely taken off her coat and begun sorting through the morning's mail when the doorbell rang. As if, she thought, someone had been waiting for her. Or had followed her home.

It was Colin Asch, whom she had not seen for weeks, with a bouquet of flowers. "I hope you don't mind, Miss Deverell! I just wanted to drop by, you know, to congratulate you!"

Dorothea was startled to see him, so tall, so blond, so palpably *there*—yet rather happy too, for she'd been thinking of him, and in a way missing him. She invited him inside, and offered him tea or some sherry—

"Thank you, you're very kind, why don't I have whatever you're having: tea?"—and put the flowers in a vase. A half dozen gorgeous flame-colored gladioli. Each stem was about three feet tall, each blossom the size of a man's fist. Dorothea laughed aloud at the prodigality of her young friend's gift. She felt suddenly quite giddy, festive. "Sherry," she said. "And what the English choose to call 'digestive biscuits.' "

They sat in the living room, Colin Asch rather shyly, at first, on the sofa, whose excess of little pillows seemed initially to confound him; Dorothea in a facing Queen Anne chair. How larger than life her visitor appeared, and how enlivened, keyed up, physically *busy*—leaning forward to examine books and magazines on Dorothea's coffee table, craning his neck to see the framed Oriental woodcut on the wall behind the sofa, smiling, smiling, like a child on a rare excursion, or a lover newly admitted to the very bower of bliss. He wore a sports coat in bright Harris tweed, and striped tweed trousers, not quite matching—the latest in men's fashions presumably; his white-gold hair was cropped short at the sides and back but rose in thick tufts at the crown of his head. A scrim of pale beard glimmered on his jaws and cheeks, and this too Dorothea seemed to know was fashionable—though why it should be, she hadn't the slightest idea. And was that an earring in the young man's right earlobe? Not an earring precisely but a sort of clamp, gold or brass and rather cruel-looking?

In a high rapid self-conscious voice Colin Asch was explaining to Dorothea, as if some sort of explanation were expected, that he had actually heard of her good news from his Aunt Ginny days ago—"But she cautioned me not to be premature. To wait, you know, for the official release." His expression shifted as if in mimesis of his days of anticipation and impatience.

"It's such wonderful news, Miss Deverell—I mean, Dorothea! And so deserved!"

Dorothea thanked him and tried, after a discreet pause, to deflect the subject from herself, asking after Colin Asch's job at the television station and where he was now living—she'd heard, she said, that he had found an apartment somewhere in Lathrup Farms? It struck her at the time, though less forcibly than it would afterward, as odd, just slightly odd, that a young man whom she scarcely knew should be so impressed by—indeed, so emotionally caught up in—her modest professional success. And the way he looked at her, his beautiful eyes widened in respectful admiration: it was all rather odd. But flattering.

When Colin Asch told Dorothea that he no longer worked at WWBC-TV but had a "much more challenging" job in public relations with a firm here in Lathrup Farms, she recalled vaguely that Ginny Weidmann had told her something of this and of Colin's rather abruptly leaving the Weidmanns' house. She recalled too that there had been some unpleasantness—hurt feelings on Ginny's part—and something more, but for some reason it had all faded from her memory; perhaps she hadn't wanted to believe anything less than good of Ginny's extraordinary young relative. He was saying, with an embarrassed shrug of his shoulders, "They didn't want me to leave the television station, and it was all rather awkward at the end. In fact, a competitor of theirs found out I was leaving and made me an offer *over the telephone*—which left me a little breathless. But I had had it up to here, Dorothea," he said, drawing a forefinger swiftly across his throat, "with the media and their pitiless emphasis on *popularity*. The only question such people ask themselves is, 'Will it sell?' Or, 'Will advertisers like it?' The content of a typical television program is always subordinate to so many other factors, so many other *triv-*

ial factors—I mean, it's an insult to the human species!
At least,'' he said, lowering his voice, ''it was an insult to *me*. They practically begged me to do a pilot
show, a sort of high-level interview program like on
public radio, you know, where the interviewer really
knows his material, reads a lot of books and things,
to prepare, and I was tempted, sort of, but not, you
know, really seriously—what the media takes from you
ultimately is your soul, Dorothea: nothing less. So I
quit. Walked away. And had the good luck to walk
into another—well, a much better job.''

Dorothea Deverell, rather dazzled by the rapidity of
her young friend's recitation and the intensity with
which he regarded her, could only murmur, banally,
''Good for you!''—though the thought occurred to her
that public relations, as she understood the field, could
not really be much of an improvement over television.

Colin Asch finished his glass of sherry, and licked
boyishly at his lips, and laughed, and said, ''I know
what you're thinking, Dorothea—''

''Yes?''

''—that a job in public relations is the same kind of
thing as a job in television, that the goals are sort of
basically the same—an emphasis upon surfaces, images, and all that. But no, actually,'' he said, frowning, ''it isn't like that, actually. I mean, it can be, and
probably is, in most circumstances, but this position
that I have, assistant to the art director at L.L. Loomis
and Company—d'you know them? ever heard of them?
they're a state-of-the-art kind of company, first-class,
upbeat, sort of wired, but wired in a *good* way—the
director's a guy about my age, only a few years older,
really great to work with. In fact I was thinking, Dorothea, on the way over here—I mean, I have another
reason, a primary reason, for being here—but I was
thinking, sort of, I could help you out, I mean at the
Institute, with publicity for your programs and exhib-

its, that kind of thing—I mean,'' he said, breathless, ''if you wanted me to.''

Dorothea smiled, as if ruefully, and said, ''Yes, publicity hasn't been one of our strong points. I never seem to—''

''It isn't just *informing* people of what you're doing, it's *forcing* them to take notice,'' Colin Asch said passionately. ''Some of the programs you sponsor, they're so good, they're so deserving of a much wider audience—they're as significant as anything going on in Boston, in my opinion, or in Cambridge—but the masses have to be alerted. Not that you'd want too many people of course; the auditorium wouldn't hold them. But the art exhibits, that's different, they'd space themselves out sort of naturally I'm sure.'' Seeing Dorothea's smile he asked, ''Is something wrong?''

''I was just thinking, Colin, that it has never yet been a problem for us, at the Institute: an excess of people—of 'masses.' ''

''Well, I know,'' Colin Asch concurred, with a sheepish smile, ''it's been a small operation, mainly local, serving the community and all that. But now that you're in charge it's a new era, sort of—has got to be. Maybe you could give me your schedule for this spring—before I leave—so I could get started, just sort of unobtrusively? I mean just on my own.'' As if to discipline himself for speaking so excitedly he came to a full stop; Dorothea saw his jaws clamp. Then he said, ''I mean *just* on my own, Dorothea. Don't worry about a fee. *Pro bono.* ''

Dorothea said, uncertainly, ''That would be very kind of you.''

''Oh, no! I'm not kind! I'm just—a cultural emissary!''

Colin Asch had settled almost comfortably into the sofa, with the pillows neatly positioned beside him. He now crossed one long lanky tweed-clad leg over the other and chose a biscuit from the plate Dorothea offered him. She saw that he was wearing enormous running shoes, in shades of lavender. And—was it possible, in 20 degree weather?—no socks.

He said, as if to prod her into speaking a bit, "But it *is* a new era, Dorothea. With a woman in charge, and all."

Dorothea Deverell did indeed have plans for change, and newness; but she supposed she had better go slowly and not worry, or annoy, or offend the rather conservative board of trustees and the faithful little corps of volunteers, mainly female, who supported the Institute. But she confided in Colin Asch that, yes, she was intending to broaden the scope of the lecture series in particular: the former director had not wanted her to bring in a "controversial" speaker, a woman defense attorney who worked with battered women and children in Boston, and this excellent woman she would certainly engage for next year; and she would invite poets now and then; and in two or three years, when a former professor of hers at Yale retired, a distinguished art historian in the Renaissance, she might arrange a sort of *Festschrift* in his honor, inviting a number of art historians in his field, including former students, to give public lectures . . . and it would be tied in, of course, with an art exhibit.

"Those are wonderful ideas," Colin Asch said, staring at her. "Those are—I mean, those are *brilliant* ideas."

So encouraged, Dorothea Deverell was led to confide in her young friend even more, some of it sheerly speculative, and all of it unformed, inchoate: she foresaw an education series, she foresaw extensive renovations in the building, she foresaw new additions—a wing better suited for art exhibits, a new auditorium. She said, breathless, "I was telling a close friend about some of these things the other day, Colin, and he said, as if he were startled, 'I hadn't realized you had such ideas, Dorothea,' and I said to him, 'I've never had power before, and power brings ideas.' He looked at me strangely, then, and said, 'I suppose it *is* a matter of power ultimately, the realization of ideas.' I couldn't help replying—though I didn't at all want to offend him!—'Not *ultimately,* but *immediately.'* And then,'' she said, laughing almost girlishly, ''and then he really did look at me strangely.''

But Colin Asch was not to be drawn in with Dorothea Deverell's laughter. He said soberly, brushing a crumb or two fastidiously from his lips, ''Yes, the average man is very jealous of a woman's 'power.' Who did you say was your friend?''

''Charles Carpenter,'' Dorothea said. (But why had she told Colin? She hadn't meant to.) Her cheeks pulsed with warmth; she added, apologetically, ''You wouldn't remember him, but he—''

''Of course I remember him,'' Colin Asch said. He cast his eerily dazzling smile up at Dorothea as if she were teasing him. ''A lawyer. A friend of the Weidmanns'. His wife attacked me on the issue of my vegetarianism. She was drunk—she was a drunk. Yet, do you know, Dorothea, Mrs. Carpenter tried to make it up to me afterward? Sent a check for two hundred dollars to me for the Animal Rights League, by way of my aunt.''

Dorothea Deverell stared blankly. ''She did? Agnes Carpenter?''

''Wasn't that kind of her?'' Colin Asch said. ''Even if she was expiating a guilty conscience.''

''Yes,'' Dorothea said slowly. ''It was kind of her.'' She added, not knowing what she meant, ''Many of the most generous things in life, I suppose, are done to expiate guilty consciences. Which doesn't make them any—''

''Any less generous.''

There was an uneasy pause. Dorothea offered her visitor a second glass of sherry, which he accepted with thanks—''It's delicious!'' She had the distinct impression that he was turning over in his mind a question of some blunt direct sort regarding Charles Carpenter, and she wanted neither to hear it nor answer it.

She said, ''Ginny was telling me you've found a new apartment?''

Colin Asch nodded and caressed the metal clamp in his ear. ''It's called Normandy Court, do you know it? No? I'm on the eleventh floor, overlooking a little park. A friend—a new friend—is sort of helping me finance it, until I get settled in at L.L. Loomis. That's her Porsche I'm driving too—though maybe you didn't see me drive up in it?—a 1986 model I have an option to buy if I like it. Sweet little car, and *fantastic* apartment. Which is why I'm here, Miss Deverell, I mean Dorothea—I hope you'll come to see me there, and let me make dinner for you? I was thinking some sort of celebration dinner, you know, in honor of your promotion? I'd invite Aunt Ginny and Uncle Martin too, they're such wonderful people, and anyone else you'd like, and my friend Mrs. Hunt, Susannah Hunt, I guess you know her?—sort of?—she says she knows you. Just a small intimate dinner. *Please say yes.*''

''Why, yes—of course,'' Dorothea said slowly. ''If—that is—''

''It would mean so much to me! It would be such an honor!''

''If you don't think it would be too much—''

''How does March fifth sound to you? A Saturday? Eight P.M.?''

''As far as I know that date is—''

''The actual reason I have to postpone the dinner so long,'' Colin Asch said with a pinched, pained look, ''is I can't depend upon the furniture people to get the furniture to me before then. This beautiful glass and chrome dining room set—first they promised it in three weeks, now they've extended it to five, the bastards! And this beautiful Halogen lamp I bought on sale, right off the floor, marked down from $460 to $399, a real bargain, when they delivered it the base was scratched—so I refused to pay the C.O.D. charges and sent it back. *But I still want it.* Some items are in the apartment, like a nice off-white sofa, actually sort of resembling the one I'm sitting on, but others aren't, so Susannah has lent me some stuff of hers in the interim. But by March fifth everything should be perfect. By March fifth everything *will* be perfect.''

Dorothea said weakly, ''But I can't allow you to go to any trouble, Colin. Or spend much money—''

''How can it be trouble, Dorothea,'' Colin Asch asked, regarding her with hurt eyes, ''if I am doing it for *you?*''

Dorothea was holding her sherry glass in both hands, to prevent its trembling. She thought, what does he want from me?—and why? With a pang of chagrin she remembered the Christmas present, the unexpected and, indeed, unwanted gift; and meant to mention it to Colin Asch before he left the house. And Susannah Hunt: how did this ingenuous young man become involved with *her?* Dorothea Deverell could claim no firsthand knowledge of the woman but had heard startling tales, over the years, revolving around her legendary rapacity for men (including young men) and her squabbles, legal and otherwise, with her former husband, a prominent local physician. Once, at a cocktail party, Dorothea had spent an anguished half hour observing, out of the corner of her eye, her beloved Charles Carpenter in a spirited, laughter-punctuated conversation with the glamorous divorcée; to her mortification she had happened to glance across the room to see Agnes Carpenter similarly observing the couple . . . staring at them with a Gorgon's un-wavering eye. How sisterly she'd felt toward poor Ag-nes in that instant! How united in their mutual helplessness!

She had never said a word about the episode to Charles Carpenter, nor had he said a word to her.

Now she said to Colin Asch, in a neutral voice, "Are you no longer seeing that young woman from the tele-vision station? What was her name?—with the lovely black hair—"

Colin Asch said vaguely, *"That* didn't work out."

Dorothea said, "Didn't it? I'm sorry."

"Oh, don't be sorry! Really—don't be," Colin Asch said. He grinned, and uncrossed his long legs, and ran a hand roughly through his hair. "Hartley was too intense. She wanted too much from me. We just weren't, you know, each other's destiny. Also, Doro-thea," he said, lowering his voice, "she had a cocaine habit. An expensive one."

"Cocaine!"

There was an awkward pause, and Colin set down his sherry glass and rose to his feet. He consulted the platinum watch on his wrist and said, reluctantly, "Well, I suppose I should be leaving." Then, in vir-tually the same breath, he said, "Your house is so beautiful, Dorothea! Do you think I could see the rest of it?"

Dorothea heard herself say, "Of course."

Her mind leapt ahead to the upstairs: in what con-dition was it? Must she show her impetuous young friend everything—even her bedroom? Her closets?

Seeing her expression Colin said, "Unless it's too much trouble? I mean—you must be exhausted from your long day."

"Oh, no, it isn't too much trouble." Dorothea laughed.

And then the telephone rang.

She excused herself and took the call in the dining room, absentmindedly watching her visitor through a mirror—in fact, through two mirrors—without his awareness. The caller was a woman friend named Merle, an intelligent, rather lonely married woman with whom Dorothea Deverell sometimes went to the ballet, and though Dorothea tried to cut the conversation short it seemed that Merle wanted to talk: wanted rather urgently to talk. "May I call you back? I have a visitor," Dorothea said. She saw, in the living room, Colin Asch in his boxy Harris tweed moving with astonishing swiftness from place to place, like a big feral cat on its hind legs . . . scanning the books in her bookcase, checking the things on her fireplace mantel, lifting and setting down a little ivory box on a table . . . trying, with a practiced twist of his wrist, the lock of her terrace door . . . tiptoeing to the foot of the staircase and peering up, frowning, into the shadows. (But why? Dorothea thought, fascinated. I am not up there: I am down here.) The inside of her mouth seemed to be coated with a thin scummy fear, and it was with relief that she saw the tall blond figure pass out of the mirrors' range. She murmured to Merle in as kindly a voice as possible, "I'll have to call you back later. I can't talk now."

When she returned to the living room, however, Colin Asch was awaiting her with a quizzical, radiant smile. He held an art book of color plates by the American artist Alice Neel—"*This* is an original talent!" he said. He queried Dorothea Deverell about Neel, and Dorothea told him some of what she knew and offered to lend him the book—which he accepted with gratitude. He was so eager to learn, so much the ingenuous student, her suspicions of him seemed unwarranted.

Indeed, in the face of the young man's dazzling personality it was difficult to form any negative judgment of him at all.

Dorothea was telling Colin Asch about the background of her trio of dwarf Portuguese orange trees in their green ceramic pots, arranged along the southerly wall of the dining room—the tour of the house seemed, mercifully, for the moment at least, forgotten, or held in abeyance—when the telephone rang another time. A spasm of anger ran over the young man's face, but he clenched his jaws and said, "You're a very popular woman, Dorothea!—or I've come at the wrong time."

"I'll tell him to call back," Dorothea said apologetically.

But it was Charles Carpenter, with whom she did want to speak, as he wanted, it seemed quite urgently, to speak with Dorothea. Might he drop by, Charles asked, on his way home? He was still in Boston, and he'd had a very difficult day.

"Is something wrong?" Dorothea asked, alarmed. "What is it?"

"I'll tell you when I see you, Dorothea," Charles Carpenter said.

Dorothea said softly, "Is it—?"

"About you, and me? Yes it is, dear," Charles said. "And Agnes."

Dorothea Deverell, standing in the darkened dining room, the telephone receiver pressed against her ear, could make no reply. *She knows,* she was thinking calmly. *Now it will be all over between Charles and me.*

Charles said, "Is someone there, Dorothea?—with you?"

Dorothea, staring sightlessly at the floor, pointedly not looking into the mirrors, murmured vaguely, "No, not really."

Her lover did not register this ambiguity, or subtlety; he said, "Then I'll be seeing you soon, Dorothea. In about an hour."

Dorothea said, dumbly, "Tonight? Ah, yes. Of course."

They said goodbye; and like a sleepwalker Dorothea returned to her visitor, who was standing, as if at attention, in exactly the same spot he'd been standing when the telephone rang. This time, Dorothea suspected that he had been listening to her conversation. She could not recall if she had spoken her lover's name and was too exhausted suddenly to care.

Colin Asch was examining with reverence a Chagall lithograph of sleeping lovers framed and hung prominently on Dorothea's wall, a gift from Michel Deverell's grandfather, on the occasion of their wedding; a mysterious and beautiful work of art at which, in truth, Dorothea Deverell rarely glanced, it had become so familiar to her with the years and was, over all, so melancholy in its associations. The artist had signed *Marc Chagall* in pencil, in the lower right-hand corner, and it was to this signature that Colin Asch pointed, exclaiming, with touching naïveté, "He really did sign it himself, didn't he! This must be a real collector's item!"

Dorothea said, "It's only a lithograph—one of many copies."

She told Colin that the telephone call had been an important one, and that someone was coming over that evening to see her; she was sorry to be unable to take him on a tour of her house, but another time, perhaps . . . ?

"Yes," said Colin. "I understand."

Dorothea felt like a guilty wife or courtesan in a Molière farce, ushering out one male to clear the way for another: though why she should feel guilty, and why such circumstances, edged with hysteria, might be imagined as crude farce, she could not have said. God knows there was nothing amusing about it.

At the door Colin Asch said, "You won't forget March fifth, Dorothea, will you? Eight P.M.? I'll be sending out invitations as soon as I can, but please mark the date."

"I will," Dorothea promised. "I will mark the date."

She could make out, at the curb, in the dim light of a streetlamp, Colin Asch's borrowed sports car. Small, sleek, classy. Dorothea feared he would impulsively invite her to go for a ride in it, and that, against her will, she would hear herself accept.

On the front step Colin Asch shook her hand vigorously, clasping it just a beat or two too long. Dorothea said carefully, "What exactly do you want of me, Colin?"

It was the first time in her life she had ever spoken so, to any human being.

Colin Asch blinked at her as if she had slapped him. He said, hurt, "I don't 'want' anything of you, Dorothea. It just makes me happy to think—I mean, to *know*—"

"Yes?"

"—that you are here. That you exist." He spoke slowly and painfully, not meeting Dorothea's eye. "That, you know, our lives are . . . parallel."

Dorothea waited, but he said nothing further. Tears of relief sprang into her eyes. She said, squeezing his hand, "That's very kind of you, Colin. You're a remarkable person. I feel the same way about you—you've put it very gracefully."

"Then that's everything," Colin Asch said gravely, backing away.

She watched him hurry to his car, knowing that, before he climbed inside, he would turn and wave to her, just once. As he did.

She was thinking shrewdly, Parallel lines never meet.

Awaiting Charles Carpenter, Dorothea Deverell changed from her gray jersey dress to a plaid woolen skirt and an oversized Shetland sweater and put on low-heeled shoes. She carried the vase of tall flame-colored gladioli out of the living room, where they were far too exclamatory, and walked from room to room before setting them down in a twilit corner of the dining room. Then she made herself a cup of strong tea and stood in the kitchen drinking it. She was too agitated to sit down; seated, she would hear her heart-beat too clearly. She was thinking that her life of nearly the past decade was coming to an end and that, for all its frustration, intermittent humiliation, and heart-break, it had been a comfortable sort of life. She had been happy, really—less a married man's mistress than a married man's second, and far more companionable, wife. Her mother's words rose to her memory. "You go on for years and years doing the same things, not even thinking how happy you are, then suddenly one day everything is ended"—this sad, stoic observation on the occasion, when Dorothea was a senior in high school, of her father's first operation for cancer. Now Dorothea thought, Yes. But I will have to bear it.

And then, to her astonishment, within the hour Charles Carpenter brought her entirely unexpected news: "I've spoken to her, Dorothea. I've told her!"

He hadn't yet removed his overcoat, which smelled of cold, and was slowly removing his hat, a gray fedora Dorothea Deverell thought very handsome.

He said, "Did you hear me, Dorothea? *I've told her.*"

"Told her—?"

"I mean, I've begun to tell her. At last!"

Dorothea stared at Charles Carpenter, whom she had rarely seen so excited; so agitated. She backed off, rather frightened—then stepped forward into the man's hard, clumsy embrace—they grasped each other like guilty children and staggered together in Dorothea's little foyer.

Charles was saying triumphantly, "Last night—and this afternoon, over the telephone! I've made a beginning, at last! Now there is no turning back!"

As if yoked together they moved blunderingly into Dorothea's kitchen, where, uninvited, Charles Carpenter located a bottle of Irish whiskey in one of the cupboards and poured himself and Dorothea drinks. In the living room they sat on the sofa amid the scattered pillows, clasping hands as Charles Carpenter talked and Dorothea Deverell listened wide-eyed and disbelieving.

"Out of nowhere suddenly—we *weren't* arguing; our silences are far, far worse than speech—I simply said to her, 'We don't love each other, Agnes, why do we remain together?' and she cast me a look of absolute loathing as if I'd violated a sort of secret between us, and when I tried to continue she got up and left the room, as she has left at other times, simply walking away—*as if I didn't exist.* But I followed her, and insisted we talk, and we did, or I did. I mentioned the possibility of a separation, and she screamed at me, 'I'll never consent. I'll kill us both first!' Later, she accused me of wanting to kill *her;* I knew she wasn't well, she said; and what would my parents—'your precious parents'—say; and my business partners—'those fellow hypocrites.' She slammed out of the room, and I didn't follow her for a while; then I went upstairs where she was waiting but she'd locked the door, and—and so it went. For hours! Literally for hours!" He stared at Dorothea, smiling strangely; he was grasping her hand in his so hard she winced in pain. Several times he said, wonderingly, "But I've made a beginning, at last. I've made a beginning—at last."

Dorothea said faintly, "I'm so glad, Charles."

"My parents *will* be very upset, and I dread telling them, but it can't be helped. They've tyrannized me—us—with their good, sweet, uncomplaining, exemplary natures for too long. Being good, you know, is a kind of blackmail, it holds the rest of us in thrall. Agnes has always known this—known she could rely upon my 'good' nature, my fidelity, my absurd sense of conscience. Ah, yes, she has known! She has *capitalized!* Now she can enjoy a sort of martyr's pleasure, a mean bitter pleasure, casting me as the villain, a 'typical middle-aged asshole'—those were her words—and reaping sympathy and pity, or so she thinks. As if any of our friends are hers, any longer! As if anyone but her husband has been able to tolerate her, for years!"

So Charles Carpenter talked; and Dorothea Deverell, in a trance of amazement, listened. Could she believe what she was hearing? But what *was* she hearing? In the midst of a passionate tirade on the subject of Agnes' excessive drinking, Dorothea interrupted to ask if the word "divorce" had been uttered, and if Agnes had said anything about consulting a lawyer—and Charles Carpenter stared at her, as if unhearing.

He said, passing a hand over his eyes, "She will retain a lawyer who's an enemy of mine—I know it."

Dorothea said, *"Our* relationship should be kept a secret for the time being, shouldn't it?"

"Dorothea, I don't see how it can," Charles said. He had removed his suit coat; now he tugged irritably at his tie. A fine film of perspiration glistened on his face. "I thought, you know, that that was the point of—all this: my speaking to her, bringing things out into the open. Perhaps, in terms of timing, with your appointment and all at the Institute, it isn't ideal, but as I said I hadn't planned it—just suddenly out of nowhere, out of our damned glacial *silence,* I began talking and haven't been able to stop. You know I love you, and I want to marry you; surely you don't expect me to *deny* you? To Agnes or to anyone?''

Dorothea had to resist the childlike impulse to shut her eyes tight. She said, ''But have you told her, Charles? About—?''

''One of the things she screamed at me was, 'There's another woman, isn't there?'—and I didn't answer; I managed somehow to deflect the question, but a while later she returned to it, and said, 'Is it Dorothea Deverell?' and I'm afraid, Dorothea, under the pressure of the moment I said 'No.' I went on to say, 'The deadness in our marriage has nothing to do with any third party, as you certainly know,' and that distracted her enough to—Dorothea? Are you all right?''

Dorothea was clutching at Charles Carpenter's hand with both her hands. ''Did she—did she really say that? 'Is it Dorothea Deverell?' ''

''Yes. She did. She isn't an unobservant woman, after all.''

''But you told her 'No.' ''

''I told her 'No' as a means of telling her something else—eliding speech, in a sense—not very courageously, I'm ashamed to say, but in the desperation of the moment expediently; I didn't want Agnes, in her rage, to involve *you.* To pick up the telephone and call *you.* That would have been unthinkable, dear.''

Dorothea was still clutching Charles's hand in her hands, and now she leaned forward suddenly, as if faint, and pressed her forehead against it. She was thinking, What will happen now? What will happen—now? She murmured, ''So you've told her, Charles, at last!'' Dazedly she kissed his hand, her face damp with tears—she had not known she was crying. She whispered, "I love you," and Charles Carpenter kissed her warm forehead, whispering, "I love *you,*" passionately, repeatedly, as if he were making a formal vow.

"Now maybe we can give up all this—subterfuge. This damned demeaning subterfuge. I am at fault, for postponing a break with my wife for so long; in retrospect I'm appalled at my cowardice. My 'goodness.' My very sense of myself as citizen of a community! You've been so patient, Dorothea, a saint, really—having such faith in *me*. But now, soon, we can live together, openly—we can be married, and live together, in a house of our own—like normal people." He laughed excitedly, as if the single glass of whiskey had gone to his head; he slung an arm around Dorothea almost roughly, hugging her close. "Imagine, Dorothea darling: married. *Like normal people.*"

"Yes," Dorothea Deverell said. "Yes," she wept, though in truth she could not imagine it. Not after so many years of hope.

So, that night, after Charles Carpenter left her—they had gone at last up to Dorothea's bedroom to make love, as ardently as if for the first time—Dorothea Deverell lay wakeful, rigid, her eyes starkly open and her brain a storm of thoughts. Like maddened wasps the question assailed her: *What will happen now? What will happen—now?* Though she tried to think of Charles Carpenter, and her love for him, and the possibility—or was it, now, a probability?—of their being married someday soon and living in a house of their own—indeed, Dorothea had just the house in mind, or its type: Georgian revival, elegant, stately, though not large, in the older "good" section of Lathrup Farms— she nonetheless kept envisioning Agnes Carpenter, her rival, her sister rival, lying at the very same moment sleepless in *her* bed, in *her* bedroom, on the other side of town; she envisioned the woman's stunned, creased, aging face and those terrified glaring eyes—*Is it another woman? Is it Dorothea Deverell?*

I had so much rather be an object of her selfishness, Dorothea thought miserably, than have her be the object of mine.

So Dorothea passed a hellish night, the first, she presumed, of many to come; and *this* the consequence of her happiness—hers and Charles Carpenter's! By morning she had made up her mind, and telephoned Charles at his office, and told the astonished man in a rush of words that he should wait—they should wait, *must* wait—and not do anything further to upset Agnes.

"To upset Agnes?" Charles Carpenter asked, as if he had not heard correctly.

Dorothea said, "Please don't be angry, dear, but I—I can't bear to hurt her. I can't bear it that you and I, in our selfishness, should hurt her. In time, perhaps—in a few months, gradually—it could all be explained to her, but not so suddenly—so cruelly. It's like murder! such an assault! And there are two of us, Charles, and only one of her: think of how she must feel!"

Charles protested, *"I* don't want to hurt Agnes either, but it has to be done. In fact it has been postponed far too long, as I thought you'd agreed. If you and I are to—"

"All those years I envied Agnes and felt such bitterness toward her, or thought I did, and now I find I—simply don't want to hurt her. Can't bear to hurt her. You loved her once, didn't you? And she loved you, surely—didn't she? She hasn't been well for years; she will only begin drinking more heavily—"

"Dorothea, for God's sake, you sound hysterical.

Where are you, at home? Haven't you gone to work? I'll come over—''

"No, don't come over! Not now!"

"You sound so upset—"

"I *am* upset; we must rethink this!"

"But I thought, last night, we'd come to a kind of conclusion—"

"Did you say anything more to *her,* last night? When you went home?"

"No. Not to Agnes. But to you, Dorothea, I mean—I talked to *you*—I thought we'd come to a kind of conclusion, Dorothea, didn't we?" There was a pause; Charles Carpenter was breathing heavily, like a man who has been taxed to the limit. This side of him, this sense of an impatience, even anger, barely restrained, was new to Dorothea Deverell, and intimidating. "And now," he said bitterly, "now you're withdrawing from me. Now you mean to deny *me.*"

"I certainly don't! I love you. But there *is* Agnes, she *does* exist, other people do exist in the world, and we can't simply trample over them. Only think," Dorothea said in a hoarse frightened voice, "of how, at this moment, she must feel!"

"I'm thinking rather more urgently of how I feel," Charles Carpenter said.

"But I—" Dorothea began.

But in that instant the line went dead: for the first time in Dorothea Deverell's life someone had hung up on her.

A few days after Colin Asch's visit with Dorothea Deverell a packet came for her, special delivery, containing a sample of the invitation card Colin meant to send out to the guests for Dorothea's dinner party.

Colin Andrew Asch
requests the pleasure of your company
to celebrate the appointment of
Dorothea Deverell
as Director of the Morris Brannon Institute
on Saturday, March fifth, nineteen eighty-eight
at 1104 Normandy Court, Lathrup Farms, Massachusetts
R.s.v.p.   *Eight o'clock*
Telephone: 617-555-5825   *Black tie*

The paper was stiff ivory; the print elegantly, one
might say a bit pretentiously, engraved. Holding it in
her hand, Dorothea laughed aloud in embarrassment.
"This is impossible." Why did that good-hearted
young man forever teeter on the brink of absurdity,
making too much of too little, pouring his emotions
into vessels too frail to contain them? In his letter he
requested from Dorothea a list of people to whom he
should send invitations; informed her that, on the evening of the party, a chauffeured limousine would pick
her up and bring her back home; and that, if she had
liked it, and if she was "so disposed," she might wear
to the party a "recent Christmas gift, from an anon-
ymous admirer."

"Impossible!"

When, however, Dorothea telephoned Colin Asch to
protest, as diplomatically a possible, the unneeded
formality of the invitation and its "self-congratulatory"
tone, he countered with the argument that the appointment *was* an honor and she *was* to be publicly congratulated. "You are not congratulating yourself, after
all; it's your friends who are doing so." Dorothea had
not the heart to tell him that, indeed, a banquet of
sorts in her honor was being organized by the Friends
of the Brannon Institute for early September after

Howard Morland officially retired, and that other dinners and gatherings of an informal nature were planned, and would be planned—Lathrup Farms being Lathrup Farms, after all. In an outburst of defensiveness, as if Dorothea had challenged him on some very deep issue, Colin told her that everyone to whom he'd spoken about it thought it was a great, a fantastic idea, and his Aunt Ginny was frankly jealous. "She tried to preempt my party, in fact—'Why don't we do it at my house, Colin, we have more room over here'—but I told her absolutely *not*. It's *my* idea and *my* apartment. It's *my* celebration dinner for *you*."

Dorothea gently objected that she found the very idea of a celebration embarrassing; Colin Asch said at once, with the energy of a high school debater, speaking rather loudly into the phone, "But embarrassing for who? *Whom?* You can't think exclusively of yourself at such a time, Dorothea, you have to think of your friends too, don't you? Like, they want to honor you, they'd be cheated if you backed out—right? It's like certain great people who die, you know, and say in their wills they don't want any funeral or fuss; in a weird way it's sort of *selfish*, I always thought, to deprive people of—you know, certain ceremonies. What would human existence be like, Dorothea, without ceremonies? I don't mean crap like Christmas, Easter, that wornout dead kind of stuff; I mean, you know, something *liv*ing, springing from the *heart*—"

So in the end, fairly bludgeoned by her young friend's passion, which after all outweighed her own aversion to the project, Dorothea Deverell gave in and withdrew her objections. Even to the slightly silly formality of the card. Even to the admonition "black tie." She neglected to mention the limousine, and the Christmas gift, the lovely white lace and wool outfit— though she intended, at the time of the party, to consent to neither. Her primary anxiety about the dinner

was not in fact such details but the guest list: whether
she dared invite Charles Carpenter without inviting
Agnes, and without Agnes' knowing about the party;
how, given the protocol of such things and the endog-
amous nature of social life in Lathrup Farms, the finesse might be managed. Though Charles Carpenter
was still furious with her and might refuse to come in
any case . . . he loathed black tie occasions. And matters at the Carpenters' home were, as he grimly and
accusingly said, at an impasse.

In the end Dorothea decided simply to invite
Charles, by himself, with an invitation sent to his office. Perhaps, by March 5, he would have forgiven her.

8

What do you want of me, Colin? she'd asked, raising her lovely troubled eyes to his, and without thinking he told her what was in his heart surging and pulsing in his blood strong enough to choke him *I don't want anything of you Dorothea only that you exist, that our lives are parallel* and so saying he saw the happiness lighting up in her eyes like sudden candle flame. Backed away trembling in dread of being drawn by those eyes into saying more, revealing more, before she was prepared to hear.

"I was only the agent—yours."

Subsequently he would record in the Blue Ledger:

> Parallel lines never meet!
> Except in the eye!
> —like at the horizon!
> Thus in the eye of the mind parallel lines NEVER FAIL to meet!

He'd subsequently record too in abbreviated codified fashion how he had driven off from 33 Marten Lane, then parked the Porsche (which was handling beautifully—a dream car at last) on a side street then doubled back as he'd done in the past always with conspicuous success having calculated the most direct route that answered to the demands of safety and common sense through Dorothea Deverell's neighbors' back yards, in only one instance a dog yapping like crazy in what looked like a glassed-in rear porch—but maybe nobody was home?—but anyway C.A. never hesitated never panicked knowing this was a special night for him *nothing can touch you at certain illuminated times when all that is "out there" emanates in fact from the soul* . . . just jogging along like he's a weird local guy actually *jogging* . . . except not on the street but across the back yards of his Lathrup Farms neighbors . . . in six-inch crusty-icy snow in new Nike running shoes and no socks. So you get a little snow in your shoes, what the fuck: "The main thing is, it's healthy."

At the rear of 33 Marten Lane, Colin Asch stood panting, staring into the warm-lit interior of the very living room in which *Jesus! wild!* he'd been sitting in a few minutes before *what a weird shift of perspective!* except now Colin Asch was gone, also Dorothea Deverell was gone, that very sofa with the little pillows perpendicular to the fireplace, and the rose-colored chair in which she'd been sitting smiling at him her sherry glass held in both hands her mood gay, bright— *How beautiful* she'd said, taking the gladioli from him *thank you so much Colin, you shouldn't have*—and the gladioli were there in the tall cutglass vase proudly on the mantel *but Christ! how weird it all looked from outside the window like he almost could (like when he was acting, on stage) watch himself perform from outside himself.* He'd forgotten the fucking binoculars. Thus had to approach the house closer than the other times. Crouching just outside the terrace window, the big plate glass window that was the entire wall on that side.

D.D. had gone upstairs maybe but he waited, C.A. had all the patience in the world, warmed now by the sherry she'd given him, the cookies, the taste of the sugar still in his mouth, crystals on his tongue, all the patience in the world *there's a certain holy quality to this: shadowless* and they'd shaken hands goodbye, her eyes shining with affection for him and approval of him *Just to know that you exist* and she'd said *I feel the same way about you—you've put it very gracefully.* Thus he waited, and after a while D.D. reappeared, looking young as a schoolgirl in a plaid pleated skirt and yellow sweater but unsmiling now, worried, distracted, the man who was her secret lover was on his way but it was not a visit that promised pleasure, or solace—''Could be he's giving her a hard time.'' Colin Asch felt a stab of hurt and resentment when Dorothea removed the vase of flowers, his flowers, from the mantel, carrying them out of the room *as if by a directive of the invisible lover.*

(Whom he guessed to be the man whose name she'd uttered, ''Charles Carpenter,'' the friend of the Weidmanns'—middle-aged cautious-looking sort of Englishy fucker, lawyer, well-to-do—of course Colin Asch remembered him, never forgot a name; and the wife, Agnes. Had the audio equivalent of a photographic memory: perfect recall. He had tricked D.D. into saying the name aloud: ''Charles Carpenter.'' And shrewdly he knew by her liquidy gaze and the softness of her voice, *That's him! that's the man!*—for it's a fact that when you're in love with someone you say the name as much as possible, for instance at the present time Susannah Hunt was in that stage where she said his name constantly—''Colin, *Col-*liin''—sort of mock-crooning, caressing, teasing, parodying (lest her young lover beat her to it: S.H. was the kind of woman who'd had some bad experiences with younger lovers, Colin could sense) some of the things they were doing, or maybe just the fact that they were doing them at all plus saying the usual words like *I love you I'm* *crazy about you* like *you're so beautiful* like *Oh God that was wonderful* like nobody had ever said such words before but you had to believe they were true, and wanted to.)

And there suddenly the man was, in Dorothea Deverell's living room where, a short while previously, Colin Asch had been: Charles Carpenter himself. Looking taller than Colin remembered. And so earnest. So *excited*. A drink in one hand, and his other hand grasping D.D.'s, dragging her along. As if he had the right.

Thus Colin Asch was forced to crouch shivering in the snow amid the sharp-needled evergreens while inside the lovers had their surreptitious meeting—*an assignation* it would be termed—sometimes kissing, embracing . . . then drawing back again to talk . . . and D.D. was crying it seemed .. and Carpenter tried to comfort her when it was obvious *he* was the one causing *her* grief—hadn't she been radiant with happiness a short while before, in Colin Asch's company?

So he watched. Couldn't hear what they were saying. Not even their voices, which were seemingly raised now and then. You had to figure it: the fucker was a married man cheating on his wife, thus disloyal, dishonest; D.D. was foolish to trust him; *didn't* trust him, probably; if she was happy with him with being in love with him why was she so agitated now? Why was her face shining with tears? *And she'd hidden Colin Asch's gorgeous flame-colored gladioli for this man.*

How long this went on, the two of them talking, embracing, kissing, Colin Asch could not have said, an hour perhaps, or more; he'd slipped into a trance like dreaming with his eyes open not minding that his feet were fucking cold and there wasn't any moon to soften things, staring at the man and woman inside the house only a few yards away but *distant* . . . this weird sensation rising in him like almost coming in his pants like observing a target ignorant of being observed thus *your power is infinitely magnified while theirs is diminished* to the point finally of extinction. Then abruptly the two of them got up from the sofa and left the living room, passed out of Colin Asch's vision, so he climbed up onto the terrace to look inside—couldn't see them—in a reflex gesture tried the door: but naturally it was locked. (The kind of lock he could jimmy open, though, in maybe thirty seconds.) Was Carpenter leaving finally? *Or were they going upstairs to D.D.'s bedroom?* Colin backed off from the house, sliding and stamping in the glazed-over snow to disguise his footprints, but he couldn't hear voices at the front door or the sound of a car door being slammed and so forth, which meant the two of them had gone upstairs leaving him behind in the freezing cold like a mongrel dog, not that a dog would be treated with such insult—it was the time of evening when human beings sat down together to share a meal, to partake of a ceremony, not be kicked out into the fucking arctic cold, and he'd had the distinct impression she was meaning to invite him to dinner, of course she was meaning to invite him to dinner, after the tour of her house, then the fucking phone rang, then it was *him*—Carpenter—the fucker. In a sudden rage that came over him like a spasm of hiccuping he thought of hiding in Carpenter's car in the back seat and when finally the bastard got in and drove off he'd allow him to get a certain distance then at a light or something he'd just reach up and around and get him in a choke hold the kind that the police are trained to use *pressing on the carotid artery to cut off circulation to the brain, one two three four five! presto!*—then just calmly get out of the car and walk away—"Sure, I could do that. Easy." But he had an even more convincing flash like a dream of him ascending the stairs in the house moving like a sleepwalker like Shelley who said *I go my way like a sleepwalker until I am stopped and I never am stopped* up the stairs into her bedroom where it would be darkened but he'd see them clearly the two of them asleep, naked after love, lovemaking *though in truth it was unimaginable that Dorothea Deverell would do such a thing really* nonetheless he saw them asleep and he saw himself standing over them and he had a knife in his hand, or a razor . . . and as Charles Carpenter slept Colin Asch gracefully sliced his throat—it was part of his pride to do things with grace like they were effortless though all of his life, his ingenuity, his physical conditioning went into the smallest gesture!—and somehow Carpenter just bled to death without waking . . . nor did *she* wake . . . for he could not imagine it, could not imagine any of the scene, except that *she* continued to sleep oblivious of what Colin Asch was doing, of what must be done *for her own very sake: her happiness.*

But this vision rose and fell away in a quick flash like the flash of a car's headlights, blinding one instant then gone the next, though leaving Colin Asch dazed and weak in the knees . . . like, once, naked except for a thin undershirt, he'd stood on a carpet kneading his toes in excitement and terror and Mr. Kreuzer'd reached out to touch him, the hot little pulsing knob of him, and in that instant he'd come, standing, whimpering, scared, a stream of semen shooting out thinly from him and arcing, and falling . . . and Mr. Kreuzer said, *"That* was precipitous, Colin."

Weeks later on the afternoon of March 5, Colin Asch in his newly purchased tuxedo was setting the dining room table for dinner, his pulse already fast though he'd taken two Quaaludes that morning, whistling a jagged dissonant version of "Traumerei"—which he'd once played, straight, on the piano, aged eleven—

talking to himself to cheer himself up—*tonight's the night! after so much anticipation! Colin Asch's social debut in Lathrup Farms!*—and he stood for a long moment with the place card in his trembling fingers that read in elegant old-fashioned script *Charles Carpenter*—Colin had done the place cards himself, every one of them: black India ink, a snub-tipped drawing pen—thinking he had to make up his mind soon what to do about Carpenter. Or if he should do anything at all.

March 5: Colin Asch woke before dawn thinking at first he was in Susannah Hunt's oversized perfumy bed but, no, she'd laughingly kicked him out early the previous night, a telephone call had come from her fiancé (as she called him), this old guy sixty-two or -three who owned condominiums in the Caribbean, an ex-physician, ex-partner of her husband's, but Colin Asch didn't pay much attention to the details, nor did Susannah Hunt, most of the time, but "Honey, I have to look out for my future, don't I?" So Colin woke in his own bed, his mind immediately flooded with panic thoughts of that evening's party, the first dinner party of his life, the many guests who were coming, and Dorothea Deverell herself. . . . He was a novice at such things, a mere baby the women were calling him, thus Susannah Hunt and Ginny Weidmann were helping out and he'd contacted this fabulous caterer everyone recommended, yes the guy *costs* but it's *worth it.*

Naked and shivering with anticipation, Colin Asch walked through the rooms of his apartment laughing like a child—"I own this! Jesus! I own *this!*" Staring blinking at the mirrored walls in which his handsome form glided and the high-class furniture he'd bought, the way everything went together, the modulation of the colors, the *shapes* and *figures:* "Fantastic." At the Rhode Island School of Design and that art school in New Mexico he'd checked into for a semester Colin

Asch had been told he had a natural genius for interior
design, a magical eye, and the name of that particular
game is BUCKS they told him, none of this artistic-
integrity shit, but you just sort of naturally take for
granted a talent that comes so easily so he'd never tried
to work his way into the field. But here was this stu-
pendous apartment, the living room and the dining
room especially, looking like something in *Art & Ar-
chitecture* and maybe the Lathrup Farms weekly might
do a photographic feature on it, "contemporary bachelor living" maybe: the white walls with the brass mirrors and the wall that was almost entirely glass and
the long oatmeal-colored sofa with its dozen designer
pillows and the tub-shaped suede chairs in umber and
mustard yellow, the twin Halogen lamps (tall graceful
black poles, shallow white globes) and the thick-piled
creamy-white wall-to-wall carpeting, the dazzlingly
beautiful glass-and-chrome dining table and the side-
board and Colin Asch glided about naked partly
aroused in ecstasy, also in a kind of disbelief—"Hey:
I own *this.*" He would worry about making the
installment payments when the time came.

You're some kind of a neurotic perfectionist, Susannah Hunt told him fondly and chiding, and he'd answered proudly, You can't get anywhere in this shitty
world otherwise, and she'd laughed and said, For some
of us, trying to be perfect only slows us *down.*

Dorothea Deverell too had that insight into his character; the last time he'd telephoned her—anxious to
know if she had the date for the dinner party right, the
time for the limo, and so forth, *he couldn't bear it if
something went wrong! if he was publicly humiliated
at the outset of his social career in this affluent Boston
suburb!*—she'd said, Aren't you making too much of
this, Colin? of *me?* and he'd laughed nervously and
said, gazing at his reflection in one of the brass mirrors like some young British actor on a BBC television

program, all elegant cool, the last word in absolute fucking charm, "Ah, but I've just begun, Dorothea! *Watch me!*"

But what about the dining room chairs? They were three-legged, which he hadn't exactly noticed when he bought them. Sitting on them could be tricky because they wobbled slightly, but if you sat carefully and didn't shift your ass around they were OK. Colin Asch stood biting his thumbnail wondering if he should warn his guests tonight about the chairs, just casually, or say nothing.

He saw too suddenly that there were black scuff marks on one of the walls from the fucking furniture delivery men and it looked as if—from this angle, the sun glaring the way it was—the windows were rain-splotched, and he'd washed them himself the other day, a long hard job, thus it sickened him if he'd have to wash them a second time, not that he minded the literal expenditure of energy (he had plenty of energy) but the idea of it, the repetition of an action already performed, *asshole repetition of something you've done once and were pleased with,* demoralized him—it was a sign of the inferior man, the slave mentality, and not that of the master.

A flood of panic hit him then that even the Quaaludes could not forestall. That he'd made a mistake and could not alter the course of time to undo it. Like the car skidding and crashing through the rusted bridge railing and into the water, and not even God himself could reverse time if the fucker'd wanted to.

The day before he'd been in a weird wired state too at L.L. Loomis, bossed around by his so-called supervisor, Jay—the bastard's actual name was Jason—who behaved in a systematic patronizing manner toward Colin Asch, handing him crap assignments any asshole could do like double-checking galleys and pasting

labels on packages, running errands to the printer like
a mere messenger boy, it'd been weeks now since he
started work and he was yet to be allowed to experi-
ment with design and layouts—Jay's fear of Colin
Asch's potential talent was transparent; also, the fucker
was jealous of Colin's connection with Susannah Hunt,
who was an old, good friend of Mr. Harris who owned
the business.

Jealous too of the sexy black Porsche Colin Asch
drove, and the stylish clothes Colin Asch wore, and
the luxury apartment he knew about (from Colin's
chatting with the office girls) but would sure as hell
never see. Thus referring to him not quite behind his
back as "glamour boy," "angel puss," and "blond
beast."

Just give them a chance to see how imaginative you
are, honey, how shrewd and sharp, Susannah Hunt told
him, and this Colin certainly intended to do but had
been thwarted thus far by the selfishness of Jay—
though sensing himself a popular addition to the office
staff. But day following day his supervisor was still
with him, ignored his smile, his good-natured placat-
ing remarks, sure the bastard was jealous, paunchy
fag-looking guy in his early thirties, probably he knew
about Colin Asch's big dinner party to which he wasn't
invited so he was pushing Colin all that day, then finally when he told Colin to run some crap back to the
printers to have it reset Colin said quietly, "Fuck you:
I'm not a gofer," and Jay said excitedly, as if he'd been
waiting for this, "That's exactly what you are, glamour boy, so move your ass."

In an instant the revelation burst in Colin Asch that
the force inside "Jay" was giving permission to the
force inside "Colin Asch" to confront it and destroy
it if he could, but Colin sat quietly, unmoving, his
mind working quickly, he didn't want to disappoint
Susannah Hunt was the primary thing, when she had

such faith in him and had helped him so much, lending him money as she had and possibly there would be more to come (though "lending" was sort of ambiguous since maybe she'd never get around to actually asking for it back) and he had to be reasonable: he knew this was a trial period for him at the public relations firm and he had only to work hard and succeed and later when he was promoted to the top or had maybe moved on to a billion-dollar company in Boston or Manhattan he'd tell them all to go fuck themselves. . . . Christ, he could understand how ex-employees so frequently returned to offices and factories and this poor bastard the other day in Kansas City spraying innocent people with bullets in a post office he'd been fired from, Colin could understand that mentality for sure but he'd never fall into so crude a mold for the simple reason he was too smart. *Once you lost control it's all over.* So he lifted his eyes to those of his frowning supervisor and managed a child-like hurt smile and said, repentant, "Well, I guess you're right, Jay. Thanks for reminding me!"

Thoughts of Jay were getting scrambled into thoughts of Dorothea Deverell and the upcoming party so he spent a while with the Blue Ledger soaking in a hot bath trying to work things out *control is the essence of survival* taking another Quaalude *anything done henceforth is blessed because it emanates from the soul* but still he was feeling weird so he got dressed and drove by the caterers' to see how things were going, drove to a florist's to buy razzle-dazzle flowers—a dozen ruby-red roses, big bunch of purple dwarf iris, big bunch of mixed gladioli, Colin Asch's favorite flower—then came back home and made a few calls, one of them to the limousine rental and another to Susannah Hunt, who didn't seem to be in the apartment or in any case wasn't answering her phone, and one of them to Aunt Ginny, who said, "Colin dear, *please* don't worry—the caterer will take care of everything, or almost everything, but would you like me to come a little early, to help out?" It was only 5 P.M. but he decided to get dressed anyway, putting on the tuxedo he'd bought the week before at the Village Haberdashery, 20 percent off the ticketed price, the ivory-white silk pleated shirt and the embroidered red silk vest and the black bow tie, and staring at himself in a full-length mirror Colin Asch felt chilled, he looked so good, an old melancholy washed over him like dirty water—*Why has this young man blessed with such looks such brains such talent been treated like shit all of his life?*

To which there was no answer.

Barefoot in his formal attire Colin Asch spent an hour and a half fussing over the table settings, arranging and rearranging the floral displays, positioning the place cards—twelve guests at his table and the guest of honor was obviously to be seated at one end of the table and the host at the other but where to put Charles Carpenter, for instance? and where to put his VIPs as he thought of them, the Director of the Brannon Institute himself Mr. Morland (who had initially declined Colin's invitation but then, on the basis of Colin going personally to speak with him, consenting) and his wife, and Tracey Donovan, the young woman from the *Lathrup Farms Monitor* who covered area "social and cultural" events. Also there were the Weidmanns, and there was Dorothea Deverell's assistant, Jacqueline, and an unknown factor named Paul Wylie who was another Institute worker, Colin hoped not a guy his own age or type, and a second unknown factor but probably harmless, a woman friend of Dorothea Deverell's named Merle Altman. Five men and seven women which presented a problem he couldn't solve to his satisfaction and where should he put Susannah

Hunt, on his right hand as she'd naturally expect or midway down the table next to Carpenter maybe? She knew Carpenter, she'd said, and liked him. A lot.

Colin checked the champagne another time, counted the wine bottles—Martin Weidmann had advised him on the wine and he hoped to hell he could trust his judgment—and there was the brandy, and the crème de menthe, two or three other fancy liqueurs he picked up just in case, and on the shelf carefully wrapped in a Kleenex the pulverized pill he meant to sift into Dorothea Deverell's drink or possibly her coffee at the end of the evening: he'd forgotten the specific name of the pill but it'd been one of the giant white ones, one of a very few remaining from his stay with the woman in Fort Lauderdale. "Better put it in my pocket," he said aloud, and did.

As promised, the caterers arrived precisely at 7 P.M. so Colin began to feel a little more relaxed; then the Weidmanns arrived at 7:30 and he felt better still, in fact moved almost to tears by the very sight of them— Aunt Ginny a good-looking woman in an aqua cocktail dress with a sequined bosom, Uncle Martin in black tie like some handsome old graying business executive in an advertisement—*the only living relatives who cared a fuck about Colin Asch.* Aunt Ginny kissed him and moved on into the kitchen to take charge, and Martin seemed impressed with the apartment and the furnishings and asked after Colin's new job and told him he looked great in his tux and Colin blushed with happiness and stretched his arms to ask, like a boy asking his father, if maybe the sleeves weren't a little short?—did his cuffs stick out too much?

"They look fine," Martin said, pouring himself a drink. "Those are interesting cuff links," he added, and for a dizzy moment Colin thought the cuff links were actually Martin's, then remembered of course they weren't.

"Oh, these? They were a gift," he said, holding out his wrists for Martin to examine them, gold with ruby and onyx insets. "Sort of a private joke; this woman I used to know called me 'Colin' like with a 'K'—you know, like a German pronunciation: '*Kol*in—so she had these cuff links made up engraved with a 'K'."

"Interesting," Martin said. "And how's my old friend Susannah Hunt?"

Then it was 8 P.M. and Colin Asch's guests began to arrive; so many slow dragging hours and now everything seemed to be happening at once, everyone was arriving at once, there were guests like Paul Wylie and Mrs. Morland whom Colin had never set eyes on before, and there was Susannah Hunt in a glamorous black satin dress fairly bursting in the bosom, diamonds glittering on her fingers and at her wrists: Mrs. Hunt who discreetly pecked him on the cheek and breathed in his ear, "Hel-*lo* Colin!" And there suddenly in the crowded little vestibule stood Dorothea Deverell in her fur coat, bareheaded, smiling at Colin Asch and extending her hand—and Colin couldn't help himself, he stared at the woman for just a fraction of a second too long: she was so beautiful, she was so perfect, *she had come to him.*

Her appearance so dazzled him, he hadn't time to be disappointed that Dorothea had not come alone as he'd fantasized her, in the elegant Cadillac Brougham limousine, but had had the driver pick up two other guests, her assistant Jacqueline and her friend Mrs. Altman. As if Colin would derive any pleasure from hiring a car at $110 an hour for *them*.

But Colin Asch, greeting his guests, showed none of this; he was shaking hands, being introduced, stooping to hear names. Dorothea Deverell seemed quite impressed, perhaps even startled, by the splendor of Colin's apartment—"But how beautiful, Colin! How *unique*."

"Is it?" Colin asked eagerly. "Do you think so?"

When he helped Dorothea remove her coat he saw to his immense satisfaction that she was wearing after all the costume he'd given her—the exquisite lace jacket and the long white wool skirt. Again he stared at her, not knowing what to say. His eyes misted over. Finally he whispered, "Thank you, Dorothea," but the Weidmanns were swooping upon her, she and Ginny embraced warmly as sisters, and the doorbell was ringing again, and someone opened it to another stranger, a snub-nosed smiling woman—and Colin walked off like a sleepwalker with Dorothea Deverell's fur coat to lay it tenderly across the bed in his bedroom exhilarated by the knowledge that, if all else failed, *she had come to him: to Colin Asch.*

Through the lively cocktail hour Colin shrewdly rationed his drinking; he had a naturally speedy naturally wired sensibility which alcohol sometimes exacerbated, so he played it cool, acting the perfect host, introducing guests to one another where required—not that he knew these people but he'd quickly learned their names!—overseeing conversations then easing away tall and handsome and seemingly poised: What a remarkable young man, what an extraordinary young man, he's Ginny Weidmann's nephew, who *is* he, an actor? an artist? a young business entrepreneur? He found himself oddly shy in Dorothea Deverell's specific company but was otherwise in control, or nearly—he had only to clamp his jaws shut when there was the danger of talking too fast and too much. The tuxedo was a little warm but impeccably tailored, his new dress shoes gleamed darkly, at the age of twenty-eight he was clearly approaching the prime of his young manhood *and perhaps this evening and the night to follow would constitute the pinnacle of his life.*

"Didn't I tell you, dear? Everything is going beautifully," Aunt Ginny said.

And Colin, wiping his forehead with a handkerchief, said, "Thanks to you, Aunt, it *is*." In truth he was getting a little resentful of the woman's supervision of the caterer's assistants as they were serving the hors d'oeuvres, for whose party was this anyway? "I owe you everything!" Colin said.

He was grateful though for Susannah Hunt's glamorous presence, and for the chaste distance she maintained between them—would anyone know, could anyone *guess*, what their relationship was? And it quite flattered him that perky little Tracey Donovan, the media representative for this social event, seemed so sincerely impressed with Colin Asch's guests and with his apartment and with *him*—asking him numerous questions about his public relations career, his past television experience, his travels in Europe and North Africa—"We'll have to get together soon for a full-scale interview!" Mr. Wylie, with whom Dorothea Deverell was earnestly discussing a painter of whom Colin Asch had never heard (Burchfield? Charles Burchfield?) turned out to be, to Colin's relief, no rival of his but a stocky sweet-faced man of youngish middle age with tortoise-shell glasses; and Charles Carpenter, for whom he had a certain nervous edgy excitable feeling, was quite gracious to him, gentlemanly and charming, including Colin in a conversation (about politics? Soviet-U.S. relations?) he was having with Howard Morland and Martin Weidmann as naturally as if they were all friends—neighbors, peers, equals. Talking with them, offering his opinion, Colin was flooded with a sudden happiness: *the happiness of a man among men.* Why had he been cheated of this all his life?

It absorbed his rapt attention, that Charles Carpenter was Dorothea Deverell's lover and no one knew save Colin Asch. He was their protector, in a way. You could think of it, that way.

He yearned to draw Charles Carpenter off into a corner of the room and say confidentially, man to man, "I know, Charles. But your secret is safe with me."

Carpenter had a tall, slim, slightly round-shouldered figure, probably rather slack-muscled at his age; his hair appeared grayer than Colin recalled. His long lean horsy face was handsome but creased as if with worry or tiredness . . . still, Colin could see why Dorothea Deverell or another woman might admire him. So *reasonable*. So *solid*. So *patrician*. So like the father you'd maybe choose if you were a baby again. And had a choice.

Which wasn't the way the fucking world was constructed.

Then they were summoned to dinner, and there were exclamations at the splendor of Colin Asch's table—the scented candles, the roses, the gleaming English bone china and sterling silverware—and after all his guests were seated and the champagne poured, Colin resplendent in his tuxedo and red silk vest rose to toast Dorothea Deverell in a high, quavering voice—"our guest of honor: one of the most accomplished women of her generation"—and Dorothea laughed, exclaiming, "My God, Colin—really!" as if they were old casual friends, but Colin insisted and spoke excitedly of the several books she had written, and her years of dedication to the Institute, until he fell abruptly silent and stood staring down the length of the table at her—he had more to say but could not utter the words. In any case the mood at the table was festive and unserious, Colin Asch's awkwardness scarcely mattered, went perhaps unnoticed, so he ended, blushing, "—anyway, let's drink a toast to Dorothea Deverell, and wish her health and happiness forever!"—and the moment passed.

Colin sat down. His head was ringing as if it were inside a clapping bell.

He wanted suddenly savagely to murder everyone. All of them.

No—he was in a giddy exhilarated mood. Never in his life had he attempted anything like this: an ambitious dinner party. He was telling the women close beside him that he thought there was nothing happier on earth *than to bring people together in festive settings*. Susannah Hunt, pleasantly drunk, lifted her glass and cried, "I'll drink to that!"

Now there followed the elaborate procession of courses, the realization of Colin Asch's fevered consultation with the caterer and his several changes of mind: oysters forestière followed by chateaubriand of beef with espagnole sauce and wild rice and intricately cut vegetables followed by a salad of red lettuce and Belgian endive followed by French cheeses followed by strawberry chiffon pie followed by coffee, tea, liqueurs in tiny sparkling glasses, Swiss bitter-chocolate dinner mints . . . and though Colin Asch who'd paid for all this tried gamely to eat he had not much appetite. He'd gotten hooked on the champagne and red wine, alternating glasses until the champagne ran out, doing a good deal of talking and laughing less fearful now of getting loud *he had every right to enjoy himself freely at his own fucking party* entertaining the entire table with anecdotes of travel in Germany, Greece, Morocco . . . and then there was a general conversation about a racial incident that had taken place in Roxbury a few days previously in which Colin Asch as a former "television person" could participate, his opinion in fact solicited by none other than white-haired aristocratic Howard Morland, who was clearly quite taken with his young host . . . and talk shifted to AIDS, and to politics, and to an event that was scheduled soon to occur at the Brannon Institute, and to area restaurants, particularly several new and highly recommended restaurants of which Colin Asch had not heard, thus could inquire (of the gourmet Paul Wylie) after them . . . and the meal was passing swiftly or was it passing with dreamlike slowness . . . and Colin Asch saw that Dorothea Deverell was happy . . . *was* happy . . . engaged in conversation with friends at her end of the table and hardly more than glancing now and then (ah, how discreetly! how *skillfully!*) at her lover Charles Carpenter, who in turn did not frequently glance at her; they must be old well-practiced lovers, accustomed to such situations.

But Colin Asch had the power to end all that.

There was spirited conversation about the stock market, and Third World poverty, and the ever-imminent "global crisis," and when the way cleared for Colin to volunteer his opinion he launched into a lengthy earnest explanation of the X-factor in human genetics—did they know that one tenth of one percent of the human race is instinctively bred to lead the remainder? that there are by nature "master" beings and "slave" beings? that social institutions that fail to acknowledge this are doomed? A sharp slightly shrill edge to Colin Asch's voice signaled to certain of his guests that this subject meant a great deal to him and perhaps at the moment he was not to be contradicted, but others registered nothing out of the ordinary so there followed a lively discussion, confused and disjointed and a bit combative, until Colin heard himself talking too loudly and clamped his jaws prudently shut, making an effort simply to smile, to nod, to let the ignorant assholes talk, he was magnanimous enough to accommodate dissenting points of view. The bosomy perfumy women at his end of the table were united in any case in trying to make him eat—"Colin the food is *delicious,* you simply must *eat it*"—and Colin fumbled with his fork and chewed a bit and swallowed, washing whatever it was down with a big mouthful of red wine then shaking his head like a dog to clear it, staring down the length of the table past the tall glittering candles and the ruby-red roses in their crystal vase at Dorothea Deverell so beautiful in her white lace jacket, her eyes shining like a young girl's. He raised his voice to thank them all, suddenly, "For coming here! Tonight! For being my friends!" His mouth worked as if puzzled: "I want to be your friend! To be one of you! I *am* one of you, for Christ's sake!" He was breathing quickly, almost panting. Their many eyes both intimidated and excited him. He added, gripping the edge of the table as if he feared falling from his chair: *"I want to be good!"*

This released a chorus of protesting voices, primarily female, Ginny Weidmann's and Susannah Hunt's the most earsplittingly soprano: "But you *are* good, Colin! You *are* good! You are an *angel! Silly boy, Colin!*"

So that quieted him for a while, stirred his emotions so he was in danger of crying, his head lowered and his eyeballs sliding as if greased in their sockets: weird! Then suddenly it was nearing the end of the meal—*so suddenly coming to an end!*—and Colin Asch lurched to his feet, inspired another time, smile wide and bright as a jack-o'-lantern's, and again he lifted his wineglass high above his head and proposed a final toast: "To somebody not with us tonight who made all this possible"—and there was a flurry of amused quizzical speculation about who this mystery person might be—but Colin Asch winking and grinning refused to say, repeating, "To someone not with us tonight who made this all possible *by being not with us tonight*"—and at this Dorothea Deverell flinched visibly and cast Colin a look of such shocked disapproval, such transparent warning, he bit his lip and went silent, swaying at his place smiling stupidly the glass still lifted above his head . . . the gaiety at the table awkwardly fading . . . until Mrs. Hunt in throaty dry Tallulah Bankhead style said, "No doubt an absent parental figure—the very best kind." And this naturally provoked a fresh round of mirth, at least in those ignorant of Colin Asch's "tragic" background.

Then Colin was sitting again, his heart pounding wildly.

Thinking: She saved me.

Thinking: Saved us both.

With the excuse of wanting to help serve the coffee and tea in person Colin Asch was able, unwitnessed, to stir into the cup of herbal tea intended for Dorothea Deverell the finely ground drug he had prepared, as easily and innocently as if he were stirring sugar into it, and this he served to her without arousing the slightest suspicion, and returned to his seat at the far end of the table nursing a final glass of red wine and watching her sip at her cup—until finally it was emptied. Horse-sized barbiturates, his female friend in Fort Lauderdale had called them, prescription pills strong enough to knock out a horse, and to this, yes, Colin Asch could attest. Though he scorned reliance upon drugs, mainly.

And then it was midnight and the party was over—a fantastically successful party but now at last over—and Colin Asch stood in his miniature foyer saying good night, shaking hands, thanking his guests for having come, and there stood wrapped in her fur coat prepared for the cold lovely Dorothea Deverell with heavy eyelids and an unfocused sort of smile . . . teetering on her white satin high heels to lean forward to kiss Colin Asch on the cheek as if they were the oldest and dearest of friends *as if they had known each other all their lives.*

"Thank you, Colin. It was wonderful."

"Dorothea. Thank *you.*"

* * *

While the caterer's assistants labored to clean up in the kitchen, Colin Asch retired to his bedroom to change from his formal attire to jeans and a black turtleneck sweater and Nike jogging shoes. So wired by this time he could barely contain himself, he did push-ups on the carpet—fifty-five, fifty-six, fifty-*seven,* then gave up counting—till finally the hired help went home and things were quiet as the tomb, yet still shrewdly he forced himself to wait another forty-five minutes before leaving in the low-slung black Porsche for 33 Marten Lane.

9

The telephone was ringing persistently, jarringly, in a distant room. Or was someone speaking to her from a distant room. She could not make out words, only murmurous modulations of sound; she could not see, though her eyes were open. Nor could she move for her limbs were paralyzed . . . heavy and leaden as if waterlogged.

It was frightful, horrible: yet, becalmed in her bed, paralyzed, she was not capable of feeling such emotions. Her own interior voice, muted, solicitous, was both warning and gentle admonition: *This is your punishment. This is your reward.*

"How can it be? My God!"

When, early in the afternoon of Sunday, March 6, Dorothea Deverell finally woke from her heavy stuporous dreamless sleep—the sleep of a dead woman—it was to the appalling knowledge that she had slept for nearly fifteen hours.

Her bedside clock showed 2:40. She thought at first that the electricity must have gone off and that somehow (she was too dazed to have reasoned how) day and night were reversed.

When she tried to get out of bed she was too weak; her legs would not hold her. A tiny pin might have been dislodged in her upper vertebrae, for her head rolled helplessly on her shoulders. "What has happened to me? Was I drunk last night?" Her eyeballs were as seared as if she had been staring for hours into a naked light, and the interior of her mouth was parched, scummy, vile; her nostrils were so pathologically dry she felt them as twin passageways leading up into her brain. Not in recent memory had she felt herself so thoroughly debilitated, so ingloriously *wrecked.* "But did I make a fool of myself?" She wondered if she would dare telephone Charles Carpenter to inquire. Though surely it would be more prudent to say nothing, in the hope that nothing would be said to her.

A vertiginous five minutes was required simply to get Dorothea Deverell from her bed and into her bathroom; wherein, in the mirror above the sink, a wan, etiolated face awaited her. Another half hour was required to get her but partially dressed and downstairs . . . descending the staircase like an invalid who can no longer trust in the efficacy of her own limbs or the substantiality of the physical world to support her. How her head ached, how her eyes burned! How thoroughly wretched she felt! She saw that the folklore of the classic hangover was needed to mitigate its sickening horror. To suggest that the drinker has brought his misery upon himself, thus is, after all, in control of his fate.

Yet she could not recall having drunk more than two glasses of champagne at Colin Asch's party, and perhaps a single glass of red wine. Or had she drunk more, half consciously? Had she blacked out on her feet? She could remember virtually nothing of the ride home in the limousine, or of undressing for bed. . . . She knew herself a woman unaccustomed to alcohol; yet, more to the point, unaccustomed to such fevered celebration, such an insistent focusing of others' attentions upon her: Dorothea Deverell. It left her giddy and childlike and wholly uncritical, as if, unprepared, a reckless hiker in the mountains, she had gone too high too quickly.

She could not tolerate so much as the thought of breakfast, but stood at the sink drinking ice water and trying not to notice how her hands shook. If this is your debut into a new life, Dorothea, her interior voice admonished, perhaps you are unfit.

Toward evening, by accident, she discovered that her rear terrace door was unlocked. This was a rude little shock—though she must have left it unlocked herself since, so far as she could judge, nothing in the house seemed to have been taken, or even disturbed; there were no footprints visible on the carpet. In the excitement of the past several weeks she'd become careless, though; increasingly, break-ins and acts of vandalism were being reported in the North Shore area. You must get a burglar alarm installed, Charles Carpenter repeatedly urged her, and repeatedly Dorothea promised, yes, she would.

She checked the upstairs, and nothing there appeared to have been disturbed either.

Belatedly, still feeling rather dizzy and unreal, Dorothea made her bed and picked up, in the room, her white silk slip which the night before she had tossed on a chair, her brassiere and underpants lying on the floor, the exquisite white outfit Colin Asch had given her for Christmas unceremoniously draped across her bureau. . . . She checked it anxiously for stains but found none: white is so beautiful and so impractical. It was a costume Dorothea Deverell would never have chosen for herself, even granted the willingness to pay an inflated price for clothing, yet she liked it very much, now; prized it, in fact; for she'd looked really quite remarkably beautiful in it the night before, as if the bloom of her young womanhood had been restored. To see Charles Carpenter's eyes drifting to her, dwelling upon her, in love . . . in what must be called, for all Dorothea Deverell's mincing behavior of the past several weeks, a husbandly sort of tenderness . . . how could she fail to be grateful for *that?* And Colin Asch had been naïvely happy to see her in it, ignorant of the fact that the reasons for her having worn it were sheerly expeditious: she had so forestalled planning what she would wear to the dinner party, she'd gone through her closet only the afternoon before, in mounting anxiety, to discover that really she had nothing suitable: no evening dress except a burgundy velvet sadly worn at the elbows and seat and a long black rayon skirt that was rather battered-looking at the hem and, in any case, rayon.

But fortunately she had white satin shoes to go with the jacket and skirt, and a white beaded bag. Which went perfectly.

PART
THREE

10

The call came for Dorothea Deverell late in the afternoon of April 11, a windy, sunsplotched day. She would remember it forever as the second of the telephone calls to abruptly reorder the course of her life.

Dorothea was in her office at the Institute—her old office still, since Mr. Morland, though rarely at the Institute these days, had yet to vacate his—engaged in a somewhat groping conversation with a Lathrup Farms matron who, newly widowed, was considering giving a sizable donation to the Institute in her late husband's name with the proviso that she "maintain some say" as to its specific use. To this, Dorothea felt she could hardly object; yet, recalling past episodes in the previous director's experience, when such provisos brought with them unanticipated problems, she was reluctant to simply agree. Perhaps Mrs. Harmon would like to join the Building Committee? the Programs Committee? Perhaps she would like to be an honorary member of the Friends of the Morris T. Brannon Advisory Council?

To these suggestions the impeccably dressed Mrs. Harmon made no reply, as if unhearing, but, smiling tightly at Dorothea, said in a small, stubborn voice, "The thing is, Miss Deverell, that I want Edgar's name to be preserved. I want to be certain that it not be *forgotten.*"

"Of course," Dorothea said, nodding in sympathy, "I understand." She was about to say more when there was a sudden knock at the door, curt and sharp, and in the same moment Jacqueline entered, with a look so unlike her usual—so stricken, so apologetic—that Dorothea's blood simply ran cold.

"Miss Deverell?" Jacqueline said, "I'm so sorry to interrupt you and Mrs. Harmon, but there seems to be an emergency call for you."

"Ah, really! Is there! Then I'll take it in the other office."

Dorothea spoke almost calmly. Her family was so attentuated by this stage in her maturity, the pool of her blood relatives so shrunken, there could be no emergency in her life excepting one pertaining to Charles Carpenter.

He is dead, she thought, lifting the receiver.

For, after all, hadn't she lived through this horror already? In the distant past, as in a distant lifetime?

Thus it required several seconds for Dorothea Deverell to realize that it was Charles Carpenter who was on the line and that it was he to whom the horror had in fact happened.

He said, "Dorothea? Agnes is dead."

Dorothea gripped the telephone receiver hard and sat on the edge of a table. Uncomprehending, she said, "Agnes is—"

"Agnes is dead."

"—dead?"

"Just now. I mean—I've found her just now. In the house." He spoke in queer uncharacteristic gusts and waves. Dorothea could hear noises, men's voices, in the background. "I'm here—at the house. The police are here. The ambulance too—but it's too late, she's dead. Dorothea? I found her just now—a while ago, I mean. There hadn't been any answer all day when I called her so I came over and let myself in and went upstairs thinking she was, she might be—you know how she has been—thinking she might be sick, or unconscious, in her bed. Thinking she might have fallen and injured herself. I called her name and there wasn't any answer so I went upstairs and the bathroom door was shut and locked, and I forced my way in, and there she was—I mean, *is;* I think she still *is,* unless they've moved her—in the bathtub. In the bathroom. Upstairs. She—seems to have had an accident.''

Dorothea's eyes immediately flooded with tears. ''My poor darling,'' she said. ''Oh, my poor, poor darling Charles! How terrible! For Agnes! For Agnes, and for you! Shall I come over there, darling? What can I do?''

''It seems somehow she *drowned,''* Charles said wonderingly. ''In only a foot or so—how many inches could it be?—of water. I found her lying there in the water—the water was stone cold—her face was submerged—I checked for a pulse but couldn't find one. It was horrible! Her lips were purplish-blue. I knew she was dead.''

Charles Carpenter paused. In the background someone, a man, was shouting directions. Dorothea wiped at her eyes and said, ''Charles? Are you all right? You've had a terrible shock, shall I come over? Or would I be in the way? I had better come over.''

He said half accusingly, ''She'd been drinking. She reeked of it. There were bottles in the bedroom, bourbon and gin. That must have been it—that, and the other.''

''Yes? What other?''

''You know—I've told you. The drugs. The sleeping pills. And there were diet pills too, for a while. I don't in fact think that Agnes ever gave up any prescription willingly; I think she simply changed doctors. My God,

I *told* her, I *warned* her! And she refused to listen! These past few weeks, Dorothea"—Charles had moved to a residential hotel in Boston in mid-February—"have simply been hell. She has been—had been—simply impossible. The drinking, the raving, the abuse, the threats, the terrible, unforgivable things she said—ah, but I've told you enough of it already, dear Dorothea. I can't heap such filth upon your head, I can't—I don't dare—" He was speaking more and more rapidly until finally he stopped; and Dorothea, her heart pierced, could hear him sobbing. How she longed to hold him in her arms, to comfort him. For surely she had the right? Surely she, of all living beings, had the right?

Dorothea offered again to come to him but Charles rather curtly told her no, he didn't think that was a good idea right now; he would speak with her later, try to see her later that evening if possible—if the police were finished with him by then. "I'm sure they have questions to ask of *me*," he said, with a sudden grim gust of humor. "The husband is always the first suspect."

"But Charles—"

He hung up abruptly—in other circumstances, it would have been rudely—and Dorothea Deverell was left gripping a telephone receiver tight against her ear, listening to a dead line. She thought, Yes? What if— *if Agnes Carpenter's death were not accidental, but deliberate?* Since the Carpenters' separation Agnes had repeatedly threatened to kill herself, had several times threatened to kill both herself and Charles. Dorothea burst into fresh, despairing, bitter tears.

"That terrible woman—*it would be just like her.*"

After a tactful several minutes Jacqueline poked her head into the office and, seeing the state Dorothea Deverell was in, went to comfort her. What had happened? Why was she so upset? Dorothea said in a rapt, slow voice, "It's horrible: Charles Carpenter's wife is *dead,* she has *died,* it must have been only a few hours ago." Jacqueline expressed surprise and sympathy, to a degree: she didn't after all know Mrs. Carpenter, though she was acquainted with Mr. Carpenter. Dorothea murmured, "Horrible, horrible," pleating the fabric of her skirt, tears streaming unimpeded down her cheeks.

"But how did it happen?" Jacqueline asked.

"An accident," Dorothea said. "I don't suppose they quite know, yet. He said—Charles said, Charles Carpenter—he'd come home and found her in—oh, Jacqueline, it's so terrible! So sordid, somehow!" Dorothea began to weep harder, helplessly, for Charles's sake; and for poor wretched Agnes': and for herself too, perhaps—the guilt of it, the shame of it, the misfortune. For at this point, in the late afternoon of April 11, when, as the pathologist's report would later disclose, Agnes Carpenter had been dead approximately nineteen hours, it had not yet begun to occur to Dorothea Deverell that the death of her lover's wife, whether by accident or otherwise, might be a factor in her good fortune.

If Jacqueline was mystified by Dorothea Deverell's passionate grief, and the look of frank shocked guilty fear that showed in her face, she had the discretion not to show it; she was a kindly woman, for all her occasional caustic wit, and she seemed to look upon Dorothea Deverell—her superior at the Institute—as a personal charge, an innocent very much in need of a protector. As Dorothea wept and murmured repeatedly, "Horrible, *horrible,*" Jacqueline sent Mrs. Harmon away and must have told the others simply to go home (it was the end of the working day for the staff) without disturbing Dorothea. Afterward, Dorothea would recall how readily her assistant had absorbed, not so much the fact of Agnes Carpenter's death as of

Dorothea Deverell's emotional connection with Charles Carpenter.

Has Jacqueline known all along? Dorothea wondered.

Has everyone known, all along?

The fact of death is public: what is personal yields to the impersonal; even one's body shifts out of one's unique possession, no longer tenanted. So there was a funeral for Agnes Carpenter, which everyone in her circle, or in Charles Carpenter's rather wider circle, attended. There had been, prior to the funeral, an autopsy; there would be, in ten days' time, an inquest. The county coroner would file his report. The local newspapers would print whatever seemed "newsworthy"—not a good deal, for neither Agnes nor Charles Carpenter was a public figure—but it rankled Charles that the information should be so freely printed, that the Carpenters had been "formally separated, divorce pending" at the time of Agnes' death. Most distressing, the Carpenters' home on West Fairway Drive—in particular the Carpenters' bedroom, and Agnes' bathroom—was thrown open temporarily but aggressively to a team of strangers: investigating detectives, police photographer, fingerprint man, pathologist. Though there appeared to be no evidence of foul play in the death—no fingerprints found other than those of the dead woman and her husband, no forced door or window, no sign of theft—the investigation would turn upon whether Agnes Carpenter had died accidentally or by her own hand.

Charles Carpenter was surely not a suspect in his wife's death, as he had jokingly remarked to Dorothea, but he was questioned repeatedly, to the point of despair and exhaustion. To his distress (and to Dorothea Deverell's) two crumpled sheets of stationery were discovered in a wastebasket in Charles's former study, with the words "Charles" and "Dear Charles" written on them, in Agnes' very shaky but recognizable handwriting: raising the possibility of a suicide note, thus suicide.

"Agnes would not have done it," Charles Carpenter said, many times. "She was simply not the *type*. She was not the *type*."

But hadn't she threatened suicide, by his own account? Might not her death have had a good deal to do with the pending divorce, the separation?

With lawyerly doggedness Charles Carpenter repeated, "My wife would not have done it. She was not the type to take her own life. I knew the woman for more than twenty years—*and I would swear under oath.*"

But hadn't there been planned, the investigating officer persisted, for next Monday, a meeting between the Carpenters and their lawyers, to discuss the terms of the divorce? Did Charles believe it could be nothing more than a coincidence that his wife should die only a few days before this meeting?

Charles Carpenter said angrily, *"I would swear under oath."*

Days passed, and Dorothea Deverell was to hear many times her lover's account of how, concerned about his wife, he'd gone to the house and discovered her body; in his bereavement (and Charles Carpenter was truly bereaved) he seemed under a spell, or a compulsion, to tell and retell the story, to dredge up new details, as if desperate to get it right. And, relaying his story to others in abbreviated form, Dorothea too came under the spell of the need to get it right.

As if we are testifying in a court of law, Dorothea

thought. Like criminals on trial, to be judged by the sincerity of our words.

According to the pathologist's report, Agnes Carpenter had died in her bath at approximately 9 P.M. of April 10. Charles had last spoken with her late in the evening of April 9, and they had had a vicious quarrel. "Her final words to me were, 'You deceitful son of a bitch!' " Charles said. "And then she slammed down the receiver and practically broke my eardrum." Agnes had been drunk, irrational, vindictive—the previous week she'd telephoned Charles's parents to tell them what a "lying hypocrite" their precious son was, which greatly upset them; now she was threatening to make a visit to Charles's law partners to tell them what he was really like. "I didn't want to provoke her even by pleading with her," Charles told Dorothea. "I dreaded her guessing *you*—somehow knowing it was *you.*"

"But it seems so unfair," Dorothea said guiltily, stroking her lover's hair. "That you should bear the brunt of all that alone."

"Agnes was my wife," Charles said. "In a sense none of this had anything to do with you. I mean—I love you and want to marry you of course, but Agnes and I had fallen out of love with each other a long time before. Our marriage had been dead for years before you and I met." He spoke briskly; he was nodding, telling himself this story too as if its veracity were unquestioned; which perhaps it was. "I've come to see, Dorothea, that you have nothing to do with it— any of it. The ugliness, the scandal. You are really quite innocent, darling, of it all."

As if he knows how hopeful I am, Dorothea Deverell thought humbly, of being told so.

Yet she could not resist speculating: "I wonder if, you know, there was anything we might have—I might have—done . . . to prevent it."

"Nothing," Charles Carpenter said emphatically. "Absolutely nothing."

And then he might retell the story another time, in a slow, wondering voice: evoking for Dorothea a vision, very nearly cinematic in its fluidity, of how, having telephoned Agnes without success on the morning of April 11 and intermittently throughout the day, he'd driven to the house . . . knowing something was wrong as soon as he saw not one but several newspapers lying on the sidewalk. And that day's mail was still in the mailbox. And he'd unlocked the rear door and gone inside, entering through the kitchen, dismayed at the overflowing trash can and the plates messily stacked on the counters and in the sink and even on the floor. And the numerous empty gin, bourbon, and wine bottles in plain view. (For the past three weeks Agnes had refused to allow their cleaning woman to come to the house: she didn't want her "poking her nose in my business.")

Charles called Agnes' name but there was no response—nothing.

The radio was on in the living room, turned up high, which struck him as strange. During the daytime, when she was alone, Agnes frequently turned on the television, even when she was too restless to watch; but the radio, rarely.

"Agnes?" Charles called. "Where are you? It's Charles."

He dreaded what he might find upstairs, in their bedroom. He halfway feared she might be hiding and would rush out to attack him.

He was appalled by the condition of the bedroom: the bed unmade, bedclothes disheveled, blinds drawn, everywhere items of soiled clothing underfoot. And here too were empty bottles. And the close stale air reeking of alcohol.

"Agnes?" he called. "Where are you?"

Several times she'd fled from him in a rage and locked herself in her bathroom, so it did not surprise Charles that, when he tried her bathroom door, it was locked. "Agnes? *Agnes?*" he said. He was not yet alarmed but he seemed to have a sense, he didn't know but he *knew*, that this was no ordinary episode in their lives. He called to her, pleaded with her to open the door, and when there was no response he threw his weight against it and forced it open and found Agnes inside, naked in the bathtub, slumped over, her head partly submerged in the water. . . . He knew in an instant that she was dead: the bathroom smelled of deadness. Yet he could not believe it, really; he shouted her name, felt for a pulse, tried to lift her from the tub as if to revive her. She was not breathing and her lips had turned a ghastly purplish-blue, her skin horribly white and puckered from the water. Her eyes had rolled partway back into their sockets as he had never seen human eyes before. He knew she was dead but could not believe it: he knew the woman's stubbornness, her perversity—and this seemed to him, in his shock, in that suspension of feeling that shock initially provides, a part of her subterfuge, her ill will and hostility. "Agnes! Agnes! *Agnes!*" he shouted.

Then in a panic he ran to telephone the police. And an ambulance.

Like a terrified child he begged them to come help him. "My wife—she isn't breathing! Please help me! Help us! The name is Carpenter, we live at Fifty-eight West Fairway Drive—"

Awaiting their arrival he ran back and forth between the bathroom and an upstairs window from which he could see the street, as if under a compulsion to check every few seconds to see that Agnes was really in the state in which he had described her . . . now that he had made the calls, now that the outside world would know of what had been until now a sheerly private matter; he had a childish expectation that perhaps he'd made a mistake and Agnes was not in fact dead but playing some sort of cruel trick on him.

He thought, But these things don't happen to people like us.

And afterward, when the house was open to strangers, and teams of men entered it freely, including a police photographer, a youngish bearded man in tinted sunglasses who took numerous photographs of the naked woman in the scummy gray water who had been Charles Carpenter's wife, he thought, as a corrective: If these things can happen then we weren't the people we imagined we were. All along, we had been other people.

"I suppose I actually felt, on a purely unexamined level," Charles Carpenter told Dorothea Deverell, "that, living in that particular house, on West Fairway Drive, in Lathrup Farms—being, you know, the sort of person I believe I am—I would be spared such monstrosities. And could spare others from them."

Dorothea Deverell said naïvely, gazing up into Charles Carpenter's face, in love, "But Charles—you *are* that person!"

Dorothea Deverell was not of course the only friend who comforted Charles Carpenter during this period of grief and upset—the Weidmanns, among others, rallied to him—but she was the friend upon whom, most clearly, he depended. And with the passing of days, weeks, eventually months, it would become yet clearer that their connection, their emotional rapport, went deeper than simply friendship. For Charles Carpenter was often at Dorothea Deverell's home for dinner (though he did not stay the night), and friends who invited one to their homes began quite naturally to include the other. If a general communal curiosity was aroused by such practices—if, behind Dorothea's and

Charles's backs, gossip of various degrees of intensity made the rounds—they were not to know of it directly; though Dorothea, forever sensitive to emanations in the air, supposed that people must be talking—"They would hardly be normal, otherwise."

For gossip after all is the very soul of a community: evidence that it is not a mere mechanical gathering of individuals but a living organism with its own life's blood.

And one day Ginny Weidmann impulsively telephoned Dorothea Deverell, to ask her friend point-blank, "Are you—? And Charles—? Is it—Dorothea, _is_ it true?"

Dorothea had long ago prepared a dignified little speech with which she might explain herself to such friends as Ginny Weidmann; she would say, "I don't know precisely what you are asking, Ginny, but I can tell you—yes, Charles Carpenter and I are very good friends; yes, I suppose we are in love; but Agnes Carpenter knew nothing of it and it had nothing to do with the disintegration of the Carpenters' marriage—that marriage had been, as everyone knows, dead for years." Now, however, confronted at last with the actual question, Dorothea Deverell merely said in a quiet, hopeful voice, "Yes."

And then there came the inquest, in late April, at which, to Charles Carpenter's (and Dorothea Deverell's) immense relief, the verdict of accidental death was given.

According to the county coroner, the specific cause of Agnes Carpenter's death was drowning; there had been water in her lungs. But the alcoholic content of the deceased's blood was so high, and she had taken so many tablets of Valium, that she'd clearly been unconscious, even comatose, at the time of her death.

And she had a medical history of alcohol and drug abuse.

"So they chose not to make an issue of the 'suicide' notes after all," Charles Carpenter said. "I suppose they didn't think it was worth the effort—trying to build a case against me on such slender evidence."

"A case against you?" Dorothea Deverell asked, puzzled. "But wouldn't it have been a case against poor Agnes, arguing that she had meant to take her own life?"

"But Agnes is dead," Charles Carpenter said carefully. "And I, as the surviving husband, stand to collect her estate—and her life insurance, which would have been null and void in the case of self-inflicted death." He paused, as if mildly ashamed, not quite looking at Dorothea. "I thought you understood, dear. The usual terms of life insurance . . . ?"

And now the realization swept over Dorothea: for of course she knew, or must have known. Charles Carpenter was the beneficiary of his wife's estate as Dorothea had been the beneficiary of Michel's estate years ago. At the time, she had been too distraught with grief to think about money or to care about her financial situation; at this time, she simply did not want to know.

Charles said, placatingly, "We can give most of it to charity, in Agnes' name."

Dorothea Deverell knew that for some time, even before the Carpenters' formal separation, Agnes had been willfully negligent about money, as a way of asserting herself against Charles; her excuse was always that it was *her* money—she had inherited approximately $2 million at her mother's death. Her personal checking account was often overdrawn and her record of it unreliable; though she seemed to have little to show for it, she ran up large, frequently unexplained bills on her credit card. "She is trying to drive me mad," Charles complained, "and she is succeeding." He was the one in charge of all financial matters, as he was in charge of household matters—the overseeing of workmen, repairmen, the weekly lawn crew during the summer months. One of Agnes' chronic habits was to lose receipts and even, it seemed, to lose or misplace cash. Like many women who are affluent yet have no work, thus no salaries, of their own, she harbored a curious ambivalence about money in the abstract: clearly she relished its use, as an expression of personal power, while at the same time she disdained it. Her cynicism was not without its lyric side; Dorothea recalled her once saying, at a social gathering, "Money *doesn't* buy happiness—but it makes it irrelevant." Charles Carpenter had visibly winced.

After Agnes' death, Charles and his accountant tried gamely to make sense of the woman's financial records. There were many errors, many missing items, and, dating from the last six weeks of her life, at least one mystery: On March 7, Agnes had made out a check to an individual (or a business) called, simply, "Alvarado," for $7,000; on April 10, the day of her death, she had made out a check to the same party for $8,500. Charles had no idea who or what "Alvarado" was: a store? an independent money manager or investor? Nor did anyone in the Carpenters' circle of friends know. "She could not after all have spent fifteen thousand five hundred dollars on alcohol and Valium," Charles grimly observed.

But he was satisfied that the mysterious expenditure had nothing to do with his wife's actual death. For what connection could there possibly have been?

These matters, and numerous others, Charles Carpenter routinely shared with Dorothea Deverell; as she shared with him, perhaps to a lesser extent, matters pertaining to the Morris T. Brannon Institute. Charles's mourning for his difficult wife was taking the form of a protracted quarrel with her, which, being wholly one-sided, *his*-sided, could not fail to yield frustration and anger; this, Dorothea was more than willing to indulge, out of guilty complicity. She might try to comfort her lover in his grief, but she would never have wished to quarrel with it. She foresaw how, as if inevitably, she and Charles Carpenter would become a couple in Lathrup Farms society, even before they were married and living in the same house; as Ginny Weidmann said, they were a "perfect match."

Dorothea smiled suddenly, unexpectedly.

For she *was* happy.

Since Colin Asch's extravagant dinner party in her honor, Dorothea Deverell had been very kindly disposed to her friend Ginny's young nephew. She invited him to the cocktail reception for a new art exhibit at the Institute and there introduced him to a number of the trustees and members of the Friends—older, well-to-do men and women, for the most part, of the kind socially receptive to the emanations of "youth." She gave him inscribed copies of her handsome books on Isabel Bishop, Arthur Dove, and Charles Demuth; in lieu of the dinner party she owed them—for this wasn't after all a period in Dorothea's life when she felt up to the demands of a dinner party—she invited the Weidmanns and Colin to be her guests at a performance of the visiting New York City Ballet in Boston and took them to dinner beforehand at a restaurant near the theater. More importantly, she suggested to Mr. Morland, who immediately agreed, that Colin Asch be added to the Institute's payroll as a "consultant for publicity"—as it was, Colin had been helping in a casual, unsystematic way, placing notices for up-coming Institute events in Boston publications and getting local radio and television stations to add such notices to their cultural calendars. "Our office has been mailing out press releases, as they're called, for years, with a minimum of success," Dorothea told Colin, mystified. "How is it these people have listened to *you?*" Colin merely laughed, embarrassed, and said, "I suppose it does require a certain knack. A minor talent for coercion."

He was touchingly grateful to Dorothea for adding him to the Institute staff and thanked her repeatedly. "The consulting fee is very modest, I'm afraid," Dorothea said, pleased that Colin Asch was pleased, "but maybe, one day, we might have enough in the budget for a full-time director of publicity—"

"Oh, I doubt that I could work here full time," Colin said quickly. "It's just, you know, the honor of it. The association. The Morris T. Brannon Institute." He paused. He smiled his spontaneous sunny smile at Dorothea, which never failed to move her. "But—who knows? I can't make predictions, in terms of my career. Modeling is a notoriously unpredictable profession."

"Modeling?" Dorothea asked, amazed. It was the first she had heard of it.

It seemed that Colin Asch had quit L. L. Loomis in mid-March; he'd been approached by one of the firm's clients, Elite Models—" 'Elite Models at Affordable Prices' is how they advertise themselves"—to sign on with them as a photographer's model, primarily for men's fashions. Of course he had not ever envisioned himself as a model since he was rather critical of his appearance, and skeptical too over the very idea of peddling one's looks on the market. . . . Though he had not been particularly happy at L. L. Loomis, where his talent and energy were being suppressed, he'd hesitated to leave since a job in public relations might have led to something in artistic design, even in architectural design, someday; but here suddenly was this exclusive modeling agency begging *him* to give *them* a chance. So he suffered through a week of terrible indecision; once he had an offer to leave, and an excellent offer at that, everyone at Loomis naturally wanted him to stay—even the supervisor who had been so cold and so transparently jealous of him. "But finally I decided to quit and try my chances at modeling," he said. "After all, I'm twenty-eight years old and not getting any younger."

Dorothea Deverell listened to Colin Asch's words as she might have listened to the speech of an exotic foreigner or the song of an exotic bird. Surely he was, as canny Howard Morland had said of him, a "golden boy—hardly a member of *our* modest species." She did not envy him the adventure of his new profession—the very thought of "peddling" one's looks in public dismayed her—but she did envy him the brash vitality of youth. And she had no doubt that, if he did not give up too quickly, he might very well succeed.

Almost apologetically she said, "How meager it must seem, then, to be asked to serve as a consultant for us. The Institute isn't very glamorous, I'm afraid."

Colin Asch fixed her an almost defiant look. "As if, Dorothea, *I* should be concerned with 'glamour'!"

A week later, however, near the end of April, he dropped by Dorothea's home uninvited to show her his portfolio of photographs. "I just thought, you know, you might be curious," Colin Asch said. Most of the photographs, he explained, as Dorothea turned the pages slowly, were the property of the agency; the half dozen at the end were the first prints of a "shoot" he'd done the previous week for the fashionable men's store Tatler & Co. Watching Dorothea's face, he ex-

uded an innocent, boyish vanity. "It's weird seeing
yourself as an object," he said. "But I guess it sort
of puts things into perspective."

Does it? Dorothea wondered.

She had made them a pot of herbal tea; she'd laid
the bulky portfolio down on the dining room table and
was examining the glossy photographs in sequence,
thoughtfully, as if they were—as, indeed, perhaps they
were—works of art. It was clear that Colin Asch
wanted her to contemplate these images of himself as
a model, but it was not clear to Dorothea how she was
expected to respond. "How striking!" she murmured.
"How unusual!" She found herself staring at a photograph of a very blond very arrogant-looking young
stranger posed leaning against a Jaguar sports car
parked amid the dunes, the point of the photograph
being, evidently, the Italian designer's suit the young
man modeled, with exaggerated shoulders and a slim
waist and wide lapels. "I don't think I would recognize you," Dorothea said, laughing uneasily. "It *is*
you? Colin?"

"Oh, you'd recognize me, Dorothea," he said, seriously. "You and I would know each other anywhere."

There was the formidable young blond man posing
in jodhpurs and a polo shirt that fitted his slender yet
muscular torso tightly; there was the young blond man
in a fashionable ribbed sweater and blue jeans and
running shoes; there, lounging on sunlit stone steps
redolent of the Mediterranean (though photographed,
surely, in the Boston area), his hair glaringly blond,
his eyebrows nearly white, eyes obscured by tinted
Polo glasses. In one photograph, over which Dorothea
chose not to linger, he was nearly naked—wearing only
snugly fitting jockey shorts. In all the photographs
Colin Asch seemed far more sinewy, muscular, *mas-
culine,* than Dorothea would have thought him had she

simply envisioned him, summoned an image of him in her mind's eye. For was he not, still, the waiflike boy who had turned up at the Weidmanns' house back in November and who had stared so appealingly at Dorothea Deverell? And if he was no longer that boy, what had become of that boy?

She looked up at Colin Asch, who, standing with a teacup in one hand, his other hand crooked at his waist, elbow akimbo, was looking expectantly at her, and saw that, yes, the young man who stood before her was indeed the iconographic young man of the fashion photographs; he had supplanted entirely the skinny boy with the limp ponytail, the sallow grayish skin. The carnivore had supplanted the vegetarian.

Unless, she thought, there had never been any vegetarian, from the start. Only the carnivore.

But these were fleeting, unfocused thoughts, themselves supplanted, in the next instant, by others—for Colin Asch with childlike eagerness seemed actually to be waiting for a judgment of some sort from Dorothea Deverell. "Do you," he asked, with a gesture toward the portfolio, "do you think I have a future there, Dorothea? Or do you think it's all some sort of—I don't know—chimera? It *is* an exciting life, but it's tough, too—like, you know, 'dog eat dog'; you're in such immediate and continuous competition with other models, I sort of wonder whether my nerves can stand it."

Dorothea Deverell said, closing the portfolio carefully, "But it seems you're more than merely promising, Colin, it looks to me as if you have arrived," and a moment later wondered at the odd jocular confidence of her remark. Did she mean it? Did she even know what she was talking about? Her professional world was in no way contiguous with that of modeling.

But it was the reply Colin Asch most avidly wished to hear; his face lit up like a child's. He said, humbly,

"Thank you, Dorothea. For your faith in me. There's no one whose opinion means more to me than yours, and your—faith in me. I'll always remember it."

So Dorothea could hardly retract her statement, or even qualify it. She said, "Are there other 'shoots' planned soon?"

"The head of the agency told me that too, in effect, what you said, Dorothea," Colin said thoughtfully. "And the photographers I've been working with. 'Naturally photogenic,' they're saying—that's a sort of buzzword in the profession. Of course, I can hardly take credit for it," he said, with modest dip of his head, "it's just an accident of genetics. When I was a schoolboy at Monmouth Academy there was this teacher of mine, he was also the headmaster of the school; he'd say he had faith in me too, could see in my face I had some sort of special destiny and he wanted to guide it, he said, but . . ." Colin Asch's voice trailed off dreamily. For several seconds he stood, teacup in hand, staring not at Dorothea Deverell but through her, at a space that excluded her; she felt suddenly, though not for the first time, the fact of his extraordinary loneliness. "But something happened to him, and things changed. It's such a sad thing in life, isn't it, Dorothea," Colin Asch said, frowning severely. "That things *change?*"

Dorothea, in whose imagination visions of poor Agnes Carpenter had been dominant for days, since the news of her death two weeks before, said merely, "Yes."

"They told me I should get 'investors' in my career, 'shareholders' to help with expenses," Colin Asch said suddenly, in a derisory voice. "A top model, you know—the head of the agency thinks I'll be tops in maybe five, six months—can make a million dollars a year, two million, but there are expenses to begin with, and I have my apartment and my furniture and my car—payments; I mean, rent and insurance and that sort of thing," he said, speaking quickly, laughing. "I'm just so damned ignorant of that side of life, so helpless, like, you know, an *idiot savant* or something—Mr. Kreuzer, my teacher, he used to say, 'All you need, Colin, is someone to take you in hand, someone who loves you'—but, Jesus, Dorothea, I told them I just couldn't do anything like that!" he said vehemently. "I mean, after all, peddling myself to my friends? I told them no, I refused to do that sort of thing, I'd rather quit right now than—than do that sort of thing."

Slowly, almost awkwardly, Colin Asch took up the outsized portfolio and prepared to leave, his movements rather studied; so that Dorothea, ever conscious of her role as—and her limitations as—a hostess, had the distinct impression that her young friend was waiting for—hoping for—an invitation to stay awhile longer. It was Saturday evening; surely so handsome and dashing a young man would not be spending Saturday evening alone? Dorothea felt a pang of guilt, but her evening was taken: given over to Charles Carpenter, for whom she would prepare a meal here at home, in truth the happiest most idyllic sort of evening she could envision, though their conversation would almost surely be centered upon poor Agnes and the ramifications of her death . . . and Colin Asch, for all the appeal of his boyish loneliness and his young man's swaggering glamour, simply had no place in it.

At the door Colin Asch said, as if eerily, and not for the first time, he were capable of reading Dorothea Deverell's mind, "*That* was so sudden, wasn't it?—Mrs. Carpenter's death the other day."

Dorothea said, startled, "Yes—yes, it was."

"Did you know her, Dorothea?"

"Not really. No—not well."

"You're closer to Mr. Carpenter, I guess."

"Yes," Dorothea said uneasily. "Charles and I are quite close. He has been"—and this was vague, fumbling—"involved in activities at the Institute for years. A very cultural man, a—a man who likes to involve himself in cultural things. Though with his job it's—"

"Susannah Hunt was telling me Mrs. Carpenter had been an alcoholic for years," Colin Asch said gravely. "Sort of emotionally unstable? And the Carpenters' marriage wasn't, I guess, too happy. They didn't have any children?"

"No," Dorothea said. She would have liked to end the conversation but had no idea how, since Colin Asch was standing with his back to her front door, and the door had not yet been opened. "They didn't have any children."

"*That's* a blessing, then," Colin said. "Though I guess, at their age, the children would be all grown up, mostly. Even out of college."

"I suppose so."

"Susannah was telling me Mrs. Carpenter might have taken an overdose of pills? Like, I mean, on purpose? She'd left some letter or something behind that the police confiscated?"

"No," Dorothea said firmly, "there was no letter."

"There was no letter?"

"Not that I know of."

Colin Asch soberly pondered this: not disbelieving, merely thoughtful. The brass clamp in his ear—he was wearing it again, after an interim of weeks: fortunately he'd left it off for his own dinner party—flashed rakishly; his punkishly styled hair lifted in tufts from his forehead. He smiled suddenly and said, almost in a whisper, "Mrs. Hunt is the kind of woman, she makes things up, and it isn't even lying, really, it's just—fabrication. In fact, you know, *she* drinks a lot too. I think that's why she's going around saying all these things, these sort of unverified things, about the Carpenters—she's afraid she might end up like Agnes Carpenter.'' He paused, nodded, not seeming to see the look of apprehension in Dorothea Deverell's face, and said, in a derisive dismissal, ''Next thing you know, she'll be telling lies about *me*.''

It was a balmy misty day with a palpable taste of spring in the air, so Dorothea accompanied her young friend to the curb, to his car—the black Porsche, low-slung, polished, expensive-looking. (But was that a dent in the rear right fender? And was that a hairline crack in the front windshield?) She wondered if the Porsche belonged, still, to Susannah Hunt, or whether Colin Asch had bought it from her. The peculiar outburst about his finances, about ''investors'' and ''shareholders'' in his career—which, discreetly, Dorothea Deverell had seemed not to hear: even should she be inclined to do so, Charles Carpenter would be severely disapproving if *she* invested in Colin Asch's modeling career—indicated a concern with money of an extreme kind. (Which did not in fact surprise Dorothea, who had wondered from the start how Colin Asch could afford so luxurious an apartment, with such luxurious furnishings, and such tastes. Surely Susannah Hunt was not supporting him entirely?) Guilt tugged at her like a mild ache; she could of course help Colin out if he was terribly in need of cash but she worried that lending him money would humiliate him and giving him money would insult him. At their luncheon at L'Auberge he had looked as if she'd slapped him when she had merely suggested paying her half of the check.

''It was sort of like Krauss's death—I mean, unexpected,'' Colin Asch said, tossing the portfolio casually into the car and swinging in behind the wheel. ''But sort of expected, too, in the context of the life. If you knew the life.'' He took down a pair of Polo driving glasses from the sunscreen and fitted them on his face. Immediately he became the very blond very arrogant young man, a Greek god-like young man, in the fashion photographs. And he was wearing white: a white linen sports coat with a mint-green collarless jersey shirt. Dorothea Deverell, not knowing what he said exactly, was smiling uncertainly down at him. "If you know how to read it," he said with an enigmatic smile.

"Read it?"

"Like, you know, Dorothea, things in code."

And then, in keeping with his glamorous persona, he drove off.

Afterward, preparing dinner and awaiting Charles's arrival, Dorothea Deverell reviewed her conversation with Colin Asch and felt increasingly uneasy. What had he been talking about? She seemed to have nodded there, at the end, and given him her hand in farewell. Had Colin Asch, for all his pride, really wanted Dorothea to "invest" in his career? Or had he been sincere in his dismissal of the very idea? He had spoken almost angrily, after all, of the prospect of peddling himself to his friends.

No, Dorothea thought, finally, he can't have meant it.

She would not in any case mention the possibility—or even its impossibility—to Charles Carpenter.

For Charles did not approve of Ginny Weidmann's nephew; it seemed he had not approved of him from the start. Dorothea had several times tried to argue in Colin Asch's behalf but Charles had remained unmoved. "But Colin is so appealing, so likable," Dorothea said, "so eager, like a child, to be loved," and Charles replied, "That's in fact why I don't much like him—why I resist."

That evening, at dinner, Dorothea described Colin Asch's brief visit: his portfolio of photographs, the prospect of his new career. But Charles did hardly more than murmur in response, like a jealous husband. In exasperation Dorothea said, "*Why* don't you like Colin? He likes you; he has told me. He very much admires you."

"Does he?"

"He has told me so himself."

But Charles Carpenter was not to be drawn into discussing a subject against his will. He would rather, Dorothea supposed, settle into the sort of melancholy, tender, brooding exchanges they'd had for days on end, circling around the subject of Agnes and the degree to which they might consider themselves involved in her death.

Impatiently, Dorothea said, "You don't really have any reason to dislike Colin, do you?"

After a brief pause Charles Carpenter said dryly, "Only my sense, darling, that the young man is a psychopath."

Dorothea stared, as shocked as if her lover had reached out suddenly and struck her. "A . . . *what?*"

"You heard me perfectly plainly, Dorothea. A psychopath."

Dorothea Deverell had heard perfectly plainly but did not choose to consider her lover's words. They were cruel and vindictive; they did not reflect very nobly upon him.

Yet they abraded her nerves; and she had cause, a few days later, to remember them, meeting Susannah Hunt in a village store and having a painful conversation with the woman. Out of nowhere a voice rang out: "Dorothea Deverell! It *is* you!" She looked up startled to see Mrs. Hunt, floridly made up, elegantly dressed, headed in her direction, as if they were old, intimate friends—or enemies with a score to settle. In a louder voice than was required, Mrs. Hunt said, "I *thought* that was you, Dorothea, but you're looking— well, you aren't looking quite yourself somehow."

To this semi-accusation Dorothea Deverell could think of no adequate reply, so stood mute, smiling, expectant, a ream of typing paper in her arms. She had hurried into the Village Stationer's to make a single purchase and truly had not time to linger and chat, as the formidable Mrs. Hunt seemed inclined. "I don't believe I've seen you, you know, since the night of Colin's party. *Your* party," Mrs. Hunt said, as if Dorothea needed to be reminded. "Have you been well? And Charles Carpenter—has *he* been well? Such a terrible, terrible shock. I'm still shaken by it."

Susannah Hunt was a powerfully attractive woman, tall and full-bodied, with an air of desperate chic. She had outlined her wide mouth in a chalky cranberry shade and colored her eyelids pale blue, but both her mouth and her eyes appeared puffy. Something stylishly severe had been done to her hair, which was dyed a flat, lusterless black, razor-cut close to her head. As she spoke Dorothea was vaguely aware of a gentleman friend waiting for her at the front of the store, an older, white-haired man, deeply tanned, in a navy blue blazer with a nautical look to it; but this friend Susannah Hunt herself seemed to have forgotten. She was standing close to Dorothea and smiling rather strangely at her, asking after Colin Asch, whom, it developed, she had not seen in a while—twelve days. Uncomfortably, Dorothea said, "As far as I know, Colin is well. He seems to have embarked upon a new—"

"He's a *model*. Isn't that extraordinary? But so somehow *right*, don't you think? Since he's so very attractive and there's so little a man can do with being attractive—a heterosexual man, I mean—except *be*. A model, or an actor, that's about it," Susannah said in a bright dazzling rush of words. She smiled at Dorothea but her eyes were cold. "Did you say you'd seen him? He's always talking of course about *you*—how you gave him a start, so to speak, here in Lathrup Farms. When he'd just about been desperate—penniless. Working practically as a beach boy—in Florida, was it? Key West?"

"I—I don't know about that," Dorothea said.

"A very attractive young man, in any case," Susannah Hunt said.

"I suppose he is, yes."

"And sweet."

"Yes."

"But with such a violent temper! At times."

Seeing Dorothea's disbelieving look, Susannah Hunt drew a hand lightly across her brow, as if to indicate an injury to her eye. She gave off a rich, disturbing scent: expensive perfume, red wine. Was the woman merely drunk? Drunk and histrionic? Dorothea wished to think so. "At times, indeed," Susannah said, sighing.

Dorothea would have moved on, but the woman blocked her way. She asked her now whether she had heard from Ginny Weidmann recently, whether Ginny saw much of her nephew these days. "I don't like to call her, you know," Susannah said. "She has become so sort of mother-henish over him. So proprietary."

Dorothea thought. She had not spoken with Ginny Weidmann in more than a week but was reluctant to convey this information to Susannah Hunt, whose intimate, rather belligerent manner she did not at all like. "I'm afraid I don't know," she said. "Now if you'll excuse me—"

"He stays away overnight sometimes. Colin does. He never used to, you know—he was wild about that apartment. 'The center of the universe,' he called it. 'My sanctuary.' Now the little bastard simply disappears without explanation . . . a day and a night, two days, two nights . . . leaving me practically *frantic*. But you don't know where he is, Dorothea, you say, or whom he might be with?''

"No," Dorothea said coolly.

"Yet you and he are so *close.*"

This too had the resonance of an accusation, to which Dorothea Deverell felt no inclination to reply. The heady discomforting scent of perfume and wine was now unmistakable, emanating from the other woman; Dorothea had the idea that Susannah Hunt, now regally drawn to her full height, swaying as if indignant in her high-heeled alligator pumps, was debating whether to challenge Dorothea head on or grant her a mocking sort of victory.

Then, as if suddenly remembering her gentleman friend at the front of the store, she gave way and relented, allowing Dorothea to pass by to the cashier. She said, "Next time you do see him, Dorothea, tell him he*lo* from me. From Susannah. And that's all. And that's *all.*"

"Yes," Dorothea promised. "I will."

So, with a shudder of repugnance, she escaped. Thank God, she thought, Colin had eluded that terrible woman.

11

Where did the money go? Where, when Colin Asch had sure as hell earned it, sweated for it, did it *go?* The phrase "cash flow," which he didn't entirely understand, stuck in his brain: yeah, it *flows*, all right, sure does *flow!* "In one fucking direction."

In the Blue Ledger when he could force himself to sit still he made his calculations, in pencil, in pencil with a good eraser, but what he needed was one of those little Japanese pocket calculators. To take the burden of mathematics off his brain. . . . He'd try, God knows he'd try; then the injustice of it rose like vomit to the back of his mouth and he threw the Ledger down and walked fast through the rooms of the apartment, almost trotting, slapping at his bare thighs (hadn't he gotten dressed yet? but what time was it?), trying to figure out why Colin Asch always needed money, money and more money, always more fucking money, when there was after all money coming in: *flowing* in. Or had been until the other day when he realized he'd better stop for the time being.

Running needless risks, jeopardizing his future. And now Dorothea Deverell had trusted him with an executive position at the Institute; he didn't want to disappoint her.

Still, it was a task for Colin Asch in this weird electric kind of state that'd settled onto him to sit quietly to figure his next moves out in the Ledger, let alone meditate as his soul urged—"The kingdom of God is within! With*in*!"—let alone endure with grace the shooting sessions, the protracted scenes of passivity, even helplessness, the photographers giving him instructions, herding him here and there like a clumsy calf, or actually positioning, touching him—arms, legs, head. The other day he'd caught the fuckers exchanging glances behind his back but gave no sign, just continued smiling—compliant—"professional" in every regard. When all he wanted to do was tear their throats out with his teeth.

In a year, he'd been promised, he'd be one of the top Boston-area models. Thus he *was* trying—subordinating himself to his intellectual inferiors.

"Colin Asch is learning. A lot."

Also with Susannah: screaming at him, threatening to go to the police or to her lawyer, actually daring him to hit her like it was Colin Asch's manhood and dignity she challenged, though the cunt liked it, being hit, fairly hard but not too hard, never any blood—"They tend not to like actual blood." But he'd backed off from her, laughing, saying, Wow. Wow. *Wow*. Saying, Lady, you don't *know*. The first time she'd started hinting about wanting her money back, her "investment," he'd had the quick sort of floating idea why not strangle this woman and dump her body out in the dunes, but it wasn't a serious thought; after all there was Dorothea Deverell in his life now—just thinking of her calmed him, to a degree. So he'd kidded Susannah out of her rage or whatever it was— "All she ever needs is a good hard fucking"—and afterward in the steamy bathroom he wrote in the mirror in tall block letters HEY I WANT TO BE GOOD!!!!

* * *

The money, though. Did Freud say money is shit? For it *is* shit. Surely. Money-grubbing capitalist-imperialist society where human beings are forced to peddle themselves in the market. . . . if not their actual flesh (like your million-dollar fashion models) then their talents, their brains, their souls. If Susannah followed through with her threat to stop paying her share of his rent at the Normandy Court he'd have that added expense, plus the payments on the furniture et cetera and incidental expenses and of course the $$$ he wished to hide away as a nest egg . . . for the Emergency. (For Colin Asch sensed that the time rapidly approached when he would feel the need to terminate this phase of his life, as, in the past, he'd terminated other phases; he'd maybe have to go into hiding at an hour's notice, with Dorothea Deverell as his friend and companion perhaps or maybe just alone: thus $$$ sequestered safely away *hidden right here in the apartment* was of the utmost priority.)

"The money, though."

In the secret Ledger's account there was D.T./2300/ "M" (meaning that Tracey Donovan, the perky little plump-assed reporter for the local weekly, had handed over to Colin Asch a check for $2,300 payable to "T. Manatee"—her notion of his professional modeling name); and there was W.G./3500/"A" (meaning that a Lathrup Farms widow named Gladys Whiting, to whom in fact Dorothea Deverell had recently introduced him, had invested $3,500 in his career as "A. Avalon"), and there was C.A./7000/"Al" and C.A./8500/"Al" (meaning that Agnes Carpenter before her death had invested a total of $15,500 in Colin Asch's projected career as a handsome if temperamental blond model named "Alvarado")—*yet still it wasn't enough.*

Was he adding wrong? Subtracting wrong? Monthly expenses multiplied by twelve plus incidentals plus 15 percent set aside for the Emergency. . . . It seemed that, the more cash flowed *in,* the more cash flowed *out,* and there was nothing he could do to prevent it. "Sometimes I feel, Dorothea, as if the top of my head is about to explode. *I don't think I'm going to make it.*"

Bare-assed on his tacky little balcony leaning against the railing, his eyes filling slowly with tears. A soft spring breeze stirring his hair . . . but which spring was it? *When I'm thirty I will cut my throat. I don't want to live past thirty.* Not knowing what the fuck to do next . . . sensing he hadn't better try to see Dorothea Deverell for another few days, though he could try to calm his thoughts thinking of her. And it came back to him in a flood of warmth how one day Mr. Kreuzer had placed his hand over his when he was writing or doing algebra, guiding Colin Asch's thin hand with his, his cold faltering hand enclosed in the other's big-knuckled hand that carried such heat, guiding Colin's pencil that way, helping him, and all the trouble to come wasn't so much as a premonition then; he'd felt his eyes fill with tears . . . what kindness, what relief. Just to know somebody gives a fuck about you.

But that sort of tender solicitude is rare.

"If you know how to read it."

Watching her face: and she'd blinked at him, mildly puzzled it seemed, her brown gaze imperturbable, opaque. Silent but squeezing his fingers as if in warning *don't say it,* as if to warn *yes—but don't say it.* And he'd sped off from the curb exhilarated as a smart-ass teen-aged kid—couldn't help showing off in the Porsche.

Though Dorothea Deverell had disappointed him too. Not inviting him to stay a while longer . . . not inviting him to stay for dinner when he had a strong hunch that Charles Carpenter would be coming over and the three of them would have gotten along so well, Colin just knew it. Actually, that was his plan. Sort of. Like Dorothea Deverell and Charles Carpenter would take in Colin Asch like married couples sometimes do, especially older married couples with no children or with grown-up children like the Weidmanns. Now that Carpenter's wife was safely out of the way, the two of them owed Colin Asch a favor, after all. If only they knew.

(Did they know? Did *she* know? Sometimes Colin believed she must . . . like about Krauss; he was certain she knew about Krauss . . . but the other he wasn't so sure about, actually.)

"It's the stillness in her."

That night, after the celebration party where they'd all been so happy, Colin Asch had come to her house in secret like a sleepwalker drawn to his fate. Not knowing what he would do but knowing, trusting; his instinct would guide him, for what did not, in this blessed state, emanate from the soul? In her presence *Colin Asch was elevated he was refined he was purified* like the petals of a flower opening innocently in the sun. High on champagne and red wine and one or two other factors, the smiles and warm handshakes of his good friends—*I want to love and be loved! Is that too fucking much to ask?* And Dorothea Deverell had kissed him on the cheek, thanking him for his kindness. And flying high but fully in control he had followed her afterward to her house in the night and with a miniature screwdriver he forced the lock of the rear terrace door; then he was standing inside in the dark that was so familiar to him as if he'd been living here all his life just as she was living here, *as much at ease.* This fact he would later note in the Blue Ledger. With a pencilized flashlight he illuminated his path to the stairs and upward . . . a narrower staircase than he recalled, and strangely steep, like a staircase in a dream . . . and maybe he *was* dreaming, for there was no fear in it: Colin Asch ascending to Dorothea Deverell unhesitating and lithe as a panther *knowing no harm could come to him or to her as all emanated from the soul.*

In her bedroom in the shadows he felt his breath quicken, for there, suddenly, she was . . . asleep and breathing heavily, hoarsely, as if straining for oxygen . . . *there,* only a few feet away, unknowing! "Dorothea. I won't hurt you." He drew nearer, stood above her, staring in amazement in rapture nothing raw or crude, nothing sexual—though, yes, there was *that* (feeling the blood rush into his penis like a faucet turned suddenly on), but so much more than merely *that.*

Wouldn't touch himself. It wasn't like *that* at all.

The thin beam of light darted and snaked about the room. Seeing that the room too was familiar, the low ceiling slanted at the front windows, the shape of the windows, the doorframes, teasingly familiar as if without being conscious of their union he'd seen them for years through her eyes. Thus *he could not be touched! could not be stopped!* Standing above Dorothea Deverell as she slept staring at her sleep-struck face as (when? where? he thought, yes, it had been recent) in one of the hospitals where he'd made his way by stealthy night to a young woman's room thus to contemplate her in her sleep and that too a heavy drugged sleep, a sedated sleep, the kind mimicking death but it isn't the real thing of course. The skin like alabaster; the dark disheveled hair on the pillow; the eyes (so beautiful! so *knowing!*) shut in sleep; the lips moist and open; the breath coming deep, rhythmic, labored . . . to which he tried to fit his. "Dorothea. It is I, Colin Asch: *it is I.*" Why was he trembling, when he wasn't frightened or even unduly excited? Why did his heart pound so heavily, as if he felt he were trespassing, doing something wrong? Through the fragrant dark dense as water Colin Asch could plunge to her, dive to her, take her up in his arms . . . rescue her from all harm. It was his mission, his fate. He'd never have hesitated. *My life for hers!* he thought gaily.

But she slept, unknowing. And there was no danger. The room with the low slanted ceiling and the floral wallpaper and the gauzy white curtains like a dream solidified around the dreamer. *We could die together. Tonight.* Excited, he pulled the black turtleneck sweater off over his head and let it drop. His hands were clumsy in the tight kidskin gloves, but that couldn't be helped. On a bureau were her clothes, and on a nearby chair, tossed down; she'd barely managed to get undressed for bed he supposed: there, the white lace jacket, the long white skirt partly on the floor, a white silk half slip and a white brassiere; and touching the fabric Colin Asch couldn't help himself, he removed one of the gloves and held it gripped between his teeth and pressed the silky underclothes against his bare chest managed to force the slip (so fragrant! charged with electricity sparking in his hair, his eyelashes) down over his head, his mouth dry with anticipation, dread of what might happen, *or had it already happened and the woman was dead . . . ?*

(But only if Colin Asch was trapped, boxed into a corner. Only if there was no way to accommodate his dignity, pride, manhood. Never would he force her, however—"I promise"—or even beg as Mr. Kreuzer had in the end, fumblingly pressing the very razor into the boy's fingers, daring him, or actually wishing him to use it—"What more perfect death than death-in-union? Two-in-one? Forever?")

Afterward he would not remember precisely but it

was like a dream in teasing fragments, the emotional tone of it and not details or images or uttered words: Colin Asch crouched over the sleeping woman slowly tremblingly drawing the covers off her, ascending, like a beam of light . . . no shadows! no gravity! . . . and she continued to sleep unknowing, trusting in him—a woman in a nightgown bunched at her knees, a woman with a petite skeleton, flat-bellied, her breasts flattened too as she slept lying on her back but slightly twisted as if she had fallen from a great height—and Colin Asch bent closer, staring, the silk slip in taut tight folds over his chest, fragrance easing upward, his eyes filling with tears like pain. In an ecstasy, nearly blinded, he knelt at the bedside and pressed his burning forehead against the woman's bare foot . . . the pale bare foot, cool as stone, and as smooth.

I want to be good!
I want to destroy the world!

Days or maybe weeks later the mood shifted suddenly like the spring woods, turned shitty; Colin Asch was susceptible at this time of the year, the axis of a new fresh head-splitting season when you're supposed to be happy like the rest of the assholes, lifting your face to the sun, sniffing the earth, the moisture, the warmth, melting snow and dripping eaves and rivulets of water running fast in the gutters; and he made the effort. Christ the fuckers had no idea what an effort it was, how he loathed them manipulating his very body daring to touch his very skin which pained him, it was a true complaint—hyperesthesia, they'd called it, like the outside layer of his skin had been peeled away thus special medicines were required but he hadn't had those medicines in a long, long time—''I don't like any doctors fucking with *me* like I was just some mere body or something," he'd actually told the judge who'd heard his case, but that was a long, long time ago, in another spring. Anyway he made the effort. Allowed himself to be made up—"You're a little *pale*, Colin, also there's some shadows under your eyes: see?"— and made the fucking effort trying to joke with the photographer, to turn their relationship into *something warm something real something other than the merely commercial* for he'd been thinking he would like, really, to be a photographer—but a true photographer— taking portraits of distinguished people traveling around the world for (maybe) *Time* magazine, or *Life,* or the *Boston Globe;* it was unnatural for a man of Colin Asch's energy and temperament and imagination, above all, dignity, to be so passive, so putty- in-the-hands like the other models (those narcissistic assholes, pretty-boys crazy in love with their own re- flections), when he was an artist himself: and that pri- marily. Thus he gritted his teeth, and smiled, and tried hard, showing how serious he truly was, how eager to cooperate, during one of the breaks asking the pho- tographer about his background, what kinds of work he did, what kinds of contracts were necessary, and was photography school actually a good or necessary thing or could you sort of pick it up on your own— "Provided you had good advice, I mean." Of course Colin Asch had been enrolled at the Rhode Island School of Design. He'd been told he had almost too much talent for one individual—"It sort of all con- denses, y'know, if you have too many things to think about, too many currents pulling at you—like a par- agnosiac fugue."

Bob the photographer peered at Colin Asch over his heavy white coffee mug steaming coffee and said, "Like a *what?*"

"Paragnosiac fugue."

"What the hell's that?"

Blinking and smiling his dazzling white smile, drawing his fingers swiftly through his newly shampooed hair—"Oh, I forget."

Then seeing how Bob looked at him not knowing if he should smile or not as (maybe) Bob'd looked at Colin Asch a few too many times for his own good (the fucker: telling tales on him like all the rest he didn't doubt), Colin Asch quickly added, "Just like a nervous spell, sort of."

"Oh," said Bob, still looking at him, still holding the coffee mug steaming in front of his mouth. "Is that it."

He wanted to plead with her; he was surrounded by mental and spiritual inferiors—except of course for her! and Charles Carpenter (if Charles Carpenter would only *see!*)—thinking sometimes he was swimming to save his life, desperately flailing his arms to keep from sinking, drowning: "The worst kind of death, Dorothea. You don't know."

It was moist warming air that upset him. It was the acceleration of the earth. The approach of the summer solstice *before he was prepared*. This year held a threat of being worse than the year before, scaring him with its excitement and violence like pelting rain against the windows and the roof of the car, like thunderclaps, the smell of lightning—his sense of smell was so heightened at these times, like a dog's actually: "I'd have liked to be a dog, just, y'know, trotting around sniffing, seeing the world through my nose," Colin Asch had told one óf his doctors when the fugue had just about lifted and he was himself again or nearly; the fault lay with the impure PCP he'd dropped which left one of his temporal lobes short-circuited (or so he surmised: the doctors gave him and his fellow victims double-talk in which you couldn't believe or confidently disbelieve)—all this he would explain to Dorothea Deverell one day soon. That it scared him, things speeding up as they sometimes did. "And I haven't touched any PCP for years."

Which was true. Absolutely incontestably true.

Of course Colin Asch could not confide in Dorothea Deverell *everything*. That he was tortured not knowing, not being able to decide, what exactly to do about the Carpenters: to eradicate the husband, or the wife. There were powerful arguments on both sides. There were voices yammering on both sides.

For one thing, he hated Charles Carpenter, didn't he, for supplanting Colin Asch in Dorothea Deverell's affections; if Charles Carpenter died it would fall to Colin Asch to comfort her, and no one else. *Our mutual tragic lives. Life?*

But he couldn't be blind to the fact that if Charles Carpenter died, or was killed suddenly, Dorothea Deverell would be terribly upset: brokenhearted. "Christ, it might *kill* her." And he didn't want *that*. No—scrutinizing his soul—he didn't want *that*. "What I want is happiness for her, and happiness for me. But Dorothea must come first, otherwise there is no *me.*"

Knowing this he was flooded with relief like simple happiness, or happiness like simple relief. He did after all want only to be good *in homage to the goodness in her.*

Thus he inwardly debated. Thus the thoughts rose and fell and drifted and faded and reemerged in his head as he stood on his balcony in the soft spring rain . . . or drove the Porsche along unfamiliar highways . . . or posed near-naked, his head tilted at an insufferable angle, modeling sea-green swimwear coyly bulging at the crotch, eyes opened wide despite the glaring brain-frazzling lights. For hours, or was it weeks, Colin Asch analyzed the possibilities open to him, and to her. Yes, he wanted only what would yield happiness to her—"So Mrs. Carpenter must die." It was that simple. Inescapable.

XXX performed out of humane indifference, disinterest. For he had nothing personal against the woman, in fact he felt clean and neutral toward her, he'd forgiven her for challenging him that night at the Weidmanns'—in truth, she'd played into his hands like the two of them were performers and the others mere spectators—and he had been pleased he could convince her that the young blond New Wave model "Alvarado" had so promising a future why not invest $10,000 in his career? and she'd thought about it awhile then said she would limit herself to $7,000: "But don't tell my husband! Don't anybody"—she'd begun giggling, the alcohol flush warm in her cheeks—"tell that coldhearted *prig.*"

Of course not, Mrs. Carpenter.

Thus in his unhurried reverie Colin Asch came to the conclusion clear as Euclidean logic that Agnes Carpenter, and not Charles Carpenter, must die. So clearing the way for Dorothea Deverell and Charles Carpenter to wed. So ushering in, in time, a new ménage in which more and more frequently young Colin Asch would be included: weekends, special holidays, birthdays. It would be the most natural thing in the world; older childless couples often take up younger unattached men. A kind of spiritual adoption.

"You will never be lonely again."

"Why, Colin. That is, Alvarado. How *nice. Finally.*"

Seven-thirty P.M. of April 10, Colin Asch has rung the doorbell of the residence of Charles and Agnes Carpenter, 58 West Fairway Drive, Lathrup Farms, Massachusetts, eight-inch stainless-steel switchblade knife in his right-hand coat pocket, small tidy fragrant bouquet of flowers (daffodils, carnations, yellow tulips) in his right hand, and after a wait of five minutes or so he's being invited inside by the lady of the house: his second visit to this house, and his last. "Come in, come in," Agnes Carpenter says airily, "Just in time for a drink"—swaying a little on her feet leading the way into the semidarkened not-entirely-clean living room where the smell of cigarettes and alcohol is strong. Colin Asch thanks her and goes out into the kitchen himself to fetch a vase and water for the flowers, since it's the least he can do under the circumstances. From the other room Agnes Carpenter calls to him half accusing half teasing and he doesn't quite know what she is saying but he answers, "Right! Good! Great! *Yeah!*" Bottles on the kitchen counter, on the floor, dirtied plates stacked in the sink; his nostrils pinch in fastidious disdain. For who would think, contemplating the outside of the Carpenters' fine old colonial, it would be in this condition inside?

In the living room Agnes Carpenter has prepared Colin Asch a drink, a dandy big Scotch to match her own, handed him with shaky beringed fingers, and Colin Asch sets the bouquet atop the fireplace mantel (*"That's* nice, thank you," Agnes Carpenter barely murmurs) and accepts the drink, smiling his sweet cheery boyish dazzling smile but not drawing off his tight black kidskin gloves; he's too shrewd to be leaving fingerprints anywhere around here. He sees that the poor bitch had hurried to make herself up when she heard the doorbell—quick-powdered face, sad-glamorous crimson lipstick, some attempt at fluffing out the permed dry-as-straw colorless hair; and she'd buttoned (crookedly) up to her wrinkled throat the emerald-green brocaded Japanese housecoat or kimono she's wearing: not knowing who might be ringing her doorbell this time of evening but hoping for a pleasant surprise. Peering worriedly at her lanky vis-

itor through the squares of stained glass framing the
door until, yes, yes, finally, she recognized him—her
young friend Colin Asch, her secret investment "Alvarado." Recognized him and opened the door wide.

"It *has* been a long time . . . hasn't it? At least a
month?"

Giving Colin Asch a pug-dog look of reproach,
moist eyes narrowed, and he likes it since there's invariably an edge of flirtatiousness to such reproach,
allows him to shake his head, baffled, and smile
sheepishly. "Gee, Mrs. Carpenter—I mean Agnes—I
meant to call but I've been so busy these past six
weeks, I guess your investment is really going to pay
off 'cause Alvarado's phone practically never stops
ringing—"

And Agnes Carpenter exercises her power by inter-
rupting, careless-seeming, "Not at all! Not at all! I've
been busy too! I quite understand!" She lowers her
voice mock-dramatically: "All I was, actually, was a
tiny bit concerned, Colin, that you *were* still around.
That you hadn't disappeared."

Tall blond natural-aristocrat Colin Asch fixed the
woman with his wide-open quizzical eyes. "Disappeared? But *where?*"

Agnes Carpenter laughs sharply as if he has said
something intentionally comic.

They sit; and Agnes talks. In surges and gusts like
someone who has not had the opportunity to talk in a
long time. She is semi-drunk; not quite slurring-drunk;
some color in her sallow cheeks and a look of sudden
light in her bloodshot eyes. *With a tinge of regret C.A.
touches the weapon through his coat pocket. Why is it
the fate thrust upon some of us, to bring not peace but
a sword?* Self-consciously Colin Asch settles himself
in a velvet loveseat facing Agnes; close by a brass and
mother-of-pearl mahogany cabinet that looks Mediterranean and antique. He listens politely to his hostess's

yammering, crosses his long sinewy legs, shifts his shoulders inside his striped boxy double-breasted coat, nervously straightens his tie (a beauty, a creamy silk Dior with a pattern of tiny black horse-figures—Valentine's Day gift from Susannah Hunt): all to suggest that he's charmingly ill at ease in this plush bourgeois setting—he's an innocent, even naïve young man, of the sort the modeling profession might well take advantage of: and predatory women. Agnes Carpenter pauses in mid-sentence, to squint at him. "Your gloves—why are you wearing *gloves?*" she asks. Colin Asch says, embarrassed, "Oh, these? I'm so anxious these days, I'm back in an old bad habit of biting my nails till they bleed—the thumbnails especially—so the doctor said, he said the very best method, the most practical, is just to wear gloves. Until the anxiety lifts."

"Until the anxiety lifts," Agnes Carpenter echoes, suddenly touched. "But you know, Colin dear boy, that might not happen for a long time. With some of us—a long, long time."

Surreptitiously Colin Asch glances at his platinum-band wristwatch. Seven-forty already: he hopes to be out of here and in rapid motion by nine-thirty.

Unless he can wrap it up earlier? The woman *is* getting drunk.

And there is another drink, for Agnes, while Colin Asch (like a young athlete in training) nurses his, and more talk, the conversation swerving and lurching along a track very like the one it took on Colin Asch's previous visit in March. "I suppose you have heard? I suppose everyone is talking about it, laughing behind my back? Charles wants a separation; he says he wants a *divorce*. And only out of spite! Only to hurt me! Because"—and here Agnes begins laughing, laughing and coughing, wheezing, her jowls quivering, in mirth and indignation—"he knows I know *him,* inside and *out.* There's no mystery to Charles Carpenter to *me!* To his wife! I don't doubt he has a woman friend with whom he imagines himself madly in love—some cold greedy ambitious young woman twenty years younger than he who flatters him sexually—if it's possible to flatter my husband sexually without bursting into laughter. These pseudo-'liberated' young women to-day, they're all stalking other women's husbands since there aren't enough heterosexual men to go around. But the hilarious part of it, Colin, or the tragedy, take your pick, is that no man is a mystery to his wife—no wife is a mystery to her husband." Agnes Carpenter pauses, laughs derisively, succumbs to a fit of coughing, wipes her mouth on her sleeve, *the lovely emerald-green fabric despoiled by a gesture of slovenly drunkenness that fills Colin Asch with revulsion and pity. And anger.*

"Someone should put you out of your misery, Agnes."

"What? Don't mumble, please!"

"Someone should take you out, out on the town, like," Colin Asch says, wildly improvising, as if he too is on the brink of being frankly drunk and in a party mood, as, perhaps, having swallowed down a bennie or two before coming over, he is. "A good-looking woman like you, cooped up in here. It's a great house but, well, it's just—an interior."

Agnes Carpenter laughs shrilly, as if her young male visitor has said something not only intentionally comic but profound. "Christ. Are you *correct.* It's, whatever it is, just an *interior.* "

So the minutes pass. Colin Asch tries to calibrate the degree of the woman's drunkenness vis-à-vis the actions he requires her to perform.

Since as "Alvarado" he is hoping for another generous check, another gesture of faith in him as a top-rank model, he naturally turns the conversation in that direction, and Agnes Carpenter willingly follows, for isn't there something titillating? salacious? about the very notion of a male fashion model? Thus, minutes of banter, some of it gay and flirty and some of it—"D'you think, dear Colin, or, I mean, 'Alvarado,' d'you think, being in such close contact with some of those people, there's any danger? for instance, of getting AIDS?"—rather nasty, and at last Agnes Carpenter heaves herself up from her chair to lead Colin Asch into another room—Charles's "den" as she bitterly calls it—and to make out a check for "Alvarado" (who has, so very shrewdly and prudently, his own savings account in an area bank from which all monies will be withdrawn first thing in the morning of April 11) for the sum of $8,500. The grim satisfied smile on the woman's pug face suggests that she is doing this primarily to take revenge upon the absent, so conspicuously absent husband: there is a happy violence in the very swash of her signature. The bedrock of personality shows through the scrim of girlish intoxication: flushed and panting slightly, Agnes Carpenter hands the check to Colin Asch as if handing the young man her virtue, or her very life, and says very nearly the same words she'd said the first time: "But don't tell my husband, he would so strongly disapprove. That coldhearted"—and she searches for a word—"bastard."

"Of course not, Mrs. Carpenter," Colin Asch says courteously, examining the check to see that the date, the sum, the spelling are correct and the signature reasonably legible. " 'Alvarado' never tells."

"I've asked you to call me Agnes, for heaven's sake!"

"Agnes, then," Colin Asch says, suddenly high with sheer simple happiness *that sometimes though not always precedes the entrance to the Blue Room,* "for heaven's sake!"

* * *

Now that the financial transaction is completed, Colin Asch is all business. When Agnes Carpenter turns as if to leave her husband's den, asking if Colin would like his drink freshened, he says quietly, "No—we have a little more business here." The check is safe in an inside pocket and the eight-inch stainless-steel switchblade knife is in his hand, opened. "Pick up the pen again and write a note to your husband," Colin Asch says, having located, in one of the messy desk drawers, a rose-tinted and -scented stationery pad with *From the desk of Agnes Carpenter* engraved at the top. There is a pause of several seconds, several long seconds, during which Agnes Carpenter stares uncomprehending at Colin Asch and at the knife he holds, its gleaming point not precisely aimed in her direction but its significance unmistakable. At last she says, hoarse, blank, *"What?"*

"I'm not going to hurt you, Agnes, you have my word on that, but like—as I said, there's more business here. Write a note to your husband. Here. On this pad here. With this pen here. 'Dear Charles.' Come *on.*"

But Agnes Carpenter continues to stare. Too shocked, too puzzled, too—oddly, even now—trusting, to be frightened. "But Colin, what are you—? What on earth is—? That knife—what *is* this? Colin? What—"

"I'll explain it all later if there's time," Colin Asch says briskly, handing her the pen, nudging her to write. "But for right now I'm requesting your cooperation: 'Dear Charles.' Write, right here. Right *now.*"

"But Colin—that knife? Is that a real knife? Are you—is this—are you going to rob me? After I did so much for—"

"And now a little more, Agnes," Colin Asch says. Ah, what a model of calm, equanimity. Afterward he will record in the Blue Ledger, *XXX performed clean & ingenious & UNCONTAMINATED BY DESIRE.* He explains to the astonished woman that he isn't going to hurt her—naturally not—he doesn't want to hurt her 'cause he likes her, admires her, but he's pressed for time and will she cooperate? It isn't a robbery, no such thing, Colin Asch is above the crudeness of armed robbery, housebreaking, pillage, desecration, that sort of thing, but she had better obey his instructions since he has a complete scenario in mind—"And I'm pressed for time."

Several times Agnes Carpenter, now beginning to be frightened and, so suddenly, quite sober, asks, "Are you going to hurt me? Please—are you going to hurt me? Oh, Colin, why do you want to hurt me?" and several times, with growing impatience, Colin Asch says, baring his perfect teeth in a smile, "I don't *want* to hurt you, Agnes, that isn't my *intention,*" and, finally, the blood beating hotly in his eyes, a sort of choking band tightening invisibly around his chest, he says, *"Take up the fucking pen, Agnes. Do as I say."*

So Agnes Carpenter takes up the pen and, as Colin Asch stands over her, begins to write, in a badly shaking, terrified or drunken hand, *Dear Charles*—but Colin Asch nudges her hand, and the pen makes a wavering skidding mark. "Start again. Do it over. This time just 'Charles.'" And as Agnes Carpenter writes *Charles,* Colin Asch again nudges her hand and spoils the second note, and Agnes Carpenter has begun to cry in helplessness and terror and, just maybe, hurt feminine pride, for she'd thought this young man had liked her, had been in an oblique way attracted to her as women of any age and any condition of physical decline or mental disorientation are led to think despite the strong counterminings of rationality.

"Thank you, Agnes," Colin Asch says quietly, taking up both notes and crumpling them and dropping them—how very mysteriously! how seemingly purposelessly!—into the wastebasket beneath the desk. "And now," he says, waving the knife as if negligently, as if it were but an extension of his hand, "now we go upstairs."

"Are you going to hurt me? Oh, Colin, please—"

"No one is going to hurt you, on that you have my word," Colin Asch says, as if speaking prepared lines, calm poised controlled at the very brink of an outburst of euphoria but knowing how to keep himself from being sucked over the brink like forestalling the moment of orgasm for as long as possible. "But we're going upstairs now, Agnes. We're taking along something to drink and we're going to continue our visit upstairs."

So Colin Asch leads his tottering hostess into the other room and loads his arms with bottles, Scotch, gin, bourbon, whatever, and he helps her forcibly up the stairs as she shifts from terror to defiance to pleading to weeping to threatening—"If you don't let me go, If *you* don't go, and go *now,* I-I-I will call the police"—and back to pleading again, which is the note upon which, mainly, her life will end: "But *why,* Colin?—how *can* you, Colin?—when I gave you more than fifteen thousand dollars; I've been so *nice* to you, Colin—"

Upstairs, briskly efficient as a film director. Colin Asch instructs Agnes Carpenter to go into her bathroom and draw water for a bath—yes and dribble in some bath salts, like that—and take off her clothes— *as if quite naturally she is going to take a bath.* When she balks he lifts the knife to her throat: "Do it, Agnes." So she does it. Obeying clumsily yet eagerly, like a frightened child, for after all Colin Asch gives the impression (no matter what his actions suggest) that he will not harm her if she follows his instructions step by step, for why should he harm her (he's behaving so rationally!) if she follows his instructions step by step? "Do it. And you have my word, I won't hurt you."

Agnes Carpenter, naked, is a piteous sight. Her stout fleshy self quivers with animal fear. And, in these awkward circumstances, Colin Asch isn't able (as in truth he would like for *there is nothing personal about this sacrificial action, nothing contaminated with mere desire*) to glance away. Large flaccid drooping breasts . . . large flaccid drooping belly . . . creased lardy hips, thighs, buttocks . . . a rough patch of graying-brown pubic hair . . . knees oddly bruised, discolored . . . but the calves of the legs rather slender, and the ankles . . . and the small white feet, the very toes quivering with terror. *Don't hurt me.* And Colin Asch assures her, *Of course not.*

The luxurious bathroom with its lemon-yellow tiled walls and its several mirrors and its gleaming ceramic sink and oversized tub is filling up quickly with steam. There's a festive air to this, the heady scent of the Scotch (which Colin Asch urges Agnes Carpenter to drink: it will make things much easier for her), and the bath salts (it's one of the scents Susannah Hunt favors and were he a nostalgic person which of course he is not *he hasn't time* Colin Asch would recall how in the early days of their friendship he and Susannah splashed about in Susannah's oversized fake-marble tub together playful and conscienceless as children and *not once did Colin Asch fantasize killing or even humiliating the cunt),* and swaying dangerously, with Colin Asch's assistance, Agnes Carpenter manages to lower herself into the warm lapping water, and then she's settled weeping and shaking her head from side to side as if in disbelief, why why *why* has this young man turned against her, *why* is he doing this to her when she meant only well she meant to be good to be kind to be generous to open her heart to him, and now he's handing her her glass of Scotch and urging her to drink, and he has located a container chock full of Valium capsules in her medicine cabinet, and these capsules one by one he is urging her to take, to swallow down—like this, Agnes, come *on*—he gives the impression of an individual both plunging headlong into the future and restraining himself, under extreme duress, like a precision machine vibrating finely with energy.

For the next forty-five minutes, never hurrying the action, Colin Asch forces Agnes Carpenter to swallow down approximately fifteen tablets of Valium, and at times she resists, and at times she acquiesces, her feebly hysterical weeping now intermittent. Near the end of the siege she tries to shake herself awake, tries to open her eyes, unfocused crescents of bloodshot white, and her swollen lips move—"Let me go, don't hurt me; *why?*"—so faint Colin Asch can barely hear but he says, laying one of his gloved hands lightly atop her head, "I won't hurt you, Agnes—you won't feel a thing." Then her head rolls slack on her shoulders, her pale breasts appear to float like dead things, her mouth falls open . . . she is out, unconscious: breathing heavily, hoarsely.

Colin Asch, sitting on the toilet seat, sweating amid the fragrant steam, waits a few minutes longer. It is eight-thirty-five. Maybe Agnes Carpenter will cease breathing, with no violence done to her? Maybe, by herself, she will sink helplessly into the bathwater and drown?

Colin Asch doesn't want to contemplate the doomed woman too intimately. *Pity is the most destructive and the most useless of all human instincts* he'd written in the Blue Ledger years ago, after an incident long since forgotten. *Pity weakens. Pity unmans.* Hadn't Colin Asch once lost all control and run outside half naked, barefoot in the snow?

"You won't feel a thing."

The mania is almost upon him like a giant bird gripping its talons in his shoulders but how calm! how cool! how controlled! he remains. Carefully emptying bottles of liquor into the sink and running the water hard to carry the smell away then taking the bottles into Agnes Carpenter's bedroom (where in fact there is a half-empty bottle of Dewar's on the bedside table) and letting them fall where they will. The bedroom is large and luxuriously furnished like the rest of the house but in extreme disorder, bureau drawers hanging open, clothes underfoot, bed unmade, a lampshade crooked, over all a sour sickish odor: "Disgusting." It is an irony not lost upon him that, before he leaves, he will have to straighten things up a bit, for, though he intends to take one or two or three small items of a kind that won't be missed, he doesn't want the police to suspect that there was a stranger in the house, an intruder . . . the first thing the fuckers will look for is evidence of theft.

In the bathroom Colin Asch carefully wraps towels around both his hands and stoops over Agnes Carpenter, or over Agnes Carpenter's body—the woman is so insensible now, so comatose, it hardly seems that any spirit inhabits that flesh. But as he forces her head down into the water she begins to resist—not fighting exactly, or struggling, but tensing—and suddenly her hands rise out of the water as if to grip his, so Colin Asch releases her and steps quickly away.

"Not true violence but a death by natural causes. Or nearly."

So he waits. Patiently. A trifle impatiently. Beginning to pace about. In and out of the bathroom . . . in and out of the bedroom . . . down the stairs . . . where, in the living room, it occurs to him suddenly to switch on the radio. The fucking house is too *quiet*. What if Agnes Carpenter wakes up and begins screaming hysterically into that *quiet*?

Through a front window Colin Asch nervously observes the street, the sidewalk. Deserted. Peaceful. (He parked the Porsche blocks away, of course.)

It is eight-fifty. He finds himself lifting the telephone receiver, involuntarily dialing Dorothea Deverell's number. He stands listening to the ringing, the ringing, the ringing . . . his heartbeat pleasantly fast. As if he is in two places at one time. As if he has forgotten some danger close by. "Hello? Yes? Who is it?" Dorothea Deverell says, a little breathless. Colin Asch listens to her voice but does not speak. *I am your agent. I am Death's force.* "Hello? Is anyone there?" Dorothea Deverell asks. Even now she is composed, rather excessively formal; as if guessing that, whoever it is who has called her, he means no harm. *My love for you is beyond any love previously known to man.*

Dorothea Deverell hangs up the phone and Colin Asch thinks, Yes, good, it would be wrong to bring her into this action unprepared. XXX performed in utter solitude and dispassion.

"I will tell you sometime. There is nothing I will not tell you, sometime."

He returns the receiver to the cradle and hurries back upstairs, imagining he has heard Agnes Carpenter struggling in the bathtub but to his relief (he doesn't want violence!) she is lying slack-jawed, boneless, unconscious . . . and when, this time, his hands wrapped in towels, he squats over her to force her head beneath the water she no longer resists. "Yes. Like this. It will be over in a few minutes." The life seems to have gone out of her already, leaving her rubbery and docile, like a balloon; he presides over her drowning, her death, with no extraordinary difficulty, XXX performed with an almost surgical precision, holding her there for a long, long time . . . a long dreamy heartpounding time. Feeling the joy of release bubbling in his veins. In his very spinal column. Sweet and explosive as sexual orgasm but cleansing. And innocent. Blameless. Shadowless.

"Didn't I promise you, Agnes? You wouldn't feel a thing."

Recorded in the Blue Ledger as *C.A.888104am.*

> *A sensation of extreme lightness as if a weight was being removed* from my chest. And I could breathe again LIKE SURFACING FROM WATER.
> *AND NOW FOREVER AND EVER I AM FREE! FREE TO BE GOOD!* FREE TO BEGIN MY ENTIRE LIFE OVER AGAIN PURIFIED AND BLESSED!!!

"But Dorothea, it didn't last long this time. In the Blue Room, that good feeling—something went wrong!

"Dorothea? Something has gone wrong!"

Afterward, and in the days following, he scarcely took much interest in reading about Agnes Carpenter's death in the newspapers, for it wasn't (after all) a murder case . . . the police, the assholes, considered it an accident. They had found no evidence of foul play and no evidence of theft. And Charles Carpenter seemed to have believed that no one was with his wife at the time of her death and that "nothing was missing" from the house. (When of course, following his custom, Colin Asch had appropriated a memento or two. And he'd taken $130 from a surprisingly large wad of bills— $288—he'd found in Agnes Carpenter's purse.)

But the pleasure of it all seemed diminished, he didn't know why.

* * *

And there were worries about money: expenses, monthly payments.

Even with Agnes Carpenter's check for $8,500 Colin Asch didn't have enough money.

"It's all so demeaning, Dorothea."

The capitalist-imperialist society was at fault. Forcing its citizens to sell themselves on the open market, *prostitute themselves like mere meat*. Colin Asch was coming to despise all that had to do with modeling, with the exploitation of his physical being, the contamination of the spirit within.

And, by the end of April, by the first days of May, Colin Asch was in a stage in which he could barely tolerate Susannah Hunt's presence *yet dared not offend her irrevocably*.

Her voice, her air of perpetual hurt and reproach, her melting eyes, her painted nails drawn slowly and seemingly provocatively up his arm: "Colin? Honey? Don't you love me anymore? God damn you, what *is* it?"

Colin Asch shut his eyes, and kneaded her flesh, and buried himself in her, and fucked her, as best he could. He did not want to hurt her, still less did he want to kill her. Knowing well that, in such cases, the lover is always the first suspect.

"So demeaning, Dorothea!"

And the new season. Spring.

"Too much light."

12

 Late in the warmly sunlit afternoon of
May 8, a Sunday, Dorothea Deverell was working at
the rear of her house, in her garden—if "garden" was
not an overly ambitious term for so modest and cir-
cumscribed a space, in which, this spring as most
springs, she intended to plant only the hardiest, most
reliable of annuals—when she heard, in alarmingly
rapid succession, the doorbell to the front door ringing
and a hard and prolonged knocking. Her immediate
sensation was fear, even dread—but there could be no
more bad news, could there? so soon? Charles Carpenter was coming over, but not until six; nor would
Charles Carpenter, even under extreme duress, have
made such a racket at her door. Dorothea envisioned
a neighbor come to inform her that her own house was
on fire, or an official serving a subpoena.

 She was hurrying to the front door when the knocking abruptly stopped. And when she opened the door
she saw no one there.

 Yet she had scarcely time to consider if it was a
prank or something more urgent, for already, at her
rear—calling to her through the house from where he
stood on the terrace—her importunate visitor announced himself: Colin Asch. "Dorothea? I'm here,
I came back here, I thought you might be back here,"

the young man said apologetically, and rather excitedly. "I'm sorry to disturb you. I hope I didn't scare you!"

Dorothea, who was in fact quite shaken and annoyed but supposed she would readily recover, said, "No, Colin, of course not," not seeing at first as they approached each other to shake hands in greeting that Colin Asch looked distinctly odd: his smile stiff and excessive, his forehead creased, his eyes moist and blinking and narrowed as if the sunlight blinded him. "Of course not, Colin," she said, as if a conventional femininity (in which the perhaps bolder accents of femaleness did not obtrude) obliged her to tell lies, to put others at their ease.

"I thought maybe you'd be out back, just not answering your door 'cause it's Sunday or something," Colin said, shaking Dorothea's hand—in fact, squeezing it, hard—and fixing her a look in which subtle reproach and forgiveness contended. "Or maybe somebody else was here. But there's nobody here? Or is somebody coming over? Later, I mean? You can tell me: just be direct. *I'll leave if I'm not welcome.*"

Dorothea saw to her mild surprise that her young friend was carrying a duffel bag of remarkable shabbiness slung over his shoulder, and that his clothes, though no doubt "fashionable" in the new aggressive style she made no effort to comprehend, were strangely rumpled, even creased, as if he had been sleeping in them. A metallic blond stubble glinted on his jaws, which had, as he continued to smile, a predatory thickness to them Dorothea had not previously registered; a bluish vein, wormlike, angry, defined itself prominently in the center of his forehead. His eyes *were* alarmingly moist—was he about to cry? Or had he in fact been crying? Dorothea, sensing an emergency, her instinct for maternal solicitude immediately aroused, assured Colin Asch that no one was expected for some time and that in any case he was welcome, of course. "Please sit down," Dorothea said, "and tell me what's wrong."

"How do you know—why do you *think*—something is wrong?" Colin Asch challenged her.

"You seem so—"

"You *know* something is wrong," Colin Asch said reprovingly, letting his duffel bag fall at his feet, "so why ask?" But he sat on Dorothea's sofa heavily, as if suddenly exhausted, his shoulders hunched and his head lowered, turning his head in jerky little tics from side to side as if he were trying to ease its stiffness. Dorothea could hear him panting and seemed to sense, from a distance of several feet, the powerful emanations of heat that rose from him. Even as she ventured to take a seat in a chair facing him Colin Asch got abruptly to his feet, as if too restless to remain in one place. "You left this open," he muttered; he strode to the terrace door, and shoved it shut, and locked it. Then, for a brief moment, he stood at the plate glass window staring out. What did he see? Did he see anything? Beyond the young man's tall, rangy, somehow electrified figure the solace and simplicity of Dorothea Deverell's garden—the evergreens and newly leafed deciduous trees, the whitish slanted sunshine itself— seemed now remote, inaccessible. Something terrible has happened, Dorothea Deverell thought. And I am involved.

Yet with reasonable calmness she asked, "Colin, what *is* it? Please tell me."

"Oh, I think you know," he said quietly.

"What, Colin? I didn't quite hear."

"I think you know, Dorothea."

"Know? Know what?"

He rattled the handle of the terrace door, saying, "This is the kind of lock that burglars can force easily. It isn't a *safe* or a *smart* kind of lock."

He returned to Dorothea's sofa and sat, again heavily, sighing, belling out his cheeks, in a juvenile expression of extreme fatigue. But his skin was flushed with excitation; there were slight tremors in both his eyelids. With increasing uneasiness Dorothea waited for him to explain himself but instead he made a desultory show of examining books on her coffee table— a gigantic *Matisse* with hundreds of color plates, a well-worn paperback of Montaigne's *Essays*. (Dorothea had brought the Montaigne back with her from Vermont but had never quite finished reading it.) Colin frowned over the *Essays;* said, with no transition, "Except for today, I mean—this morning—not *that; that* was only a mistake." He paused, watching Dorothea. "The other two, I mean."

Dorothea said, swallowing, "I'm afraid I don't understand, Colin."

"Don't you!" he laughed. Then: "Who did you say was coming here today? You said somebody's coming? Is it Carpenter? *Him?* When is he coming?"

"At—at five."

"*Is* it Carpenter?"

Dorothea winced inwardly at the name, so unceremoniously uttered. "Charles Carpenter, yes."

"He's coming at *five?*"

For a long strained moment Colin Asch stared at Dorothea as if he were trying to determine whether she lied or spoke the truth. Dorothea was beginning to be seriously alarmed. He has hurt someone, she thought. Or someone has hurt him.

"*He's* a friend of mine too but he doesn't know it," Colin Asch said slowly. "He thinks—I can sense that he thinks—he doesn't like me."

"Of course Charles—"

"He doesn't *know* me. He's *prejudiced.*"

"Oh, but I don't think—"

"But you're my friend, Dorothea, aren't you? and I can trust you?"

"Of course, Colin, you must know by—"

"You can trust *me*."

"Yes?"

Seeing Colin Asch's look of bravado and hurt Dorothea Deverell felt a sudden urge to go to him, to lay a hand on his overheated forehead and brush his damp hair from his eyes. How unlike his usual composed self he appeared, how raw-edged, how without defenses! Yet she was not so forthright a person; she remained seated, fixed in place, staring, in dread and fascination.

"No, I have to modify that, I'd have to say that you are my only friend, Dorothea," Colin Asch said, shaking his head gravely. "Not Charles Carpenter. Not now, and maybe never. And I don't trust him—how the fuck could I trust him—he's a lawyer, isn't he? And a lawyer is an officer of the court, isn't he? Isn't that his allegiance?"

"Colin, dear, please—you're frightening me," Dorothea Deverell said. She would have risen from her chair but she seemed to know that the sudden movement would upset him; and she had after all nowhere specific to go. "Can't you tell me what has—"

"Dorothea, I'm just not *happy!*" he said petulantly. "For years, in school, I was the good boy, the 'little angel,' the superachiever, and now, headed for thirty, I'm getting frankly *tired*—I mean spiritually and morally and not just physically *tired*—fucking *tired*. This constant pressure to excel, to claw my way to the top. Competing with people who might be friends, forced into savage competition like you are in a mercenary society like ours—it's invariably the shitty end of the stick for someone who's sensitive. I know you probably don't feel it, Dorothea, you're different—you've always been different; you hold yourself above such things—but *I* feel it—Christ, do *I* feel it!''

Dorothea said, inspired, ''Did you quit your job, Colin?''

''Yes,'' Colin Asch said vehemently. ''I quit my job.''

''But—so soon?''

''Quit Elite Models—'Elite Models'!—Friday morning, in the midst of a big-deal shoot! Told them all to go fuck and just—quit. Walked away.''

''But, Colin, I thought you—''

''No, I never liked it, Dorothea: I loathed it. Peddling my flesh like I was some kind of—meat, or a prostitute, or something. I saw the look in your eyes when you examined the photographs, Dorothea, I *saw;* it was for that revelation I came.'' He paused, breathing hard; he was rummaging through the duffel bag at his feet. Dorothea could not imagine what connection there might be between the young man's fierce contemptuous words and his pawing about in the duffel bag, but she sat watching, fascinated. He has hurt someone, she thought calmly. It is for that reason he has come to me.

''Y'know this Roman emperor Caligula, Dorothea?'' Colin said conversationally. ''My teacher Mr. Kreuzer—Mr. Kreuzer was headmaster of the school but he taught English too—he told us how Caligula said he regretted 'the world didn't have a single neck so he could strangle it'—*wild!* That stayed with me all these years: 'a single neck so he could strangle it.' I know you won't agree—you're so *good,* so *nice*—but that's the way a lot of people feel a lot of the time. Winding up invariably with the shitty end of the stick year after year.''

And then he spread out on the carpet the several items he wanted Dorothea Deverell to see and was gazing expectantly up at her, his pale eyelashes trembling and his eyes brimming with moisture. In that instant Colin Asch reminded Dorothea Deverell of her mother's father, elderly, partly paralyzed, aphasiac after a severe stroke, gazing up at her from his hospital bed with his single sighted eye and waiting with intense excitement for her response.

A pair of man's gold cuff links, a smart new-looking man's leather wallet, a square-cut jade dinner ring edged with small diamonds—how could Dorothea respond? What could these items possibly mean? "My treasure, Dorothea," Colin Asch said, lightly mocking "for *you.*"

The beautiful dinner ring, so large as to resemble costume jewelry, did look teasingly familiar to Dorothea; the other things meant nothing at all. She smiled uncertainly at Colin Asch as if this were a mere game: a riddle, perhaps. "But Colin, what are they? Whose are they?"

Still lightly mocking, Colin Asch said, "You know, Dorothea."

"But Colin, I—"

"Don't you?"

Dorothea Deverell, on the verge of exasperation, spread her fingers wide, helpless. "Colin, I'm afraid I don't. *I don't know.*"

Is there an authentic premonitory instinct, Dorothea Deverell would afterward wonder, or do we simply fill in the spaces of our ignorance retrospectively, claiming a superior wisdom where there was only—ignorance?

It was true, she had thought intermittently of young Colin Asch often that winter, and well into spring; she had brooded in her customarily inconclusive way upon certain actions of his, and certain enigmatic remarks ("Oh, you'd recognize me, Dorothea—you and I would know each other anywhere"), and had been haunted by, if not indeed frankly baffled by, certain postures and assumptions, granted even the profundity of her involvement with Charles Carpenter and with his grief and distress over his wife's death. (Weeks after the accidental drowning it was the rude shock of its initial pronouncement that lingered, still, in Dorothea Deverell's imagination, possessed of the nearly cryptesthetic power to arouse in her, at weak, unguarded moments, a paralyzing sense of guilt and shame.) Yet she would have to confess that she had not thought of Colin Asch in any exact, any *real,* relation to herself; she would have said that she did not think of the unique young man in any exact relation with anyone at all—not excluding Ginny Weidmann, his very blood kin. For surely there was something innocently transitory about him? For all the blond, muscular, sinewy *physicalness* of his person, something fleeting and insubstantial? To which the words "fickle" or "shallow" or "unreliable" or "uncontrolled" did not in all fairness apply?

How very strange Dorothea Deverell thought it, that, having expressed such childlike delight in his "position" at the Institute, Colin Asch had twice failed to show up for meetings in April; what news she had of him, from Ginny Weidmann, was scattered and vague. She had the impression of a life being rapidly lived, too rapidly, perhaps; but it was not *her* life, and she had no right, certainly she had not the requisite knowledge, to pass judgment. For, involved with Charles Carpenter as she was, and more in love with him than ever before, she simply did not have time to think about Colin Asch, still less to worry about him. Since that peculiar episode when, unbidden, the young man had dropped by Dorothea's house to show her those amazing photographs of himself as a model, she had heard very little of him, or from him: and had not sought him out. Maybe later, in another year, when she and Charles Carpenter were in some way settled, "established" . . . maybe at that time, if Charles were willing, she might befriend young Colin more attentively: invite him for dinner, include him in gatherings, help to advance and promote him. Until then, her own life and her own work claimed all her energies. And what was Colin Asch but a being *sui generis*, of no age precisely, speaking with no discernible American accent, possessed seemingly of no background, no personal history? "He is a will-o'-the-wisp," Dorothea Deverell decided, as if she were affixing a label to a work of art and having done with it.

She did not consider that in fact she had no clear idea of what a "will-o'-the-wisp" actually was; it was the lightness, the musicality of the term, that charmed her.

Now Colin Asch sat on her sofa, smiling, watching Dorothea Deverell with moist glittering eyes, informing her in a matter-of-fact voice that he had killed both Roger Krauss and Agnes Carpenter—and he'd done it for her. As her agent. In her name.

"Not that they didn't deserve it, Dorothea," Colin Asch added, with a derisive twist of his lips. "They did! Him especially! It was a *pleasure*, with him! The son of a bitch!"

And Dorothea, bathed in cold as if a glacial wind had penetrated the walls of her snug little stone house, simply stared at him, her mind blank with growing horror. "What—what did you say?" she several times asked in a whisper. She could not believe Colin Asch's words yet knew, as if a lock were clicking into place, that they must be true. She knew—yet could not believe. This so very kind so very generous so very warm and affectionate and sympathetic young man—a killer?

What had Charles Carpenter called him? A psychopath.

Yet Dorothea said faintly, blunderingly, "I—don't believe it. It isn't possible."

And Colin Asch said, as if reprovingly, "Look, Dorothea: there's nothing to discuss. I mean, like, what's there to *debate?* They weren't the first people I've killed and I doubt they'll be the last. You know what Shelley said of himself: 'I go my way like a sleepwalker. . . . I go until I am stopped and I never *am* stopped.' Sure! It's like that! If you cover your tracks, if you're reasonably careful and brainy—who's to catch you? The police don't know that much, they work with probabilities and not possibilities . . . *probabilities,* not *possibilities.* You supply them with some clues that fit together—with a baffle, some little story they can tell themselves—they fall for it every time; you know why?" He smiled so broadly at Dorothea, his lower face seemed nearly split in two. " 'Cause they're human! They want to believe that things add up, make sense, come neatly together. There's never any motive for any single thing Colin Asch does that anyone could calculate, which is why nobody will ever catch Colin Asch—nobody."

"But why—"

"These things I brought you, they're mementos, the ring especially—take it, try it on! Like I said, there's nothing for us to *debate;* it isn't a matter of *talk.*" Colin Asch kicked the ring in Dorothea's direction— it rolled along the carpet toward her chair. His action was the most wayward, abrupt, and unexpected that Dorothea Deverell had ever encountered in him; she couldn't help flinching. He said, as if confidentially, "The weird thing is, Dorothea—I mean this really makes you believe in destiny, karma—the thing is, I picked out that ring in five minutes, at Aunt Ginny's that night, y'know, when she made me join you people and sit at the table; there I was in your presence, Dorothea, without knowing *you*, and there I was looking at a woman's big fancy glamorous dinner ring, without knowing *her*, but sort of guessing I'd get that ring one day, one day I'd slip it into my pocket—Colin Asch restoring a little balance to the world. Go on, Dorothea: try it on.''

Dorothea was staring at the ring at her feet—a square-cut jade stone edged with small diamonds, in a white gold setting. It was exquisitely beautiful. She could not bear its lying like that on the floor; she picked it up, turned it in her trembling fingers. Yes, it was Agnes Carpenter's; she remembered it now. ''But how, Colin, did you get it?''

''Took it.''

''Yes, but how?''

''Out of her bureau. In the bedroom. A fancy little jewelry box with a lock that wasn't locked—the ring was the only thing I wanted.'' He sighed and squirmed about on the sofa, as if with irrepressible energy. ''Though Christ!—I could use the money.''

Dorothea swallowed. ''I mean, Colin,'' she said carefully, ''how did you get it? How did you get the opportunity? I don't understand: this is Agnes Carpenter's ring, and Agnes Carpenter is dead; she died by—''

''She didn't die: I killed her.''

''You—killed her?''

''I *told* you, Dorothea,'' Colin Asch said, making a snorting noise, bemused, dismayed, and slapping both hands against the sofa. ''I *told* you I killed her, and I killed the other one—who else was there to do it? Your boyfriend Carpenter? Like hell!''

''But I can't—''

''No need to look at me like that, Dorothea, it wasn't any special effort. I mean, it was *easy*—it's always been *easy*. What's so fucking hard is''—and here his voice dipped, and his face took on an expression of simple regret—"this sort of life here, that you have—this sort of daily life, *living* it, making sense of it as you go along or maybe not making any special sense of it but just—going along. *That's* hard. The other is *easy.*"

"You are telling me, Colin, that you actually—killed?"

"Sure! Why not? People get killed all the time, don't they—somebody's got to do it!" He laughed, as if he'd said something extravagant and witty. "Once I get the idea figured out it isn't difficult to execute it. Like, you know, making up your own movie or play in your head. Everything that exists in civilization, Dorothea," he said, tapping his forehead, "comes from in here—the human brain. Once you get the idea, the rest comes naturally. But the idea, first—that's the trick. That's genius."

Dorothea laid the jade ring carefully on the coffee table. The gold cuff links and the leather wallet remained where Colin Asch had deposited them. She was blinking rapidly, for her eyes were filling with tears of shock and disbelief. *Was* she in shock? Her hands and her feet had gone icy cold, the interior of her mouth extraordinarily dry; she feared that, if she got to her feet, she might faint; yet she had to get to her feet. She had to get away from Colin Asch—had to go for help.

But it was Colin who rose, fairly leaping to his feet. "I'm dying of thirst!" He went out into Dorothea's kitchen; she heard him open and shut the refrigerator door. Somehow, on tottering legs, she followed him, a terrible roaring in her ears, her vision nearly gone. "This is delicious—just what I need!" Colin said happily, drinking orange juice directly from the quart bottle. He stood, head back, legs spread, emptying the bottle.

Dorothea felt rather than saw the floor rise swiftly toward her; there was a sharp cracking blow against the side of her head. She'd lost consciousness for what could not have been more than a split second—then woke, lying on the dining room carpet, her head ringed with pain, while Colin Asch crouched over her. Repeatedly, he uttered her name, begged her to be all right. "Don't die, Dorothea! Don't *die!*" He ran into the kitchen to dampen a towel to press against her face. When she was sitting up and had more or less recovered, he said, repentantly, "It's my fault. I upset you, I guess. You're a sensitive woman—I should have known."

He helped her into the kitchen, where she sat, sat and stared at him: stunned, perplexed, rather blank. What had he been telling her? That he'd killed two people, or more? That he was a killer. He—her friend? Her friend Colin Asch? She thought, I must telephone the police. I must get help. It had not yet occurred to her that she was in the presence of a dangerous man.

Nor did he seem to her mad. He was pacing about the kitchen talking excitedly but lucidly, berating himself for his "insensitivity" and then, in the next breath, declaring that "it couldn't be helped"—Dorothea had to *know* because she had to *help him.* (But what was he expecting, Dorothea wondered. What did he want of her?) If his manner was extravagant, histrionic, hadn't it always been so? The brass clamp flashed in his ear as his eyes flashed, and his quick nervous smile; the heat that almost palpably radiated from him might have been mere high spirits, energy, the hyperkinesia of youth. Dorothea said, "You didn't really, Colin, did you? What you said—"

"Didn't really *what?*"

"—Agnes Carpenter, and Roger Krauss—"

"Yeah? What?"

"Didn't—*kill?*"

The very word stuck in Dorothea Deverell's throat.

Colin Asch regarded her with bemused eyes. She saw that his face was angular and lean, the bones of the cheeks, brows, and forehead far more prominent than she'd remembered. He had lost weight—too much weight. His face gleamed with perspiration like anger, and his striped sports shirt was soaked through beneath the arms. "What did you want me to say, Dorothea? No? Is that what you want to hear—no?"

"Just—tell me the truth."

"OK: the truth is yes."

"But—why?"

"I told you, Dorothea: for you."

"For me?"

"For *you*. But also, like, 'cause I wanted to—Colin Asch never does anything that isn't *ordained*."

"But I don't understand," Dorothea said gropingly. "You have come here today to tell me—"

"I've come here today to tell you that I'm not *happy* the way I deserve, that things are *fucked up,* that I need your *help,* Dorothea—your *advice* and *consolation!*" he said in a high plaintive voice. "I need some sign from you that things are all right. That, you know, things are—in place again."

"In place?"

"Like you said once about appetite, people doing what they have to do, like carnivores, and their victims—I forget the exact words; I have them written down—it was a way of explaining, it made sense. And you looked at me too like you knew me, you recognized me. And I recognized you."

He fell silent, contemplating Dorothea Deverell; Dorothea could only shut her eyes. She tried to comprehend: if Colin Asch were a murderer, and if he were confessing two of his crimes to her, did that mean that a murderer was confessing to her—to Dorothea

Deverell? And, if so, did that mean she must bear witness against him?

But I am his only friend, she thought.

She said, with more resolve than she felt, "But, Colin, you must know that I will have to inform the police. If what you say is true—"

"The police? You think so? Yeah?"

"—there seems to have been a terrible, tragic mis-understanding, and I—"

"Nobody's informing the police of anything, Dorothea," Colin Asch said matter-of-factly. "It's got nothing to do with them; they're completely at a distance. It's got nothing to do with Krauss and Mrs. Carpenter either, much—it's just between you and me. Which you knew all along."

"But—"

Colin shouted her down: *"Which you knew all along!"*

Dorothea flinched as he went to the telephone and knocked the receiver off the hook. In an instant he was enraged, out of control. "You're not telling the police and you're not telling anyone! I'd have to kill us both right now, right here, and I'm not fucking ready!"

After several seconds the telephone began to emit a series of harmless warning beeps; then went silent.

How silent, indeed, Sunday afternoons were, in the leafy cul-de-sac at the end of Marten Lane!

Dorothea thought, So that is his plan.

She thought, So Charles and I will never marry after all.

She'd begun to cry without quite knowing it. Colin Asch said sullenly, "We'd better go." When he went into the living room, to retrieve his duffel bag perhaps, Dorothea decided to make a run for it—thinking, in her desperation, she might go next door, scream at her neighbors to call the police—but of course Colin Asch easily caught her: she'd barely gotten out the side door, would have had to grope her way through the darkened garage to another, outer door. Hurt, fierce, incredulous, Colin Asch cried, "I knew it! *Now I can't trust you either!"*

His grip on Dorothea was surprisingly strong, practical, not in the least hesitant. Dorothea, struggling, weeping, felt his warm moist breath like a dog's against her face and smelled the harsh acrid odor of his perspiration. For the first time the fact of the young man's physical self, his sexuality, struck her.

"We'd better go," he said. "Before Carpenter comes. 'Cause I *am* ready for him."

Seemingly out of nowhere Colin Asch had drawn a pistol. It had a long smooth barrel and a handsome carved wooden handle, like a work of art.

So, at 4:50 P.M. of Sunday, May 8, began what would be Dorothea Deverell's nearly one hundred hours of terror: though "terror" as such, with its intense, visceral, adrenaline-charged distress, could hardly be sustained for so prolonged a period of time. Afterward, contemplating the wild, doomed flight on which Colin Asch took her, Dorothea would recall feeling alternately resigned and fatalistic as if, in a sense, she were already dead and merely enacting a prescribed role; and alternately hopeful, even optimistic—as, perhaps, condemned prisoners feel, anticipating the reprieve they know cannot come.

Before they left Dorothea Deverell's house, Colin Asch forced her to go upstairs to her bedroom so that she could change her clothes; it was his idea that they would be less readily identified if they looked like two men. That was the first baffle, he said. (Dorothea believed the word was "baffle" but did not inquire.) So, trembling, biting her lip to keep from crying, Dorothea Deverell, her captor close by, changed from the

attractive clothes she had so deliberately put on earlier
that day—a beige pleated skirt in light wool, a hand-
decorated wool-and-cotton sweater—into navy blue
rayon slacks, and an old gardening shirt, and an old
sweater. Colin Asch insisted that she pin up her hair
and wear a hat, and to this too Dorothea acquiesced,
though the only suitable hat was a very old mothball-
reeking green angora cap she'd worn one winter to
keep her ears warm and forgot she still owned. Take
whatever you need, Colin Asch instructed, having gallantly located one of Dorothea's suitcases and holding
it open for her—underclothes, socks, another shirt and
another sweater, toiletries—then he led her into her
study where he insisted she bring along some books
and "things you're working on—you might not be back
for a long time." In the kitchen he loaded several grocery bags with food from Dorothea's cupboards and
refrigerator, whistling as he did so, exclaiming to himself, not unlike a boy about to embark upon an out-
door adventure. How innocent he seems, Dorothea
thought, in wonderment. The long-barreled pistol was
stuck, with rakish insouciance, in his belt.

"OK! Great! Let's go!" he said.

Not the black Porsche but another automobile entirely awaited them in Dorothea Deverell's driveway
(later to be identified as Susannah Hunt's 1988 Audi,
though outfitted with license plates from the Porsche:
Mrs. Hunt would be found dead, strangled, in her bed
in her Normandy Court condominium), its rear seat
and trunk partly filled with Colin Asch's things; but
there was space for Dorothea's too. Handing her the
keys Colin told her she should be the first to drive. "It
will be more practical for me to drive after dark." He
spoke with a husbandly solicitude.

And, later, when he took over the wheel for a long
siege of driving—by that time they were well into New
Hampshire, on northwest-bound Route 89—he ex-

tracted from Dorothea the promise that she would not try to escape from the car by doing anything crazy or reckless like opening her door while they were in motion, nor would she make signals at people in other cars; if she involved others, Colin warned her, he'd be forced to shoot them dead: "You'd be signing their death warrants, Dorothea."

So she obeyed. Rather like a zombie, or a robot.

Thinking repeatedly, this can't be happening . . . such things do not happen to people like us.

It seemed like a very long time before they stopped for what remained of the night. Somewhere, Dorothea had the groggy idea, in upstate New York, in a desolate wooded area off the expressway. Colin Asch, unable to stay awake any longer, positioned himself to sleep with his arm around Dorothea's shoulders and his head resting hard against hers, so that he would be immediately wakened if she tried to slip free. That way, there was no escaping him, even in sleep. Even in the fitful, twitchy, hallucinatory bouts of sleep to which each succumbed.

"Won't you please reconsider?" Dorothea Deverell was not quite begging but speaking quietly, practicably. "I'm sure that allowances might be made if you haven't been well, if you've been"—she hesitated to say the word "hospitalized"; now driving the Audi, her eyes aching with the light as if she'd been ill, she scarcely dared glance over at Colin Asch, her captor—"not *well*. I mean, if you have a history of—of episodes."

Colin Asch, arms folded, lying back in the passenger's seat with his head against the window in a sullen sort of pose, merely grunted.

"I would tell them how considerate you've been of me," Dorothea said carefully, wetting her lips, "how you haven't"—and again she hesitated, not wanting to say the word "hurt"—"haven't threatened me" —though this was not quite true: he'd threatened her after all. In a desperate little plea she concluded, "But you're so intelligent, Colin! You must know the police will pick us up soon!"

"A lot of things can happen, Dorothea, before that happens."

They stopped for gas. They stopped at a truckers' restaurant where Colin, pistol inside his shirt, bought hot food, coffee. They stopped on a lookout point—a "scenic site"—in the Adirondack Mountains not many miles from the Canadian border. Dorothea's mind worked swiftly and with seeming proficiency but to no purpose. She would signal someone (at a gas station, at a restaurant, beside the road, in another car) to get help; she would escape from her captor (perhaps wrestling with him for the gun); she would call attention to them, or to the car, in some way: the same few thoughts repeating endlessly, to no purpose. She thought of Charles Carpenter, who had by now come to her house and found it empty—her car still in the garage but some of her clothes and possessions missing, food missing from the kitchen. Would he know? But how would he know? And when he called the police how would they know? Several times she broke down, sobbing, near-hysterical, and Colin Asch said, rubbing his own eyes roughly with a fist, "Just don't give *in*, for Christ's sake."

As if, Dorothea thought, amazed, their predicaments were identical; they were united in their desperation to escape.

It had been Colin Asch's bold intention to cross the Canadian border into Quebec, but each time they approached the customs and immigration checkpoints— at Trout River and Hogansburg, in New York, and at Derby Line, Vermont—he changed his mind; wisely, no doubt, for by this time there must be a police alert

out for them, or for their car. (Dorothea did not know
that Susannah Hunt was dead but Colin had told her
that the car was registered in Mrs. Hunt's name.)
On this protracted giddy headachy second day of flight
they drove in wayward looping circles, so far as Dorothea could judge, mainly along narrow mountain
roads, where dusk came prematurely and brought a
feathery barrage of snowflakes. "This is madness,
Colin," Dorothea said. "We simply can't keep this
up."

Colin Asch yawned brutally and said, "You want to
stop, then? You're ready?"

At least, she thought, Charles has been spared.

But Colin Asch's mood was rather more nervous,
petulant, and distracted than murderous; he drove
along ever-narrowing roads, turning up forks, recon-
sidering, backing out again, as if guided by instinct;
bringing them at last to a deserted lakeside area of
cottages and lodges, Glace Lake the name. Was this
near the place where his parents died? Dorothea wondered.

At the far end of a rutted lane was a lodge of weath-
erized logs in mock-Swiss chalet style; a shingle above
its front door announced LAND'S END. As Dorothea
Deverell, reeling with exhaustion, stepped out into the
freezing air, it struck her as the most bitter sort of
irony that she might very well die here.

Colin Asch adroitly forced a door at the rear of the
house and let himself in and came to the front door,
where, not having moved an inch, Dorothea awaited
him. She'd begun to cough helplessly. She was on the
verge of illness: a raw burning ache had established
itself in her throat, and she felt the early symptoms of
bronchitis. Almost shyly, apologetically, Colin said,
"OK, Dorothea, come inside! I'll unload the car.
Maybe you can find a hurricane lamp or something."

"Yes," Dorothea said tonelessly.

She came stumblingly inside the unfamiliar house where the long-confined air, smelling of dirt and damp, was as cold as outside. A cruel parody of a homecoming, she thought. A parody of a honeymoon.

Fearing a caretaker at Glace Lake, Colin hid the car somewhere to the rear of the house and shrouded the windows; smoke from the chimney was unavoidable— he had to start a fire in the fireplace. (The gas stove in the kitchen was disconnected; the electricity was turned off.) Clumsily, her fingers stiff, Dorothea prepared a makeshift sort of meal for them, using the fireplace. It was sobering, how ferociously hungry each of them was—no matter the metallic taste of the soup, heated in a stained saucepan, or the bread's staleness. They devoured hunks of cheese, slices of turkey breast, raw carrots. Like animals, Dorothea thought, feeding.

Then she slept close beside the fireplace, or tried to, in a kind of delirium: her teeth chattering with cold, misery, simple dread of what was to come; waking to spasms of coughing and pain in her throat and chest. Her captor was too excited to sleep—he'd boasted that he needed no more than three or four hours of sleep for every twenty-four—he spent much of the night (Dorothea gathered) prowling about the house with a flashlight; then, near dawn, she woke with a start to a pressure on her leg—and there was Colin Asch, curled up innocent as a child, or a large dog, heavily asleep on the floor close by her with his face pressed against the calf of her right leg. His pale beard glinted like silver, his mouth was slack, his breath moist and gurgling. . . . Dorothea hugged herself in the frowsty-smelling blanket Colin Asch had located for her in one of the closets and stared at her captor, her friend, her former friend: whom after all she had never known. Colin Asch was mad, but what *was* "mad"? That the young man had evidently killed two quite innocent people, and for a purpose he could not explain; that he felt not the slightest twinge of remorse, or, indeed, full consciousness of his actions; that he fervently believed Dorothea Deverell's life and fate were inextricably bound up with his own: these were mere facts that lay upon the surface of his being like the fact that he had blond hair, brown eyes, a strong-boned angular face. Such facts described but did not define him.

In the morning a chill glowering sunshine penetrated the coverings Colin had affixed over the windows; with the return of day, or daylight, a sense of ever deeper malaise overtook Dorothea Deverell. As, noisy, ebullient, whistling to himself in a display of cheery high spirits, Colin prepared breakfast, Dorothea made little effort to help; she was sick and would be getting sicker: her limbs stiff, tears dried in her eyes. She could not imagine what she looked like, what desperation flickered feebly in her face; nor did she care. She wondered why, during the night, she had not taken advantage of the darkness and fled. . . . Surely Colin Asch would not shoot her in the back? Surely that was not to be her fate at his hands?

That day, intermittently, when she dared, Dorothea tried to engage Colin Asch in conversation, frankly pleaded with him. What did he hope to accomplish, hiding out here in the mountains? How long could they endure it? What did he intend to do next—or if they were discovered? Colin Asch told her airily that he was sorry things had turned out exactly as they had. "But, Dorothea, after all, none of this is my *fault.*" In a tone of mild reproach he told her that he would have continued on his way, back in November, pursuing another phase of his life, if it hadn't been for her—"Like there was a promise you made to me, Dorothea. That first night."

"Promise? I don't understand."

"Yes, Dorothea. You do."

Colin removed the coverings from the windows, and opened the rear door of the house, but did not leave the house at all; nor did he allow Dorothea to do so. He was jumpy, apprehensive, breaking off in the middle of a sentence to cock his head and listen: was it a loon on the lake? an airplane passing high overhead? a chain saw in the distance? a scrambling, as of squirrels, in the eaves? He fingered the pistol, checked the bullets in the revolving cylinder, laid the barrel alongside his nose as if in a parody of contemplation, strode about with the gun loosely stuck in his belt. Dorothea eyed it, thinking: Am I required to try to take it from him and use it against him? Is that expected of me? There was no vision of Dorothea Deverell, no extravagant cinematic daydream, in which, for even a fleeting moment, she could imagine such an act: she no more wanted to shoot Colin Asch than she wanted to be shot by him.

Colin squatted on his heels in front of a ramshackle bookshelf, pulling out and leafing idly through old copies of *National Geographic, Audubon, Arizona Highways*. There were United States and world atlases; an incomplete set of *Collier's Encyclopedia*. He told Dorothea in a dreamy voice that he'd always been fascinated by maps and travel. Maybe he was Marco Polo, reincarnated! "If I had my life to relive that's all I would do, I think—get in motion, and stay in motion—let momentum carry me. And you could do the same, Dorothea! Evil begins with stopping: with entrophy."

From time to time during that long hallucinatory day and the next, Dorothea was uneasily aware of Colin Asch regarding her in silence; she perceived, with a despondent heart, that he was contemplating her death. Hers, and perhaps his own: murder and suicide. Was that not romantic? Was that not the logical end to their story? As if merely conversationally, Colin Asch said, "My book here—I'm going to be writing in it soon. I have to think what I mean to say 'cause there isn't a lot of time, you know? You could write in it too, if you wanted. I mean at the end. The last pages."

"Is it a journal?" Dorothea asked.

"It's my life. In words."

The notebook was oversized and substantial, with badly worn blue-gray covers: a kind of account book, or ledger. Colin was not precisely offering it to Dorothea (who did not in any case want to touch it), but he leafed through it in such a way that she could see some of the pages: tight, condensed passages of script, lines that were presumably poetry, sections meticulously crossed out in bands of black ink. Stroking the pale stubble on his jaws he said dreamily, "What I want to do is bring it up to date. Up to the present hour. From a perspective, you know, of great distance. Like God looking down." Dorothea murmured a vague soft assent but drew no nearer. "You couldn't read it, actually, most of the pages," Colin said apologetically. "It's in code."

"Ah, yes, I see—code," Dorothea said.

"To keep the fuckers from sticking their noses in my business," Colin said, smiling bitterly. "After my death."

The interior of the lodge was furnished in a spare yet slapdash manner, the large main room in particular: there were dusty old woven "Navajo" rugs laid upon the floor, and mismatched stained furniture, and lamps with torn shades, but, here and there, substantial and attractive items like the Shaker-style rocking chair in which Dorothea sat and the long narrow churchly-looking table at which Colin Asch sat for hours, writing in his notebook, alternately rapidly, as if he were inspired, and then very slowly. For long dreamy periods he simply gazed out the window (he was seated in such a position as to have a clear view of the lane, and the lake) or in Dorothea's direction. We are a grotesque parody of domesticity, Dorothea thought, but of what sort of domesticity *is* the parody?

She seemed to know that, if she survived, she would remember this interlude for the remainder of her life: not the episodes of confusing action and violence (for she understood that violence was unavoidable) but this protracted and seemingly idyllic scene in which, only a few yards away, her young blond captor Colin Asch sat brooding over his notebook like an unusually intense schoolboy immersed in his lesson. Outside the day was slowly warming; the air smelled wetly of spring and of plenitude. In the Scotch pines that ringed the house, jays called to one another in urgent, throaty, liquid notes, a spring song that, to Dorothea's ear, had always the sound of bubbles musically ascending.

Colin Asch read to Dorothea Deverell a stanza of a poem of Shelley's he had transcribed, he said, eleven years before, "Never guessing how I'd be reading it to *you, today!*" It was not a stanza Dorothea immediately recognized, nor could she in all honesty have attributed it to Shelley, for she had neither read nor thought of Shelley's poetry in months.

" 'The everlasting universe of things
  Flows through the mind, and rolls its rapid waves,
  Now dark—now glittering—now reflecting
     gloom—
  Now lending splendor, where from secret springs
  The source of human thought its tribute brings—' "

Colin Asch's voice trailed off as if this were not in fact the end of the stanza but a weariness had passed over him suddenly, touching Dorothea Deverell as well. And outside, in the pines, the jays continued to sing.

* * *

In all there would be four days of captivity; it would
end, and end abruptly, in the late afternoon of May 11.
But almost immediately Dorothea Deverell began
to lose her sense of time and of spatial distance, as
one whose proprioceptive instinct is dislodged loses
all sense of the body's unique and indefinable territo-
riality. Or as the web of memory itself is altered by
the mildest of brain lesions.

It seemed to her in her weakened emotional state
that Charles Carpenter's love should have had a greater
power to protect her. But it was distant, and its force
hourly ebbing. She thought, I am alone.

Except for my captor.

She was sick: wrapped in her frowsy blanket though
it was midday and May. From childhood she'd had
respiratory illnesses of varying degrees of severity, and
certain symptoms frightened her, for they might signal
a headlong plunge into fevers, wracking chills, convulsive coughing spells. Her lungs were congesting,
and her chest felt as if an invisible band were slowly
tightening around it. Her eyes watered with tears of
hurt and indignation.

But she was watching (and could not help but admire) Colin Asch on the floor in front of the fireplace
doing push-ups—how rapidly!—how like a slightly
frenzied machine!—as the little blue vein defined itself
ever more palpably in his forehead and his face grew
visibly hotter, ruddier. He counted ninety before stopping. And then he did sit-ups: fingers linked at the
nape of his neck, elbows expertly swung around to
touch his knees in an alternating pattern. And then—
as if his mad energy could in no other way be contained—he jumped up and, panting, glistening with
sweat, chinned himself on the doorframe. Though he
was so thin that his ribs showed through his damp

T-shirt, the muscles of his shoulders, arms, and back appeared hard and prominent. ". . . twenty-eight, twenty-nine, *thirty!*"

Performing for Dorothea Deverell but never so much as casting a single glance in her direction.

In plain view, atop the table, lay the long-barreled revolver.

Dorothea, eyeing it, thought, *I must make the effort.* She calculated there were six feet separating her and the gun; and that, when Colin was distracted, she need only throw off the blanket, lunge forward, snatch it up in both hands. . . . She would turn it against her captor and stammer out an entreaty, or a threat: *I will pull the trigger if you don't obey me!* But hallucinatory images assailed her of Colin Asch simply wrenching the gun from her grasp or, worse yet, the gun firing by accident, a bullet tearing through Colin Asch's chest or face.

"You could have taken the gun any time you wanted, Dorothea," Colin Asch said, as, at dusk, they ate one of their crudely improvised meals. "But you didn't. You could have shot me down dead and you'd never have been charged for a thing, and that means you don't want to go back any more than I do."

Dorothea said quietly, "That isn't true."

Colin said, "Yeah, it's true."

Dorothea said, "Colin, you must know—it isn't true."

"It *is.*"

So with the stubborn purposelessness of true intimacy, they quarreled; until finally Dorothea turned away, choking with indignation, hurt, dismay. She seemed to recall how, in childhood too, the salt taste of tears was the very taste of humiliation.

"If you're wondering, the way I did it was I got her drunker than she was, and fed her some Valium from her medicine cabinet, and held her head under the water till she stopped breathing. She didn't feel a thing!—just like I promised her. Not like that son of a bitch Krauss,'' Colin Asch said with a spitting gesture. ''I wanted him to feel it all the way, and he did.''

It must have been very late. Dorothea's watch had stopped running. Colin Asch was feeding, page by single page, the book he called his ''blue ledger'' into the fire. Dorothea did not want to ask why.

''It's a weird thing,'' he said almost conversationally, ignoring the look of revulsion on Dorothea's face, ''how good you feel doing something you know is right. Like, after all, there're so few times in your life you really know you're standing in exactly the right place at the right time. Like you're not even yourself any longer but an agent of history. Of Death.''

Dorothea shuddered, and said, ''I should think it would be better to be an agent of life.''

''When I kill someone I am the agent of Death,'' Colin Asch said slowly. He was detaching pages from the front of the notebook, ripping them carefully from the binding: he'd rekindled the fire, and it burned with a disconcerting Currier & Ives cheeriness. The lighted warmth, cast upward on Colin Asch's angular, pale face, gave his cheeks a look of boyish ruddy health. ''When it's done it's done forever. *And no one can controvert it.* Think of that! Try to realize that, Dorothea! When you put something in the world, or love something in the world, or, say, you yourself are in the world, it's all fucking vulnerable—it can end at any minute. But the agent of Death—that's different.'' His voice rose tremulously. He grinned into the firelight. ''Yeah. *That's* different.''

''You're talking simply about destroying things, taking life away—''

''You don't know what I'm talking about, Dorothea," Colin Asch said, " 'cause you've never done what I have done. And if you had, you'd know."

"But—"

"If you had, you'd know."

Dorothea began sobbing, and the sobbing turned into a spasm of coughing that left her throat raw. Earlier that day Colin had expressed concern for her and murmured something vague about taking her to a doctor or to an emergency room. "Or maybe I could go by myself to some drugstore and get you penicillin." In a nervous reflexive gesture he'd checked the pistol another time for bullets, swinging the cartridge holder out. Dorothea had wondered how he'd known her bronchial condition required penicillin but she said nothing about it, and in any case Colin seemed to have forgotten within the hour.

Now he said, as if talking to himself, "You don't want to go back any more than I do. I know. It's a matter of honor and integrity—think of Christopher Columbus carried back to Spain in chains! The fuckers! What they want is to make people like us grovel, beg for mercy. But why the fuck should we? It's a question of freedom. It's power—doing things the way you want them done, becoming the agent of your own life. And death."

Dorothea made an effort to control herself. "But I don't want to die," she said.

"When I was twelve, and my parents died, there was this weird force drawing us off the bridge and through the railing—into the water—I could *feel* it, almost," Colin said, beginning to speak in an agitated voice, "but I thought—you know how you do at that age—I thought I could fight it, *controvert it!* There I was, diving into the water, swimming down, trying to get the car doors open, trying to pull them out—my mother, my father, first the one then the other then first one again then the other—like there was some

kind of crazy thing in me too so that after a while I
wasn't even thinking, didn't have any volition, or will;
it wasn't Colin Asch but just my body, my muscles.
But the fact was I failed. The lesson I was meant to
learn was—I failed. Life goes in one direction only,
like a river flowing or like gravity—you can't controvert it.''

Deeply moved, having dreaded another sort of nar-
ration entirely, Dorothea said, "But you were very
brave, Colin! And so young. . . .''

Colin shook his head violently. "There was nothing
brave about it; I don't know what 'brave' is. It was
just this asshole kid trying to do something he wasn't
meant to do so a lesson could be taught about it. Life
goes in one direction only.''

"Ah, Colin, surely not!''

He tore off another page and dropped it into the fire.
Dorothea had a glimpse of a surface of neat block
letters in a variety of shades of ink; there were tiny
drawings too, or doodlings, in the margin; she would
have liked, in that instant, to snatch the page out of
the fire and save it. But it burst into flame and van-
ished.

"Did that happen anywhere near here?'' Dorothea
asked. "Your parents' accident?''

"No. Nowhere near here,'' Colin Asch said. "Hundreds of miles to the south.''

Dorothea Deverell did not believe she was asleep but
there, unaccountably, was her mother . . . her young
mother with loose flying hair and dark smooth golden
skin . . . striding through a meadow of tall grass,
shading her eyes and calling *Dorothea! Dorothea!* A
scattering of tiny yellow butterflies surrounded her.
The game was that Dorothea's mother could not detect

the giggling little girl crouched hiding in the grass so Dorothea leaped up to surprise her, feeling a wave of joy so intense it turned to pain in her throat . . . and then she was coughing violently, and awake, returned confusedly to herself, sitting in a patch of wan sunlight in an opened doorway strange to her in a place strange to her and someone was approaching, speaking to her in a peremptory, suspicious voice: "Hey, what the hell are you doing here, lady?"

A burly old man in soiled overalls and a railway worker's cap, with a flushed bewhiskered face and small narrowed eyes: the caretaker for Glace Lake?

And some thirty feet away, behind him, beside a pickup truck parked in the lane, stood a teen-aged boy with what appeared to be a rifle slung loosely in the crook of his arm.

Dorothea waved at the old man to come no nearer, trying to warn him, her voice raw, cracked. "Get away! Don't speak to me! There's danger!"

But the old man took no heed; excitable and emboldened, having sized up Dorothea Deverell as no one he need fear, he said loudly, belligerently, "Just what the bejesus are you doing here, lady? This is private property—don't you know?"

At this point two events happened with near-simultaneity: the boy by the pickup truck shouted out something to the old man Dorothea could not quite hear (except for the word "Grandpa," which she would retain for a long time), and, easing up noiselessly behind her, as if, these many hours in "Land's End," he had primed himself for this very moment, Colin Asch gracefully leaned over Dorothea's head in the doorway, and aimed the pistol at the old man's chest, and fired. Dorothea screamed as the old man spun partway around and fell; Colin leaped to the walk crying "Fucker! That'll teach you! I'll kill you all!" He sighted the boy in the lane but the boy turned to run; Colin pursued him and fired a single shot but almost immediately returned, cursing, infuriated, as Dorothea knelt beside the dying old man whose chest was already soaked in blood and whose face had gone, with terrifying swiftness, a sickly ashen gray. "A doctor—call a doctor! Oh, Colin—an ambulance!" Dorothea said.

Colin Asch stood over his victim and almost idly aimed the pistol again, at the old man's forehead.

"Here's your doctor, you old fart. *Didn't I warn you all!*"

And then it was the end, or nearly.

Dorothea found herself cringing in a corner of the kitchen, then in the tiny lavatory adjacent to the kitchen, sobbing hysterically, as Colin Asch, enraged, incredulous, stomped from room to room, from window to window, shoving furniture into place to establish what reports of the siege would subsequently call a "barricade," cursing, talking loudly to himself and to Dorothea, whom he berated for having been discovered and for having forced him to shoot the old man without adequate preparation. First, Colin had had the idea that they must flee, in the car, but he'd immediately changed his mind, reasoning that "they" would be waiting for him since the road led in only one fucking direction thus they'd have him trapped like a sitting duck; they'd set up a roadblock or wait in ambush; the only strategy was to stay where they were and see how long they could hold out—"Fucking Christ I've already wasted three bullets!"

Banging on the lavatory door with such violence that the feeble lock sprang open he shouted at Dorothea, "It's all happening too fucking fast! I'm not ready! *You're* not ready!"

And indeed from this hour everything happened with dreamlike rapidity and logic, as if the unnatural stasis of many hours were breaking, pent up and malevolent, about their heads. There came to Dorothea's ears, within minutes it seemed, the sound of a police or ambulance siren, and a second siren, and a man's voice, garishly amplified through a bullhorn, shouting instructions to "you!—inside that house!"; the sound of other voices; and Colin Asch's at first unrecognizable shouting (so raw, so despairing and *young*) from one of the barricaded windows—he was armed, he said, and he had a hostage. And there was the deafening sound of gunfire, and breaking cascading glass. The image of Charles Carpenter's face passed swiftly through Dorothea's vision, but it was a face of studied calm, remoteness. He knows nothing of me, she thought. It was all a dream.

For the duration of the siege—three and a half hours in all, though most of that time was spent in shouted instructions, commands, repartee of a kind—Dorothea Deverell remained where she had crawled to hide, shivering with a hot rank animal fear and gradually passing beyond panic and into a stage very like catatonic bliss: as if, in this nearly sculptural mimicry of death, she might magically be spared death.

Yet even then, amid the chaos of men's voices, random and seemingly theatrical displays of gunfire, and the outraged heavy footsteps of her abductor as he charged past her hiding place to commandeer one or another window (it would have been held grievously against him by the county sheriff and his deputies, had he survived, that Colin Asch had given them so pointlessly difficult a time in "rescuing" the fallen old man whom they could not have known with certainty was dead)—even then, in the very cynosure of madness, Dorothea Deverell would have found it exceedingly difficult to believe that Colin Asch who so admired her and was her friend truly wished her harm.

"He would *not*—would he?"

But at last Colin Asch came for her, and presented her briefly at a window, to prove, since proof had been demanded, that his "hostage" still lived; then he walked briskly away into a room at the rear of the lodge, presumably the safest, most barricaded of the rooms, a bedroom with a fieldstone fireplace in which, so very unexpectedly, a fire was burning—for Colin was occupied in tearing pages from his mysterious blue notebook and feeding them to the fire, and in this he wanted Dorothea's help. Repeatedly he said, with jaw-gripping fury, that he wasn't ready! wasn't ready!

Finally he threw what remained of the notebook into the flames and watched it ride their crest for a long moment, and that was that.

He had then, in his right hand, a long smartly gleaming knife at which Dorothea stared without recognition; staring too at Colin Asch's face—why had she never noticed it before, that thin sickle-shaped scar over his left eye? His mouth moved but she could not make out the urgent words. There was too much that was urgent, that was loud and jarring and unceremonious, for her to absorb. Colin Asch was telling her what must be done since there was no escape and no going back. "All that's finished now."

He pressed the knife into her fingers and closed his strong fingers over hers, saying, "Like this," and Dorothea was uncomprehending but not at first resistant for was this young man not her protector?—but when the edge of the blade touched her throat Dorothea screamed and pushed away.

So Colin had to forcibly reposition her—by now the two of them were squatting beside the fireplace and Dorothea's back was close against the wall—and press the knife into her fingers another time, saying, in a pleading, accusatory voice: "But it's time! Don't make me do it to you alone!"

"No—let me go!" Dorothea cried.

And Colin said, as if reasonably, bringing the blade up against her throat, harder this time, "We love each other, Dorothea—we haven't had to say so."

And Dorothea said, "I don't love you well enough to die with you!"—struggling against the young man with a reserve of strength she could not have known she possessed. She succeeded in prying the knife from Colin's fingers, using her nails to lacerate the backs of his hands and his face. "Let me go! Let me go! Let me go!" she screamed. In the startling sweaty intimacy of their near embrace she sensed in him an absolute surprise—consternation—as if he could not believe that Dorothea Deverell would resist this death ceremony, or would resist with such hysteria.

The knife clattered to the floor—but Dorothea's strength, having flared up, now died away; a moment's struggle had consumed it. Colin snatched up the knife and held it as if threateningly against his own throat, saying, hurt, reproachful, "Dorothea? Don't you want to? Don't you love me? You'll let me do it alone?"

"Don't."

"You'll let me do it alone?"

Regarding Dorothea Deverell intently yet calmly, as if he were staring into a mirror at his own reflection, Colin Asch brought the end of the blade against his throat, against an artery he'd groped to find with seemingly practiced fingers. In the instant in which he brought the blade powerfully downward and slantwise against his throat his eyes became entirely black, all pupil, as if with an unspeakable pleasure. Dorothea screamed for him not to do it, shutting her eyes, steeling herself against the warm splash of arterial blood that would explode upon her and mark her for life. For of course it was too late.

13

"**D**orothea?—where are you?"
Too much light.

EPILOGUE

They were not yet married but were
shortly to be so, on the last Saturday in September—
the very eve, coincidentally, of Dorothea Deverell's
fortieth birthday; which would subsequently prove to
be the happiest birthday of her adult life. But for
months, on the weekends, they had been house-
hunting, looking for the perfect house: the house that
would somehow erase, or at any rate counter, their
memories of the past. In secret they hoped for a house
that might combine the most prized qualities of the
houses they were leaving while suggesting, publicly,
neither house—for Dorothea Deverell and Charles
Carpenter, as lovers, were duly guilt-ridden and supposed they would forever remain so, in a luxury of
self-recrimination no amount of penance could ab-
solve.

Many have sacrificed, Dorothea thought, who dare
not give themselves in love. *That* prim virtue, at least,
she would be spared.

The house they had almost definitely decided to buy,
in an older residential area of Lathrup Farms near the
Brannon Institute, was, finally, not perfect, but they
were keen to buy it just the same—a small white brick-
and-stucco with Greek Revival features, tall slender
fluted columns, an elegant portico, tall windows; an

interior that, in its current unfurnished state at least, with high ceilings, white walls, and gleaming hardwood floors, suggested the austerity of a Dutch interior out of Vermeer—a tabula rasa of a kind that cast an immediate, potent charm over them both. Walking through the house on her initial visit, Dorothea Deverell had squeezed Charles Carpenter's arm in a fearful sort of delight. Yes! Here! This is it! We are home! She would retain the house's quality of austerity, a wonderfully light-flooded sharp-angled purity; but there would be hanging plants, and richly colored carpets, and interesting but not obtrusive contemporary furniture. She had not the slightest intention of relocating her charmingly mismatched things in a new setting: she would sell some of them and give the rest away to Goodwill. Like Charles Carpenter she wanted most desperately to make a fresh start on neutral territory. After all, neither was lacking in funds.

The sale of Dorothea's house had brought her unexpected revenue: as if by magic the property had quadrupled in value during the nine years Dorothea had owned it. And Charles Carpenter's Fairway Drive house had sold for much more. And there was his late wife's estate as well—estimated, even after inheritance taxes, at more than $2 million. For Agnes Carpenter, though having filed for divorce from Charles, had not yet cut him out of her will; her husband remained her chief beneficiary.

When first told this astonishing news Dorothea Deverell had felt a pang of chagrin, a sense of sisterly hurt, for Agnes' sake. "It does seem so unfair for her, somehow," she told Charles Carpenter. "So much the sort of thing that, in her ironic cast of mind, she might have anticipated."

"But only in essence," Charles said. "If she'd truly anticipated it she would have cut me out at once."

"Still," Dorothea said, "it seems unfair."

"But why, Dorothea? If *I* had died when Agnes had died, if that madman had killed me instead, *she* would have inherited everything," Charles said reasonably. "It hadn't crossed my mind to cut her out of my will, so long as she was my wife."

Thinking of these things—even as she'd resolved not to think, still less to brood over them—Dorothea Deverell drove to the beautiful white house on L'Arve Place one afternoon in early September: twenty-two days, to be specific, before the wedding. She had picked up a key from the real estate agency; she wanted to make another final visit to the house (she'd already made several "final" visits) before she and Charles signed the purchase papers. The house loomed in their imaginations with the monumentality of an Egyptian pyramid, nearly!—they joked that buying it together seemed a more daunting step somehow than getting married.

It was past 5:30 P.M. when Dorothea arrived and let herself into the house by way of the front door; Charles was to meet her there as close to that time as he could manage. But she liked it that she'd arrived before him; she walked through the beautifully empty rooms breathing in with gratitude the ineffable odor of vacancy. . . . There were no mirrors remaining on any of the walls and no casual reflecting surfaces. What pleasure, Dorothea thought, to be so totally *alone:* not even one's own face to intrude.

Though, these days, Dorothea Deverell was looking extremely attractive; her skin plumped out slightly with health, and less pale than it had been; her eyes clear, if frequently bemused; her hair richly dark and glossy, its several strands of gray, silvery-gray, and white hairs quite distinctive. Since the terrible events of the previous spring she had become less fretful over trivialities, less impatient, demanding, and critical of herself.

It was a quality of middle age, she supposed, but not of middle age exclusively. The persistent narrating voice of thirty-odd years, forever detached, clinical, judgmental, and subtly disappointed in Dorothea Deverell's performance, whatever that performance was, had been, during her convalescence, replaced by other, more benign and forgiving and even encouraging voices. These were to be quite explicitly traced to their sources: the excellent doctor who had attended her in the hospital (Dorothea had been there for three weeks); her warm and unfailingly supportive circle of friends; her associates at the Institute; Charles Carpenter above all. As a hospital patient Dorothea Deverell had learned the virtues of passivity and obedience in small things; she had pleased others simply by regaining her health. She had pleased herself too by recovering sufficiently to return to work on the first Monday in June and to take up quarters in Mr. Morland's old office.

There had been a good deal of disagreeable, even sensational, attention focused upon Dorothea Deverell, of course, but Charles Carpenter had shielded her from most of it. No media interviews, no strangers knocking at her door. He had not shown her the newspaper accounts of the abduction and its aftermath, nor had Dorothea asked to see them. It would have given her no pleasure to see Colin Asch's photographs in the newspaper; the less so, since, by way of an incidental remark of Jacqueline's, she gathered that some of the modeling shots had been used.

But the police had been very nice, very courteous, patient and undemanding in their questions. There were the three Boston-area killings credited to Colin Asch, and the killing at Glace Lake, and it seemed there were others in other states, or their likelihood; but the evidence was inconclusive. Dorothea told the police, and retold them, all she knew of Colin Asch or could honestly recall. By way of her experience as

a "witness" she came to understand why, in criminal
cases, reports of eyewitnesses are notoriously unreliable: what the witness believes to be clear remembering is in fact fabricating, filling in the gaps,
misremembering, and what is "remembered" becomes subsequently this misremembering, ever more
emphatically reiterated. The precise events of the abduction—for "abduction" was the public, the inevitable word—had begun to fade in Dorothea's memory
almost immediately afterward, as our dreams so
quickly and teasingly fade even as we labor to recall
them; her physical collapse had surely exacerbated the
emotional trauma (the bronchial condition had become lobar pneumonia by the time she was taken to a
hospital in Massena, New York, following the siege at
Glace Lake), thus her memory was further confused
by delirium, feverish bad dreams. Extreme illness frequently mimics psychosis, in which the cacophonous
images of the unconscious fly loose: Dorothea Deverell was so sick as to have conflated, to her shame
and distress, the deaths of the mass murderer Colin
Asch and her young husband Michel Deverell . . . as
if Colin Asch's death, which she had witnessed, were
in some way Michel Deverell's death, which she had
not.

For these reasons her account to the police was tentative, hesitant, qualified. Most of her statements were
preceded by *I think* or *I seem to remember*. There was
revealed to be an intermittent amnesia concerning the
one hundred hours—"one hundred hours" being the
neutral euphemism Dorothea Deverell herself pre-
ferred—which Dorothea could not penetrate. Had her
abductor struck her, pummeled her, tried to strangle
her? No, said Dorothea Deverell; yet the medical reports listed bruises on her body, reddened marks on
her throat. Had her abductor threatened her life? No,
said Dorothea Deverell, not exactly. Yet hadn't he tried

to kill her, at the end? Hadn't he held a knife blade against her throat, at the end? Yes, said Dorothea Deverell but . . . but it was somehow not *that*.

Asked to explain herself, Dorothea could not, quite. Her words were faltering and inadequate.

She was capable, however, of recalling vividly the details of the "cold-blooded" shooting of the caretaker at Glace Lake: the exact circumstances of Colin Asch's first shot, and his second. Only Colin Asch's words, if he had spoken at all, eluded her.

Over all, she could not remember much of what Colin Asch had said to her during the one hundred hours. The doorbell had rung at the front of her house, she had hurried to answer it, and then. . . . The sound of the young man's voice was beginning to fade; even more strangely, his face. "It's as if Colin stands on the far side of an abyss," Dorothea told Charles Carpenter, "speaking to me, trying to explain himself, in a normal voice—but a normal voice, under the circumstances, isn't sufficient. *I can't hear.*"

"Then don't, for Christ's sake," Charles Carpenter said. "Let it go, Dorothea."

"But—"

"Let *him* go. The contemptible son of a bitch."

When he was forced to speak of Colin Asch, Charles Carpenter's usually composed face was contorted by a grimace of sheer loathing; the mere name upset him. For it was the general if unproven hypothesis that Colin Asch had had an exploitive sexual relationship with Agnes (thus the two checks to "Alvarado"—identified by bank tellers as Colin Asch), as he'd had with Susannah Hunt and almost certainly with Roger Krauss. Of this, Charles Carpenter simply could not bear to think.

Her medical examinations had shown of course that there had been no sexual assault upon Dorothea Dev-

erell, no sexual activity of any kind. But had Colin
Asch threatened her with rape? with any sort of sexual
violence? "No," Dorothea Deverell said, "he did
not." For this she knew with absolute confidence.

Now Dorothea found herself standing on the stairway,
her hand resting on the banister, in the house on
L'Arve Place, thinking of these things: the very things
she had vowed she would not think about, particularly
in this new setting. "Let it go!" she said aloud, and
hurried up the stairs.

The master bedroom had tall windows facing south
and west; the westerly windows were flooded with
sunshine of a mellow, autumnal cast; Dorothea felt
its warmth on her face like the gentlest of caresses.
In this room there were faint rectangular marks on
the walls from mirrors and other hangings, the ceiling was blistered in several spots, thus they would
have it all redone; the walls repapered in something
light and restful to the eye . . . *not* a print of any
kind . . . an ivory-beige perhaps. Dorothea liked that
color and hoped that the Carpenters' master bedroom, which she had never seen, had not had walls
in that shade.

And plain curtains, satin and damask. And a new
carpet laid upon the floor.

At a front window she watched as Charles Carpenter's car was parked at the curb; she watched as the
man's tall, elegant figure emerged. Like a young girl
awaiting her first lover she watched him approach the
house, then ran breathless to the staircase outside the
bedroom door to wait for him to appear below: she'd
left the front door unlocked.

"Dorothea? It's Charles." His voice lifted uncertainly. "Where are you?"

Dorothea Deverell leaned over the banister; there

was something wonderfully playful, prankish, about seeing the top of Charles Carpenter's head while he had no awareness of her presence. She laughed happily and called down, "I'm here, Charles—come up!"

About the Author

ROSAMOND SMITH lives in Princeton, New Jersey. She is now writing a new novel.

SHADES OF SUMMER CONTEST

WIN ONE OF 60 PAIRS OF FOSTER GRANT SUNGLASSES!

On the form provided, or on a plain piece of paper, fill in your name, address and phone number and send your entry to:

"Shades of Summer Contest"
c/o Penguin Books Canada Limited
2801 John Street
Markham, Ontario
L3R 1B4

Name: _____

Address: _____

_____

City: _____ Province: _____

Postal Code: _____

Home Phone: _____

Bus. Phone: _____

Contest closes August 31, 1990
For complete details, see reverse

SHADES OF SUMMER CONTEST RULES

1) On the form provided, or on a plain piece of paper, fill in your name, address and phone number and send your entry to:

"SHADES OF SUMMER" Contest
c/o Penguin Books Canada Limited
2801 John Street
Markham, Ontario
L3R 1B4

2) Enter as often as you wish. All entries must be handwritten, not mechanically reproduced. Each entry must be in a separate envelope bearing sufficient postage. No purchase necessary.

3) Contest closes August 31, 1990. Three separate random draws will be held, on June 30th, July 31st and August 31st, respectively. Each draw will award 20 prizes, each consisting of one pair of Foster Grant sunglasses. The approximate retail value of each prize is $30.00

4) Entrants who submit entries prior to the first draw date of June 30th, 1990 will also be eligible to win in the draws on July 31st and August 31st. Entrants who submit entries prior to the second draw date of July 31st, 1990 will also be eligible to win in the August 31st draw.

5) To win, the selected entrant must correctly answer a time limited mathematical skill-testing question to be administered at a mutually convenient time. The chances of winning a prize in each of the draws are dependent upon the total number of entries received prior to each draw date. Decision of contest judges is final.

6) All entries are subject to verification for eligibility, become the property of Penguin Books Canada Limited and will not be returned.

7) Penguin Books Canada Limited is not responsible for entries lost, misdirected or delayed in the mail or otherwise.

8) Prize must be accepted as awarded (no cash substitutes).

9) By entering, entrants agree to the use of their name, address and photograph for publicity purposes and agree to abide by all the rules of this contest.

10) Contest is void where prohibited by law and is subject to all federal, provincial and local regulations.

11) This contest is open to all Canadian residents except residents of Quebec, employees (or members of their immediate families) of Penguin Books Canada Limited, Foster Grant and their respective affiliates.